Travelling Hopefully

ALSO BY MAGGIE MAKEPEACE

Breaking the Chain

TRAVELLING HOPEFULLY

Maggie Makepeace

C

Century · London

First published by Century in 1995

Copyright © Maggie Makepeace 1995

Maggie Makepeace has asserted her right under the Copyright, Designs
and Patents Act, 1988, to be identified as the author of this work

First published in the United Kingdom in 1995 by
Century, 20 Vauxhall Bridge Road, London SW1V 2SA

Random House Australia (Pty) Limited
20 Alfred Street, Milsons Point, Sydney
New South Wales 2061, Australia

Random House New Zealand Limited
18 Poland Road, Glenfield
Auckland 10, New Zealand

Random House South Africa (Pty) Limited
PO Box 337, Bergvlei, South Africa

Random House UK Limited Reg. No. 954009
A CIP catalogue record for this book
is available from the British Library

Papers used by Random House UK Limited are natural,
recyclable products made from wood grown in sustainable forests.
The manufacturing processes conform to the environmental
regulations of the country of origin.

ISBN 0 7126 6169 7

Printed by Mackays of Chatham PLC, Chatham, Kent

To travel hopefully is a better thing than to arrive,
and the true success is to labour.

Robert Louis Stevenson

I

'JUST listen to this,' Barnaby Redcliffe said in tones of disgust, brandishing a note from the dustbin men. He quoted: ' "In order to more effectively pick up the domestic refuse would you please: Place your bin outside your house for collection each Thursday." Do they think that's English? *I* don't want to pick up my refuse, effectively or otherwise, *They* do. How can they write such rubbish? It's so sloppy!'

'Well it's obvious what it means,' Imogen observed from behind her breakfast coffee. 'It may be ungrammatical but it serves its purpose perfectly well.'

'People don't care any more,' Barnaby said. 'They're so keen on expressing themselves freely, that's the phrase isn't it? Their . . . dammit, I've lost the word . . . making things . . . imagination . . . *blast*!' He looked exasperated.

'Workmanship?' Imogen suggested. 'Flair?'

'No! Look it's bad enough forgetting the bloody words without you suggesting all the wrong ones. It's on the tip of my tongue . . . *creativity*, yes that's it. People nowadays think their creativity shouldn't be stunted by wearisome rules. I mean, novels these days are full of sentences with no *verbs*! What they don't seem to realize is that grammar is there not to obstruct the language but to clarify it; to make it unambiguous. That's the beauty of it.'

'More coffee?' asked Imogen, wearily. She looked across the kitchen table at her husband and wished she were able to leave him.

'Had enough. You don't care either, do you?'

'Not as much as you do, clearly.'

'You should. Our generation is the last bastion of civilization against the illiterate hordes.'

'Oh well,' Imogen said easily. '*Après nous le déluge* and all

I

that.' If only he was in good health, she thought, then I could go tomorrow, but only a total shit leaves a partner with an incurable disease.

'Time to go to work,' Barnaby said with a sigh, getting to his feet. He refused at all times to use a walking stick, and had a tendency to lurch sideways or trip over the slightest irregularity underfoot. After years of uncertainty he had been diagnosed as having multiple sclerosis ten years before, the day after his fortieth birthday, and Imogen's first response, to her shame, had been *I've been cheated!* It was as though she had bought damaged goods in good faith and had only discovered the fault after the guarantee had run out. A good woman would have been flooded with compassion for Barnaby first, and only secondly filled with regret for herself. I'm not a good woman, she had thought. How shall I endure it?

'I must get off too,' she said. 'Will you be home at the usual time?'

'Probably.' Barnaby picked up his briefcase and his driving glasses and walked towards the door. 'See you this evening.'

'Right.'

As she piled the breakfast things into the machine to be washed later, Imogen glanced through the window and saw him getting rather awkwardly into his car and driving off towards his office. I suppose, she thought, I should be grateful that he's got a relatively benign kind of MS, the slow sort, and not the dramatic disease which sometimes paralyses people into wheel-chairs or even kills them in a very few years. I should be grateful too to Butcombe, Nempnett & Thrubwell, Solicitors and Commissioners for Oaths, who took him on as a partner years ago, and who now make allowances; I should be, but somehow I'm not. She glanced round the kitchen to check that everything was turned off, heaved her own bag on to her shoulder, took her mac off the hook in passing and checked her face in the hall mirror, before closing the front door firmly behind her and setting off for her stint at the Citizens' Advice Bureau.

Her friend Carol passed her in the corridor as she arrived. 'Not long now,' she said, 'you lucky devil. Have you had all your jabs and things?'

'Tetanus, hepatitis, and boosters for polio and typhoid,' Imogen said, counting them off on her fingers.

Carol sighed. 'I really envy you,' she said, 'but I reckon you've earned it.'

'I like working here,' Imogen said, 'but even so, I shall be very glad of the change.' By Saturday, she thought gleefully, we shall be in Seychelles in heaven, and nothing else will seem important. Barnaby will have no syntax to moan about, and our dustbin will be securely out of sight in the garage, so the bin men can go and be effective wherever else they choose.

Barnaby drove to work gloomily, anticipating the pile in his in-tray which would certainly not get dealt with by the time he went on holiday. He would have to sort through it for the priorities, but it niggled him to leave even the smallest thing uncompleted. These days he kept forgetting things. He was quite capable of losing a whole conversation which had taken place only the day before. Imogen kept nagging him to write things down, but Barnaby felt that this would be giving in to old age. After all, that was all it was. It was just a question of keeping the old brain going. Once you started leaving yourself little notes all over the place, you might as well retire to the geriatric ward. Today he would have to make an extra effort to make sure he'd forgotten nothing vital. After all, he could hardly ring the office from the Indian Ocean . . . He sighed. He was not convinced of the merits of this holiday anyway, but Imogen had been so insistent. It was all right for her, but the thought of spending fifteen days with a load of cripples (even if it was beside warm turquoise seas and palm trees) did not fill him with any enthusiasm. Oh, he saw the logic of it all right. It was a clever idea to run two parallel holidays for 'sufferers' and 'carers' so that they could 'share in the experience, but each according to his/her physical capabilities', the carers being let off duty to do energetic walks whilst the poor bloody disabled commiserated with each other and, no doubt, compared symptoms from a sitting position, somewhere in the shade. Barnaby had looked up from the *Leisure Doubletrips* brochure which Imogen had brought home in triumph, and had said,

'I'm damned if I'm going to join a party of no-hopers in wheelchair races on the coral strand in a sort of tropical *Gladiators* crossed with *Hearts of Gold!*'

3

'Don't be ridiculous,' Imogen said. 'It wouldn't be anything like that. It's for people with your sort of MS who aren't badly incapacitated but who can't walk quite as far as the rest of us. There won't be *any* wheelchairs. It will just give us both a chance to do as much as we can.'

'Instead of me holding you back all the time, you mean?'

'Yes!' She looked exasperated at being made to say it.

'Perhaps you should go without me, then?' he suggested, 'to give you a clear field.'

'Oh please don't be a martyr. I'd rather you were bad-tempered! Look, Barnaby, why won't you try it once? You don't know anyone else with MS because you've always refused to join a group. You never know, you might find the others very supportive and interesting. You don't moan about having it. Why should they?'

'I'm afraid I don't like the idea of being herded about with a crowd of strange people; being . . . arranged? sorted? No. Hell! Don't tell me . . .' He thumped the table in frustration and then remembered what he was trying to say. '*Categorized* – just because we've all got the same disease, but probably damn-all else in common.'

Imogen giggled. 'Like that ghastly woman at your office party, who introduced those two painfully shy wives to each other by saying "Here, Sue, you must meet Sally. You'll have so much to talk about since both your husbands have just had vasectomies".'

Barnaby made a face. 'Precisely,' he said.

'But I'm sure it won't be like that. There's bound to be someone interesting on the trip and at least half of them will be – ' She had almost, he knew, said normal – 'won't have MS. Anyway – ' she gave him her little-girl look, which had disarmed him in their youth but now just looked silly – Seychelles are paradise on earth, or so they say. They're some-where I've always wanted to go. We both need a break and it would be so good to experience it together.' Wishful thinking, or did she believe that?

'Oh well, I suppose . . .'

'Marvellous!' She rushed over to kiss him. 'You won't regret it. I'll make sure of that. Oh I can't wait to go!' Then she made a mock-frown and said, 'I never knew you watched *Gladiators* or the other one, hearts of something?'

'I see them by mistake when I'm waiting for the news,' he said firmly.

'You are sweet,' she said, laughing indulgently. Barnaby had noticed that she was always – well, sweet was the only word for it – to him when she was getting her own way. Once he had thought it charming. Now he saw it merely as manipulative. 'I wonder what the leader will be like,' she said. 'Roger Dare. Apparently his wife has MS and he's been doing this sort of thing for several years. I admire someone like that, I really do. And his assistant's a GP called Claire Mainwaring. That's handy!'

'Well it would be if there were convenient little pills she could dispense, which would cure MS.'

'One day,' Imogen said encouragingly. 'One day there will be. They're doing masses of research.'

'Then they'd better get a move on.'

Thinking of time jolted Barnaby back into the present. He had been driving on autopilot, but apparently successfully. He glanced at his watch: five minutes to nine, he should just do it. The modest queue of cars funnelling into the small Somerset town could barely be termed rush-hour traffic. He was glad he didn't live and work in London. He was glad he was going on holiday too, if he were honest. He could do with a rest, and Imogen diluted by a dozen or so others might be a lot more liveable with. He made a wry face at the thought.

'Now then,' Daisy Mann said to her friend and companion, Dorothy Petrie. 'All set? Got your tickets? traveller's cheques? bathing suit? torch? notebook? sunblock and hat?'

'Yes I think so.'

'Right. Now I've got the bird book, my binoculars and the map.' She ticked them off on her checklist. 'I still think you'll wish you'd got yourself a snorkel and mask like these old ones of mine. There will be lots of opportunities to explore the coral reefs, you know. After all, that's what we've been training for at the swimming baths all these months, isn't it?'

'I like swimming,' Dorothy said. 'I even used to be quite good at it. I got my bronze life-saving certificate at school, you know, but I don't like getting my head under water and I'm too old to change that now.'

'What rubbish! You're the healthy one and you're years younger than me, and I'm certainly going to have another go at it.'

'Which stick are you taking?' Dorothy asked. She wondered why Daisy had been so keen to go, yet again, on one of Roger Dare's holidays. It was true, she and Dorothy had enjoyed the other trips, but others hadn't. There had often been quite a lot of unpleasantness. When Dorothy talked to herself it was usually in euphemisms. She concluded that Daisy must secretly be studying Roger. Once a psychotherapist, always one, she thought, even if retired.

'I shall take both sticks,' Daisy said. 'The folding one may come in useful if I lose the other, and I suppose it's entirely possible that I may need two at once if it's frightfully hot and tiring.'

'Perhaps we should have opted to go to the Isle of Wight after all?' Dorothy said. 'Oh I do hope it won't be too much for you.'

'I shall see to it that it isn't,' Daisy said crisply. 'Ah, here's the taxi now. You are sure you've got your tickets?'

'In my handbag.' Dorothy opened it, drew a blank, and started scrabbling desperately through it. 'They're not here!' Panic-stricken, she emptied the contents of the bag onto their dining-room table. 'Oh my goodness!' she exclaimed, running her fingers through her fluffy white hair until it stood up all over her head like froth. The taxi hooted outside.

Daisy made an imperious gesture at it through the window. 'Perhaps you put them in your little green bag?' she suggested patiently.

'Oh *yes*, perhaps I did.' Dorothy unzipped the smallest pocket of her hand luggage and peered inside. '*They're here!* Thank goodness for that!'

'Come along then,' Daisy said. 'Just get yourself into the taxi and do try to remember to take your head.'

'I'm so sorry,' Dorothy gabbled, picking up her handbag and sweeping everything off the table and back inside it. 'I remember now. I thought that pocket would be such a safe place, and so easy to get at . . .'

'What would you do without me?' Daisy said. She picked up her walking stick in one hand and her hand luggage in the other, and limped to the front door. Then she rested the stick carefully against the hat-stand while she opened the door and beckoned to the driver to come and help.

'I'd be lost,' Dorothy said simply. 'If you hadn't come along after Albert died, I just don't know how I should have managed . . .' Her eyes filled with grateful tears.

'Silly old thing,' Daisy said gruffly. 'Ah, driver, would you be good enough to carry these two? Thank you so much.'

Dorothy climbed into the taxi and mopped her face with a lace-edged handkerchief. Her eyes were prone to leaking spontaneously and she had long ago ceased to feel any embarrassment about being seen to weep in public. It was just that she felt emotions more keenly than most other people; her skin was thinner. She wondered what the group would be like this year. She asked herself how Roger's saint of a wife could possibly put up with him? She hoped that Philip Blunt, Daisy's protégé from the local bird-watching club, would be fit enough to enjoy the trip. Multiple sclerosis sometimes raged through the young at a terrifying pace. What future has he got? she thought. What a wicked waste!

The taxi called at Philip's house and he climbed in, beaming all over his face. 'Morning Daisy, Dorothy,' he said. 'Isn't this great? I've got a brand new 500-millimetre mirror lens specially for this trip. Can't wait to use it!'

Dorothy noticed that his flight bag was bulging with photographic equipment, so much so that the zip wouldn't do up. She watched as his anxious mother waved them off, and wondered whether the poor woman would be comforted in years to come by the albums of photographs her son would leave behind. She dabbed at her eyes again. Philip waved encouragingly at his mother as the taxi set off again, and sat down on the jump seat opposite the two elderly women.

'She worries,' he explained, 'but I've told her I'll be in good company.'

He's so handsome, Dorothy thought, and has such expressive eyes. It's so unfair!

Dr Claire Mainwaring travelled south on the train from Edinburgh to London in optimistic mood. Outside it was raining, and the November countryside looked brown and dreary. Claire looked forward to hot white beaches, lazy swimming and wonderful Creole food. She was glad to leave Edinburgh just now. Magnus was becoming a nuisance, but Murdo (with whom she went rock-climbing at weekends) was simmering encouragingly and could be relied upon to come to the boil in just over a fortnight, coinciding nicely with her return, all languorous with sunshine and fetchingly tanned. She smiled to herself. She knew Roger Dare would not be a problem on this, her second Seychelles trip as his assistant. He was fun it was true, and he was pretty good in the sack too, but once Claire had got to know his wife, she had come to understand that Ruth had known what was going on right from the beginning but was quietly putting up with it. Claire, who had seen Roger as a fellow free-spirit and hadn't given a thought to anyone else, was shocked at Ruth's acquiescence, and troubled for the first time in her life by feelings of guilt. So after a week she had told him to sling his hook, and he had accepted her decision, albeit rather childishly.

Ruth must be some sort of masochist, she now thought, to put herself in that situation year after year. Claire had no illusions about Roger. She was sure that if she herself were not on offer, he would chat up someone else. Why didn't he piss off on his own once a year, she wondered? It would be much kinder to spare Ruth from being a resigned witness to his verbal foreplay, and would give him far more freedom. Perhaps he couldn't afford to, unless he made money out of it? She didn't know anything about his home situation, except that he lived in Cheshire and had once been a probation officer. She supposed that he could hardly lead Leisure Doubletrips without Ruth, since that would invalidate his own brilliant idea of running parallel holidays for the able along with the infirm. Perhaps he didn't care if he hurt Ruth? Claire smiled grimly. It didn't say much for Roger's character but it still made Ruth a wimp, and of the two, Claire preferred the heartless chancer any day. She looked out of the window and wondered idly what the punters would be like this time. Then she got the group address list out of her bag and studied its salient points.

Mr Barnaby and Mrs Imogen Redcliffe from Somerset – he with his age (50) and MS beside his name, she with (48) and AB (able-bodied).

Dr Daisy Mann (70,MS) Splading, Lincolnshire.
Mrs Dorothy Petrie (64,AB) ditto.
Mr Simon Overy (45,MS) Islington, London.
Miss Shirley Gage (62,AB) Sheffield, Yorkshire.
Mr Brian Gage (60,MS) ditto.
Miss Annabel de Beauchamp (25,MS) Cambridge.
Mr Philip Blunt (21,MS) Spalding, Lincolnshire.
Mr Leslie Cromwell (55,MS) Birmingham.
Mrs Janice Cromwell (53,AB) ditto.

They were mostly pretty ancient, but that was to be expected. Few people in their twenties and thirties could afford such a trip. Perhaps Simon Overy would be amusing? She wondered what they all did for a living. She had tried to guess the previous year, and had got it badly wrong. Daisy and Dorothy (the retired psychotherapist and nursery school teacher) of course she knew already. They were regulars, and harmless enough. Brian and Shirley Gage had also been on other trips, but not with her. They and the others would reveal themselves at Gatwick and be identifiable by their red LEISURE DOUBLETRIPS luggage labels. Claire hoped that there would not be any moaners, mopers or malingerers amongst them.

The train was half an hour late into King's Cross, but Claire had plenty of time to spare and finally arrived at Gatwick unflustered and full of anticipation. She walked across the concourse and saw them all at once: the little knot of people at the Air Seychelles desk. Roger and Ruth had their backs to her. Daisy and Dorothy were bent double and seemed to be unpacking one of their bags onto the floor. Claire approached slowly to get a good look at all of them before having to declare herself. The two youngsters stood out. The young man (who must be Philip) was demonstrating an expensive camera to the young woman. Mmmm . . . Claire thought, he's a bit of all right. Pity he's not older. The woman (Annabel) was not as sophisticated as her elegant name would suggest. She was intelligent looking and quite attractive, with shoulder-length ginger hair, good cheekbones and a pale skin, but she looked vulnerable and shy. The short, bearded man in glasses, standing a little apart from the rest, must be Simon. He didn't look promising.

9

The rest of them looked pretty undistinguished: plump/thin, grey-headed/bald, all irrevocably middle-aged and to Claire (who hadn't got there yet and didn't know any better) all very much past it. She amused herself trying to predict which of the women Roger would make a play for. It wouldn't be Annabel, that was for sure, not because Roger was overawed by breeding or brains, or even seduced by youth and beauty, but (a) because she was unmarried and (presumably) available on too permanent a basis, and (b) because she was likely to become a health liability fairly soon. Roger always went for married ladies, or women like herself who were clearly allergic to commitment and would therefore cause no long-term problems. Claire smiled inwardly. It looked as though Roger was in for rather a thin time this year. Serve him right! Was everyone here? She counted heads; two missing.

'Claire!' Daisy had seen her and was waving enthusiastically. Claire went forward and joined the group. 'How nice to see you again,' Daisy said. 'How are you?'

'Very well. Lovely to see you too. Hi, Rog! Hello, Ruth, here we go again then.'

Roger winked at her and put an arm round her shoulders. 'Now this,' he said, presenting her to the group, 'is the delicious doctor I was telling you about. Claire Mainwaring, pronounced Mannering (don't get it wrong, or she gets very uppity). She's the best GP I know; totally unsympathetic, doesn't believe in pills, but is wonderful in a crisis. What more could you ask?'

Claire smiled apologetically at Ruth and began shaking hands as she was introduced to the others. 'Who's missing?' she asked Roger.

'The Redcliffes,' he said, 'Barnaby and Imogen. I hope they get a move on.' He looked round. 'Oh, this looks like them now.'

Claire turned round also and saw a couple with red-tagged luggage approaching them. The man was tall, going a little thin on top and with a friendly, distinguished sort of face. He looks nice, she thought. He lurched when he walked, like someone intoxicated, but he was not using a stick. At his side walked a slim well-dressed woman who looked ten years younger than the 48 Claire knew her to be. She had large blue eyes, short curly hair (which was too evenly dark to be natural) and she was smiling broadly. Roger stepped forward to welcome them and took her hand first, in both of his.

'Mr and Mrs Redcliffe?' he said. 'Hello to you both. I'm Roger Dare.'

Claire, watching him, thought, Oh Roger you jammy bastard!

2

As Imogen approached the check-in desk with Barnaby, her
heart sank. The rest of the party looked so uninspiring, so
elderly. She hoped the trip wouldn't turn out to be a complete
disaster. If it were to be so, Barnaby would say it was all her
fault. Everything always was; she was sure that he had married
her in order to have someone to blame. As they got closer she
became determinedly optimistic, and smiled widely to encourage herself. Then an athletic man in his late thirties with thick
blond hair and unlikely brown eyes, stepped forward to greet
them. He introduced himself as Roger Dare and held onto her
proffered hand for longer than was just polite. He told them
the other people's names and she nodded and shook hands, and
forgot them instantly. She was thinking: At least Roger seems
genuinely delighted to see us. Maybe it will be all right after
all?

They checked in their suitcases and went as a group to the
departure lounge for the 17.45 flight to Mahé via Frankfurt.
Some people seemed to have got to know each other already
and were chatting away comparing cameras. I've never had a
camera, Imogen thought. I prefer to live life, rather than to
waste time recording it. She glanced sideways at Barnaby to see
how he was taking it so far. He looked inscrutable as always.
They sat down in rows of seats to wait.

'I'm never going to remember all their names,' she said to
him under her breath.

'You will when you know them better,' he said. 'Try associ-
ation of ideas. For instance, Roger's wife looks the opposite of
ruthless.' Imogen felt obscurely that he was getting at her, but
in such a subtle way that she could not retaliate. She hoped he
wasn't going to make a habit of it over the next fortnight.

Barnaby had also felt unimpressed at the sight of their travelling companions, but since he hadn't expected to enjoy the trip anyway, their appearance had not disappointed him. They were more or less what he had anticipated. He distrusted Roger Dare on sight. The word 'bounder' sprang to mind, but he sat on it firmly. Barnaby had been led astray by first impressions before. But surely no *gentleman* sported such a startling anomaly of hair and eye colour? Barnaby grimaced to himself and was glad he had not spoken his thoughts aloud. He was beginning to sound exactly like his father! It was alarming how relentlessly heredity caught up with you, once you'd got to 50 . . . characteristics you'd always sneered at in your parents suddenly started to manifest themselves in you . . . It was inexorable and depressing. He looked about at the assembled group as they all sat themselves down, and nudged Imogen towards Brian (wild grey hair) and Shirley (fat), the couple who looked the least boring. He had got several of their names fixed in his head already, and was about to offer more word associations to Imogen to help her to remember them, but after the first one she had looked irritated, and he gave up. It was true, Ruth did look the sympathetic sort; compassionate. Ruthless, on the other hand, described Imogen rather well.

'Hello,' said Brian as Barnaby sat down next to him. He held a stinking pipe up to his mouth and drew on it, looking at Barnaby over the top. 'Have you been on these junkets before?'

'No,' Barnaby said, momentarily disconcerted by trying to work out which of Brian's eyes was the one to talk to, since they didn't seem to be co-ordinated. Was wall-eyed the term for a divergent squint?

'We have,' Brian said. 'This is our third time, isn't it Shirley?' He leant back so that Barnaby could see the woman on the other side of him. 'My sister,' Brian explained. 'We live next door to each other in Sheffield. She cooks for me and I keep an eye on her.'

Only one? thought Barnaby unkindly.

'Where are you from?' Shirley enquired.

'Somerset,' Barnaby said.

'Lovely part of the world.'

'Yes.'

'And is this your wife?'

'Yes, Imogen . . . Shirley and Brian.' He leant back so that Imogen could see the other two.

'Are you looking forward to the trip?' Shirley asked her.

'Enormously,' Imogen said, 'and it's such a relief to be escaping from real life for a while.'

'What do you do?' Shirley asked.

'I work for the Citizens' Advice Bureau.'

'What a coincidence! Roger used to work for the Social Services too, I believe. Not that it's the same thing, of course.'

Huh! Barnaby thought, I should imagine that's the only possible thing they've got in common! He looks more like an intellectually defective ski instructor to me.

'What about you?' Imogen asked Shirley.

'Oh I'm retired now, but I was a district nurse and Brian here was a sanitary engineer until MS struck. Have you had it long, Barnaby?'

'About ten years that I know of.' I do hope we're not going to discuss symptoms, he thought. I really can't take too much of that sort of thing.

'Well, you look good on it,' she said cheerfully, 'but if you need any information or anything, then Brian's your man. He's researched the whole field in depth. He even lectures on the subject.'

'Really?' Barnaby tried to lift his voice at the end of the word to make it sound less dismissive, but he knew he hadn't fooled Shirley. She gave him a knowing look.

'And he's an artist too,' she went on proudly.

'Really?' Imogen said (in just the tone of voice he should have used).

'I dabble,' Brian said modestly, 'nothing more. But I have brought my sketchpad on this holiday. What do you do?' This to Barnaby.

'I'm a solicitor.'

'Oh that must be very interesting,' Shirley said. Then the conversation lapsed.

Very British, Barnaby was thinking. We've done just enough of the preliminaries to be able to categorize each other into our proper pigeon-holes. The Gages now know that we are 'professional people', speak 'properly' and are upper middle class. We have heard their Yorkshire voices, assessed their occupations, and can place them with some confidence as upwardly mobile but still working class. And that's all we need to know. Conversation over. Who says Britain is a classless society these days? We're not even half-way there. He smiled and quoted Matthew Arnold silently to himself: *Thus we have got three distinct terms, Barbarians, Philistines, Populace to denote roughly the three great classes into which our society is divided.* Am I a Philistine? he thought. I'd hate to think so.

The woman on the other side of Imogen leant over and said confidentially, 'I must say I'm really looking forward to getting away from my hubby on this holiday, aren't you?' She jerked her head backwards towards the man sitting on her other side, who clearly didn't notice his wife's gesture.

Imogen, who had thought very similar thoughts only a few minutes before, was nevertheless rather shocked to hear them articulated so baldly, especially by someone whose manner was distinctly off-putting. She immediately felt like contradicting the woman flatly.

'Oh I don't know – ' she began.

'We all need a break,' the woman said. 'They're so demanding, aren't they?' Her mouth turned down at the corners and she looked permanently affronted. 'I'm not a fussy woman,' she said, 'but . . .'

Imogen wondered why people gave themselves away like that. She might equally well, and more truthfully, have said, 'I'm an extremely tiresome woman, and I'm giving you fair warning that I won't put up with much'!

' . . . I never get a moment to myself these days. It's want, want, want from him all the time and they get worse as they get older, don't they? Worse than children!'

'Do you have any?' Imogen asked, hoping to change the subject.

'Any what?'

'Children.'

'Oh my son's grown up. He flew the nest years back, but he's still on at me all the time. It's a life sentence with them, isn't it? You're never off the hook.'

'I don't see it like that at all,' Imogen said. 'I just wish my two daughters lived nearer.'

'It's Isobel . . . is it?'

'Imogen.'

'Ah well, pretty close,' she cackled.

'I'm sorry. I've forgotten . . .?'

'Janice Cromwell, and this is my old man, Leslie. We're from Birmingham.'

That much is patently obvious, Imogen thought. It was the one regional accent she couldn't bear. She glanced past Janice to look properly at the husband and nearly laughed aloud. His head was shiny-bald and almost completely spherical. A more typical Roundhead would be hard to find.

'How-de-do,' he said. 'Pleased to meet you.'

'Hello.'

'Do you think short-sleeved shirts look common on a man?' he asked.

'Um . . . no I don't think so.' She'd never thought about it.

'Well I'm not sure meself, but the wife went out and bought me four anyway, for this do. Two have even got flowers on them.'

His wife raised her eyes in a gesture of exasperation for Imogen's benefit. 'Men!' she said. 'See what I mean?' Then with barely a pause for breath she changed the subject, as though switching abruptly to another topic was the normal way to converse. 'I've noticed your husband doesn't walk too steady,' she said. 'You should get him a stick.'

Right, Claire thought, looking along the rows of the departure lounge, I've got them all sussed . . . I think. Let's see what Simon Overy is really like. She went over to sit next to him.

'Hello,' she said, 'I'm Claire.'

'Oh yes,' he said. 'The lady doctor. I hope we're not going to waste any time on this holiday?' He regarded her challengingly from behind horn-rimmed glasses. Thick black hair sprouted from his nostrils and ears, and fringed his mouth in a ragged beard. She wondered whether it grew all over his back, like a gorilla, and repressed a shudder.

'Well I'm not. I don't know about you,' she said lightly.

'No, no,' he said impatiently, 'I'm talking about those of us with MS. I hope you don't expect us to sit about in Bath chairs while you able-bodied people do all the exciting things, because I warn you, I won't stand for that.'

'It won't be like that at all,' Claire said stiffly.

'Mind you,' Simon said in an undertone, 'looking at the rest of them, I reckon I'm just as fit as some of the so-called able-bodied. I haven't come on this holiday as a second-class citizen, you know. I want to get as much out of it as the next person.'

'I'm sure you will,' Claire said.

Simon ignored this. 'I'm not going to be held back by a load of deadbeats,' he said, 'not on an expensive holiday like this!'

'No one's going to hold you back,' Claire said, carefully polite. 'I think you'll find that there's a lot more to the rest of the group than meets the eye.' A look of disgust sailed across Simon's face and dropped anchor, leaving him with a permanent sneer.

He's a pain in the neck so far, Claire thought. No wonder he's on his own. She couldn't think of anything else to say to him. He was clearly not interested in small talk, so she turned instead to the girl on her other side. Annabel was eating a sandwich from a lunchbox on her knee and bending forwards so that her face was hidden by a shiny screen of red hair.

'I expect there'll be food on the plane,' Claire observed.

Annabel blushed. 'It's usually meat,' she said, 'and I'm a vegetarian, so I always bring my own. Would you like one?'

Claire, who hadn't eaten since breakfast, was tempted by the fresh look of the chunky brown bread and took one. 'Thanks very much.' She bit into it gratefully, but found it disappointingly bland.

'What's in them?' she enquired, chewing exploratively.

'Mashed potato,' Annabel said. 'It's my favourite.'

Imogen sat in a window seat and watched as England faded away beneath their plane. They were off, and she was happy. She loved beginnings, when experience opened up ahead and anything could happen. She knew she was a courageous and enterprising person at heart; the sort who could cope with anything. This she believed firmly was not only part of her character, but was an unquestionable virtue. She didn't understand people who were not restless with hope most of the time, and she couldn't bear to have her enthusiasms and enterprises punctured by sharp logic or caution. Why would anyone want to shoot you down when you were flying, unless of course they were jealous or mean-spirited, or both? Barnaby was a bit like that. He called himself a realist, but Imogen knew him to be worse than a pessimist. He was a saboteur of joy.

She sighed. In truth she was bored by him; by his worthiness and his refusal ever to risk his own dignity in any way. He was always the one who did not wear his paper hat at parties. The essence of living, Imogen thought, is taking *risks*. Barnaby didn't *live*. He didn't drink and drive, in fact he never drove at all above seventy. He didn't wear man-made materials next to his skin. He refused to have a microwave oven in the house. He collected all his credit-card receipts in a little wallet. He argued with Radio 4 every morning. He never *ever* admitted that he was wrong. He always went precisely the same way to work, at exactly the same time. Those things individually were admittedly trivial, but (together with all the other annoyances that had temporarily slipped her mind) they were guaranteed to drive one mad. It was like being married to an automaton.

But worse than that, far worse, was the niggling certainty that Barnaby's brain was being affected by his MS. It had deteriorated very slowly, so it was difficult to know whether she was imagining things, but she was sure his character was changing. He was always tired and increasingly bad-tempered. His memory was more and more unreliable. He was slower on the uptake, denser, even wilfully obtuse in arguments. He had formerly been so articulate, but now he forgot words all the time, got angrily frustrated about doing so, and took his rage out on her . . . Imogen had tried discussing it with her friends, but they had dismissed it lightly with phrases like: 'Oh my husband forgets things on purpose, so he can get out of having to do them!' or 'Bill forgets his words too – everyone gets a bit vague when they get older, don't they? It's nothing.' They didn't understand the *degree* of the problem! If he was just the same as everyone else, she wouldn't be worrying, but he *wasn't*. However, she knew that if she tried to explain Barnaby's special case, her friends would think she was making a fuss about nothing. Imogen was convinced that there was more to it than mere age, and she suffered. She found that slowness in mental processes led to irritation and impatience on her side and a general loss of spontaneity in conversation. It was like trying to talk in a foreign language where nuances get lost and wit falls flat. Failing memory was even worse. It led to the eradication of shared jokes and memories; an undermining of their special relationship. If the past became incomplete, the future looked disjointed too. In the end, Imogen had talked to their GP about it, but he had been no help at all. 'You don't get cognitive dysfunction with MS,' he had said at once. 'I shouldn't worry about it.' But Barnaby *was* different, she knew. He was not the same as the man she had once loved.

I've been married for nearly thirty years! she thought. I've had a comfortable, protected, standard sort of a life. I've brought up two good daughters and contributed some valuable work to the community, but I've never gone off and done my own thing. I've never had a fling. I've only ever slept with Barnaby. There hasn't been time for others and I've never had the energy. How could I have been so unenterprising? Of course I've constantly tried to get out of the rut, but I've always included Barnaby in my schemes. I've dragged him behind me from one interest to another; hobbies, concerts, local events, good causes, and each time the dead hand of his cumbersome caution has ground me down and eventually brought me to a standstill. Even when all our friends were having interesting holidays in foreign parts, I couldn't get him to do the same. He always had to go to his mother's old cottage in Devon, saying that it was pointless to own a second home if one didn't make use of it (and anyway it wasn't safe to drink the water, abroad). Why didn't I take him up on his offer this year, and go off on holiday on my own? Imogen found the answer with reluctance and admitted it to herself only because its truth was self-evident. Over the years Barnaby had brainwashed her into conforming to his own concept of the ideal country solicitor's wife, so much so that she hadn't questioned it at all.

It wasn't just Barnaby. Their friends also conspired to preserve the status quo. Most of them were divorced or otherwise dislocated from proper family life. They held up her marriage to Barnaby as an example to them all. They asked her advice and confessed their failings. She restored their faith in human relationships, they said. Imogen, who had been flattered initially, soon began to feel a fraud and then kept up the deception purely out of pride. Now she wondered why she had cared what anyone thought.

She looked at Barnaby sitting beside her. His seat belt was buckled obediently across his stomach. His hands were folded on his lap. Even this annoyed her. It was so prim! She glanced up. He was asleep, of course. He was always asleep these days. Perhaps on this holiday, she thought, I'll shake him out of his complacency, just a little, surprise him. Then maybe I'll find out if there really is any *spirit* in him. I need to know.

Ruth Dare had stood anxiously beside her husband as the group assembled, waiting to find out what fate had in store for her on this trip. She wasn't worried about Claire any more. Roger had come off worst in their encounter the summer before, and was unlikely to want to repeat it. Ruth felt almost grateful to Claire for turning the tables on him, but she would never admit it. She had not discussed Roger's behaviour with anyone. She would rather that outsiders thought she didn't know about Roger's affairs, than realize that she condoned them, which would make her appear so inadequate. Ruth knew that she wasn't really feeble, not deep down. It was just that all her emotions were overlaid by a punitive blanket of guilt. She subconsciously assumed that it was somehow her own fault that she had MS, and that Roger had been unfairly caught in the same incurable trap. By marrying him, she had deprived him of a normal life. She felt she couldn't blame him for going off with other women for sexual adventures; he had to have some consolation. Of course it was very hurtful (and there were times when she wanted to hurt him back) but it was better than losing him altogether. Anything, she felt, was better than being totally alone. She bolstered herself with the knowledge that Roger *did* care for her, and that he demonstrated this by doing good works for other people with MS as well as for her. Leisure Doubletrips was entirely the product of his vision, and together they brought it about. It did well, and apart from the fact that it was now their only way of earning a living, it assuaged some of her guilt. It was a service worth preserving. Ruth reminded herself of this each time Roger fell for another female, and told herself firmly that this too was just a transient fling. No woman knew the real Roger like she did. He always came back to her afterwards.

This year she felt more hopeful than usual. There didn't seem to be any obvious candidate for his attentions. She liked the look of the Redcliffes at once, particularly Barnaby. It was not just that he had a nice face, but his whole manner spoke to her of stability and comfort and responsibility. Here was someone you could rely on, Ruth thought. Lucky Imogen! She could see that they were one of those rare things, a happily married couple. It did one good just to be with them; repaired one's trust in human nature. Roger might well fancy Imogen (what man wouldn't?) but he wouldn't get anywhere. To her eye, Imogen wore her contentment like impenetrable armour. Ruth looked forward to watching Roger bounce off it.

Their plane, a Boeing 707, was almost empty. The first time Ruth had travelled to Seychelles, it had been the same. She had wondered how the operators made a living. Then she had thought, Good! we shall all be able to spread ourselves out later on three seats each. That way we might even be able to sleep. It's going to be a long twelve hours otherwise. This time she knew that that was a forlorn hope. Barnaby seemed to be asleep already, she noticed, glancing up at him. Even at rest he had a sort of authority. He was so neat, hands clasped, breathing regular, everything under control. Ruth looked across the aisle at Roger. He was slumped in a seat which clearly did not offer him enough room. His left leg stuck out into the aisle and his hand luggage (which was too bulky for the overhead bins) didn't fit properly under the seat. She knew that he would be the first to bag a free trio of seats to kip on, if any remained available, once the meal was over. She caught his eye and he winked at her, reaching across to pat her arm encouragingly.

'All right?' he asked.

'Fine.' In front of her, Brian and Shirley were chatting away to Annabel. She and Roger didn't chat these days, but then, what married couple did? That was how you could always spot them in restaurants.

On arrival at Frankfurt, the plane filled up with German passengers. The group had fallen silent as they took off again and were served with a free drink and a hot meal. Imogen, glancing across at Roger, thought, Blond hair and brown eyes are certainly very striking! This is going to be a wonderful holiday. I feel it in my bones. At the approach of food, she heard Ruth telling Roger rather crossly to get his foot out of the way to let the stewardess get past with the trolley. Then she caught Ruth's eye as she finished speaking and raised her eyebrows at Imogen in mock exasperation.

'Mine keeps falling asleep,' Imogen said to Ruth, leaning over a yawning Barnaby. 'You'd never think this was his *big* holiday, would you?'

'Oh well,' Ruth said, smiling understandingly at Barnaby. 'Of course he can't help that, can he? After all, fatigue is often the most debilitating symptom of MS, as you probably know.' Imogen, who in fact did not know this, was piqued and thought, Whatever happened to female solidarity?

3

A T 6 a.m. (10 a.m. Seychelles time) and only half an hour late, the plane landed on the island of Mahé and the passengers walked down the steps on to the airport tarmac to be engulfed in a stifling atmosphere which was not only hot but also heavily laden with moisture from the surrounding thousand miles of sultry ocean. Imogen, feeling the sweat breaking out all over her body thought, I'll never cope with this humidity. It's like living in a sauna! She looked up at Barnaby for his reaction, but he just raised his eyebrows and exhaled through his mouth in a wordless display of surprise. Not everyone was so reticent.

'Oh my Lord!' Janice exclaimed at once, 'I don't call this hot; I call it *suffocating*! I won't be able to stand this for one day, never mind a whole fortnight.'

'You'll soon get used to it,' Roger said encouragingly. 'You'll get acclimatized in no time.'

Imogen saw him exchange a glance with Claire and was pleased to find that her initial reaction to the Cromwells was shared by others. They all went by bus from the airport to their first hotel on the north-west coast, on small roads which zigzagged up through a profusion of thick dark green tropical vegetation, with glimpses of the vivid flowers of oleander, frangipani and bougainvillaea, past low wooden houses with corrugated-iron roofs and gardens of red earth full of things Imogen recognized as house plants. She felt elated by the strangeness and the simplicity of it all. Here at least, man and nature seemed to have come to an understanding. No buildings showed above the palm trees, and everything was in scale with everything else. There were few cars, and the people they passed, walking on the roads, were not all ethnologically homogeneous. Although mostly brown skinned, some had straight black oriental hair. A few were pale or even blonde. Imogen wondered if racial tensions existed amongst them. They all looked relaxed and confident. Some of the children even waved. At least so far, she thought, they haven't been contaminated by tourism. I wonder for how much longer?

Their hotel was right beside a wide arc of beach with white coral sand and a clear pale green sea. There were people swimming and sunbathing, but the beach was more than able to accommodate them, and its very length dwarfed them all. There was a rather suburban swimming pool ringed with sun-beds between hotel and beach, and tables with conical parasols, small editions of the thatched roof over the round, open-sided bar.

'Hey!' Leslie said. 'Talk about la dolchey vita, eh?'

They were allocated their rooms as couples and the odd singles, Shirley and Annabel, Brian and Philip, agreed to share. Simon got his single room and Claire, by default, did also. Imogen was relieved to find that theirs was air conditioned and had its own bathroom. She felt tired and crumpled but was longing to rush out and discover everything at once. Barnaby lay down on the bed in his travelling clothes and closed his eyes.

'What d'you think of it all?' Imogen asked him eagerly.

'Bloody hot,' he said.

'Yes, but isn't the scenery fantastic? And aren't the flowers and trees exotic looking?'

'Mmmm,' Barnaby said, eyes still shut.

'Is that all you can say?'

Barnaby opened one eye. 'I would agree that it seems to be all it's cracked up to be, yes: spectacular, beautiful, unspoiled, breathtaking, stunning, jewel-like, in fact a tropical-jungle-island-paradise,' he said. 'That's the trouble with clichés; sometimes they are the only things that answer!'

'You are glad you came, then?'

'Ask me in a week's time. At the moment all I can think about is how exhausted I am, and how we've got to do that whole ghastly journey again in reverse.'

'Have a cool bath,' Imogen suggested. 'Then you'll feel much fresher.'

'You go first.'

Imogen lay in her bath and mentally hugged herself. So far

it was all she had hoped it would be. She couldn't wait to explore this island, let alone the others on their itinerary. Barnaby, true to form, was being a wet blanket, but even he would perk up in time. His fatigue was understandable; it had been a very long, uncomfortable night. Now they had some time before lunch to recover, and then there was to be a gentle walk with the whole group. She lay back with a sigh of pleasure at being sweat-free and clean again, and looked forward to putting on fresh clothes, making her hair look nice, and perhaps to having a quick walk on her own before lunch, while Barnaby slept.

Roger made some telephone calls to his Seychellois contacts, to check that all his long-distance arrangements were in place and then, satisfied that all was well, went for a solitary walk along the beach. In the distance a motor boat roared through the shallow waters, towing a small figure hanging from a brightly coloured parachute which was ascending high into the air above the water. From where Roger stood, the rope connecting the two was barely visible and it looked like magic. Roger looked forward to leaving Mahé soon to go on to other, smaller, islands where such vulgar amusements were not available and where the environment was not subjected to such unnecessary disturbance. He always tried to include some wildlife interest in all his Leisure Doubletrips holidays. At first this had been solely for Ruth's benefit, but now it had become a plus for him too. Before she had become ill, Ruth had taught biology, and she was still a keen amateur botanist. Roger wanted her to be able to maintain that interest, and with that in mind, he made a point of stressing to his punters that the trips would not be glitzy or for the lazy. Accommodation would in the main be simple and members of the group would be encouraged to push themselves as much as possible to get the most out of their holiday. Roger (never having been ill) had a brisk approach to disease, a quality he also recognized and approved of in Claire.

Roger thought briefly about Claire as he walked along the edge of the sea, letting the warm water lap over his toes. If she wasn't careful, she'd miss the boat altogether, marriage-wise. Perhaps it wasn't important to her? He was not sorry their brief affair was not to be repeated this year. It hadn't been a great success anyway. This was his third trip here and her second. Whether he would use her again as assistant leader, he wasn't sure. He would have no trouble replacing her; most of his friends would jump at the chance. He wondered idly what sort of man would be brave enough to marry Claire? She tended to be impatient, which was off-putting.

The sun was hot on his back through the loose cotton shirt and he could feel the sweat gathering at the waistband of his shorts. He supposed he would have to wear something to protect his head sooner or later, but a little natural bleaching of the hair would make a nice change. He smiled to himself. After lunch he planned to take the whole group on a gentle stroll and at the same time assess their various capabilities. Daisy Mann and the chap with the funny eye, Brian Gage, seemed the least mobile at first glance; not surprising really, since they were amongst the oldest. Roger wondered whether he had done the right thing in bringing two younger people along this time. He didn't usually accept people with the relapsing/remitting form of MS in case they had an attack on the trip and needed hospital treatment. It was a gamble. He hoped it would be worth it. It had been Daisy's idea to bring Philip (and to pay his fare), and she had worn Roger down with her insistence that it would be quite all right. Then Annabel had applied to come too, and he'd thought, why not? It will balance the numbers. He wondered how they would all gel as a group. Sometimes it worked a charm. Other times they were like a bag of mixed magnets, with little clumps attracted together and like-poles repulsing one another; impossible to manage all together.

The sand squidged between his toes and was washed away with each warm wave. Paper-white fairy terns flitted gracefully overhead. Roger saw that there were dark clouds gathering over the sea beyond the aptly named Silhouette Island and behind the headland at the end of the bay. Then his eyes were caught by a slim woman in a yellow dress who was crouching on the sand a few hundred yards away, apparently looking down at something. As he got nearer he saw that it was Imogen Redcliffe.

She looked up and smiled as he approached. In front of her

lay a long, thin, newly dead fish gleaming silver in the sun. It had large eyes, small fins, and an extended pointed beak which gaped, exposing rows of tiny sharp teeth.

'Isn't it strange?' Imogen said to him. 'Somehow I never think of fish having teeth.'

'Piranhas do.'

'True, but this looks more like a fat eel. Do you know what it is?'

'Haven't a clue,' Roger said. 'Ruth might know. She's got a book on the coral reef fish. We'll see even better ones than this when we go snorkelling.'

'I'm a bit worried about that,' Imogen confessed. 'I'm not a very strong swimmer.'

'You don't need to be,' Roger assured her, 'and in the unlikely event that you get into trouble, I'll save you myself. I was a life-guard once.' He made a self-mocking face.

'My hero!' Imogen said, teasing. They stared at each other. Imogen looked away first. She was tough, Roger thought, more of a challenge than some women, definitely not a pushover, but certainly worth it. She shouldn't be rushed though, just taken very slowly and carefully . . .

'Isn't this a fantastic place?' Imogen said. 'I'm so glad I persuaded Barnaby to come.'

'He was reluctant?'

'Well he hates organized fun, that sort of thing.' She inclined her head towards the distant parascending man.

'Him and me both.'

She appeared surprised. 'I'd have thought you'd be keen on water sports,' she said. 'You look the type.'

'No one is ever a *type*' Roger said. 'We're all different inside and we all change, all the time.'

'How true,' Imogen said soberly.

They walked back towards the hotel together. Roger asked her about her job and fed in pieces of information about himself at the same time, picking those which showed most clearly how much they had in common. He discovered that he could make her laugh, and felt encouraged.

After her walk, Imogen found Barnaby in their bathroom, standing naked at the mirror, about to shave. Compared with

27

Roger, his legs looked rather spindly and very pale but he had a good figure for his age and his back was still a little brown from the English summer before. She felt a wave of affection for him, born of her pleasure in her surroundings and her gratitude that he had, in spite of himself, agreed to their being there. She was still smiling inside after her conversation with Roger. She felt unaccountably randy.

'When you've finished shaving, why don't we have a quick snuggle?' she suggested to Barnaby.

'What d'you mean, a cuddle-type snuggle, or the more active sort?'

'Does it matter?'

'Well it does to me.'

'Couldn't we just be spontaneous?'

'I need notice of that sort of question.' Barnaby smiled, looking smug.

'And then we can go down for lunch,' Imogen went on, ignoring this.

'Don't you think that sort of thing is better in the evening?'

'You're always too *tired* then,' Imogen said crossly.

'People usually are, after a hard day's work.' He sounded carefully casual. 'You don't mind, do you?'

Imogen wanted to say, *Yes I mind*. Some people go on having active sex lives well into their eighties. *Of course I mind!* She felt all her old irritation with him resurface. On this special holiday she didn't want to feel sorry for him. She wanted *fun*. She realized of course that he was hoping for reassurance, but felt unable to give it to him; to lie to him just to make him feel better. Instead she avoided the question.

'We're very unadventurous,' she said. 'We never make love anywhere except in bed after dark, and hardly ever then, these days.'

'Oh well, *anno domini* and all that,' Barnaby said, preparing his face for shaving and peering at himself in the mirror.

'We're not that old!' Imogen protested.

'And it's far too hot. I like my sex in comfort.' He began scraping the foam away with a razor, and dabbling the razor into the half-filled basin to clean it between strokes. As usual he seemed careless of her needs, brushing them aside as if they were of little consequence. He always did this when Imogen

28

tried to talk to him on subjects which were important to her. It was as though, sensing a Big Issue in the offing, he would quickly shut the door to exclude it. It was at this point that Imogen usually got angry and forced him to confront whatever it was, by shouting at him. He always maintained that she initiated their rows. He always had the moral high ground.

This was different. She had never before invited him to make love to her. She wished she had anticipated how crushing it would feel to be turned down, then she would never have put herself at such a disadvantage. I won't ask him again, she thought. He's had his chance. Now he can bloody well do without!

'I wonder what the food will be like here,' she said, changing the subject crossly.

'No idea,' Barnaby said, making a monkey face to shave his chin.

'Well of course you haven't! I wasn't asking, just wondering out loud.' He's so *infuriating!* she thought. How do I stand him?

Ruth walked at her own pace along the road behind the hotel with the group on their first exploration of the island. It was slow going, for in spite of half of them having had a rest before lunch, everyone was tired from the journey and overwhelmed by the enervating atmosphere. Still, she was so glad to be back. It felt almost like home. She had looked out of her bedroom window at the rear of the hotel and greeted as an old friend the lumpy mountain peak with its covering of lush vegetation right to the summit. She would get used to the heat and to the fact that cotton clothes never got properly dry. She would put up with more than her usual quota of fatigue. She had done so twice before and it was worth it. She felt almost proprietorial about the place, as though three visits and much studying of the few books about the island flora and fauna had conferred upon her the right to belong there. She looked forward to imparting her knowledge to anyone in the group who might value it, and was surprised and pleased when Leslie was the first to ask.

'What's them sparrow-size birds?' he asked, 'the bright red jobs.'

'Madagascar fodies' Ruth said, 'sometimes known as cardinals. The males are red but the poor females are just a drab brownish colour.'

'Oh, right. And the bigger black ones with yellow on their faces?'

'Indian mynahs, introduced here in the early nineteenth century.'

'My auntie had one of them in a cage in her lounge,' Janice said. 'It made a terrible racket, dawn til dusk. I don't know how she stood it.'

'Poor thing!' Annabel said.

'Well it was her own fault. She would buy it in the first place; wouldn't be told.'

'I meant, poor bird,' Annabel said, colouring.

Ruth wondered whether Annabel and Philip would get together on this trip in solidarity against the wrinklies. She looked round for Philip, but he was yards ahead of the straggling group, striding towards the beach apparently unimpaired by MS, and stopping every so often to stare through his binoculars or hold his camera up for yet another photograph. He was enthusiasm personified, she thought, smiling; a man in his element. She looked around her at the trees above their heads, identifying them again with the pleasure of recognition: the planted coconut palms, the feathery casuarina trees by the shore, the badamier with its red leaves amongst the green, and the takamaka with its laurel-like foliage.

'Isn't it strange,' Barnaby said at her elbow, 'to be in a landscape where nothing is familiar? It makes me feel that I've suddenly escaped from the real world.'

'Is that good?' Ruth asked, changing her stick to the other hand, so as not to trip him with it.

'Yes, I think it is. It engenders a wonderful sense of irresponsibility.'

'That must be an odd feeling for someone like you,' Ruth said.

'You're right,' Barnaby said, surprised. 'How did you know that?' Ruth smiled and shrugged her shoulders. 'Very . . . bother – can't think of the word,' Barnaby said. 'It means . . . not born yesterday.'

'Perspicacious?'

'Yes! Very perspicacious of you. Thank you.'

Ruth felt like a schoolgirl who has been awarded a gold star, and smiled to herself at the absurdity of the thought.

'My God!' Imogen called out suddenly, 'look at those *huge* spiders!'

As they crowded round the webs which spanned the wide spaces between low-growing bushes, with exclamations of amazement and horror, the first enormous drops of rain began to fall. Within seconds it was a deluge, soaking right through their clothes and making running for cover quite unnecessary. The group nevertheless started to walk purposefully back to the hotel. Philip rejoined them, out of breath and bent double, shielding the top of his camera bag from the rain with his body.

'It's amazing,' he panted. 'I've just seen sanderling and turnstone and curlew sandpipers, *European waders* on the beach. Isn't that weird?! I suppose they must be migrants.'

'Like us,' Barnaby said.

'A bit of real life creeping in?' Ruth suggested.

'No,' Barnaby said, 'not for me. The illusion is still complete.'

Ruth turned round to include Roger in the conversation. He was looking the other way, and when she followed his gaze she saw why. In the wet, Imogen's yellow dress had become nearly transparent.

Imogen had noticed earlier on that Barnaby was talking in a cheerful manner to mousy little Ruth, so she felt free to walk separately and chat to whomsoever she wished. She decided to save Annabel from the awful Janice, who had clearly just embarrassed her in some way, because the poor girl's face was bright red, clashing unbecomingly with her hair.

'Isn't this great?' Imogen said to her, smiling.

'Wonderful,' Annabel said shyly. 'A lot better than working!'

'What do you do?'

'I'm a tax inspector.'

'Good God!' Imogen said involuntarily. Then, 'I'm sorry. I expect you always get that sort of negative reaction?'

'Quite often,' Annabel admitted.

'Have you been on one of these trips before?'

'No. Have you?'

'No.' It's hard work so far, Imogen thought, trying to think of some way of getting a proper conversation going. Plunging into personal things was often a good way to break the ice . . . 'You're not married, then?' she asked.

'No.' Annabel looked ready to burst into tears.

'Oh, I'm sorry, was that tactless of me?' Imogen said, making it worse.

'Well,' Annabel gulped, 'it's just that I . . . did have a fiancé three years ago, but he . . . he left me when I was diagnosed with MS. It was only two weeks before . . . before our wedding day.' She bit her lip and lowered her head, so that her hair hid her face from Imogen.

'But that's dreadful!' Imogen exclaimed. 'What a really con-temptible thing for him to do!'

Annabel was silent and Imogen wondered about her back-ground. She had a pleasant speaking voice and was clearly well educated. She was presumably reasonably well off, to be able to afford this trip. Perhaps the de Beauchamps were a wealthy family? Imogen was intrigued.

'Well,' she said, 'he obviously wasn't good enough for you. You're probably well rid of him.'

'Please,' Annabel said, 'don't tell me that there are plenty of other fish in the sea.'

'I wouldn't dream of it,' Imogen said untruthfully. 'I was going to say that marriage seems almost to be out of fashion these days, doesn't it? You're part of the trend. It's always said that a career woman like yourself needs a good wife more than she needs a husband, anyway.'

Annabel looked up, startled. 'What can you mean?'

'Well you know, someone to cook you a meal when you get home after a long day at the office, do the chores, make the bed, warm your slippers, that sort of thing. What did you think I meant?'

'Oh I see . . .' Annabel blushed again. 'Ruth does that for Roger, you know. She told me that she devotes herself to him, now she's not working.'

'Lucky Roger.'

'I was thinking "lucky Ruth" actually,' Annabel said. She gave a little smile and hid behind her hair again.

Aha! Imogen thought. Someone's carrying a torch for Roger Dare. This could prove interesting!

'You won't tell him I said so?' Annabel implored suddenly.
'I didn't – '

'No of course I won't,' Imogen said reassuringly. She looked
about for something with which to change the subject, and
found it. 'My God!' she said, 'Look at those *huge* spiders!'

'Here,' Barnaby said, going across to Imogen, as they were
making their way back through the rain to the hotel. He took
off his shirt. 'Put this round you. You look like the winner of
a wet T-shirt competition!'

Imogen looked down at herself and then snatched the shirt
and put it on.

'Bloody dress,' she muttered, 'I'd no idea . . .' but Barnaby
saw that she didn't look especially embarrassed, just impatient.
'But won't you be cold?' she asked automatically, then laughed.

'Chance would be a fine thing,' Barnaby said. He closed his
eyes, leant his head backwards and held out his arms, so as to
increase the target area of his bare skin for the rain. 'Aaah!' he
said, 'that's better.'

'Cool baths are an excellent way to combat fatigue, even at
home,' Brian said. 'I'm not suggesting that anyone should leap
straight into a freezing bath, just like that; no one but a masochist would be so daft. But I find if you run a warm one, get
into it, and then turn the cold tap on to cool it down gradually,
it really works.'

Barnaby opened his eyes and lowered his arms. 'I hate baths,'
he said. 'I end up feeling totally knackered after one. Showers
are bad enough, but baths are the end.' He wondered why
Brian still had his teeth clamped round his pipe stem (when he
wasn't talking) when the bonfire in the bowl had clearly been
drowned out.

'Well of course,' Brian said. 'People like us shouldn't get too
hot. It's well known to make things worse.'

People like us, Barnaby thought. I am not 'one of us'. I have
no wish to join this particular club, and I wish they wouldn't
keep harking on and on about bloody MS. I'm here for a
holiday, not sodding group therapy!

'You didn't know that?' Brian persisted, surprised. 'Don't
you read the Society's magazines, keep up to date with the
research, that sort of thing?'

'No,' Barnaby said shortly.

'In my experience,' Brian said, 'if you'll pardon me for saying so, denying the existence of a disease like MS doesn't prove very helpful in the long term, especially for those of us with the chronic progressive form. Just because it's incurable so far, doesn't mean there are no useful forms of *management*.' He banged his pipe out on his palm, discarded the soggy contents and put it away in the trouser pocket with the burn mark.

Pompous know-all! Barnaby thought. 'Fine,' he said rudely. 'You do it your way, and I'll do it mine.'

In the abrupt silence that followed this, Barnaby became aware of other conversations going on around him.

Janice was complaining to anyone who would listen: 'Well if I'd known it was going to rain like this, I'd have stayed put at home. I mean, English rain is nice and gentle, but this is hammering down like stair-rods; I'm wet to the bone!'

'Well what d'you expect in the tropics?' Daisy asked her. 'Haven't you ever heard of tropical rainforests?'

'If getting too hot is bad for MS,' Leslie challenged Roger, 'then why bring us here of all places? Or is it for your own benefit? I'd have gone to Norway if I'd'a known. I was led to believe that you were an expert.'

'It has worked out fine in previous years,' Roger assured him. 'You'll have to take my word that you'll all get used to the climate in a matter of a few days, and be glad you came.'

'I do so hate the word *incurable*,' Annabel said passionately to Dorothy. 'It's so final and so terrifying.'

'It may not be so bad, dear,' Dorothy said comfortingly. 'These things are sent to try us. I mean, look how Daisy manages at 70! I think she's wonderful. It moves me to tears sometimes, just watching her.'

Simon said to Claire, 'God what a load of whingers! Are Dare's trips always like this?'

'It depends,' Claire said carefully. 'Some individuals take longer than others to shake down into a cohesive group. Sometimes it just doesn't happen.'

'Trust my luck to have picked one of the latter,' Simon said in disgust. 'What are you going to do about it, then? How are you going to earn your keep? I take it this is a free trip for you?'

'Perhaps,' Claire said deliberately, 'if some people made sure that their brains were in gear before operating their mouths, we'd all be better off.'

Barnaby found that Imogen was slipping her arm through his, and felt her giving it an urgent tug. He glanced down at her. She was wearing the determined look he'd learnt to be wary of.

'Look,' she said to him, in a fierce whisper, 'for heaven's sake don't be so *inflexible*. At least *listen* to other people's point of view. I mean, God preserve us, you might even *learn* something! What's the point of coming thousands of miles to a wonderful place if you're just going to be the same pig-headed, hidebound, impervious prat that you were to begin with?'

'Well thanks a lot,' Barnaby said tightly. Here we go again! he thought.

'Look Barnaby, whether we like it or not, we're stuck with these people. They may turn out to be quite different from our first impressions of them. They may be worth making some effort to get to know!'

'I doubt that.'

'But what's the point of being here if you won't even *try*?'

'It wasn't my idea, if you remember, to come here at all.'

'Oh great!' Imogen said furiously. 'I suppose it's all my fault, is it? Well sod you then, but I'll tell you one thing: I'm going to make this group work, *and* have the best holiday of my life, even if it bloody kills me, *so there*!'

4

WHEN Imogen woke the following morning after a surprisingly cool and comfortable night, she felt (as one of her colleagues had once described her) full of piss and ginger, and even more determined to encourage the group into a harmonious working unit. She was surprised that Roger and Claire seemed not to realize that this role was part of their function as leaders. Neither of them, it appeared, had so far made a point of approaching any potentially disaffected individuals to find out how their grumbles could be defused. Both Roger and Claire seemed to have the attitude that they'd done their job in bringing everybody here and sorting out their itinerary, and now it was up to the punters to make the most of it: a brisk, businesslike approach which wouldn't admit to any problems. Imogen could see that this probably made the holiday more enjoyable for *them*, but it didn't make for consensus. Imogen prided herself on her person-management skills. The important thing to do first was to talk to everyone in turn, find out each one's background, any problems or disasters they'd had in the past, and to discover their hopes and ambitions. That way, you really got to know the person, and could make allowances for their irritating habits or apparently groundless fears. Then you could explain these to the other people in the group, the ones that they were annoying, and thus bring people together. It was only common sense really, but very rewarding when it worked.

So Imogen set herself the task of manipulating the assorted jarring egos until they all vibrated on the same neutral frequency; until everyone got the message that it was worth while making small sacrifices for the sake of creating harmony in the group as a whole, and that they would all have a better holiday as a result. She firmly believed that it should not be beyond the wit of anyone to appreciate the merits of such a plan. Of course you couldn't expect that sort of simplistic approach to work in an open-ended situation like life, but just for a fortnight . . .?

Today they were all due to go together on a tour of the island. Imogen decided that she would sit in the first vacant seat on the coach and make a start with that person, whoever it turned out to be. Barnaby was still in a mood from yesterday, and she was fed up with him. He could sit with anyone he pleased.

Shirley was pleasantly surprised when Imogen sat down next to her, and looked forward to a good gossip while the coach drove them round Mahé on the preliminary sightseeing tour. Shirley was always interested in what made people tick. Instead, she was surprised to find that it was she who was doing most of the talking, drawn out by Imogen who proved to be an excellent listener. She found herself telling Imogen her life story: how her brother Brian had always been the one expected to have a career, and how in spite of this, she had trained as a nurse, but in later years had been obliged to give it up to look after their invalid parents, until they had died. Then, how she had just been going to regain her freedom when Brian had been struck down, and how she'd felt obliged to move into a house next to him in order to look after him in turn, because he'd had such a hard time and fate had been so cruel.

'But he's not nearly as badly affected as some people, is he?' Imogen said. 'I mean, he could be in a wheelchair or even dead after all this time.'

'Well that's what I mean about the cruelty of fate,' Shirley said. 'When Brian first knew he had MS (and it was years before they found out what it was) he was married then, and his wife was desperate for children. But Brian (he's a very honourable man, my brother) well he *knew* he was destined for total paralysis and an early grave (no one had any proper information about it then, you see) and he loved June (that's his wife) ever so much, you see. He didn't want her to suffer and be dragged down too . . .'

'So what happened?'

'He divorced her.'

'That was a bit drastic, wasn't it?'

'Well he calls it a futile gesture now (when he talks of it, which isn't often) but I think it was truly heroic, because he really did love her.'

'Poor Brian! So what happened to June?'

'Oh she was all right, married Brian's best friend in the end and had five children, did June. It worked out fine for her.'

'But it meant that you had to look after him instead?'

'Oh well that's different, isn't it? I'm his sister, and we're very close.'

'I used to fight with my brother,' Imogen confessed. 'I was horribly competitive.'

'Oh Brian and I did everything together when we were young,' Shirley said. 'Especially hill-walking. We tried bagging all the Munros (in Scotland you know; the summits above 3,000 feet), and over the years we managed 250 of them. Those were the days!'

'But *you* could still go hill-walking now,' Imogen said.

'Well maybe, but I haven't to leave him for too long, you see. He can't even make toast. He's useless!'

'Where would you walk if you had the freedom to go anywhere?'

'Oh the Himalayas; top of the world! I don't mind snow and ice, maybe it's because I'm well padded.' Shirley patted her midriff and felt it quiver. Then she laughed deprecatingly. 'What a daft couple we are!' she said. 'Fancy me going on about the cold, here of all places!'

Ruth looked happily out of the coach window as they drove along the high road behind the capital, Victoria. It was no larger than a small town, and spread only half-way up the hills surrounding its bay; scattered houses with much dark green between them. They were heading for the Rochon viewpoint where one could gaze eastwards towards Cerf and Sainte Anne and other islands on the far blue horizon. Today and tomorrow the group would go everywhere together. There would be no division into 'us' and 'them'. Ruth wished it could be so every day, but of course the able-bodied had to be allowed to explore on foot. Roger (it was always Roger – why not Claire some days?) would take them off, often for most of the day, and then she could only guess what he might be doing. She wished she hadn't such a vivid imagination. Ruth felt her thighs welding themselves to the hot plastic seat, and shuffled her bottom to unstick them. The palms of her hands were wet with sweat and she wiped them surreptitiously on her shorts, looking round at the others. Philip, who had been staring intently out of the window, was now leafing furiously through the bird book.

'Cave swiftlets,' he called to Daisy, 'and white-tailed tropic birds. Beat that!'

'Barred ground doves and a monarch butterfly,' Daisy countered.

'Cheat!'

Ruth caught his eye and smiled at him. In his excitement he had run his fingers through his fringe, and it was standing on end at the front, like baby hair. Ruth had never had any babies. Roger hadn't wanted to be tied down. Maybe it had been just as well; MS might yet turn out to be partly hereditary.

The coach turned off the road and parked in the shade of some tall trees with the horizontally spreading growth habit of cedars, but covered in white flowers.

'Albizia,' Ruth said to Barnaby as she negotiated the steps behind him.

'These trees?'

'Yes.'

'I was just going to ask you that!'

Beyond the trees there were great expanses of bare grey rock.

'Exposed granite,' Roger explained, gathering the group around him, 'called glacis by the Seychellois. Now, does anyone here know anything about geology or continental drift? No? Good, then I can speak with authority.' Ruth wondered what he would do if, one year, somebody were to challenge him. She could guess. He would hand over the job with alacrity, and maybe even learn something for the next time. He wasn't macho about his leadership. He was always happy to defer to genuine scholarship; he just couldn't bear poseurs.

'It's very unusual for offshore islands like these to be granitic,' Roger went on, 'and it probably means that they must once have been part of a continent. In this case, they were most likely to have been attached to both Africa and India as a small piece of Gondwanaland; the southern arm of the super-continent of Pangaea, 135 million years ago . . .'

The view from the glacis was very fine. Ruth looked out over the flat tops of more albizia trees, and red-flowered Nile tulip trees beside the occasional house roof, down to the bright sea and its islands. She could see half a dozen cargo boats trading to and from Victoria. It was utterly peaceful. Ruth remembered that she had found lemon grass, cinnamon and Chinese guava growing here the previous year, and inched herself rather awkwardly off the rocky outcrop on her bottom, in search of them. Roger had finished his talk and was pointing out the distant islands to Imogen.

'As far as I'm aware, there's no absolute proof that plate-tectonics is anything more than a fanciful theory,' Simon said to Daisy.

'Nonsense!' she said. 'I find it entirely convincing. I read a fascinating book about it once, called restless something . . . *Restless Earth*, yes.'

'Oh, *popular science*,' Simon scoffed. 'That's as bad as religion, in my book. In fact it's taken over from religion as the opium of the people, and it doesn't offer any more absolute truth than its predecessor. More than that, it positively misleads.'

'You're not a scientist, then?'

'Oh yes I am! but *pure* science, not popular. I'm a computer specialist.'

'How very interesting,' Roger said, and in a careless under-tone added, 'Have you tried *Intelligent Strategy Games*, or *Lemmings*, or *Fighting Master*, or is *Splatterhouse Two* more your scene?'

'Sniff these,' Ruth said hurriedly to Annabel, crushing assorted leaves between her fingers and offering them up.

'Mmmm, lovely. You could use those for aromatherapy, couldn't you? I'm really into alternative medicine, are you too?'

'Well I can't say I've ever tried it myself. I just like nice smells,' Ruth said. She held her fingers up for Claire to sniff.

'Oh that one's perfect, mmmm . . . I can't remember its name.'

'Pure cinnamon,' Ruth said, inclining her head mockingly in Simon's direction, 'and popular as well!'

'I know which I'd rather be,' Claire said.

Right! Imogen thought to herself as they boarded the coach again. If I want a challenge it's obvious who I should sit next to this time. She slid into the seat next to Simon and smiled a (convincing?) smile at him.

'That's Brian's seat,' he said.

'Well there's no need to be rigid about these things, is there? It's more sociable if we swap around a bit.'

'I'm not a great one for sociability,' Simon said.

You said it! Imogen thought. 'What do you do in computers?' she asked.

'Program them, develop new systems, find faults.'

Oh, finding fault is your career? That explains a lot! 'Is that more interesting than it sounds?' she asked.

'Well it wouldn't be for you.'

Sexist pig! 'No, you're probably right. I'm keener on people than on machines.' There was a silence. Imogen wondered how Simon had managed to get himself on to this holiday without a friend or partner, since that was the whole point of Leisure Doubletrips. Perhaps he hadn't one? 'Do you always travel alone?' she asked him.

'Do you always ask impertinent questions?'

'Yes, often,' Imogen said, unabashed. 'I find it saves time.'

'Oh well, I'm all for that.' Was there a gleam of amusement behind the spectacles? Imogen was encouraged.

'Well?' she said.

'Well if you must know, yes I prefer to travel alone.'

'One of my daughters was very keen on computing at school,' Imogen said, 'but in the end she did engineering at university.' Simon made a noncommittal noise and looked out of the window. 'Do you have any children?'

Simon turned furiously to her. 'Look!' he said, 'once and for all, I have no wife or "partner", no children of either sex, no dogs, cats, stick insects or gerbils. I don't collect things. I don't give dinner parties. I don't join clubs. I haven't a microwave, a dishwasher or a video recorder, and above all, *I mind my own business*!'

Imogen laughed. 'Brilliant!' she said, 'very slick. So you're against consumerism. Property is theft, and all that?'

'I'll bet you don't know who first said that?' Simon challenged.

'No idea.'

'A French socialist called Proudhon; Pierre-Joseph Proudhon, died in 1865. And the saying "property is theft" had nothing whatsoever to do with modern so-called consumerism, but was all about appropriating the labour of others in the form of rent.'

'Goodness,' Imogen said. 'However do you remember such things?'

'I have a logical brain, but a memory which for some illogical reason is addicted to useless knowledge,' Simon said.

'A storehouse of inconsequentia?'

'There's no such word.'

'There is now.'

'Mmm,' Simon said, 'perhaps I've underestimated you. Because you're not unattractive, I naturally assumed you to be – '

'Frivolous? Bird-witted?'

'Non-combative.'

'Why?' Imogen was taken aback.

'Because only ugly women have to fight for what they want, of course. Surely that's obvious?'

'It's obvious crap!' Imogen said heatedly. 'Where have you been for the last hundred years?'

'Nothing's really changed for centuries,' Simon said. 'Superficially perhaps, but not basic human nature. Look around you. You'll see that I'm right.' He gave her a triumphant (and at the same time, dismissive) smile and turned back to look at the view.

Oh well done, Mrs Redcliffe! Imogen told herself. That's increased the sum of human understanding by leaps and bounds.

For Janice Cromwell the places they visited on that first day all merged with each other in her memory, but the tea plantation stood out as the background for her first verbal blow in the class war. Roger had invited the able-bodied members of the group to walk ahead of the rest in order to explore it properly with a local guide, while the others either rested in the coach or wandered slowly as far as they wanted to.

Janice walked with the advance party along the dirt road

which started out through a wood of tall jungly trees. Large orange puddles of rainwater stretched right across their path and made the going awkward in places. Janice stepped carefully round their edges, but failed to keep her sandals or her toes entirely clean.

'I'm not a fussy woman but I must say, I never expected mud!' she said.

She saw Shirley and Imogen exchange a look, and felt at once defensive and hurt. It was going to be the same here as everywhere else, just as she had feared. People were going to gang up against her merely because she was straightforward and spoke as she found. After all, she only said things that other people were actually thinking but were too hypocritical to say out loud. This lot were going to be toffee-nosed as well and look down on her and Leslie. (She had told him they would, but he wouldn't listen.) None of them had expected mud either she was sure, so why pretend, and why sneer?

She decided to ignore them and began to look about her. Zigzag stems of vanilla stretched up the trunks of tall mahogany trees, each with a leaf growing from every kink in perfect symmetry, like vertical embroidery. A little green gecko with feet resembling a sparse bunch of grapes was walking upside-down on a dead stump. At the edge of the road Janice saw a brown snail in a grey shell which was twice as big as any she had ever seen before. It was huge! She began for the first time to be intrigued by the things around her. At home nature was something you fought, slugs on your lettuces, spiders in your bath, tits pecking your milk-bottle tops – but here, everything had more right to exist than she did. Snails could be as big as they pleased; she was not responsible.

'I wouldn't fancy one of them things on my cabbages,' she said to Roger.

'African land snail,' he said, following her pointing finger. 'Handsome brute, isn't he?'

'Well that's not the word I'd use,' Janice said.

Handsome was what she had considered Leslie to be in their youth, before he lost all his hair. If only they'd had money then, instead of now, then he wouldn't have had to spend nearly thirty years slaving away for the Post Office. They could have had this special holiday years ago, when they were both fit and

43

well and able to make the most of it. It wasn't just Leslie who was unfit. She herself might be only 53, but most of the time she felt a lot older. Everyone assumed that the two of them would end their lives with Janice looking after Leslie, but privately she was convinced that she would be the one to go first; that Leslie might even have to care for her instead . . .

They walked out from the trees onto an open hillside which had been cleared for growing tea. The road wound ahead of them, cut into a terrace in the red earth. On either side of it, identical regularly spaced low-growing tea bushes covered all the ground like dark green candlewick. Beyond were a few taller trees and then on the horizon, the sea. Janice had never before seen soil such a colour, brighter even than the fields in Devon. She had never considered either how tea was grown. It seemed a big leap of imagination to go from these chunky, ordinary-looking bushes to tiny bits of dried leaf, infused in boiling water and added to milk and sugar; an unexciting but essential part of everyday existence. She wondered who had first thought of it, and how many different sort of leaves they'd tried first . . . and if people had jeered at them? Suddenly she realized that she had forgotten for well over five minutes how hot and uncomfortable she felt. Even her headache had gone.

Janice was glad she had put on a cotton hat and made Leslie do the same. The sun was really beating down today. That Roger was taking a chance wasn't he? Even if he did have thick (dyed?) hair. She hated those mirror sunglasses he wore; you couldn't tell what a person was thinking or where they were looking, if you couldn't see their eyes. It was sinister. She didn't take to Roger. He fancied himself too much: the sort of man who would only notice you if you were pretty, something she had never been.

The guide was talking to them about tea production and Janice listened with half an ear, sizing up her able-bodied companions as they stood in a cluster together. I might not have had their advantages, she thought, but I'm as good as them any day and I'm going to make damn sure I keep my end up. And now they were moving back again, retracing their steps to the coach.

'It sounds ridiculous,' Imogen said, beside her, 'after that wonderful breakfast at the hotel, but I'm hungry again! Wasn't

44

the variety of fruit simply astonishing? I just didn't know which to choose!'

Janice distrusted enthusiasm. To her mind, it was gushing and insincere. She too had been surprised by the good quality and great quantity of fish, meat and local fruits on offer, both at supper the night before and at breakfast, but she wasn't going to go over the top about it. It wasn't in her nature to exaggerate; those that did usually got their comeuppance. It was tempting fate.

'Too much fruit doesn't agree with me,' she told Imogen. 'It can play havoc with your insides, you know, and I've got a very delicate digestion.' Imogen now looked as though she had a bad smell under her nose. Huh! Janice thought. She thinks she's too grand to have bodily functions, does she?

'Forgive me for asking,' Imogen said, 'but have you ever heard of positive thinking?'

'Oh yes, I can be very *positive*,' Janice retorted, thinking, Uppish snob! 'Especially about things I don't like.'

They ate a picnic lunch high up in a small open-sided hut with a panoramic view. Imogen ate her sandwiches gratefully, and drank a lot of iced water from a bottle in a cool-box. She took in the view, and watched some yellow potter wasps above her head, building a tiny nest comb on one of the rafters. They had walked here, a short distance from the coach, through an avenue of great trees with untidy roots that began too soon, before they were safely underground. The trees also had spreading buttresses to hold them up, like aircraft delta wings, which started well above their heads and met the soil with their leading edges a good ten feet away from the parent trunks.

'Dragon blood trees,' Ruth had said. 'If you cut their bark, the sap runs red.' She was talking to Barnaby now, Imogen noticed, telling him more names of trees. Imogen had never known him to be much interested in such things before. Ruth was wasting her time anyway; Barnaby would never remember them. 'That one is *bois de fer*,' Ruth pointed, 'and this one *bois rouge*.' Imogen preferred the exotic flame trees herself. They were dramatic, but entirely up-front with no concealed perversity like blood-red sap.

On the coach again after lunch, she sat by Philip and allowed him the window seat. She watched as he wrote in his notebook: *plus Seychelles bulbul, S. sunbird (subfusc.), turtle dove.* Then he snapped it shut and grinned at her.

'It's terrible,' he said, 'there's so much to see that if I photograph one thing, I miss ten others!' He turned back to the window. They were down at sea level again, and passing a small relict mangrove swamp which had so far escaped being reclaimed. On the open patches of water between the gnarled whitish trunks, pale tips of hundreds of aerial roots pierced the dark surface. 'Did you see that?' Philip asked her. 'The water looked like a fakir's bed of nails, but in negative; white on black!'

He's my sort of person, Imogen thought, an enthusiast. It would have been nice to have had a son – a healthy son.

'You seem very fit,' she said to him. 'It's good to see how well you walk.'

'Yes,' he said, 'I've been lucky. Only one bad attack so far, when my right arm became paralysed and I went temporarily blind. That's when I found out what I'd got.'

'How did you cope?'

'Oh they took me to hospital and pumped me full of steroids and then gave me rehabilitational physio, and I got better eventually. I never think about it actually, just carry on as before. Don't let's talk about it now.'

'Sorry,' Imogen said, and cast about for something else. 'Are you and Daisy competing as to who can see the most birds?'

'Yes. She's great, isn't she? A really tough old bird herself. Trouble is, it's unfair on her because I can walk further so I see more, but she says she doesn't mind if I win. In fact it's neck and neck at the moment.'

'Can I have your attention?' Roger said, standing up at the front of the coach. 'We've got time for a quick dip on this western side of the island where the sea is more interesting, before we go back to the hotel. Any takers?'

Only Roger, Claire, Shirley and Imogen herself went for a swim, the others being too tired or too lazy. The waves were huge and salty and the water as warm as an occupied bed. She swam strongly beyond the wall of breakers and then lay on her back and floated with her eyes closed. It was bliss.

'You're a good swimmer,' Roger said approvingly, swimming

up beside her and treading water. 'I thought you said you weren't?'

'Mmmm.'

'I'm going for a swim from the hotel beach after supper tonight. It's a great feeling, swimming in a hot sea in the dark. Fancy joining me?'

5

On the second day Claire got up early in a now re-established routine to breakfast with Roger and Ruth and discuss the day ahead. She sat in the dining room at a table right next to the beach in what would normally be called a window seat, except that here it was without glass, its blinds rolled up out of the way, open to the air. Outside, hotel staff were smoothing out the white unblemished sand with garden rakes. Claire wondered whether she would get through the whole holiday without having to cope with any significant medical emergencies? Judging from past experience it was ironic, but true, that all the problems would come from the so-called able-bodied members of the group. Those with MS were stoical, or perhaps they already had the sympathy vote and didn't need more attention of that kind? From this group, it was obvious who had decided to extract value for money from the resident GP. Janice had already been to Claire, complaining of a pain in her temple and hinting darkly that of course she wasn't making a fuss, but there might be more to it than a simple headache. Claire had given her no-nonsense aspirin and wondered why she hadn't had the wit to bring some of her own? She was clearly a hypochondriac, the sort who never has a headache where a migraine or a brain tumour will do . . . She's probably jealous of the attention Leslie gets and is seeking to equalize things, Claire thought. It's not an unknown phenomenon; sad, though.

Claire ate her breakfast, savouring the delicious scents and textures of the fruits on her plate: the pineapple and mango, the papaya and guava. The weather was too hot for her to have much of an appetite, but small amounts of these she found positively ambrosial.

'Morning,' Roger said, appearing at her table bearing a large cooked breakfast.

'Hi.' Claire looked round for Ruth. She was getting herself some toast from the far counter. 'Sorry if Shirley and I queered your pitch last night,' she said, grinning knowingly at him, 'but Imogen was most insistent that we should join her on your midnight swim!'

'Of course. Why not?' Roger said dismissively. 'The more the merrier.'

Oh, I get it, Claire thought. New rules this year; cessation of sexual relations precludes any more intimate conversations. Well that's fine. What you get up to is a matter of supreme indifference to me anyway.

'Hello Claire,' Ruth said, as she too arrived. She put her plate of toast and fruit down on the table and hung her stick on the back of her chair before sitting down. 'I always look forward to glass-bottomed-boat day,' she said. 'I find it so much more enjoyable than snorkelling.'

'I'm just the opposite,' Claire said. 'Pity the weather's so grey today. I expect Moaning Minnie will hold us personally responsible for it.'

Ruth laughed. 'Poor thing,' she said.

'Poor thing be blowed,' Roger said. 'You can see the chip on her shoulder from a thousand paces! And what's more, she positively glories in disappointment.'

'Sssh!' Ruth said. 'Here she and Leslie are now.'

'Hollywood was said by somebody to be like a trip through a sewer in a glass-bottomed boat, wasn't it?' Imogen said to Barnaby as she got dressed. She had decided to wear a long-sleeved shirt and cotton trousers, to avoid sunburn.

Barnaby frowned. 'I don't remember who.' He paused in the act of shaving for a moment and then quoted: ' "He proposed seven times once in a hackney-coach once in a boat once in a pew once on a donkey at Tunbridge Wells and the rest on his knees" – *Little Dorrit*, and a good example of – '?

Imogen glared at him, exasperated. 'Oh do shut up!'

' . . . syllepsis.'

'So you *always* say, but what's that got to do with anything at this precise moment?'

'Well the boat bit reminded me, and it's about as relevant as your remark.'

'No it isn't. How can it be?' She stopped buttoning up her shirt and stared at him. 'You've forgotten, haven't you?'

'What?'

'You've forgotten that we're going out in a glass-bottomed boat today. How can you have? We were only discussing it last night.' She frowned. 'I'm getting worried about you.'

'It's of no consequence,' Barnaby said crossly. 'Don't go on so.'

Imogen held her breath for a few moments to prevent herself from rising to this, and then tried another tack,

'I'm discovering that the group are much more interesting when you get to know them,' she said. 'Some of them have had real tragedies in their lives, things you'd never guess just by looking at them.' Barnaby didn't comment. Imogen said, 'Do you know, Brian even divorced his wife because he loved her so much, and then Shirley sacrificed her entire career to look after him! Actually, to me that proves that Shirley is a doormat, but a heroic one.'

'A heroic doormat? Isn't that a – damn! you know what I'm trying to say – a contradiction in terms. Hell! . . . oh yes, I've got it: an oxymoron?' Barnaby expelled air down his nose in a contemptuous snort and went on shaving.

Imogen frowned, but went on, 'And Annabel's fiancé ditched her days before their wedding. Wasn't that cruel?'

'Perhaps it was all for the best.'

'What d'you mean?'

'Well, better before the wedding than afterwards.'

'Before their relationship was confirmed and inevitable, you mean?'

'No, I mean at least it saved them the expense of getting divorced!'

'What a heartless thing to say! I bet you'd have a less flippant attitude if it had been the fiancé who had been ill and Annabel who had walked out on him.'

'Why should it be any different?'

'I don't know, but it is. Women are supposed to be more unselfish, more self-sacrificing, I suppose.'

'I'm not sure that I believe that.'

'You think women should behave just like men in those circumstances?'

'Why not?'

'After marriage as well as before?'

'Why not, if they can afford to.'

Why not indeed, Imogen thought. It was typical of Barnaby to have seen the problem simply in terms of money, entirely unmindful of any emotional connotations. To Imogen, any unilateral separation of lovers at any stage was a betrayal, regardless of whether or not they were legally bound together. Barnaby clearly did not share that view. He seemed to be saying that it was all right as long as no contracts were broken, but if they were, and you could afford it, then that wasn't so bad either. Taken to its conclusion, that line of reasoning would argue that money solved everything.

'So you'd say that the very rich don't suffer as much in divorce as the less well off?' she challenged.

'Probably true,' Barnaby agreed.

'But that's utter nonsense!'

Barnaby looked at his watch. 'Are we having any breakfast today, or what?' he asked.

Remember, Imogen told herself firmly, *no arguments*.

'Oh come on then,' she said ungraciously.

'And Imo . . .' Barnaby put both hands on her shoulders and looked down at her – 'let's have less concentration on the case-histories of members of the group, eh? You're not at the CAB now and there's nothing you can do for them in this short space of time, so why don't you just relax and enjoy your holiday?' Imogen shrugged off his hands crossly. It was no use explaining to him what she was trying to do. He would be determined not to understand.

Imogen went down to breakfast with Barnaby, still reflecting on Annabel's fiancé's behaviour and the ethics of leaving someone. Barnaby's attitude had surprised her. She had thought that, after all their years together, she knew him inside-out. She would have predicted that he would have been much more stuffy about the breaking up of relationships, and yet here he was preaching sexual equality! It's fine when it's just theory, she thought, but he'd do a smart ideological U-turn if he himself were ever faced with divorce.

Over breakfast, Imogen glanced briefly at Barnaby across the table as he chatted to the rest of the group about nothing much. She wondered if other people ever divorced their husbands because they irritated them, or because they had become boring? Each was too trivial an offence, surely? People tended to proffer grander reasons: *Our love has died.* But when you thought about it, what did that mean? Wasn't it exactly the same thing? Of course illnesses like MS complicated the problem, but did they make it insoluble; make marriage indissoluble? Clearly not in some cases. If it had been her with the MS, would Barnaby have left her? By all accounts men in that position did so more readily than women. Imogen had to admit to herself that he probably would not have done so. He was too conventional, too *inert*.

'And what were you doing while all this was going on?' Imogen looked up with a start to see Brian and the rest of the group smiling and looking quizzically at her. She focused carefully on Brian's dominant eye.

'Sorry. I was miles away. What?'

'You appear to have missed a good story, but I expect you've heard it a few times before. Most wives have, haven't they?'

Imogen looked round blankly, and it was only when she finally looked at her husband and saw the smirk of satisfaction on his face that she realized it had been his story that she had missed. Barnaby was suddenly the life and soul of the party? That was ironic! Who here would believe that only half an hour before he had been tetchy and determined to disagree with everything she said? They probably all thought he was wonderful. She had thought that too, once.

The glass-bottomed boat looked to Brian like the back of an open-sided lorry which had been sliced off and, by some miracle, made to float. It was oblong in cross-section and had few concessions to boaty-ness and no streamlining at all. Vertical rails supported the fibreglass roof, and could be covered by awnings, at present rolled up to the top in sausages on either side. When he climbed awkwardly aboard, he saw that the glass bottom at the centre of the boat could be looked down upon by standing at the central rail which surrounded it. It was a lot lower down than he had imagined, in a sort of pit like an empty paddling pool. Through it he could see the water, but nothing much else. It was a cloudy day. Presumably more was visible when the sun shone? Two local crewmen and a girl helped the rest of the group in, and they settled themselves sideways on the narrow bench round the inside of the hull. The whole contraption seemed to Brian to be about as seaworthy as a cardboard box. Well, he thought to himself, if we drown, we drown. There's nowt I can do about it. He felt about in his trouser pockets for his pipe and tobacco pouch and sat contentedly stuffing it as they motored slowly past the commercial shipping berths and out of Victoria harbour towards the nearest small islands.

'That ship's from Vladivostok!' Philip exclaimed, lowering his binoculars momentarily. Everyone followed his pointing finger and smiled indulgently.

'Vladivostok,' Barnaby said, 'the terminus of the Trans-Siberian railway. Now that's a trip I'd love to take.'

'I did it last year,' Simon said unexpectedly. 'It was expensive, but mostly worth it.' He allowed himself to be drawn on the subject. Brian lit his pipe and threw the match over the side, listening with only half an ear.

'Brian?' Imogen spoke quietly and touched him on the arm to gain his attention. 'Could I talk to you privately some time, about MS? I feel I know so little about it, and our doctor is worse than useless. He just pats me on the head and says don't worry.'

'That's a common experience,' Brian said. 'Yes of course you can. Barnaby too, if he wants.'

'He doesn't,' Imogen said. 'That's part of the problem.'

'I gathered as much.'

'I can't think why. I mean, "knowledge itself is power", and all that.'

'I agree with you, but it's surprising how many people prefer to ignore reality in the hope that it will go away. Tell you what, why don't you wait until after I've given my lecture on the subject? It'll get things more in focus for you.'

'You're giving a talk?'

'I have done on past trips. Roger usually asks me to, if there's enough folk expressing an interest.'

'Oh good,' Imogen said, 'that will be such a help.' She smiled

53

warmly at him. She was a good-looking woman, Brian thought, lovely blue eyes. Not a good subject for sketching, though – features too regular. Now, someone neurotic like Annabel was much more of a challenge. She was sitting on his other side with her back to him as she gazed out over the sea. He studied her profile with a practised eye, and at that moment the boat reached the coral reef and slowed down to linger over it.

'Blimey,' Leslie said, peering over the central rail. 'It's like one damn great aquarium down there, isn't it?'

After the reef-watching, as the boat made its way onwards between the cluster of islands, Philip got into the swing of his juggling act between camera and binoculars and stopped worrying about the tangle of straps round his neck. The light wasn't as good as he'd hoped for but perhaps it would improve. He felt buoyantly optimistic and determined to miss *nothing*. He had never been abroad before and he was captivated by the strangeness of the flora and fauna and the promise of rarity. True, he was feeling knackered a lot of the time, but he was going to fight it all the way.

'That one,' Claire said in his ear, 'is said to be owned by an Englishman.' She pointed at the small low island, a rocky green-covered cone with palm trees, surrounded by a ring of white sand on a lapping turquoise background; the perfect desert island. 'I wouldn't mind being marooned there!' she added.

'Yeah,' he agreed out of politeness.

When they landed on the stone-built jetty on Round Island, Philip was the first off and itching to be everywhere first, in case any birds got scared away by the crowd before he could see them. He judged the island to be so small that he could walk all round it in no time. He set off straight away, walking where possible on the beach where the going was easy and lurking behind the large granite boulders at its upper edge to search out anything that moved, without being seen first. He was so intent upon his plan that he failed to notice that Claire was keeping up and was not far behind him as he ducked down to avoid alarming a small upright bird standing on a rock at the water's edge. He had just got the picture composed and well focused, and was about to squeeze the shutter-release button, when it took fright and flew off.

'Damn!' He scowled over the top of his camera at the departing bird.

'What was that?' Claire asked.

'Oh . . .! I didn't realize you were there. Green-backed heron. It must have seen you.'

'Sorry about that.'

He started to continue his walk and was dismayed to find that Claire matched her stride with his and walked alongside. He was lumbered.

'Um . . . would you mind ducking when I duck? If you're going the same way as me, that is.'

'Sure.'

Philip would rather have gone on alone, but could think of no tactful way of getting rid of her. In fact she behaved impeccably and followed his lead so well that he had no grounds for complaint. The next shore bird was a familiar European wader, and Philip took a particular pleasure in capturing it on film in such an exotic location.

'What's that one?' Claire whispered as he let out his pent-up breath and lowered the camera.

'Grey plover, another one of ours.'

'Have you always been interested in birds?'

'Since I was ten, or so.'

'So is your job connected with wildlife?'

Philip laughed. 'No way, I'm a chef.'

'God! I simply hate cooking. How do you stand it?'

'I love it. I love being here too.'

'Isn't it great,' Claire said fervently. 'We're so lucky.' She smiled brilliantly at him. He realized that she might have been quite good-looking in her twenties. She was slim and had good cheekbones, but now she was going grey at the edges and had fine lines round her eyes and mouth, which this light rather cruelly emphasized.

'I've never met a chef before,' she said. 'You must give me some tips.'

'I never mix business with pleasure,' he said, raising his binoculars and scanning the shoreline.

'That's a shame,' she said lightly. 'Life's so much more interesting when you do.' When he lowered his binoculars again he saw that she had walked away from him and was just disappearing amongst the trees. He had an uncomfortable feeling that he had offended her, without in the least knowing how.

It was not until he had walked all round the island and encountered the others again that Roger took him confidentially on one side.

'One word of warning, Philip,' he said, glancing round to make sure he was not being overheard. 'Claire can be a bit predatory at times, know what I mean?'

'Uh?'

'Over-sexed. But forewarned is forearmed and all that.'

'Oh . . . yes . . . right.'

After Roger had rejoined the rest of the group and left him on his own again, Philip became aware that his mouth was still agape in astonishment. He shut it firmly. Surely to God Claire hadn't been trying to chat him up? It was unthinkable. Claire was *old*, for Christ's sake! And yet he suppposed that she might have been giving him the come-on, now he thought about it. He had as usual been tuned to a different frequency. When I do get involved in a 'relationship', he thought (if I ever do), it certainly won't be with someone like her! My ideal kind of girl would be much softer, more like my mum . . . Then he thought, But maybe I never will? There's a lot to be said for celibacy. Women always want kids and security and I've got nothing to offer.

It did not occur to Philip to wonder how Roger knew about Claire's alleged libidinous behaviour. He was not curious about other people's affairs. He kept his own life very private and respected the rights of all to equal privacy. 'The last thing I need,' he said under his breath, 'is some middle-aged man-eater in hunting mode.' Then it occurred to him that this was patently ridiculous, and most probably Roger was just taking the piss. He laughed shortly and raised his binoculars again.

Ruth found herself helped off the glass-bottomed boat by Imogen, who gave Daisy and Dorothy a hand as well. The four women set off together for a gentle stroll. At the top end of the jetty on Round Island was a notice headed: ST ANNE MARINE NATIONAL PARK enjoining all visitors not to disturb the wildlife and ending with the injunction: REMEMBER TAKE ONLY PHOTO-GRAPHS AND LEAVE ONLY FOOTPRINTS.

56

'Oh,' Dorothy breathed, 'isn't that a beautiful way of putting it?' She got out a hanky and blotted her eyes.

'Would that humans would always leave so little evidence of their presence,' Daisy said, 'but it takes more than a well-turned slogan to deter us, I fear.'

'Perhaps we shouldn't be here at all?' Imogen suggested.

'Oh I don't know,' Ruth said. 'I think people like us who care about the environment can only do good, by travelling and spreading the word.'

'Well of course you'd have to say that, wouldn't you?' Imogen said it teasingly, but with an edge to her voice. Perhaps, Ruth thought, she isn't as sweet as I thought.

As they made their way slowly along to the beach, Ruth looked round to check where Roger was. He was talking to Annabel or rather, Annabel was talking to him. Ruth could tell by the bland look on his face that he was merely being polite and was itching to get away. Annabel on the other hand looked serious and intense, pushing her hair off her face with one hand and gesticulating with the other. It was an amusing novelty to witness Roger in silent retreat from a female veg-etarian in full cry – the uneating in pursuit of the unspeaking, perhaps? Ruth smiled to herself.

'Share it?' Daisy suggested, giving her a probing glance.

'Oh it's nothing. I was half remembering a saying by Oscar Wilde.'

'You should get together with Barnaby,' Imogen said. 'He has quotations on the brain. It drives us all mad at home.'

If that's the only thing that drives you mad about your husband, Ruth thought, then you don't know you're born! She was already getting tired, and looked round for somewhere to rest.

'I'm going to sit down for a while,' she said, 'on those low boulders under the trees.'

'Good idea,' Daisy said at once. 'I'll come too.' Ruth had noticed that Daisy would never admit to being tired, but if anyone else sat down she would invariably join them. If I'm half as tough as her when I'm 70, she thought, I'll be doing well.

'Shall I . . .?' Dorothy offered, hovering.

'No no, you carry on with Imogen,' Daisy said. 'Have a

good walk round. Roger says there will be time for some snorkelling before we leave, but I'm not bothered today. Why don't you swim, though? Do you good.'

'Well I don't know. I might . . . You're sure . . .?'

'Yes yes, I'll be fine,' Daisy said briskly and waited until her friend was out of earshot before saying to Ruth, 'The dear thing. Dorothy is under the illusion that it is she who looks after me, you know, not vice versa.'

Ruth smiled. 'She's very devoted to you,' she said.

'It makes her happy,' Daisy said. 'She needs a project, and I'm it.'

That sounded rather cold and impersonal to Ruth, but she supposed that Daisy was looking at their friendship from a professional viewpoint. Ruth looked out over the beach and the sea, towards other islands. On her left she could see the one-storey block buildings on Prison Island and to the right, in the background, there was the dark shape of the main island of Mahé with its tallest mountain Morne Seychellois decapitated by heavy clouds.

'I'm afraid it's going to rain,' Ruth said.

'No matter. We've all got waterproofs.'

'I always feel that people blame Roger personally for the weather,' Ruth said, 'as though he'd deliberately contravened the Trade Descriptions Act.'

Daisy grunted. 'It mentions the possibility of rain in your brochure.'

'Yes but people never really believe it.'

'More fool them.'

Ruth, seeing something red lying out on the beach, got to her feet and walked across to investigate. It was a stranded starfish of a deep crimson colour with brilliant scarlet rounded spines, each joined at the base to a raised lattice of the same colour, which ran the length of all the five arms and met in a kind of crown at the centre. It was startlingly beautiful. Ruth touched it gently with her stick, but it was quite dead and gave off an evil smell when she turned it over. She pushed it back again and glanced behind her at Daisy. She was sitting with her back against a tree and looked as though she had fallen asleep. Ruth looked seawards again and saw Philip crouching behind some boulders near the water's edge with his binoculars raised, and someone else – Claire – striding away from him rather briskly. She looks cross, Ruth thought. Funny how you can tell that from a person's carriage even when they're so far away that you can't read the expression on their face. Body language carries further. She wandered back across the sand and sat down again.

Daisy opened one eye. 'Are you happy?' she asked.

Ruth was taken aback. It was a question she usually tried to avoid asking herself. 'Well . . . I don't know,' she prevaricated. 'Is anyone most of the time? Happiness isn't a commodity you can go in search of, and capture. It's a by-product, isn't it?'

'A by-product of what?'

'Well . . . living a good life, doing your best, being as optimistic as possible, that sort of thing.

'So you don't see it as a right?'

'Certainly not.'

'And Roger? Does he feel the same?'

Hold on, Ruth thought. Why does she want to know that? What business is it of hers? 'You'd better ask him yourself,' she said. 'I've no idea.'

Imogen was astonished and delighted by her first experience of snorkelling. She floated lazily on the surface, head down, hands and flippers moving just enough to maintain her horizontal position, and eyes wide with the wonder of it all. There were walls and plateaux of coral in an abundant variety of patterns and structures and fish of every shape and colour, jinking about in the green water, and so *tame*. It was like being transported into another dimension where everything was mutable, even the laws of physics. Here you were free from all bodily constraints. Gravity barely existed. If you wanted to see something close up you approached it flowingly, almost dreamily, face first. Even your hair didn't get in the way. It rippled behind you, or billowed in a cloud like kelp. Imogen was pleased to discover that her new face mask remained watertight and that she could clear her snorkel easily with one sharp exhalation. She gained confidence and ventured deeper. She found she was desperate to know what all the corals and fish were called, and started to try to memorize their various colours and configurations with a view to looking them all up in Ruth's book later on. After half an hour she was very reluctant to stop and change back into her clothes, but it was already time to leave for another island where there would be a barbecue and the promise of more delicious salads and fruit. This place, she decided, truly was heaven. What could be better?

The rain came just as they approached Cerf island, and caught the glass-bottomed boat in a solid downpour. There was much rustling and a flurry of elbows as the group hunted about in their day-packs for their kagoules and rain-hats. It's nonsense really, Imogen thought. Half of us were wet through in the sea not five minutes ago, and now we're all desperately trying to stay dry! She could already see the open-sided thatched hut on the beach ahead, where the lunch would be served safely under cover.

'Right,' Roger announced, a few yards from the shore. 'This is as far in as the boat can go. We have to wade from here, but it's a flat calm and only knee deep. OK?' He began to help everyone to clamber over the square stern of the boat and steadied them as they found their feet on the sand or were handed their walking sticks. Those who had shorts or skirts on had it easy, Imogen thought, ditto those whose trousers would roll up above the knee. Hers were far too tight for that, so she had the choice between getting them wet or taking them off and hoping her shirt would be long enough to cover her pants. She waited until everyone was off the boat but her, and was still undecided when Roger, apparently appreciating her dilemma, put one arm round her waist but instead of helping her down, scooped her legs from under her with the other, and walked towards the beach, holding her well above the water like an offering.

Imogen had wanted Barnaby to do the very same thing years before, when they had bought their first house together and she had crossed its threshold for the first time. He hadn't, of course, and she had never voiced her disappointment. Now, in Roger's arms, she felt suddenly triumphant and entirely at ease.

'Thank you kindly, St Christopher!' she said as he put her down on dry land.

Roger bowed. 'My pleasure,' he said.

Imogen turned, laughing, to the rest of the group and was startled by the expressions on some of the watching faces.

Annabel looked stricken. Daisy looked weasel-sharp. Ruth looked stunned. Shirley looked triumphant. Dorothy seemed about to burst into tears. Claire looked resigned. It wasn't until they were well into yet another delicious meal that Imogen remembered she hadn't bothered to look to see what Barnaby's reaction had been.

6

THE eventual journey back to Mahé in the glass-bottomed boat was less pleasant than the outward one. A wind had arisen, whipping up the surface of the sea into a confused jumble of conflicting waves. The boat weltered and lurched unexpectedly. Annabel turned green and held on to one of the upright rails, tight-lipped and mute. Brian re-lit his pipe and clamped it hard between his teeth. Leslie leant over the side and was loudly and colourfully sick.

'He's always like this,' Janice explained to Ruth in a narked undertone. 'He could get poorly floating on a lounger on a swimming pool. He's even had sunstroke in Birmingham! But he *would* come on this holiday. I warned him, but he wouldn't budge; he's that stubborn.'

She was clearly trying to dissociate herself from all responsibility for her husband's failings, as though the unfortunate man was vomiting on purpose! Imogen thought, overhearing her and concealing a smile. Poor bloody Leslie; how did he stick it?

Once back on Mahé again, they bought stamps and cards in Victoria and drove back to the hotel, where Roger announced that there would be a talk after supper by a local naturalist, on Seychelles birds. Imogen went up to her room, had a bath and changed, and then sat on the bed writing postcards to her daughters and friends.

'What shall I tell them?' she asked Barnaby, who was lying full length with his eyes shut. Silence. 'Mmmm?' There was no reply. He was asleep again. She knew she shouldn't feel annoyed about this, but she did. It seemed like a deliberate ploy on his part to avoid having to communicate.

Darkness fell suddenly and completely here, early on in the evening. By 6.45 it was night and that was that. Imogen felt restless. She had decided that she might as well go to the bird talk, but there was still an hour or so before supper. She had written enough postcards, and didn't feel like reading. She brushed her hair, touched up her lipstick, sprayed scent liberally round her neck and left Barnaby sleeping. At the entrance to the hotel's indoor bar, she looked around without success for other members of the group. There seemed to be a German beer festival going on, with loud singing to an accordion and a lot of back-slapping.

Oh gawd, she thought, stepping backwards. This is definitely not my sort of thing. 'Oh . . . sorry!' She had landed on someone's foot.

'No worries,' Roger said, pretending to limp. 'I've got another one. Are you going in for a quick drink?'

'Well I was, but . . .'

'Come on then. We'll find a non-singing area somewhere.'

'Where's everyone else?' Imogen asked, as they sat down with their drinks at the far end.

'Ruth's having a kip. I expect most of them are resting as well, after the rigours of the day.'

'It was a lovely day.'

'Good.' Roger sat back in his chair and stretched his legs in front of him. 'Tomorrow's day trip should be even better.'

'To Fregate?'

'Yup. We'll get the chance of a good walk up through the forest to the top of the island.'

'What will the non-able-bodied do?'

'Oh Claire will see them OK. There's a good hotel where they can rest, with grounds for gentle walks and gardeners growing things in vegetable gardens and the odd giant tortoise lumbering past, not to mention other wildlife.'

'Philip says he saw some tame tortoises today on Cerf, in an enclosure.'

'Yeah. The ones on Fregate are wild. Sometimes the damn things even start mating on the only airstrip and prevent the inter-island planes from landing!'

'That's a bit public, isn't it?'

'They have no shame.' He gave her a long look. The corners of his mouth twitched upwards. His greeny-brown eyes narrowed slightly, humorously. Imogen took another sip of gin and resisted the temptation to giggle. 'Azure . . .' Roger said, regarding her face steadily. 'No, cornflower blue, I think.'

'What?'

'Your eyes. Beautiful colour.'

Blow me, Imogen thought, the man actually fancies me!

'Barnaby says they're steely blue,' she said, milking the compliment for all it was worth.

'Barnaby clearly has no soul,' Roger said.

'He admits he's an empiricist with a strictly limited experience of the sublime.'

'Would you care to translate that?'

'Well, he might say for instance that your eyes were the colour of winter cow dung.'

Roger raised his eyebrows in feigned offence. 'And you? What would you say?'

'Mmmm,' she said, studying them with mock professionalism, 'I'd say they were avocado green with a hint of amber, a sort of tawny khaki.'

'You mean, half-way between a bathroom suite and army uniform?'

'That's it exactly!' God, Imogen thought as she laughed aloud, for some extraordinary reason I'm acting like a bloody teenager.

'Very sublime,' Roger said drily. 'Have another drink?'

'Perhaps . . . one more. Thanks.'

Imogen watched him as he went to the bar. She wondered if he dyed his hair. She began to consider whether it would make him less appealing if he did. Then she dismissed these thoughts as academic – she wasn't going to *do* anything about him anyway. It was just so pleasant to be flirted with . . . It was, after all, the perfect setting for a little harmless dalliance. It might even pep Barnaby up a bit; stop him from taking her for granted. One thing is certain though, she told herself firmly. *I'm not going to sleep with him.*

'You look very determined,' Roger observed, as he sat down again at their table with two more gins.

'I'm that sort of a person.'

'So am I,' he said, smiling at her, 'not to say dogged.'

'Dogged Roger!' Imogen said, gulping her gin and giggling. 'For some reason that reminds me of the pirate flag, the Jolly

Roger.' I'm talking absolute crap, she thought, and I'm not even drunk . . .

'Oh I can be fairly jolly too,' Roger said. 'You should see me when I get my cutlass between my teeth.'

The beer festival had been expanding ever since they had come into the bar, and now threatened to take over the entire room. The volume of the singing swelled like the aura of a migraine, blotting out odd words completely; making their conversation patchy and confusing.

'What?'

'Never mind,' Roger said. The Germans stamped their feet, slapped their thighs and sang even louder.

'I don't think I can stand much more of this,' Imogen shouted into Roger's ear. 'I'm not accustomed to this fortissimo style of night life!'

'Come on then. Drink up.' He took her arm as she got to her feet, and steered her through the crowd and out of the bar.

'That's better,' she said. He was still holding her arm. 'Thanks for the drinks. Now I'd better go and see how Barnaby – '

'Not yet,' Roger said. 'There's still time before supper. I can show you some much quieter night life.'

'Where?'

'Outside.'

'But it's pitch dark.'

'Not when your eyes get acclimatized.'

'But . . .' Was this the prelude to an alfresco seduction? Or was she imagining the whole thing? She would look pretty foolish protesting about it, if so . . .

'But what?'

'Nothing.'

Heavens above, Imogen thought. I'm not 15 in spite of the way I've been behaving. Whatever it is he's got in mind, I can surely take care that I'm one step ahead of him.

'Go on then,' she said, 'lead the way.'

Outside in the dark, behind the hotel and away from its lights, Roger led her off the road for a short distance. He guided her until her eyes became used to the lack of light, and she could discern the shapes of the trees all around them, and until the sky had become lighter in contrast.

'Now what?'

'Sssh,' Roger said in a low voice, squeezing her hand. 'Just wait.'

Above her head a large black vampire shape flapped quietly, then another, and another, disappearing through the overhead branches.

'What are they?' she hissed.

'Fruit bats going out to feed. You do see them in daylight, but the majority are nocturnal.'

'And what's that weird noise?'

'Tree frogs singing. Now, look over there.'

A tiny blue light danced briefly up towards the tree canopy and faded. Then there were two, five, eleven, a cloud of them flitting apparently aimlessly; glowing, dying, then glowing again like reluctant embers brought briefly to life by puffs from a bellows.

'Fireflies!' Imogen whispered rapturously. 'I haven't seen them for *years*, not since I was in Greece in my twenties. Aren't they fascinating? I've always thought that Tinkerbell in *Peter Pan* must have been inspired by fireflies. Watching them, you really could believe in fairies, couldn't you? Oh I *am* glad to have seen them. Thank you!'

'All part of the service,' Roger said lightly. 'I try to give satisfaction.'

Imogen, at that moment, felt an almost overwhelming desire to be kissed; to be taken into strong arms and caressed by confident probing fingers; to have the buttons of her dress undone one by one, her bra unhooked, her skirts pushed up, her . . .

'Just for the record,' Roger said matter-of-factly, close beside her in the dark. 'Why is winter cow dung any different from any other?'

Imogen was suddenly and gratefully reunited with her resolutions.

'It's more brown than green,' she said. 'In summer the grass is lusher, so the dung is more green than brown.'

The next morning, Claire got out the Kwells at the airport and gave one in good time to Leslie. She didn't fancy even a short journey in one of the small Twin Otter aircraft if it was going to be pervaded with a lingering smell of sick.

'What about me?' Janice asked, holding out her hand.

'You don't suffer from travel sickness, do you? You were fine yesterday.'

'Oh well that's different. I mean, being up in the air's unnatural, isn't it?' There didn't seem to be a logical argument there which was worth pursuing, so Claire sighed and handed her a pill too. 'Do I suck it or swallow it?' Janice asked, oblivious of her disapproval.

'Whichever you like.' *Or shall I ram it up your bottom for you, modom?*

'Well it's important to follow the instructions exactly, isn't it? They always say you should.'

'Read it for yourself.' Claire handed her the box.

'The print's too small,' Janice complained, 'and I haven't got my glasses handy.'

'Oh give it here!' Claire said irritably, and read it out to her exaggeratedly slowly. 'One . . . tablet . . . every . . . six . . . hours . . . Kwells . . . melt . . . in . . . the . . . mouth . . . and . . . are . . . pleasant . . . tasting.'

'There's no need to take that tone with me,' Janice said huffily. 'I'm not stupid.'

Before boarding the plane everyone was weighed on a large platform scale, holding their day-packs at the same time, so that their combined weights could be added together in case they were greater than the plane's capacity. Claire, who didn't in the least mind being weighed in public, noticed that Shirley shuffled uncomfortably as the needle flicked more than half-way round the dial. Blimey! Claire thought, she's a big girl and no mistake! How can people let themselves go like that?

Claire found herself sitting next to Imogen on the twenty-minute flight in the narrow cabin, and peered past her through the porthole at the islands and coral reefs below, or forwards through the open door to the tiny flight deck, to watch the pilot and his mate flick switches and talk on their intercoms. She was aware that Philip was sitting one row ahead of her on the other side. He was busy taking photographs through the window. She watched the back of his head and his occasional profile with a wry expression. She had so nearly made a complete ass of herself over him, something she had never done before. He must be gay, she thought; stupid of me not to have

67

thought of that. Thank goodness I didn't say anything explicit to him. He clearly hadn't a clue what was on my mind. It looks as though this trip is going to be a complete washout as far as sex is concerned – my first failure!

Imogen sat and stared eagerly out of the window of the Twin Otter at the disappearing coastline of Mahé and its nearest islands. They were flying almost due east to Fregate island, and she had a first-class view uninterrupted by the propeller, having nipped in first and bagged the best seat. These planes are brilliant for sightseeing; the wings are above the portholes and don't get in the way, she thought. After a while when there was nothing much to see but sea, she turned to talk to Claire. Imogen wasn't yet sure what to make of her. She wasn't the sort you could chat to easily – she was too prickly.

'Do you still practise as a GP?' she asked her.

'Oh heavens yes,' Claire said. 'This is just a working holiday for me.'

I wouldn't call it *work*, Imogen thought, it's money for old rope! 'How did you start?' she asked.

'Roger advertised. I believe he was overwhelmed with replies, but luckily he chose me.'

'You get on well with him, then?'

'Oh yes, we're two of a kind.'

Well I find that hard to believe, Imogen thought. Roger clearly liked women very much (whether or not he actually went to bed with any of them, which she doubted) whereas Claire looked well on the way to permanent spinsterhood. People had such distorted images of themselves, she thought amusedly; no insight!

'I suppose you'll go on doing it into the foreseeable future?' she said. 'A job as good as this can't turn up very often.'

'Well I don't know,' Claire said. 'It does have its disadvantages, you know. I may have other plans.'

'Oh?' but Imogen saw that Claire was not going to elaborate. Perhaps, she suddenly thought, *I* could take over from Claire, if she gives up? I could take some time off from the CAB, and I'm sure I could do a much better job than her. I'm probably better organized. I can motivate people, and any fool can dole out aspirins or Kwells. The only problem would be the ghastly

Janices of this world . . . but I'm sure I could be more than a match for them! After all, Barnaby did suggest that I went on holiday without him. This could be the perfect way to do it.

Imogen set about encouraging Claire. 'Well, I can see that once you've been to a place a few times, it might begin to pall,' she said (thinking, I could come here a million times and it would still be paradise). 'And once it's become more work than holiday, then it would rather lose its appeal.'

'Possibly.'

'When do you think you'll make the decision?'

'Oh I couldn't say.'

Mmmm, Imogen thought, I must work on her. The more she thought of the idea, the more she liked it. She needed a boost like this. It would be a wonderful way of getting out of a rut whilst at the same time utilizing her undoubted talents. She had more to offer than Claire (apart from the obvious medical qualification). Claire, in her opinion, had severe limitations. She was probably quite efficient, but she was clearly self-centred, most likely bossy, and also rather impatient. Poor Claire, she thought, it doesn't do for women to live alone. It somehow de-feminizes them. I wonder if she's ever had a man?

It took Shirley several minutes to get over the indignity of having to stand on scales in front of everyone. Of course, she told herself, her rucksack, although small, was very heavy, and then there were her shoes and her clothes to take into account. She didn't *really* weigh nearly that much, but nevertheless it was very embarrassing and not a good start to the day. I can't help my size, she thought, I've got large bones, and it's not my fault that I don't get enough exercise. Now, if I could trek in the Himalayas I'd get fit in no time . . . She smiled ruefully through the window at the thought. The plane bumped through a patch of turbulent air, and the whole flimsy structure shuddered. Dorothy, sitting beside her, let out a muffled squeak of alarm and waved both hands in front of her, like an agitated baby.

'Are you all right?' Shirley asked her.

'Oh yes. Well, no. That is . . .' Dorothy clutched her hands firmly together in her lap, but the look in her eyes betrayed her.

'Soon be there,' Shirley said soothingly.

'Oh yes. Good . . . good.'

'Flying makes you nervous?'

'Well I'm just a touch claustrophobic, you see, and this is so small and so . . . *enclosed*. I know it's silly, but I find it . . . difficult.'

'Repressed anger,' Daisy observed from the opposite window seat. 'That's what causes claustrophobia.'

'No, dear,' Dorothy said. 'I think not. What have I got to be angry about?'

Shirley lowered her voice so that the noise from the engine kept her words from all but the two old women. 'Now there's someone who really does seem angry; him with the beard.' She inclined her head towards Simon's back. 'I mean, anything anyone says to him, he has to disagree with. I don't know how he can live with himself.'

'He's an interesting subject,' Daisy agreed. 'I had a similar case once.'

At that moment a small island appeared below them, to their left, and the plane banked and lined itself up with the grass airstrip, descending with a certain amount of buffeting, and bouncing several times on landing. Then it taxied along by the boundary of tall palm trees and came to a halt beside a small hut.

'All right now?' Shirley saw that Dorothy had unclasped her hands and started to breathe again.

'Oh much better, yes thank you.'

The pilot opened the door and helped them all down the steps.

'No tortoises. What a let-down!' Shirley heard Imogen say to Roger, and managed to intercept the amused look of complicity between them.

Aha! she thought. So I am right. He *is* at it again. You'd think he'd give it a rest sometimes, wouldn't you? I'm surprised at Imogen; her with such a pleasant husband too. What can she be thinking of? It's Ruth I feel sorry for. She's the victim in all this.

Shirley looked to see how Ruth was taking it, but found that she had already set off to walk the short distance to the hotel entrance. It's not right, Shirley thought. It ought to be stopped. I suppose I could keep an eye on them for Ruth. I could even make things difficult for them? Brilliant idea! She smiled grimly to herself. It could be a kind of moral crusade, and would give her the sense of real purpose that she usually found lacking on most of her holidays with Brian.

Barnaby was beginning to enjoy himself in spite of his previous misgivings. Yes, some of the group were oddballs, and he still distrusted Roger Dare, but the place itself was marvellous, and it was very pleasant to have someone else making all the arrangements. Exhaustion was his chief problem, but at least they were not expected to do much in the evenings, and he found that a good hour or so's sleep before supper made all the difference to how he felt afterwards. He had enjoyed the talk on birds the night before, and surprised himself by his growing interest in the natural world, especially the tropical trees. It wasn't something he had ever cared for before.

Imogen had always been much more *au fait* than he with all things pertaining to natural history. Now it seemed she was trying to become an instant expert on coral-reef fish. She had borrowed a book from Ruth, and had made lists of all the ones she'd seen, even getting him to test her on their names until she was word perfect. Barnaby wondered how long this particular craze would last. Imogen was a great one for going overboard on one hobby for five minutes, and then being caught up in something completely different apparently moments later. He found it hard to take her current obsession seriously. It was as though she was flailing about, trying desperately to find some meaning to her life, and always hoping that this was *it*.

Barnaby, on the other hand, thought he might well go on being interested in trees for some time to come. Near the entrance to the hotel on Fregate was an enormous tangled banyan tree with curtains of tresses hanging in a matted fringe, tough enough to swing from. They had been cut off at head height just where they hung over the path, to make a passage beneath. Barnaby wished he were ten again, imagining how he would climb amongst the multiplicity of roots and trunks, and make a den, from which he could swing down like Tarzan on a liana and ambush people on the path below. He sighed. He would never admit it to Imogen, but he felt his ever-decreasing mobility keenly. It was true he'd never been a great walker, but he'd always known he *could* if he'd wanted to. Now it was simply too exhausting. His right leg felt heavy most of the time, so ordinary walking had become more like wading through treacle. His right foot dragged and he was never sure where it was, so he was forever tripping up. However, one undoubted benefit of this holiday was the realization that, all things considered, he wasn't so badly off at all. At least he hadn't got it young like Annabel and Philip, and he wasn't as badly affected as Leslie or Brian, or Ruth. He supposed he and Simon were at much the same level; he didn't use a stick either. If he was lucky, he might age as well as Daisy. He resolved to try to be grateful. Up until then he had coped with his illness by simply ignoring it. He was now prepared to admit that there were other ways. He wasn't keen on Brian's . . . damnit! what was the word? . . . yes – *proselytizing*, though. He didn't like being preached at.

He looked casually ahead for Imogen and saw her in conversation with Roger. As he watched, she threw her head back in peals of laughter. Well, he thought, I can't admire her taste in friends, but it certainly gives me a break!

At the hotel they were given drinks in long glasses rimmed with sugar, and sat on the terrace fending off the Madagascar fodies who seized every opportunity to dart in and peck it off.

'They're no better than vultures,' Leslie complained, waving his arms about, 'never mind red sparrows!'

'There!' Philip said to Daisy, pointing.

'What?'

'Seychelles fody or toq toq, the rare endemic one amongst the brown female Madagascars; that darker brown bird, there.'

'Now that one is a bloody sparrow,' Leslie said in disgust. 'Beats me how you can rave about that boring-looking thing.'

'It's just a form of train-spotting,' Simon put in nastily, 'compulsive collecting and one-upmanship fused into an unattractive pastime for the cerebrally challenged.'

'I'm not a twitcher,' Philip said, quite rudely for him. 'I'm interested in the whole thing – habitat, behaviour, diet, migration, conservation, the lot! I don't just tick them off. If you can't see that there's more to it than that, then I feel sorry for you.'

'Right,' Roger said breezily, 'now for those who want to, we're going on a short walk in the cultivated area, round the hotel gardens and in the plantations. With luck we'll see the magpie robin you heard about last night. Then we'll have lunch here, and afterwards some of us will walk up to the glacis at the top of the island and have a look at the view.'

'Why not all of us?' Simon asked.

'Because,' Roger said patiently, 'it's a bit steep and rough and rather too far for some of us.'

'Well, I'm not being left out.'

'Suit yourself. You're welcome to try it. OK let's go, then.' He set off, leading the way.

'I didn't come all this way to be patronized,' Simon grumbled in an undertone, but no one took this up.

Imogen found Shirley beside her, making a face at Simon's back. 'He's a right pain and no mistake,' Shirley observed confidentially. 'Why do people like him come on trips like this?'

'Perhaps he's lonely?'

'Well if he is, he's only got himself to blame!'

'He seems to be very well off,' Imogen said. 'He's been telling Barnaby about all sorts of trips he's made.'

'I suppose computer people are well paid?'

'Must be.'

'Talking of which,' Shirley said, 'I'll tell you something that bothers me. How do you suppose Leslie and Janice can afford a holiday like this? I mean, it's hardly in their price bracket, is it? What was he before he was forced to retire early – a postman, wasn't it? I mean, they don't earn a lot, do they? And his disability pension can't be much.'

'Perhaps he's spending his golden handshake,' Imogen suggested lightly, 'or his ill-gotten gains from robbing mailbags.'

'Now that *is* a thought!' Shirley's eyes lit up. 'I'd love to know.'

Imogen would have preferred to be at the front of the group with Roger. It's not that I fancy him, she told herself. It's just that he's more fun than all the others put together.

An ancient tractor and trailer passed them as they made their way towards the banana and coconut plantations, where they found Seychellois women and children husking coconuts on sharp vertical poles amongst piles of potential coir fibre. Everywhere there were skinks; lightning-fast little grey lizards. Ruth pointed out cashew nut and breadfruit trees, and hibiscus with rampant red flowers. Imogen looked about her, taking it all in, trying not to miss anything at all. Then she saw, dead on the path in front of her, a giant millipede, dark brown with a million legs and over eight inches long. She called excitedly for Philip to come over and photograph it.

'Oh my God!' Shirley said, right beside her. 'Thank goodness it's dead!'

'I think it's beautiful,' Imogen said. 'The colour of polished rosewood.'

'Now here,' Roger said, a little later, 'is where we may, if we're lucky, see a magpie robin.'

They had arrived at a more mature coconut grove where brown cows wandered grazing between the tall grey trunks, and most of the undergrowth had been cleared away.

'Well if it's that rare,' Shirley said, 'we're hardly likely to see one, are we?'

Imogen wondered if it was her imagination, or was Shirley deliberately sticking next to her all the time? It seemed that every time she stopped to look at something, Shirley did too.

'Apparently they're very tame,' she said (weren't you at the talk last night?) 'which hasn't helped their survival, of course.' She saw Philip, ahead of the party as always, suddenly stiffen and stare through his binoculars. Then he turned, raised his thumb triumphantly, and moved stealthily forwards.

'Quietly!' Imogen admonished Shirley, and they crept up to join him.

And there it was – one individual of a world population of less than fifty, found on two tiny islands in the Indian Ocean, and nowhere else: a black thrush-like bird with a cocked tail, large white wing patches and a beautiful blue sheen on its head and neck, jauntily hopping about foraging for insects amongst the twigs and coconut husks, only a few feet away.

Imogen was spellbound. She watched fascinated as it continued to feed, apparently unconcerned by the gathering group of people or the noise of Philip's camera shutter as he photographed it from every conceivable angle.

'Oooh it's quite sweet, isn't it?' Shirley whispered. Imogen didn't reply. After several minutes of perfect visibility, the magpie robin simply flew off.

'OK,' Roger said, 'we'd better not disturb it further by trying to follow it. How about lunch?' He began to lead the group away again.

Imogen glanced at Philip. His expression was beatific. 'Good?' she asked.

'*Wonderful!*' he said. 'Now I can die happy.'

7

A T the end of their day trip to Fregate, when they were
back again in their hotel on the mainland, Imogen began
packing up their things in preparation for the flight northwards
the following morning, and the start of a week's stay on the
island of Praslin. Barnaby sat propped up by all the pillows on
their bed, deep in a paperback she didn't recognize and apparently oblivious to all her bustling about.

'What's that book called?'

'*The Blind Watchmaker* by Richard Dawkins.'

'Whose is it?'

'Ruth's.'

'What's it about?'

'Evolution.'

'Oh.' What an odd book to lend him, Imogen thought. It's
not his subject at all. 'What's it like?' No answer. She was
miffed. On holidays Barnaby usually read thrillers by Gavin
Lyall to 'help him unwind'. Today's total abstraction in a non-
fiction book which was not connected with his work was out
of character. 'What's it like?' she asked again.

Barnaby frowned, put his forefinger on the page to mark the
spot and glanced up briefly. 'Fascinating.' Then he went on
reading.

'How was your afternoon, then?' Imogen persisted.

Barnaby sighed loudly, 'Fine.' He didn't look up.

'What did you do?'

'Wandered about a bit, sat and talked, watched a giant
tortoise.'

'We got a really good view from the top of the island. We
could even see La Digue and Marianne, and there was this
great expanse of bare granite, and I found a tortoise turd nearly
as big as my foot!'

'Mmmm.'

'And do you know, Janice never even bothered to look at the magpie robin. She said she'd seen plenty of magpies and robins at home, so what was the big deal! Can you believe it?'

'Mmmm.'

'And I think Shirley has a sort of schoolgirl pash on me. She was following at my heels all afternoon like a faithful terrier. It was quite touching, actually.'

'Mmmm.'

'And Simon-pig-headed-Overy insisted on coming all the way, and he kept stopping for a pee and then got left behind and we had to wait for him. Roger almost had to *carry* him the last bit. That's why we nearly missed the plane!'

'Mmmm.'

'You're not bloody listening to a word I'm saying!'

'Can't you see I'm trying to read?'

'I just wish you'd *talk* to me sometimes,' Imogen said crossly. 'We are supposed to be *sharing* this holiday, after all.'

'Oh?' Barnaby looked up. 'I thought the whole idea was to dump me while you enjoyed yourself?'

'That's totally unfair and you know it!' Imogen snapped shut one of the suitcases and stood it upright. 'You can pack the rest. I'm going down for a drink before supper.'

She found Roger and Annabel in the bar, having a discussion which appeared to be about all the rainforest plants that might have a potential for herbal remedies. Annabel, clearly in her element alone with Roger, looked particularly displeased to see her, but Roger got up smiling and offered to fetch her a drink.

'We saw Madagascar periwinkle growing on top of Fregate,' Imogen told Annabel as she sat down.

'But that's the plant that's the source for two new cancer drugs!'

'Yes, I know.'

'Oh I do wish I'd seen it.'

'It was very attractive,' Imogen said, rubbing it in. 'Lovely pink flowers.' Annabel looked downcast. 'How was your afternoon?' Imogen asked her.

'Very nice, actually,' Annabel blushed. 'Brian started doing a sketch of my head, I can't think why. He's really very good. He even says he wants to do more; make a sort of study . . .'

77

but at that moment, Roger came back with the drink, and Imogen stopped listening.

'Tomorrow,' Roger said, 'we start the best bit of the trip.'

'On Praslin?' Imogen said.

'Yup. I really believe it's my favourite place in the world.'

'You sound just like my children,' Imogen teased. 'They were forever designating things their "favourite" or their "least favourite". I could never make such sweeping judgements myself.'

'How old are your children?' Roger asked.

'Oh, grown up. I'll probably be a grandmother any moment now!'

'Nonsense,' Roger said, leaning towards her. 'You don't look nearly old enough.' Annabel choked on her pineapple juice and fought for breath.

'You're supposed to swallow it, not inhale it,' Imogen said cheerfully, thumping her on the back.

'CUHHAAA . . . hrrrrh!' Annabel gasped, and when finally she could speak again, she said, 'Um . . . actually I think I'd better go and finish packing. What time does the bus leave for the airport tomorrow?'

'Ten o'clock,' Roger said.

'Right. Um . . . see you then.'

'Don't forget supper.'

'Well I'm not very hungry . . . in fact.' She got to her feet awkwardly, knocking her chair sideways. Roger caught it and set it upright again, but Annabel had gone without a backward glance.

Well well! Imogen thought to herself, smiling at Roger. I can't be that far over the hill; I can still see off the opposition!

'Oh, hello Shirley,' Roger said, looking up over her shoulder. 'Care to join us for a drink?'

The hotel on the Grand Anse at Praslin was a dispersed collection of thatched huts whose walls were wooden uprights clad with palm leaves held in place with batons. The sleeping huts had two double rooms each with their own entrance and shower, and a veranda with folding chairs outside under the projecting thatch, which itself was shaded by a grove of takamaka trees and faced the flat-calm sea. In between were a few tables with palm parasols, some coconut palms and low-growing green scaevola bushes, and then the long white beach itself.

'I've put Ruth and me, and you and Imogen in this one,' Roger said. 'OK?'

'Fine,' Barnaby said, putting his case down on the veranda.

'Isn't this fantastic!' Imogen exclaimed, looking all round. 'Real desert island stuff. I'd like to live here for the rest of my life.'

'You'd be bored rigid in six months,' Barnaby said. He sat down heavily on one of the chairs without first checking that the bamboo rod which held the seat in place was properly engaged. The chair simply folded up around him and trapped him upside-down, dangling from its frame with his knees above his head like a trussed chicken in a canvas bag. Imogen caught Roger's eye and let out an involuntary shout of laughter. Serve him right! she thought. It was left to Ruth to make the first move to help him out.

'Are you all right?' she asked, taking his arm and trying to pull him up.

'Well I would be if I could sodding well move!'

'Here,' Roger said, 'mind out, Ruth. We'll have to lift the chair off him somehow. Can you give me a hand, Imogen?' Together they managed to disentangle Barnaby and then stood back as he got stiffly to his feet, rubbing his thigh.

'Stupid chair!' he looked embarrassed.

'Have you hurt yourself?' Ruth asked.

'It's nothing, just a bit of a bruise. Give me a proper British deckchair any day. The design of these things is quite ludicrously inadequate.'

'More than that, they're really dangerous,' Ruth said. 'You could have damaged your spine!'

Imogen could see that it was only Barnaby's pride that was hurt, and that Ruth's fussing would merely make things worse. Then she was conscious of Roger's eyes upon her, and she looked up to meet them. He raised a quizzical eyebrow and she acknowledged him with a quick smile. Unlike Barnaby, she thought, Roger doesn't try to cut me down to size all the time. He's an *adult!*

'Isn't this Creole food absolutely heavenly?' Shirley said to

Dorothy as the group wandered through the village of Grande
Anse after lunch, doing a little gentle sightseeing. 'I'm never
going to get thinner at this rate!'

'Why worry?' Dorothy said. 'You are what the Good Lord
made you.'

'Perhaps you could try vegetarianism,' Annabel suggested,
from behind them. 'I never put on weight.'

'Oh I couldn't live without sausages,' Shirley said, 'although
I do agree with you that I'd probably be a more principled
person if I did.'

'I know what you mean,' Dorothy said. 'If I had to kill my
own food, I could never bring myself to do it. Vegetarians are
certainly less hypocritical.'

'Adolf Hitler was a vegeterian,' Simon put in.

'Not a *true* one,' Annabel said, quite fiercely. 'He didn't do
it out of *conviction!*'

Simon raised his eyes to heaven and changed his stride to
drop back behind them. Philip was in front, walking fast away
from Janice, and the group began to change fluidly from a
clump to a straggle as each of its members settled into his or
her most comfortable walking speed. Shirley looked ahead to
check where Imogen was. Sure enough she was with Roger,
talking and laughing. I can't stick beside her all the time, Shirley
thought; there's no point. But I can make sure that they never
get the chance to be *alone* together.

She began to wonder why Roger behaved in such a risky
manner. Surely sleeping with clients was as good as professional
negligence, wasn't it? How could he jeopardize his business like
that? Hadn't it got him into trouble before?

'Do you know why Roger stopped being a probation officer?' she asked Dorothy in lowered tones.

'No idea,' Dorothy said, 'but I can guess . . .'

'Hanky-panky, you mean?'

Dorothy nodded vigorously. 'Daisy says – '

'I don't think you ought to gossip like that about Roger,'
Annabel interrupted defensively, flushing bright red. 'I'm sure
the stories about him are all made up. It's just jealousy and spite
because he's so good-looking and fit.' She looked about to burst
into tears.

'I'm sorry, dear' Dorothy said at once, half turning round.

'We meant no harm.' Annabel bent down and stopped, ostensibly to re-buckle her sandal, and they went on without her.

'I'd forgotten she was right behind us!' Shirley confessed to Dorothy in a careful undertone. 'I've to watch what I say to her.'

'Of course, you and she share a room.'

'Yes. She's sweet really, but ever so intense; quite unhappy, I reckon. Hardly surprising under the circumstances I s'pose. I must get Brian to sort her out.'

'Or she could talk to Daisy.'

'That reminds me; I'd love to hear about some of Daisy's cases . . . Where is she, by the way?'

'She's resting at the hotel. She gets very tired.'

'Yes, she would.' They had got to the end of the village. Shirley glanced ahead and then looked wildly all around. Imogen and Roger had vanished!

Ruth was one of the dawdlers bringing up the rear with Brian, Barnaby and Leslie. This trip was better than most, she thought, in that there were so many men with MS. She usually got left with a bunch of women. She tried to tell herself that it was some consolation for Roger's behaviour. She was no longer able to delude herself that this trip would be any different from any other. She had been so sure that Imogen would be proof against Roger's blandishments, but now she was forced to believe the evidence of her own eyes. The first blow had come when Roger had carried Imogen ashore on Cerf Island. Even then, Ruth hadn't been positive, but lately there had been meaningful glances and laughter and (even more telling) the bandied mock insults that people who are interested in each other so often employ; to Ruth's jaundiced eye, juvenile and too obvious a ploy. Who did they think they were fooling? Themselves, perhaps? Ruth supposed that over the years she had become an unwilling expert in such matters. Was she going to resign herself to fate yet again? Somehow, this autumn, she felt more confident. She even minded less, but she did still mind.

To distract herself from such worries, she concentrated upon her little coterie of men and allowed herself to be pampered by them. Even poor Leslie made her feel better by comparison, and both Brian and Barnaby were very supportive.

'In point of fact,' Leslie was saying, 'my legs haven't deteriated as much as I was afraid they would.'

Ruth caught Barnaby's eye and controlled a smile as he silently mouthed 'det-er-i-*or*-ated' above Leslie's pink cotton sunhat, for her benefit.

Brian said, 'Well I've researched that very thing, you know. Of course MS has almost as many different symptoms as there are sufferers; that's what's so confusing. It all depends on which part of your nervous system has been damaged by it, but it does seem to be true that if your disease has progressed slowly over the last ten years, then there's a very good chance that the next ten years will be slow too.'

'I think that's enormously encouraging,' Ruth said to Barnaby, 'don't you?'

'Yes I do.' He sounded surprised.

'Oh look at those beautiful flowers!' Imogen said to Roger as they walked ahead of most of the group down the street of Grande Anse past the small shops, the magistrates' court bungalow, the football field and the police station. 'Aren't they delicate and strange?'

'White spider lilies,' Roger said, smiling at her enthusiasm, '*Lys de mer.*'

'Why have the coconut palms got numbers on them?'

'The locals collect the sap and ferment it into a lethal sort of toddy. That's what the ladders are for too.'

'And what are those little pink pear-shaped fruits on that tree?'

'Jamalac. Try one?' He picked several and gave her one, watching as she bit into it. She has good teeth, he thought, and sensuous full lips . . . Judging from her behaviour the night before when she had laughed at Barnaby's misfortune with the folding chair, she wasn't perhaps as firmly devoted to her husband as at first he had feared. Was now the time to make his move? He felt his heartbeat quicken at the thought.

'It doesn't taste of much.'

'No,' he agreed.

They had caught up with Janice who was walking (Roger thought, rather defiantly) alone. 'These shops don't sell Kwells,' she complained as they overtook her.

'That's a shame,' Imogen said in conciliatory tones, 'but I expect Claire's got some more.'

'Huh!' Janice said, 'I'm not going to ask *her* again. Some doctor!'

Come on! Roger silently implored Imogen, *for God's sake let's not get tangled up with Moaning Minnie!*

'Oh!' Imogen cried, pointing, 'there's the church. I've never seen one with a corrugated-iron roof before. Do let's look inside.' She seemed about to quicken her step but then stopped and, turning to Janice, asked, 'Why don't you come with us?'

'Not me,' Janice said with some satisfaction. 'I'm chapel, meself.' She looked belligerently at Roger. 'What you grinning at, then?'

'Nothing at all,' he said, 'sheer *joie de vivre.*'

Imogen walked into the small church first and was enchanted by its simplicity. It was cool inside and empty, and she sat down on one of the chairs to rest her feet and take it all in. Roger sat down beside her and Imogen was conscious of his eyes looking sideways at her, rather than at their surroundings. It had been a long time, she thought, since she had enjoyed a man's admiration, and she was going to make the most of it. Perhaps she would allow him an occasional snatched kiss, just to keep his interest topped up. Well . . . maybe. She wasn't going to show him that she'd guessed, though. If he wanted any favours from her, he was going to have to work hard for them!

'I feel really sorry for Janice,' she whispered. Talking aloud seemed inappropriate for such a place. 'She must feel so alone.'

'She's a miserable old bat,' Roger said, also in a low voice. 'How can you possibly feel sorry for her? You should see it from my point of view. It only takes one prize whinger to screw up a whole group, and we've got two – three, if you count Leslie. No, she's definitely a heart-sink client.'

'A what?'

'The sort of person who, when you first meet them – and forever afterwards – your heart sinks.'

Imogen laughed. 'Oh I like that,' she said. 'I must remember it.' She looked at him. 'You do enjoy this job, though?'

'It has its moments. Now is a good one, for instance.' He had crinkly bits round his eyes when he smiled, Imogen noticed. Otherwise his face was boyish and unlined. He is so different from Barnaby, she thought, so full of charm and vigour.

'How old are you?' she asked.

'Thirty-eight.'

'God! You're a babe in arms compared with me!'

'Ruth is four years older than me,' he said, 'and I don't notice that at all, so what's a further six years between friends?'

'Are we friends?'

'I'd like to think so.'

Perhaps now would be a good time for the first stolen kiss, followed by a little righteous indignation? Imogen thought. I'm sure I can engineer that.

'Barnaby always gets very jealous of my friends,' she lied. 'It's so silly. It really upsets me.' She looked down at her lap and bit her lip.

'Hey,' Roger said gently, putting out a hand and lifting her chin so that they were face to face again. 'We can't have you being sad, now can we?' Imogen almost closed her eyes and peered through her lashes to check that Roger's face was approaching her own in a satisfactory manner. She felt his breath on her cheek. She parted her lips slightly. 'Oh Imogen . . .' he whispered.

There was the sound of a heavy footfall at the church door and a sharp female exclamation, 'Ah!'

' . . . of course that's probably the French influence,' Roger said in his normal voice, whipping his head back and pointing in the general direction of the altar. 'Very charming, I always think.'

Imogen, lost in admiration for his quick reaction and impec- cable acting, did not have time to wonder how he had managed to get it to such a fine art.

'Oh hello,' Shirley said, slumping down beside them and panting. 'Isn't this a dinky little church? Which bit's French?'

While Barnaby rested before supper, Imogen washed half a dozen pairs of pants and a T-shirt and hung them from a piece of string on the veranda. She supposed she should have asked Barnaby if he had anything he wanted washing, but then thought, Let him do it himself. So she had left the Travel-wash stuff obviously on the edge of the washbasin as a hint. Now she stood for a long moment with her hands on the rail, looking towards the sea. The sun was setting and the sky glowed. If I nip down to the beach, she thought, I'll see it better, without all the trees in the way. She heard the other hut door open behind her and turned to see Roger emerging. He put his finger to his lips and closed the door quietly behind him.

'Let's go for a walk,' he said.

'What's Ruth doing?'

'Sleeping. And Barnaby?'

'The same. Doesn't the sunset look marvellous?'

When they got to the beach and looked out to the west, the two small islands of Cousin and Cousine showed up black on the horizon. Lines of thin cloud above them, and the sand, and a dinghy at anchor nearby were black too. It was a two-tone landscape of darkness and flame. The sky was every possible shade of copper, in streaks and patches from primrose yellow via marmalade to shell-pink. The sea was a silvery smooth orange lagoon, lapping the shore with tiny wavelets. It was absolutely quiet and the air was still heavy with the heat of the day.

'Aaaah,' Imogen breathed, 'just look at that!'

'Why are you whispering?' Roger sounded amused.

'I don't know. I suppose I don't want to disturb the perfect peace.'

'Let's go up the beach a bit.'

'Aren't we lucky,' Imogen said, walking beside him and feeling the cooling sand between her toes. 'Imagine having to live in a high-rise inner city flat and never having the chance to escape like this.'

'I'd rather not, if you don't mind.'

'But we're so privileged!' Imogen said passionately. 'People in our position should realize that; not take it all for granted.'

'You're right of course,' Roger said. 'You feel such things deeply, don't you?'

'I care about the inequalities of life, yes. That's why I do the work I do.'

'You and I are very alike,' Roger said.

'Why did you leave the Probation Service?' Imogen asked.

'I mean, their loss is our gain, naturally, but it seems such a waste.'

Roger sighed. 'I don't know. I suppose in the end the bureaucracy of it all got me down, and the stress of coping with impossible people. I felt emotionally drained, and then there was Ruth's MS . . . I woke up one morning and thought "Is this it?" and decided it wasn't enough.'

'You don't miss it, then?'

'Now and again, but mostly not.'

'I wonder if I would?' Imogen said.

'You're not thinking of starting something new?'

'Not very seriously. Maybe it's just that I've got to the "is this it?" stage too, and I'm sort of hoping that there'll be more to life. Barnaby can't live without routine, but I sometimes feel that I can't live with it!'

'Perhaps you need taking out of yourself.'

Imogen laughed shortly, 'You mean, have a head transplant?'

'Oh very droll.' He put an arm casually round her shoulders. 'No, I was thinking more along the lines of some TLC.'

Aha! Imogen thought, now we're getting somewhere. A modicum of tender loving care would be most acceptable.

'Mmmm,' she said, affecting non-comprehension, 'TLC? A tight lacy cardigan . . . a thought lasting centuries . . . a tremulous little creature . . . a third legitimate child . . . or maybe even a tiny liquorice crocodile?'

'Oh shut up and come here!' Roger snorted, stopping abruptly, pulling her to him in one skilful movement and kissing her with fervour.

'*Jesus!*' Imogen thought, Why have I wasted the last thirty odd years on *Barnaby*?

8

Next morning on the bus on the way to that day's outing, Philip sat next to Daisy and they compared wader notes.

'Great sand plover and crab plover on the beach first thing this morning,' he said, 'Two ticks!'

'And whimbrel,' Daisy said, looking at her own notebook.

'Yes, that too. I hope you don't mind . . . me winning the bet, so far?'

'Of course not,' Daisy said. 'That's what it's for.'

They were sitting right in front of Imogen, but she barely heard them. She was watching Roger covertly and with a certain proprietorial satisfaction. It was only with the greatest difficulty that she had torn herself from his embrace the evening before, and she had quite forgotten to employ any of the righteous indignation which might have kept him interested but still under her control. As it was, she reminded herself, she was in danger of going completely overboard. She had got to get a grip on herself and remain in charge of the situation, even though the sensation of being swept away on a tide of emotion was wonderfully novel and seductive. I must not lose my head and make a complete fool of myself, she thought. I will not.

She wondered what Roger was thinking about. He appeared to be exactly the same as always, but every now and again when he was sure no one else was watching, he would glance at her conspiratorially and raise an eyebrow, or wink, or just smile briefly, knowingly . . . Imogen was astonished to find herself responding with a quickened heartbeat and a secret thrill of complicity. The clandestine nature of their new intimacy heightened her pleasure in it. It gave her ego a tremendous boost to think that she and Roger shared something that excluded the rest of the group. She thought delightedly to herself, *If they only knew*! She felt young again, vital, irrepressible. She wondered what Roger would do next. So far it had been just kisses and a bit of a grope in the dark. Presumably he would want to take things further? Imogen had been married and monogamous for so long that she had forgotten how to conduct a developing affair. She felt like an adolescent again with a list of preliminary 'stages' to be worked through in the correct order (and giggled about with friends). What had been the sequence all those years ago? Wasn't it 1 to 5 above the waist, 5 to 9 below? And then 10 which was *it* . . . She couldn't for the life of her remember what all the numbers had stood for. Now, too, she didn't need buddies to discuss it with. This was her own special secret, to be acknowledged with a brief meaningful glance every so often, but mostly to be kept fermenting, alert and delicious within herself. But was she going to let it get as far as 10?

Of course I could never do this at home, in real life, she thought. I suppose it's the archetypal holiday romance, so common as to be ridiculous. I don't care! It was ironic really, she had come on the holiday to spend time with Barnaby in paradise; to share it with him. That had been her honest intention. He had clearly seen it differently, and it was certainly turning out to be different — a self-fulfilling prophecy on his part? If he hadn't been so uncommunicative and such a killjoy, Imogen thought, then perhaps I never would have got involved with Roger in the first place. It was a valid thought.

'You're very quiet today,' Shirley said, next to her.

'Yes.'

'What were you thinking about?'

'Oh this and that. You know the old codger's saying: "Sometimes I sits and spits and thinks. Sometimes I just sits and spits".'

The bus stopped in a car park and Roger stood up at the front. 'Right,' he said. 'We're at the Vallée de Mai national park and we're meeting a local ranger who will take us round. Claire's group will do a shorter walk, but don't worry you'll still see the important things. You'll be back at the bus for lunch and then be taken on a short scenic drive before going back to the hotel for a rest or a swim. My group will stop and eat on our way round, which will take a couple of hours, so don't forget to carry your packed lunches with you. We'll also be walking back down the hill to our hotel afterwards. Anyone who doesn't feel up to that should go with Claire's group. OK? Good.'

'Anyone would think we were schoolkids,' Janice grumbled. 'Ordering us about!'

'It's called organization,' Imogen told her. 'You'd have a lot more to complain about if Roger hadn't got everything sorted out in advance.'

Janice ignored this. 'Well I'm not walking all the way back and that's flat,' she muttered as they all started getting off the bus.

Annabel got off in her turn and went over to Roger. 'Is it all right if I come with your group?' she asked him. 'I think I'm up to it.'

'Fine,' Roger said, 'why not?' They set off along the path towards the entrance gate.

Ever since Brian had started drawing her, Annabel had felt increasingly good about herself. Was it the fact that he considered her to be worth drawing, she wondered, or was it the result of the conversations they had while it was going on? Annabel had never before had the opportunity to discuss her illness with anyone else who knew how she felt. It was wonderful to be understood. He confirmed that she had the relapsing/ remitting form of MS and that she was at the moment in remission. In the past three years she had had two attacks, each of which had come about in very similar ways. She had woken in the morning both times with her lips feeling cold and numb. When she got out of bed, she had stumbled and fallen down. Then the numbness had spread throughout the left side of her face and she found she couldn't walk without staggering. The next day, her left arm and face were numb and her speech became slurred as she found it more and more difficult to articulate clearly. Her whole co-ordination system and balance seemed to have deserted her. If she was not supported, she fell downstairs or lurched towards walls . . . Both attacks had been at their worst for about two weeks, and after each she had gradually got better, almost back to normal, but she lived in terror of the next one. She had decided from the outset of this holiday to stay with Claire's group, so that she wouldn't get too exhausted or risk precipitating another attack, but Brian had now disabused her of this idea. He had worked hard to give her more confidence in herself.

'Exercise is fine,' he had said. 'You shouldn't – and can't – wrap yourself in cotton wool at your age. Just be aware that you must pace yourself, and if you get very fatigued then you must *rest*. Don't worry, though, it won't make you any worse.'

Well, Annabel thought to herself, let's hope he's right. She had desperately wanted to be with Roger, and had been disappointed to discover that he always led the able-bodied group. Today she could join it too, and not feel second best. The only fly in the ointment was Imogen. She was so pushy! She was always up ahead with Roger, or sitting in the most favoured seat, or getting the best view. She was the sort of person who always seemed to get what she wanted.

They arrived at the entrance gate and were taken through it by a smiling dark-skinned young man in a bush hat. 'This is Gilbert,' Roger said.

Annabel looked up and immediately forgot petty irritations. On either side of the narrow path, instant primeval jungle crowded in. The daylight filtered down in greens and yellows through a thrusting mesh of palm fronds, all toothed and pointed. From some of the palms, long pendant spikes of small pale flowers hung in ragged cascades like spaghetti. Others were bushy with epiphytic ferns. Some were chained to the earth by the rampant climbing stems of philodendron (last seen by Annabel in her aunt's drawing room, cowed, and trained into 'an arrangement'). Dead brown fronds hung down. Fallen ones covered what could be seen of the forest floor in a papery deep-litter of leaf skeletons. Annabel gazed about her in awe. One palm, close to the path, sported an amazing drooping inflorescence which looked for all the world like an exhausted elephant penis covered in tiny yellow bees . . .

'Male *coco de mer* flower,' Roger said, following her gaze. 'It's enough to make your eyes water, isn't it?' and he winked familiarly.

Perhaps, Annabel thought, rather discomfited, I'm wrong to admire him. Perhaps he's a trifle common? N.Q.O.C.D., as her grandmother would have it: not quite our class, dear.

Roger smiled round at the group. 'The fruits are even better. Look, there's one.' He pointed out a ripe nut on the ground.

It was huge and brown and shaped like a three-dimensional human female bottom, even to the extent of having bristly fibres on the front, where the pubic hair would be.

'Wow!' Imogen exclaimed, 'isn't that extraordinary?' She picked it up and held it in front of her at hip level, laughing, while Philip and Leslie took photographs. Trust her! Annabel thought uncharitably.

'One leaf of the *coco de mer* can be thirty feet long,' Roger said, 'if you measure from the bottom of the leaf stalk to the top of the frond, and there are trees here a thousand years old.'

'Crikey,' Leslie said. 'Eat your heart out Kew Gardens!'

Imogen found Gilbert the ranger to be a fount of knowledge. He told her that there were large numbers of exotic species of trees and shrubs which had been introduced to Seychelles from outside and which did not naturally belong there: jack fruit, mango, cocoa, breadfruit, pineapple, and many flowering plants. Beautiful or edible though they were, the park authorities planned to eliminate them to restore the forest to its native state.

'How long will that take?' Imogen asked.

'Who can tell?' Gilbert's face creased into a wide white grin. Then he pointed above their heads where bunches of red fruits were strung like beads along hanging stems, and upon which two rather unimpressive chunky brown birds were feeding. 'Seychelles black parrot,' he said.

'Philip . . . over here – quick!' Imogen called as quietly as possible, so as not to scare them. 'Let him get past, Shirley! He's got to get these on film.' She wondered rather irritably why Shirley always had to stand so close to her, blocking the view and generally getting in the way. She quite liked the woman, but . . .

Philip and his camera were now immediately below the parrots, who continued to peck at the fruits as he banged off shot after shot.

'What are those bits of tin round that stump?' Shirley asked Gilbert.

'It is a parrot nesting tree and that is to keep the rats from climbing.'

Oh, Imogen thought, so even in paradise there are rats?

They walked down a long gentle flight of steps and came to a small stream and the end of one path. Then they waited for the whole group to assemble. Imogen looked about her as the stragglers caught up. Here there were strange palm trees, each growing from a cone of stilt roots as though they were all perched on top of a group of uncovered tepees.

'*Verschaffeltia splendida*,' Ruth said to Barnaby rather breathlessly as they arrived, 'or *Latanier latte*, in Creole.' She pointed at the stilt-rooted palms.

Imogen laughed. 'What impossible names!' she said. 'I hope you aren't expecting Barnaby to remember them? His memory is like a sieve.'

'He's doing very well so far,' Ruth said, and then, turning to Barnaby, 'There are five of the six Seychelles endemic palms and three of the four Seychelles screw pines all together in this area. I'll see if I can point them out to you.' Imogen made a face behind Ruth's back, but Barnaby seemed not to notice. He was busy following Ruth's pointing finger and scribbling things down in a small notebook.

How ridiculous! Imogen thought rather huffily. He's never taken the least bit of interest in nature before, when I've tried to foster it in him. And now he's getting all keen with nondescript Ruth. He's probably only doing it to annoy me! She resolved to ignore them both.

Daisy and Dorothy were the last to catch up. Daisy was now using both her sticks and lurching forwards slowly but doggedly.

'So sorry,' Daisy said for both of them as they arrived. 'I'm getting a little fatigued, I fear.'

'Take your time,' Roger said, 'no rush. This is where we part company anyway. In a few minutes Claire will take you back the way we've come. All you have to do is to turn right at each junction. OK? The rest of us will do a longer circuit and see you back at the hotel later.'

Roger led his group back to the fork in the path and turned left. Annabel followed them, feeling as though she had just been promoted to the first team but was on probation only. I don't feel tired, she thought. I'm fine. I'm no worse than Philip. Brian was right.

Ahead of her were Roger, Gilbert the ranger, Imogen, Shirley and Philip. Behind her was Dorothy – and Simon. Shouldn't he be with Claire? Surely he wouldn't be able to walk the rest of the way round the reserve *and* back to the hotel? Annabel wondered what to do. Should she say something to him? Perhaps he hadn't heard the instructions? Did Roger know he was following? Annabel was unwilling to challenge Simon directly and risk his sarcasm, but Roger was too far in front for her to speak to him. It's not my problem, Annabel told herself, but she felt anxious about it anyway. What if she and Simon both found that they were unable to walk the distance and became an encumbrance to the others? Annabel couldn't bear the thought of being a liability to anyone. She would rather go nowhere than risk that . . .

She took a long breath and looked resolutely ahead. *You are here to enjoy yourself,* she told herself firmly. Make the most of it! She noticed that Imogen was certainly doing just that. She had monopolized Gilbert from the outset, and was still talking to him. Now they had stopped and Gilbert was pointing something out. As she caught up and looked in the direction of his outstretched arm, she saw a tree trunk which at the base was green with white bands but higher up, with no gentle gradation of colour, was suddenly a brilliant pillar-box red.

'Sealing-wax palm,' Roger said.

'Now that one has got to be plastic,' Simon said. 'It's positively unnatural.'

'What on earth are you doing with this group?' Imogen demanded, rounding on him. 'This is the *long* walk. There's no way you're going to make it all the way back and you'll just foul everything up for the rest of us. How can you be so selfish and bloody-minded?'

Well! Annabel thought, I may not like her very much, but she's certainly not lacking in courage!

After he had defused the situation with as much diplomacy as he could muster, Roger wondered what to do next. It was clearly going to be too much for Simon to complete the walk, and he had told him this as kindly as possible (the awkward sod!). Now he supposed he would have to escort him back to Claire's group and let Gilbert take the able-bodied the rest of the way.

'Why should you?' Imogen said, on hearing the suggestion. 'It's his own stupid fault!'

'It's none of your damn business!' Simon said, furiously. 'Who d'you think you are anyway? Typical bloody voluntary do-gooder; officiousness gone mad!'

'Just cool it,' Roger said, '*both* of you, OK?'

'If I may make a suggestion . . .?' Dorothy said.

'I can quite well go back alone,' Simon said. 'I most certainly do not need someone to hold my hand. It's a ridiculous fuss over nothing!'

'Yes Dorothy?' Roger said.

'I'm happy to go back with Simon if that would be of any help,' Dorothy said. 'It's fairly straightforward and I'm pretty sure I can remember the way; first left and then two right forks. Yes?'

'Yes.' Roger was impressed. Dorothy was perhaps not as daffy as he'd always thought. 'Well, if you're happy with that . . .?'

'Absolutely. I used to be a Girl Guide, you know.' Dorothy looked splendidly determined.

'I've told you, I don't need an escort,' Simon protested.

'I think,' Roger said firmly, 'that you can't afford to turn down a good offer at this stage. I'm not going to allow anyone to go off on their own, and that's flat. It's up to you.'

'Oh all right then.' Simon turned on his heel and started walking back the way they had come, with bad grace.

'You're sure?' Roger asked Dorothy.

'Don't worry,' Dorothy said. 'Leave him to me.' She set off after Simon, trotting to catch up with him. Roger watched the two of them until they were out of sight round a bend and then turned to apologize to Gilbert. Gilbert tapped his forehead meaningfully and giggled. Then they continued on their way.

'Good old Dorothy,' Shirley said in surprise. 'Somehow I didn't have her down as a knight in shining armour.'

'Me neither,' Annabel said.

'More like Boadicea in a liberty bodice,' Imogen put in, and they all laughed.

Roger heaved a sigh of relief. Is it all worth it? he asked himself. There must be easier ways to make a living. He was going to have to watch Imogen. If there was one thing he didn't need, it was someone else doing his job for him, and doing it moreover with all the tact of half a brick! Oh yes, he fancied Imogen rotten and he lusted after her body, but there were aspects of her personality that he could certainly do without. Why couldn't women just lie on their backs and keep their mouths shut, he wondered? That would be the best of all possible worlds.

'Penny for your thoughts?' Imogen said, walking alongside on a wider stretch of path and smiling up at him.

'They're unrepeatable,' Roger said, and added, *sotto voce*, 'in public that is. Remind me to tell you later.' Her smile widened. It's easy really, Roger thought, as long as you tell them what they want to hear.

They began walking up a drier slope with sparser vegetation until at the top they came to a concrete plinth which had once supported a building. They stopped to admire the view and to eat their packed lunch. To the west, a valley led down to the sea at Grande Anse. On the far blue horizon, Silhouette Island was visible. Roger sat under the shade of a large *bois rouge* and ate his sandwich and drank water from a flask. Imogen had sat down too far away for him to touch her surreptitiously. She was wearing shorts today and her legs were slim and very inviting, hardly middle-aged at all. Roger watched her covertly with sidelong glances and a keen anticipation of pleasures to come. So far she had not disappointed him . . .

He felt another gaze upon him and looked up to meet Annabel's eyes. She was looking at him rather critically, he fancied.

'How're you doing?' he asked her.

'Very well,' she said. 'Better than I dared hope.'

'Good. And you, Shirley?'

'I'm fine,' Shirley said with her mouth full.

'Hey!' Philip said, grabbing his binoculars, still chewing, and without taking his eyes from a lurking bird, 'Seychelles blue pigeon. Brilliant!'

Roger lay back with his eyes half closed, dozing. Get things into perspective, he thought. This is a doddle really. Little shits like Simon are peanuts compared with what I used to have to deal with in the Probation Service. I don't know I'm born, here. I think I'll have five minutes' kip.

Further round on the circular path after lunch, they did a

brief detour up a cul-de-sac to another high viewing point where there was a small open-sided shelter with a few benches and a sunshade thatch of palm leaves. Here they were able to look out over the varied tree canopy below them and sit and rest for a few moments. Above their heads, clinging upside down to the roof with suction-padded feet was a bright green gecko. Then, sliding very stealthily beside the ridge pole towards the garish little lizard, Roger noticed, was a thin brown snake. He pointed this out silently, and then had physically to restrain Annabel from interfering and preventing nature from taking its course.

'Wait,' he said. 'Let's see what happens.'

The snake inched its way over the pole and down between the palm fronds, creeping nearer and nearer to the apparently unsuspecting gecko, which stayed motionless and unprotected on the open expanse of roof.

Right, Roger thought to himself, watching the developing drama intently. I'll make a wager with the fates on the outcome of this. If the snake catches the gecko, then it means that I'll get to screw Imogen. But if not; not.

The snake made a lunge. The gecko shot sideways to safety and the snake ended up dangling and writhing from the roof, held up by only a narrow strip of palm leaf under one of its coils.

'It missed!' Annabel cried, delighted. 'Oh *good*!'

Shit! Roger thought.

9

'The purpose of this short talk,' Brian said, stuffing his pipe with tobacco as he spoke, 'is not to set myself up as some sort of guru, but just to share with you various bits and pieces of information and experience I've picked up over the thirty-odd years that I've had multiple sclerosis, and to debunk some of the quackery about MS that's so rife.' He looked round from his high stool at the interior of the small circular hut which did service as the hotel bar, and at the assembled group. They were all present and had the place to themselves. The warm night air blew in gently between the top of the half-boarded wall and the bottom of the pointed thatched roof. The women had mostly changed into cotton dresses, and the men into long trousers. They were relaxing in easy chairs with pre-dinner drinks in their hands, and looking up at him with interest. Brian lit his pipe on the third match and puffed it alive.

'Perhaps the worst time is when you're first told that you have MS, usually after years of uncertainty,' he went on. 'You feel anger, despair, loneliness, depression and, above all, "Why me?" You straight away think of the life and death of Jacqueline du Pré and you know for certain that all you have to look forward to is paralysis, humiliation, deterioration and dying. Well, I have to tell you that in all probability it won't turn out like that at all.

Certainly 5 per cent of people with MS do die of it within five years, but at the other end of the story there are 90-year-olds with precious few symptoms. Only a third of the MS population ends up in a wheelchair. A third need walking aids, and a third have it in what's called the benign form and are only mildly affected.' Brian pulled on his pipe and then waved it about to underline certain points. 'People with MS feel very powerless, even guilty and become very vulnerable to quack remedies, just so they can *do* something about their condition,' he went on. 'Personally I don't believe in the efficacy of hyperbaric oxygen, evening primrose oil or special diets, although there is some evidence that eating sunflower oil may help . . .' He found that the words came easily and that he enjoyed getting his ideas across. Maybe he should have been a teacher instead of an engineer? He had decided to run through all the common problems and misconceptions encountered in MS and then summarize them at the end. He ticked off the headings mentally as he came to each one: exercise, stress, sexual dysfunction, fatigue, urinary symptoms, psychological disturbance and heredity.

Any one of these could be a worry at any stage in anyone's disease. They were not just the concerns of those who were obviously disabled. It was sometimes interesting to watch his audience's response, and it was often possible to pick out who suffered from which problem by their reactions to his words. Leslie had stared fixedly at the floor at one point. He was clearly impotent, poor chap. Brian made a note to tell him privately about an injection which could give him up to thirty hours of reliable erection, although . . . come to think of it, looking at Janice, maybe not! Dorothy had sat up and taken notice when he had discussed stress. Perhaps, Brian wondered, she was in the habit of giving in to Daisy in order to save her from stress? Probably. Simon most likely had trouble with his waterworks, but Brian was pretty sure he wouldn't admit to such a thing and would probably rather die than consult his local continence adviser . . .

When he got to the end of his talk, he recapped briefly. 'Exercise *doesn't* make you worse in the long term. Pain is not uncommon in MS. Stress is *good* for you. Infections make you worse. MS is about as heritable as heart disease, cancer or diabetes; the tendency to it does run in families but there are probably also environmental factors. MS can make you forgetful, selfish and irritable. Fatigue is often its most upsetting symptom. *Don't* get too hot in bed or eat heavy meals. *Do* pace yourself. Mornings are usually better than afternoons; your body temperature is lower then. Oh yes, and the MS Society is the best source of information. Doctors often don't see enough MS patients to know what they're talking about – sorry

Claire, present company excepted of course! I think that's it. Any questions?'

Imogen listened intently to Brian's talk and learnt a lot, so much in fact that she didn't think she would bother to speak to him privately after all. There was no need. She was also surprised and pleased that Barnaby had deigned to attend, and hoped that he too would get something useful from it. She herself had had all her major queries answered and she felt supported and vindicated. Half of MS sufferers *did* have cognitive dysfunction; 10 per cent moderately to severely, and 40 per cent only mildly. It was not correlated to physical disability and it was worse in people with the chronic progressive sort of MS; people like Barnaby. It apparently showed up in an inability to retrieve information from the brain, in difficulties with abstract reasoning and problem solving, in a slowed-down speed of information processing, and in a lack of verbal fluency; the inability to find the right word. So Imogen was *right*, and she felt surprisingly reassured by this knowledge. Barnaby was clearly only mildly affected. No one who didn't know him well would notice any problems at all, but she did, and now she knew she wasn't just imagining things. Something else that Brian had said struck a chord with her too. People with MS could be 'hard to talk to' or 'don't listen', which could seem like indifference, stubbornness, hostility or even a personality problem. That last was Simon to the life! It was also in a lesser degree, she recognized with something like gratitude, Barnaby also.

As they sat at the table waiting to be served their dinner, Annabel questioned Brian about the values of spiritual healing and yoga.

'Yes,' he said. 'Aromatherapy too. If it feels good, do it. Those three certainly won't do you any harm. I'm all in favour of knowledge first and then free will. The thing is to *know* what you're doing. I mean, I know smoking is a bad idea and I still do it, but at least it's a conscious choice.'

'What about passive smoking?' Simon challenged. 'We may not all relish inhaling essence of bonfire.'

'I only smoke in well ventilated places,' Brian said, 'but if it's a problem, I'd be happy to keep as far away from you as possible.'

'Can't say fairer than that!' Imogen said. Simon pointedly ignored her. She thought, I haven't been doing what I told myself I would. I haven't spoken in depth to everyone in the group yet, and it should have been *me* who escorted Simon back today, not Dorothy. If I hadn't been so keen to be with Roger, I would have done so. This 'thing' with Roger is stopping me from being true to myself. Then she thought, To hell with that! I'm on holiday. Why should I try to sort out other people's problems? I have enough of that at the CAB. *At the CAB*, her conscience reminded her, *you would never have spoken to Simon in that brusque way. It would have been more than your job's worth.* So what? she told it. Here is different. Here I'm liberated from normal restraints, and just for once in my life I'm going to be completely selfish and enjoy it. I deserve it. I deserve food too. I'm starving! Ah good, here it comes now.

'What's this?' Janice demanded of the waitress.

'Octopus, madam.'

'It never is!' Janice looked outraged. 'I'm not a fussy woman, but this is ridiculous!'

'It's very good,' Barnaby said encouragingly. 'Try it.'

'It's all right, duck' Leslie said to her, rolling a piece round his mouth. 'It's not a bit slimy.'

The octopus was followed by mackerel, beans and rice and pineapple fritters.

'Oh no!' Annabel suddenly cried. '*Oh my God!*'

She touched a hand to her forehead and then stared wildly at the table, clutching its edge convulsively with her other hand.

'Whatever's the matter?' Dorothy asked.

'I can't see properly. Everything's blurred and I'm going one way and the table's going the other . . . oh *no* – ' She began to cry noisily. 'I'm going to have another attack, I just know it!' She stared blindly ahead of her, with tears pouring down her face and dropping from the end of her nose. She appeared to be stuck to her chair, afraid to move.

'Come on,' Claire said, jumping to her feet and going over to her. 'Don't get upset. You've probably just overdone it today; unaccustomed exercise and all that. Best thing is to go to bed and have a good rest. You'll be fine tomorrow.'

'I won't,' Annabel wailed, 'I just know I won't', but she

allowed Claire to help her up and support her, and they left the room together.

'Oh dear,' Dorothy muttered, getting out a handkerchief and dabbing at the tears which were starting from her own eyes.

'Hmmm,' Simon said. 'One down, seven to go. I wonder who will be next?'

'I'd be grateful,' Roger said, carefully controlled, 'if you'd be good enough to keep such thoughts to yourself in future.'

'I'll just go and make sure she's all right,' Shirley said, getting to her feet, still chewing her last mouthful.

Poor Annabel, Imogen thought. Thank goodness Barnaby doesn't have 'attacks' as such . . .

'Looks like your advice to Annabel was duff gen,' Simon observed to Brian. 'She'd have been better off staying with the poor bloody disabled, like I had – '

'Has everyone finished?' Roger interrupted. 'Good. Well if anyone's interested I'm going out to look at the stars and try to find some tenrecs.'

'What's a tenrec when it's at home?' Leslie asked.

'A sort of Madagascan hedgehog. They come out at night.'

'I'm for bed,' Barnaby said. 'I'm whacked.'

'Me too,' Ruth said, to mumbles of agreement.

Imogen discovered with mixed feelings that it was just herself and Roger who were walking down the main street in the dark with a couple of torches, and being barked at but allowed to pass unmolested by the local cowardly dogs. For once there was no Shirley panting at her heels, large, insensitive and ubiquitous. When they got beyond the village, Roger led the way off the path. The sky glittered unobstructed above their heads. It was hot and sticky and pitch dark but for the stars.

'There's Orion and Cassiopeia *upside-down*!' Imogen exclaimed. 'Now I know for sure that this isn't the real world. Where's the Southern Cross?'

'Up there,' Roger said, pushing her face gently so that she was looking in the right direction. 'It is in the form of a cross, but there are two stars together on the left-hand side, not one.'

'Oh yes,' Imogen said after a while, 'I've got it. It's not very big, is it?'

No tenrecs obliged that night, and they heard only frogs. Roger inspected Jupiter through his binoculars and said he could see three of its moons. He offered the glasses to Imogen without taking the strap from around his neck, so she had to get very close to him to see through them. Roger stood behind her and cupped her breasts with his hands while she tried unsuccessfully to find the planet in the narrow field of view amongst the vast expanse of the night sky.

'I give up,' she finally said.

'I don't,' Roger said, turning her round to face him. 'I've hardly begun.' He started kissing her then, and squeezing her bottom with one hand while the other held her firmly against him.

Imogen felt her blood thumping through her arteries and tingling in neglected places. It was, she thought, rather like pumping up an old tyre whose sides have almost stuck together with disuse. Suddenly it inflates, fully turgid and ready for action; rescued just in time . . . Just in time for what?

Why am I letting this happen, she asked herself, if I don't intend taking it to its natural conclusion? It's crazy. I hardly know him. I'm a married woman. And anyway, I need to reassess my relationship with Barnaby now I know *why* he's like he is . . .

'No,' she said. 'I'm sorry, but *no.*' She pulled away from him.

'Come on,' Roger said. He sounded out of breath. '*Come on.*' He put out a hand to hold her close to him again, but she anticipated the move and sidestepped him in the dark. Then she began walking briskly back the way they'd come, shining her torch to see her path. She heard him patting the ground and swearing behind her and realized that he must have dropped his torch, but when he finally caught up with her, he had got hold of it again. He was also obviously making a big effort to sound both sensitive and reasonable.

'What's the problem?' he asked. 'I thought we had something going?' She was silent. 'Imogen?' He shone the torch at her face.

She blinked and put a hand over her eyes, but not before he had seen the determined expression on her face. He lowered the torch and waited for her to give him an explanation.

'Oh look,' she said brightly, 'shooting stars!' Then she sighed deeply. 'Poor Annabel,' she said. 'I do hope she'll be all right.'

Daisy settled her bony rear on a small inflatable cushion on the deck of the catamaran *Amazing Grace*, making sure she was shaded by the canopy which had been draped over the fixed boom to give them all some shelter from the sun. She leant her back comfortably against the central cabin roof, took off her sunhat and ran her fingers through her cropped grey hair. So far, so good. The day before she had felt particularly exhausted and had gone to bed straight after supper and slept right through. Roger had assured her that this boat had four double cabins, a saloon and two loos, and was at their disposal all day, so if the worst came to the worst she could spend the whole time lying down and not disembark for the island of Aride at all. It was a reassuring thought, but Daisy had no intention of missing the excursion. It was the seventh day of their holiday and she had kept going up until now . . . She looked across at Annabel to see how she was doing. After the night before's dramatic departure, Annabel was clearly subdued and anxious. Her vision had apparently been restored again and the feelings of vertigo had disappeared too, but she was unable to believe that her symptoms had simply been caused by extreme tiredness. She's frightened, Daisy thought sympathetically. She lives every day in terror of another attack. Poor young thing! I wonder if psychotherapy would help her? Thank goodness Philip is doing so well . . . Daisy felt guilty then, as though Annabel's loss had been Philip's gain. How absurd! she told herself. Philip was, after all, her special concern and she was delighted that he was feeling so well and clearly relishing every moment of his Seychelles experience. Daisy watched him affectionately as he stood at the front of the catamaran on a narrow length of decking with one arm round the forestay for support while he scanned all around them for wildlife. It was a beautiful day; flat calm and burning hot. The *Amazing Grace* motored slowly through a gap in the reef and out onto the open sea.

Philip is the nearest thing I'll ever get to a son, Daisy thought. It's a pity his own mother is so over-protective. It's narrowed his horizons so, up to now. Perhaps this trip will convince her of the merits of letting go a bit; allowing him to grow up. She wondered if he had ever had a girlfriend. She thought not. He was shy with girls of his own age, but happy to relax with her and Dorothy who posed no challenge to him. A late developer?

Daisy thought that she had detected an interest in Philip from Claire (thoroughly unsuitable, if so) but then concluded that she must have been mistaken. Claire seemed rather down this year. Last year Daisy had considered her almost to be a younger version of herself, but this time she lacked spirit. Perhaps, after all, she was dependent for her morale upon male approbation? She would go down in Daisy's estimation if so.

Daisy looked round at her fellow travellers, doing an update on each as she went. Janice appeared for the moment to have found nothing to criticize, and therefore looked supremely discontented. Leslie was trying to pretend that this was his normal mode of transport, with which he was absolutely at ease. He was wearing a navy peaked go-faster cap and an air of studied insouciance. If he had any sense at all, Daisy fancied, he would cover up that rather unattractive weedy torso with one of his horrible flowery shirts. It's also time he gave up the pretence of drinking gin and tonic, which he clearly hates, she thought, remembering the evening before. He should take beer instead, like a proper working man; be proud of his origins. After all, who does he think he's bamboozling?

Now Brian, Daisy thought, knows exactly where and who he is. He puts on no airs and he speaks his mind, but never unkindly. He's a good honest Yorkshireman, the sort I admire. She watched him as he relaxed on the deck next to Annabel (he could be an excellent influence on that girl . . .). He always wore long trousers, never shorts, and he never got flustered. He was a creature of comfortable certainty and fixed habits.

How different from Imogen, Daisy thought. Now there was a butterfly if ever she saw one; a woman who always had to win, but who kept moving her own goalposts! When Daisy had asked her if she had studied coral-reef fish in other parts of the world, Imogen had looked blank and then had laughed and told her she'd only just discovered them. Before that she had been keen on wild flowers, and before that deep into geology and geomorphology. 'Have you always stuck with bird-watching?' she'd asked, as though that sort of loyalty was some-how pedestrian and unworthy. She has no depth, Daisy thought. It's all instant gratification and pragmatism with her. She wondered how far her fling with Roger had progressed, and chuckled inwardly at the thought that maybe this time Roger had bitten off more than he could chew.

Today Roger looked rather sulky, although it was difficult to read his expression behind those evil-looking mirror sunglasses. He was standing up at the stern, chatting to the man on the helm; being 'one of the staff'.

Shirley and Dorothy were basking in unashamed luxury on the deck, happy to be tourists and avid for the next revelation. Shirley had taken off the white plastic sandals she invariably wore when swimming (to protect her feet, she said, from the sharp coral) and her plump naked toes looked like a row of suckling piglets. Daisy admired Shirley's courage, if not her sense of style, in wearing pink stripy Bermuda shorts. It was daring of so confirmed a gossip to provide such grist for another critic's mill! In comparison to Shirley, Dorothy was almost invisible. She was sweet, Daisy thought fondly, almost childlike at times. Daisy didn't suffer fools, gladly or otherwise, but Dorothy had charmed her from the outset by her vulnerability. It was good to see her enjoying herself so much.

Was Barnaby enjoying himself too? Daisy couldn't quite fathom him, so he intrigued her. Ostensibly he was a country solicitor and not particularly exciting, but Daisy felt that there was more to him than that. She had her eye on him. He was sitting next to Simon and Ruth, but too far away for her to overhear any conversation. I ought to be interested in Simon, Daisy told herself. He does remind me of another case I once had. I wish I could remember the details . . . He's got a good brain, but somehow no humanity. He is interesting but there's so little in the man that I can find to *like*, that somehow I can't be bothered with him.

She was distracted by Philip. 'Look Daisy! Dolphins *and* flying fish!'

Ruth sat next to Barnaby on the deck of the *Amazing Grace* with Simon on her other side. She was feeling unusually content. It was a blazingly hot gorgeous day, and here they were on the equivalent of a millionaire's yacht over deep turquoise water in the middle of the Indian Ocean. She had just caught sight of part of a green turtle as it slipped down under the calm surface. Frigate birds flew overhead. Islands had passed earlier, but now it was just open sea as the catamaran's diesel engine burbled them northward towards Aride. Ruth looked round at the two men nearest to her. Simon appeared to be asleep and didn't acknowledge her. Barnaby smiled back at once. Ruth had noticed that he rarely sat by his wife, and wondered why. Perhaps she had initially been quite mistaken about the strength of their relationship? Imogen wasn't behaving like a happily married woman (or was she? Ruth didn't know for *sure*). Ruth wondered what went on inside Barnaby's head.

'I was just thinking how lucky we are,' she said to him. 'This time last year it rained. How about you?'

'I was mentally juggling words,' Barnaby said reflectively. 'I've been trying to think of appropriate ones. I mean, how would you describe the sea at this moment?'

'Aquamarine?' Ruth suggested, then she laughed disparagingly. 'No, that's as unimaginative as describing an orange as orange! I'm hopeless.'

'You're too hard on yourself,' Barnaby said. 'My own efforts were even worse, so I cheated and fell back on Robert Louis Stevenson. I think this would count as one of his "blue days at sea", don't you?'

'I don't know . . . It sounds lovely.'

'It's from his *Songs of Travel*. I'm not sure I can remember it properly:

"I will make you brooches and toys for your delight
Of bird-song at morning and star-shine at night.
I will make a palace fit for you and me
Of green days in forests and blue days at sea."

Bother . . . I've forgotten some, but it goes on:

"And you shall wash your linen and keep your body white
In rainfall at morning and dewfall at night." '

He was entirely unembarrassed at mentioning a white body, Ruth noticed. He was clearly not thinking of hers. She wished immediately, confusingly, that he had been.

'I like that,' she managed to say. 'I like it very much. We've had green days in forests too.' Barnaby was smiling again and looking straight at her. She felt encouraged enough to go on, 'I love words and I really hate the way the language gets all messed up nowadays. I loathe the way people will keep on using nouns as if they were verbs. You hear it all the time on the radio and read it in the papers.'

'Like *to scapegoat*, you mean?' Barnaby suggested, his face lighting up with enthusiasm, 'or *to target*.'

'Yes, and *to impact*,' Ruth agreed.

'*To doorstep!*'

'*To access!*'

'*To program!*'

Ruth laughed aloud. 'Simon must be asleep,' she said, 'or he would have defended the last two as computer-speak and therefore respectable.'

'Nothing,' Barnaby said firmly, 'about computers is respectable. I hate the things!'

'So, you're a flat-earther then?'

'Well I may be boringly old-fashioned but at least I was properly educated in the classics and I know that it should be *stadia* and *referenda*, not stadiums and referendums; that *viable* really means capable of living, surviving, germinating or hatching, and not "likely to succeed" and that in football a *whitewash* and a *walkover* are not synonymous!'

Ruth laughed. 'Am I right in recognizing those as your particular bugbears?' she asked, 'and do you feel better for that mini-outburst?'

'Yes, and immensely so, in that order. It's so good to meet someone who even understands what I'm talking about. You wouldn't credit how rare that is. These days you're lucky if you can find someone who can spell, let alone worry about grammar. I had to appoint a new secretary recently, so I gave all the hopefuls a one-word spelling test and, would you believe it, they all got it wrong but one.'

'So you chose her? or even him?'

'Her. No, she was nearly 60 and couldn't drive the apparently essential word processor. I was lumbered.'

'What was the word?'

'Liaison.'

'I can spell that!' Ruth said, delighted with herself, and proceeded to do so correctly.

'Full marks,' Barnaby said. 'If you ever need a job . . .'

Ruth didn't hear him. She was thinking, Why did he choose liaison in particular? Was that really the word he'd used, or was he trying to tell her something? Did he suspect about Roger and Imogen? Should she tell him? No, Ruth thought, I simply can't. I may be wrong . . . But hasn't he the right to know?

IO

RUTH stood on the hot white beach on the island of Aride with her bare feet occasionally washed by creeping waves, and watched as the second and final load of passengers from the *Amazing Grace* were brought ashore by pirogue. It was a long slender wooden boat of local design, which had been modified to take a modern outboard motor. It was crewed by two of the warden's staff from the island, one at each end. Between them there was just room for four pairs of passengers, sitting close together one behind the other, clutching their cameras and binoculars and holding tight as the pirogue reared and bucked through the fringing surf, covering them all with spray, and making for the waterline where it would emerge from the sea and graze its prow up the beach. Ruth hoped that everyone had taken Roger's advice and wrapped all their valuables tightly in waterproof plastic bags. It was always a wet journey, even when the weather was good. It was a paradox, she thought, that there could be such huge breakers at the edge of such a calm sea. She supposed it must be something to do with the slope of the beach.

Leslie was busy beside her, snapping away, so it was apparent that his camera had survived all right. She looked at the scene he was photographing and was amused to see that Simon, towards the front of the incoming pirogue, had bent down and was covering his face with his hands. She had noticed that he always refused to be in anyone's pictures, but wasn't this taking modesty to ridiculous lengths? And surely modesty was an unlikely component of his make-up anyway? Simon was a weirdo altogether, Ruth thought. He had booked the holiday at the last moment for himself and a woman friend, and then when she had for some reason been unable to come, he had gone ahead with the booking anyway, even to the point of paying a penalty late-cancellation fee for her, losing one deposit, and having to stump up extra for a single room.

'Money no object, it seems,' Roger had remarked at the time.

'Won't it mess up your arrangements?' Ruth had asked. 'You usually like your clients in twos.'

'Oh well, that system is a bit screwed up this year anyway, because Daisy insisted on bringing Philip, and then I agreed to Annabel as well. I don't suppose it much matters. It's just easier finding hotel rooms if everyone is in pairs.'

'Say cheese!'

Ruth looked round with a start to find that Leslie, having finished pointing his camera at the new arrivals as they stepped ashore, was busy taking a photograph of her. 'Oh . . . don't waste film on me,' she said, flustered. 'There's so much else that's far more worth while.'

'I'm getting at least one of everybody,' Leslie explained, 'for my album. I want to be able to look back on this experience when I'm old, and I reckon it's people that count. They make memories come alive, don't they?'

'Yes . . . I'm sure they do.' But why, Ruth asked him silently, why on earth do you want to remember these particular people? Most of them treat you like dirt.

There was a shout of command and a rumbling noise. The warden, with two more of his Seychellois staff, plus Roger and one of the crew from the catamaran, were now running the empty pirogue up the shore on rollers, taking them from under the stern as they emerged and re-using them under the bows until the boat was high and dry, in front of the few simple buildings at the top of the beach. Ruth recognized two of the locals from the previous year. They were both young men, wearing shorts and singlets and with gleaming brown graceful limbs and wide smiles. But it was their hair that was so striking. They wore it long, down to their shoulders in dreadlocks, and it was not the usual curly black African hair, but matted and thick, dry-bleached by the sun into a pair of tawny lion's manes. Now those two *are* worth capturing on film, she thought. They're beautiful.

Ruth mused about beauty as they all walked up the beach and into the shade of the trees. It seemed to her such an arbitrary gift; the permutation of genes and circumstance, such a lottery. Yet it conferred upon its lucky recipients an over-whelming advantage in life. Even if it faded as you got older, you still knew you'd had it once. You'd still had a head start in the acquisition of self-esteem. Ruth felt that she'd never had a fair chance to prove herself. She wasn't good-looking, but she wasn't ugly either. She wasn't outstandingly clever, but certainly not stupid. She was outwardly calm but inwardly volatile; appar-ently acquiescent but actually dissenting. And now she was ill, and she found that coping with that extra burden took up so much of her energy . . . I'm 42, she thought. Time goes by too quickly. How can I change anything? I feel as though I've gone aground, stuck fast, and that there will never be another spring tide.

As Roger led the active group on a walk and scramble to the top of the island, the cripples (as Barnaby had got into the habit of thinking of his fellows) settled down to a more leisurely exploration round its edge, stopping often to rest, and gaze upwards as white-tailed tropic birds flew overhead trailing their streamer tails against the blue. Ruth pointed out nesting fairy terns each balancing its single egg on the bare branch of a tree. They found a solitary brown noddy on the beach with an injured wing, and a ghost crab tearing across the sand and disappearing into a hole at their feet.

'That's called a Lou Lou,' Ruth said to Barnaby, as it went, 'and a hole in French is of course a *trou*, so its burrow is a *trou* Lou Lou!'

Barnaby laughed. He looked forward to Ruth's company. She was restful without being boring; companionable was the word. He looked around. Simon appeared to have accepted his limitations today, and was walking ahead with Claire. Daisy and Leslie were some distance behind, deep in conversation. Anna-bel also seemed to have decided to take things gently. She and Brian had sat themselves down under the filamentous shade of a casuarina tree and were continuing with their series of portraits.

'I wonder why he specially wants to draw her?' Ruth said, following his glance. 'I'd have thought Imogen was much better looking.'

'I don't think looks count for much,' Barnaby said. 'They often get in the way of character formation.'

'Oh . . .,' Ruth said, pleased, 'do you really think so? I'd never thought of it like that. I've always considered beauty to be an unalloyed blessing.'

'No, no,' Barnaby said positively. 'It can be a snare and a delusion. People who haven't got too much of it are lucky.' I must be careful what I say, he thought. It would be so easy to offend her, and I really do not want to do that. He looked at her again, sizing her up. Beautiful she was not. Her nose was a little too long. Her straight hair was mousy brown and a little too thin. Her face was not quite generous enough, and her chin was a little too pointed. She had a good figure though, and although her gait was awkward (worse than his own), she wasn't a clumsy sort of person. He felt he'd known her for years.

Isn't that odd? he said to himself.

'I don't know about lucky,' Ruth said. 'I certainly haven't got too much beauty, but I'm not sure that my character is any better formed. I haven't enough self-confidence and I suppose I worry too much.'

'What about?'

'Everything; whether Leisure Doubletrips will succeed or go bust, whether Roger would find another job, how we'd manage if he didn't.'

'The company isn't in trouble, is it?'

'Oh no. It's quite irrational of me really, but Roger has had lots of different jobs. We always seem to be on the move, so there's always the nagging thought . . .'

'You never had children?' Barnaby asked. 'That's what settled us down.'

'No. I never felt safe enough. Oh!' she stopped and looked up at him. 'How strange.'

'What is?'

'I've never admitted that to anyone before, about not feeling safe, I mean.'

'I'm always accused of being safe to the point of suffocation,' Barnaby admitted wryly. 'I suppose the grass is always greener on the other side?'

'Perhaps. I expect you're good with money too?'

'Well, I like to think so.'

'Roger's hopeless. It's always feast or famine with him. I don't mean he isn't generous; he is, but it's not dependable, and the older I get the more I seem to need that. I've actually just had a small legacy from one of my aunts, and I'm afraid it will be frittered away just like all the rest.'

'Keep it separate,' Barnaby suggested. 'It is yours, after all.'

'Well yes, but we have joint accounts for everything . . .'

'I could help you,' Barnaby offered. 'Advise you how to invest it in your own name, either for income or for capital growth, whichever suits you.'

'Could you really?' Ruth said. 'That would be *such* a help.'

'That's settled, then. I'll be your . . .'

'My what?'

'Forgotten the words . . . they'll come to me . . .'

'Financial consultant?'

'That's it exactly. Thank you.' Imogen always feeds me precisely the *wrong* word, he thought to himself. It drives me mad!

Imogen found that she was thinking about Barnaby as she sweated up to the top of Aride. In places the path went through piles of rocks, and it was necessary to get down on all fours to haul oneself upwards, grabbing hold of bushes and trees in passing. The warden, Philip and Roger were ahead of her, and Shirley, panting loudly, was right behind, leaving Dorothy and Janice to bring up the rear.

Imogen asked herself whether knowledge of why Barnaby was like he was in fact made any difference to her day-to-day experience of it? Would it be easier to make allowances because it wasn't his fault? If a person was slow or forgetful or bloody-minded on purpose, that clearly was worse than unwitting bad behaviour. But if that person was brain damaged (no matter how mildly) wasn't that in fact a greater problem for others, like her, to live with? If someone was deliberately unkind or vague, you could always hope for improvement, for a change of heart. But with this, there was no real chance of change. The personality had been irrevocably compromised. Can I live with that? Imogen wondered. Then she thought, Am I over-reacting and being ridiculous? No. This is how my situation seems to me to be, and if that's how it feels, then that's how it is. The one positive thing to hang on to, is that Barnaby's condition is likely to worsen only slowly. He probably won't have to retire early. He'll get his full pension. He'll be fine.

But if he's fine, the thought struck her, then there's no reason why I can't leave him! It wouldn't be like abandoning a helpless disintegrating dependant. It would be just another marriage that waited until the kids had grown up before falling apart, like a million others; no big deal . . . Imogen stood at the top of Aride and seriously considered freedom for the first time in years.

The view to the south-east from Big Head Rock was magnificent. She stared down the green slope of the island to the strip of pale beach with its band of blue-green shallows, and out over the shining sapphire sea on which the *Amazing Grace* sat at anchor, a small white speck in a vastness of ocean. There were no other boats in sight, no other people. they had the world to themselves. On the horizon were other islands, Curieuse, and the small blue humps of Les Soeurs. Here one could look down on passing frigate birds, and in the far distance even see whales blowing, so the warden said. Philip spotted a red-tailed tropic bird flashing past, and was jubilant.

So far everything has gone according to plan, Imogen thought. We've been shown the special things we wanted to see and we've enjoyed getting there. I have to hand it to Roger. He's certainly got the organization of it all sussed out. This day's speciality had been Wright's gardenia, which grew only on this one island. Imogen hadn't expected much, but its flowers had been worth seeing with their five white reflexed petals dotted with crimson, if only for their rarity value.

'We hauled Ruth up to see it, the first year,' Roger said as they stood beside one large bush, 'and she reckoned it was marvellous.'

Ruth must be a burden to him, Imogen thought. I can really sympathize with that. She had kept an eye out as they toiled up to the top of the island, but Roger hadn't given her any special acknowledgement so far that day. He's probably fed up with me and thinks I'm just a tease, she decided as they all stood at the top. She felt quite justified in her behaviour. She just hadn't been sure, that was all. Now she'd had time to think things out. She'd needed the space to do that, and now she thought she really did know what she wanted. Maybe it was also time she sounded Roger out on the chances of her taking over from Claire as his assistant?

'Claire seems a bit subdued,' she said to him. 'I imagined her to be a lot more bombastic, from your description.'

'Yes, she is quieter than usual,' Roger agreed, scanning the sea with binoculars.

'Perhaps she's losing interest in co-leading these trips?'

'It's possible, I suppose.'

'If she does give up, I was wondering if you'd consider me as a replacement?'

'*You?*' Roger jerked his head from his binoculars and looked at her. She couldn't see the expression in his eyes behind his sunglasses, so it was impossible to read his thoughts, although his tone of voice was not encouraging.

'Why not?'

'Well . . . it's an interesting idea . . . but I expect Claire will carry on for some years yet.'

'But if she doesn't?'

'Well I think we should cross that bridge when we come to it, don't you?'

Imogen took his lack of enthusiasm to be temporary pique, and was confident that she could quite easily talk him round.

'But you aren't a doctor,' Shirley put in, 'and that's important.'

'Claire's done nothing so far that I'm not perfectly capable of,' Imogen retorted, irritated with her for interfering. 'And anyway this is one of the safest places I've ever come across. Everyone walks round in bare feet. Even the wildlife is friendly. All you need is a jar of aspirins and a box of Kwells.'

'Oooh,' Shirley breathed, 'for goodness sake don't tempt fate like that. Find some wood to touch.'

As they made their way downhill again, Imogen's irritation with Shirley increased. It was like being trailed everywhere by a vast child. If she stopped to look at something, Shirley would cannon into her. If she let Shirley go ahead of her, Shirley would keep stopping to make a point, which was worse. Either way, she talked and talked . . .

Imogen wanted to take in her surroundings in peace: the millions of skinks darting away everywhere you looked, the huge granite boulders, the giant millipedes lurking on the shady side of tree trunks, the bronze geckos . . .

' . . . And so I reckon he stole it from the Post Office,' Shirley wittered on behind her. 'It happens all the time. One postman the other day was found with a room full of mailbags. He just couldn't be bothered to deliver them, see. Now Leslie could have gone through his ones for money, postal orders and such. You could collect up a tidy sum like that – enough to finance this trip, anyroad. I mean, let's face it, he's hardly likely to have earned enough is he? I'll be – '

'Why don't you ask his wife?' Imogen said cruelly. 'She's right behind you.'

Shirley whirled round in confusion, almost losing her balance. Janice was a long way back, well out of earshot. If looks could kill, Imogen thought to herself with some amusement, then I'd be dead several times over! Perhaps that will cure Shirley of her pash on me.

Both groups got together again near the boathouse in the shade, to eat their packed lunches and drink iced water from Thermoses. Brian's artistic efforts were praised. Leslie completed his set of 'people' photographs (much to Simon's disgust), and Daisy, who had taken it easy all morning, announced her intention of joining the snorkellers for the first time.

'Aren't the waves rather big?' Dorothy asked her nervously. 'I don't think I'll swim here myself, although I might paddle.'

'Once you get through the surf it's perfectly all right,' Daisy said. 'Snorkelling is just a question of floating about and keeping your eyes open. I think even I ought to be able to manage that!' Really! she thought, Dorothy is awfully *feeble* at times. 'I'm sure Roger will escort me through the breakers,' she said. 'That's all the help I need.'

'With pleasure,' Roger said. 'More than that, I'll lend you some flippers too. They make swimming a lot faster.'

The hard core of non-swimmers settled themselves down for an after-lunch zizz. Leslie lay full length with a handkerchief over his face. Brian, Barnaby and Ruth decided to have a sit down first and then maybe a little walk. Janice complained that she was afraid to lie down for a rest in case skinks ran all over her.

'You never know where they might creep in,' she said. 'It doesn't bear thinking about!'

Sexually frustrated! Daisy diagnosed as she changed into her swimming costume behind a towel held up by Dorothy. That's Janice's problem. Then she held the towel in turn for Dorothy, and when they were both changed and had put T-shirts over their costumes to guard against sunburn, and Daisy had donned her mask and snorkel, they walked down the beach together. Roger helped Daisy to put on the flippers and then took her arm and supported her as they left Dorothy behind and waded, and then swam out through the reef via a channel opposite the boathouse. Once on the calm surface of the sea, it was possible to swim up and down in deep water on the outside of the reef, parallel to the shore. Daisy, encouraged by the seven busy masked heads around her, began the enjoyable business of marine exploration. She found the flippers rather awkward at first as she was used to doing breaststroke, and the frog-like leg movements which came naturally to her didn't work at all well. But in a short while she discovered she could paddle her feet up and down after a fashion and began to make progress. She wasn't going to put her head any deeper than just below the surface, so her snorkel would remain open to the air at all times. She felt more confident that way.

She became enthralled by what she saw: blue and yellow surgeon fish, turquoise and green parrot fish, bright blue blennies . . . Then she became aware that water was somehow seeping into her mask. It was quite a few years old. Perhaps the rubber bits at the edge were perishing? It had never leaked before. Damn! Daisy thought. I must clear it or it will get up my nose, even though I'm not breathing through it at the moment. It was confusing, when you weren't used to it, to remember only to breathe through your mouth. She decided to tread water while she sorted herself out. She looked round as she started to do so, to see who was nearby, but she seemed to have floated further down the coast than the others, and they were all unaware of her, heads down, intent upon the treasure house below. She could no longer see Dorothy paddling at the water's edge. Perhaps she's changed her mind, Daisy wondered, and come in for a swim? But before she had time to verify this by taking a head count, she realized that she couldn't tread water in the only way she knew how, because the flippers dragged at the wrong angle and prevented her from rising properly to the surface. Her snorkel gurgled and filled up, and the next breath she took was not of air but of water. She started to choke and thrash about furiously. *Christ!* she thought. *This is it. I'm going to drown!* Don't be so stupid, she told herself. All you've got to achieve is to breathe *air!* She tore the mask off her face and let go of it, still struggling with the flippers in an effort to get her nose and mouth above water. She managed to take in a gulp of air, and thus encouraged she forced herself to paddle her feet backwards and forwards in the approved way, which maintained her in such a position that she could continue to cough out the rest of the seawater and regain some semblance of normal respiration.

I think I've done enough snorkelling for one day, she thought. I can't make directly for the beach because the reef's in the way. What I've got to do is to swim back beside it until I get to the gap, and then I can get through it and back on to dry land. Pity I've lost my mask and snorkel, but too bad. She began to swim but realized straight away that she was making no progress. There must be a current sweeping her down the shore. Perhaps that was why she had gone so much further than the others in the first place? She found she couldn't keep up the unaccustomed leg movements to work the flippers properly. She had completely exhausted herself. Her muscles just wouldn't function any more. Daisy decided that the flippers had to go too. She could swim better without them, or at least keep afloat.

She took a deep breath and sank below the water while she pulled at the ankle straps (that Roger had so carefully tightened) to wrest the flippers off. It was not as easy as she had expected.

Dorothy watched Roger take Daisy safely through the waves, saw her begin snorkelling and relaxed fractionally. The sea did look wonderfully inviting and it was so oppressively hot on the beach; just cooling one's feet was not enough. I'll swim down as far as where Daisy is and back, she decided. After all, I've swum much further than that for three days every week for ages at the pool in the leisure centre at home. It's just a question of confidence and getting through the breakers . . .

Dorothy had seen the expression on Daisy's face when she had told her she might merely paddle, and had felt rather stung by it. Daisy could be very condescending to her sometimes, almost disdainful. There were times when Dorothy did feel – yes, angry – with her, although she would never have admitted it to her face. She took a deep breath, launched herself at the sea and pushed through the battering waves to the smooth water beyond.

It was strange to be amongst a crowd of snorkellers who rarely looked up. They were like a band of self-absorbed moles tunnelling through the surface waters, snorkel tubes sticking up like blind periscopes. Daisy seemed to have swum further away than the others. I hope she hasn't overdone it, Dorothy thought, searching for her grey head as she swam. Then she saw her. Dorothy frowned. Daisy wasn't wearing her mask any more. Was she in trouble? She was swimming but apparently making no progress. Suddenly to Dorothy's horror Daisy suddenly folded up and vanished below the water. A burst of adrenalin shot through Dorothy's system and spurred her to a superhuman effort. She swam like a mad thing in Daisy's direction, and just as she was in a panic that she might have overshot the spot, Daisy surfaced again bursting for air. 'I can't get them off,' she gasped and began to go under again.

Dorothy grabbed her shoulder and in an abrupt movement detached one of Daisy's hands, which broke the surface wildly and tried to cling on to her arm, dragging her down too.

'On your back!' Dorothy managed to say in unaccustomed tones of command. 'Lie still. I've got you.' She grasped the back of Daisy's head with firm hands, one over each ear and held it out of the water just above her own chest. Then, kicking out with her feet she began to swim on her back in the life-saving position she had mastered nearly fifty years before.

'Got to take . . . flippers off . . .' Daisy said, still persevering with one strap.

'Stop it and lie still, you old fool or you'll drown us both!' It just came out like that, and it worked! Daisy stopped struggling and lay limply on her back, helpless and spent. Dorothy soon realized, as had Daisy before her, that there was a strong current pulling them in the wrong direction. She was not going to be able to tow Daisy all the way to safety. She simply wasn't strong enough.

Dorothy then did the only sensible thing. She began shouting for help.

II

IMOGEN, totally absorbed in watching life on the coral reef and impervious to noises off, was unaware that there was a drama of any kind in progress until she happened to glance up and saw both Roger and Claire swimming like rockets past her. She watched briefly as they reached Daisy and Dorothy and began towing them both to safety, before putting her head down again and continuing her exploration. Probably got cramp, poor old ducks, she thought. Good thing Roger's nearby. Then she dismissed them from her mind and lost herself again in technicolor fish.

When she reluctantly stopped snorkelling and got back to the beach, it was to find that Dorothy was the heroine of the hour and that Daisy looked both chastened and humiliated.

'Dorothy undoubtedly saved your life,' Claire was saying to Daisy. 'If she hadn't got to you first and held you up, Roger and I wouldn't have been in time to get you back.'

'It was the stupid mask's fault,' Dorothy explained. 'If it hadn't leaked, she would have been fine.'

'Thank you,' Daisy said gruffly, 'but I don't need excuses made for me. I was a damn fool and that's all there is to it.'

'I think Dorothy deserves a medal,' Shirley said, and turning on Imogen as she joined the cluster round the survivors, said, 'This is all your fault. You should've touched wood when I said!'

Imogen ignored her. Poor Daisy was looking rather grey, she thought, in contrast to Dorothy who was pink and all of a twitter. The reversal of roles would probably do her a power of good, and do Daisy no harm either. It might even things up between them. Imogen looked round for Barnaby and saw him coming towards them across the beach with the warden and Ruth. His bad leg flopped as he moved, kicking up little spurts of sand with each step. He walks just like a camel, she thought, and then wondered why it both annoyed and touched her.

'We've been saving a young shearwater,' Barnaby said as they arrived. 'It was completely helpless and all entangled in horrible sticky . . . something . . .'

'Mapou seeds,' Ruth supplied, 'but the warden managed to pick them all off, so it was fine in the end.'

'That's nothing,' Shirley said, bursting with the news. 'Daisy nearly *drowned*!'

Imogen watched as the whole story was told again and Dorothy got pinker and pinker, and Daisy seemed physically to shrink within herself. If she wasn't so tough, Imogen thought, I'd feel quite sorry for her.

Shirley was one of the first to get aboard the small boat which was to take them back to the *Amazing Grace*, and was ushered up to the bows where she would be less of a grounding weight. They were not using the pirogue this time but a modern fibreglass dinghy, as the warden and one of his men were to hitch a ride on the catamaran and take the dinghy with them to Praslin. It was much wider than the pirogue and altogether a more sensible boat, Shirley thought as she settled herself on the wooden seat and smiled her thanks at the men who were standing in the sea to steady it as they boarded. Simon squeezed himself in beside her, Janice and Leslie followed, and then the man who was to drive it. What happened next was confused in Shirley's mind because she wasn't paying attention at the time. Whether the outboard motor failed as they were launched at the breakers, or whether it was just an extra large wave, she wasn't sure. At all events the boat was completely swamped and Shirley found herself flung out into the sea, banging her elbow on the boat and grazing one knee painfully on the sandy bottom. It wasn't deep and there was no real danger, but all Shirley's confidence evaporated at that moment and she blamed Imogen anew for tempting the fates and bringing bad luck upon them all.

Strong brown hands caught at her arms and pulled her out. Smiling faces reassured her. She found herself back on the beach with a furious Simon and Janice and a despondent Leslie, whose camera (not having been properly secured in its plastic bag) had been invaded by seawater and was making spontaneous popping noises as the electrical connections inside it shorted out.

'Has the water got right inside? Is it ruined?' Simon asked, perking up at the thought.

'Yes it bloody has,' Leslie said. 'It's totally buggered. Just when I'd managed to get snaps of everyone too.'

'It's a disgrace!' Janice said.

Shirley summed up the situation. 'That's two,' she said, shaking her head portentously. 'Disasters always come in threes. I dread to think what the third one will be.'

Ruth was grateful that she had not been flung into the sea on her trip and that Philip's expensive camera equipment had come through unscathed, although it was very sad about Leslie's. From where she was sitting she looked across the deck of the *Amazing Grace* to see how he was taking it, and was surprised and touched to see that Janice had hold of one of his hands and was patting it consolingly. After they had successfully baled out the dinghy and got the outboard working again, it had made several successful trips from the beach, and everyone was now back on board the catamaran including the warden and the lion-haired assistant Ruth called Dreadlocks Two.

'Well!' Shirley said, standing still dripping beside her, 'whatever next?' Her knees were level with Ruth's face and Ruth could see that one was quite badly grazed and bleeding. 'I'm sorry I have to say so,' Shirley went on, stooping down and in confidential tones, 'but if Imogen had touched wood when I said, then things wouldn't have started going wrong.' Ruth made an awkward movement of the head to indicate to Shirley that Imogen's husband was sitting within earshot, so that it might not be tactful . . . but Shirley went on regardless. 'She's nothing but trouble, that one. It beats me how you, of all people, can put up with her goings on. If Roger was my husband I'd have something to say about it and no mistake – '

'I think you should get that leg seen to,' Ruth interrupted fiercely to head her off. 'Look, Claire's over there. She always has first aid with her.'

When Shirley had mercifully taken the hint and gone, Ruth stared straight down at the deck in front of her and hoped against hope that Barnaby hadn't heard what she had said. He had, of course.

'What goings on?' he asked Ruth. 'What did she mean?'

'Nothing,' Ruth said, blushing. 'You know what Shirley's like. She doesn't just get hold of the wrong end, she invents the whole stick!'

'So what's the right end of this particular stick?'

'Nothing, just silly gossip.'

'Come on Ruth, you're not being straight with me.' He frowned, and then looked at her with one eyebrow raised. 'I thought I could trust you, too. You've always struck me as being a woman of great integrity. Don't let me down now.'

'You wouldn't want to know,' Ruth said, colouring even more painfully.

'Well you must let me be the judge of that.'

'If I do tell you, will you promise me you won't tell Imogen you know? I just can't be responsible for everything falling apart at this stage!' Memories of similar near-disasters in previous years rose up to overwhelm her.

Barnaby frowned again. 'I can't make promises before I know what I'm promising.'

'You *must*,' Ruth said desperately, 'or I won't be able to tell you. It would only be until the end of this holiday; only another week or so. Please?' She looked directly at him. He looked confused but not upset. Ruth dreaded seeing his expression change.

'Well, all right then. But surely it can't be such a big deal?'

'I'm afraid it is.'

'Go on then.'

Ruth looked all around to see if anyone else could hear. No one was particularly close and most of them were crowded together at the bows watching a hawksbill turtle swimming away from the catamaran.

'I don't know how to say this,' she began in almost a whisper, 'but . . . I'm pretty sure there's something going on between Imogen and Roger . . .' She didn't dare to look at him. There was a silence and then Barnaby laughed, harshly, disbelievingly.

'You're not serious?' he said.

'I'm afraid I am. Shirley obviously thinks so too.'

'How long have you thought this?'

'Well . . . since the third day or so . . .' her voice trailed off.

'Oh come on! I find that hard to believe. And if you knew all about it, why for God's sake didn't you tell me before? You've had every opportunity.'

'I kept hoping it wasn't true,' Ruth said. She was close to tears.

'So what makes you think it might be true now?' Barnaby demanded.

'Well, Shirley saying what she did, and Roger . . . It's happened before . . .'

'You're trying to tell me that my wife is bedding some cheap womanizer with peroxide hair who regularly screws his clients as part of the service. Is that it? Then I'll tell you something for nothing. No wife of mine would be that crass; that lacking in taste! Imogen may be a lot of things, but *ridiculous* she is not. Fastidious is her middle name!'

Ruth uttered a little cry of pure pain and, scrambling to her feet, fled clumsily and precipitately to the safety of one of the cabins where she could weep unobserved.

The hawksbill turtle was a great success. It resurfaced enough times for everyone to get a view. Philip managed to take a series of photographs, and Annabel was entranced by the incongruity of such a well-armoured beast being at home in an ocean full of slippery soft-bodied life, like a walnut accidentally dropped into a pond . . .

'Soup in a shell,' Simon observed, smiling thinly at her. 'I suppose it makes a change from chicken in a basket, eh?'

Annabel twisted away from him furiously and without replying. Why did he always have to try and spoil everything? Damn! she thought as she settled herself down on the deck next to Barnaby, why didn't I tell him that it's *green* turtles that get made into soup, not hawksbills? I could have scored a point there. Why do I always think of a snappy answer when it's too late? Typical. Never mind, I'm almost proof against his sort of sick mind now. I begin to feel stronger than I've ever felt. I'm OK. It wasn't a relapse last night. I was just overtired like Brian said. I shall hold on to that and not be afraid to live life in future. I *can* learn to manage things and not be so fearful all the time . . .

Annabel looked round at the others who were sitting down again on the deck, and, wondered what they were all thinking. Had they, like her, come on this trip as a kind of quest? She doubted it. She wondered how many of them had inner lives at all? Brian did, and probably Ruth too (where was Ruth, for that matter?) but Janice, or Simon, or Shirley? She felt disillusioned by Roger and ashamed that she could ever have entertained erotic fantasies about him. It was hard to credit, but she had a nasty feeling that he and Imogen . . . She looked round casually, caught sight of Barnaby's face and did a double-take. He wasn't his usual casual self at all. He was staring out to sea and he looked really upset. What's Imogen done now? Annabel thought. It's bound to be something to do with her.

In Barnaby's mind anger fought with incredulity and eventually triumphed. Now Imogen's behaviour had been pointed out to him, it did fit with the evidence of his own eyes. How could she? And with that shallow, third-rate piss-artist too? Barnaby was so enraged on his own account that it was some time before it occurred to him what hurt he in turn had inflicted upon Ruth. After all, Roger was her husband. Perhaps she felt as badly about it as Barnaby did? Perhaps she even loved the bastard? How must she be feeling now? Did the fact that he was apparently a regular adulterer make it easier for her or worse? One thing's for sure, he thought, I've certainly not improved matters. It's not Ruth's fault, for heaven's sake. She and I are in the same boat. It's grossly unfair of me to have taken my feelings out on her.

She was still nowhere in sight. Barnaby was unwilling to follow her down to one of the cabins to try to talk to her there. It would be too conspicuous. He didn't want a scene. He didn't want anyone to know about this. Perhaps Shirley had only half guessed and was basing her suspicions on Roger's antics on other trips? Perhaps she was merely fishing for gossip? Anything he did publicly would only fuel that appetite. I won't say anything to Imogen either, he decided. Ruth's right about that. I'll keep quiet until I'm sure. There's no privacy in this environment, and I don't want my marriage eviscerated and displayed for hoi polloi to gawp at. There'll be time enough for explanations and recriminations when this holiday is over and Roger bloody Dare has taken himself off. Then a thought struck him. I wonder if anyone else (apart from Shirley) knows?

Imogen had been the first to see the hawksbill turtle and had had the best view. As she turned away from the rail, delighted with the sighting, she noticed in passing that Barnaby was looking a bit grim, but at least this time he wasn't deep in a dreary discussion on tropical trees with Ruth. Imogen couldn't see Ruth at all. Perhaps she's fallen overboard? Imogen thought flippantly. She's the sort of feeble creature who would go meekly under and perish without a moment's inconvenience to anyone. God, she chided herself, that's a bit acid even for me! She was feeling buoyant in spirits, unfettered, reckless almost. She had done her duty. She had been a good wife and mother all these years. It was time to please herself for a change. She decided to proceed with caution. Nothing was irrevocable. Perhaps she would amuse herself with Roger? Perhaps she would give Barnaby another chance for old times' sake? They were both within her grasp. Perhaps she would do both?

Claire was the only one to have noticed Ruth's headlong rush below deck. She wondered in passing what was happening. In her experience Ruth usually kept outwardly cool and pretended that everything was normal. Roger, as far as she knew, had never been overtly accused of adultery on one of his holidays. People had muttered behind their hands a bit, or sulked, or split up into factions, but never actually challenged him. Claire wondered what he would do if they did. It was an amusing prospect. And what of Barnaby? Did he know? He was looking rather fierce, so possibly he did. Would he perhaps hit Roger? No, Claire thought, Barnaby is too much of a gent for that. Would he threaten to destroy Leisure Doubletrips by some legal means? Now that could be interesting!

But how would that affect Ruth? It was upsetting to see anyone look so distraught. In a few minutes, Claire decided, she would go down and check that Ruth was all right. In the meantime she looked round at the rest of the group lazing on the deck. Shirley, who was usually to be found close to Imogen, was sitting at the opposite side of the catamaran from her. Perhaps they've fallen out? Claire wondered. She also speculated as to whether Roger and Imogen had had a row. She had hardly seen them exchange two words all day. Perhaps Imogen had told him to push off?

Claire smiled. Holidays are a great disillusionment, she thought. People wait until they've worn themselves out with hard work and then, when they're at their lowest ebb they go on leave, where they spend all their time with a crowd of indifferent, even inimical strangers, constantly packing and unpacking, rushing about on unaccustomed forms of transport, eating unfamiliar food, coping with an unnatural climate, away from their comfortable routines, and on the qui vive all the time in case they miss something of vital interest. And then they wonder why they find it all so stressful! She smiled again wryly.

'When you've finished your private joke,' Simon said, squatting down awkwardly beside her, 'is there anywhere on this vulgar gin palace where a bloke can relieve himself?' He looked both embarrassed and cross.

'Of course,' Claire said. 'Down the steps, first left. There's a choice of two loos.'

'One's enough,' Simon said tersely. 'Pity you couldn't have told me of its existence earlier!'

'You never asked . . .' but he had already gone. Claire had a mental picture of him having spent the entire outward journey with his legs tightly crossed, and smiled even more broadly. The man with the dreadlocks caught her eye and grinned back. Mmmm . . . Claire thought, admiring his gleaming skin, his perfect teeth and his lithe grace. He's a lovely specimen and no mistake. But why is it that the more I think about sex these days, the more the word 'commitment' seems to come to mind? Am I getting old? She got to her feet and followed Simon below, to find Ruth and make sure she was all right.

At supper that evening, Shirley was troubled to see that Ruth was not present, and felt guilty that it was because of what she had said to her. Then she swiftly justified herself with the knowledge that such things were 'better out than in'. After all, she couldn't be expected to act as a sort of moral policeman for the whole holiday, especially since Imogen had pulled such a nasty stroke on her on the way down from the top of Aride.

She could easily have fallen then, and been badly hurt. Shirley had at that moment seen Imogen in her true colours, and didn't like what she saw. Imogen and Roger shouldn't be allowed to get away with being blatantly unfaithful, she thought. Truth must out. It may be painful for Ruth at first, but I'm sure it's all for the best in the long run. I mean, people who take groups of other people on holiday shouldn't break up their marriages. It isn't right. Roger needs to be stopped. I probably should have said something on the trip last year, but I felt it wasn't my place . . . But now this year, in my opinion, he really has gone too far. It needed saying. Anyway, Shirley thought, now I can relax. It's up to Ruth and Barnaby what they do about their respective spouses.

The assembled group was quieter than usual at supper, almost subdued. No wonder, Shirley thought, it's been quite a day with one thing and another. I expect they're all tired. Roger and Imogen are probably the only ones who will stay late in the bar tonight. Well, let them. I've done all I can. She looked round the table and saw Leslie raising a long self-denied glass of beer in a clumsy toast to Daisy. They appeared to have struck up an unlikely friendship.

'Bottoms up!' he said.

Barnaby slipped away quickly after supper, determined to mend fences with Ruth and to check that she was all right. He lit his way along the dark beach with his torch and popped briefly into his own side of the hut to collect Ruth's book, which he had finished reading and which would now give him an excuse for visiting her. Her light was on. He knocked diffidently on her door.

'Who is it?'

'Barnaby.'

'Oh . . . well I've gone to bed.'

'I just want to talk to you for a minute.'

'Well . . . all right then.'

He opened the door and went in. She was sitting up in the narrow bed wearing a white cotton nightgown. An open book lay in front of her, face down. She had clearly cried a lot; her eyelids were still red and swollen and her face was blotchy but now dry.

'I've brought your book back,' he said, explaining himself.

'There was no hurry,' she said. She looked small and vulnerable and he felt a great rush of protectiveness towards her. He sat down on the foot of her bed.

'I've really come to apologize,' he said. 'I said some horrible things to you. I'm so sorry. I was only thinking of myself and how hurt I felt. Your feelings simply didn't cross my mind.'

Ruth smiled wanly. 'You didn't say anything that wasn't true.'

'There was still no need to say it.'

'Well it's done now.'

'Yes.' There was a silence.

Barnaby looked at her with concern and she dropped her eyes, unable to meet his. He reached forward and took her hand. 'Look,' he said, 'I want to help.' Then she started crying again, silently, but with big tears which welled up and fell down her cheeks, splashing on to the book cover. 'Please,' he said, 'don't cry. I can't bear to see you so unhappy. Talk to me.'

'What is there to say?'

'Tell me how you feel. Get it out of your system.'

'I don't know how to.'

'Why is it worse this time? You said it had happened before. Many times?'

Ruth started to sob, reaching blindly for a tissue from a box beside her bed. Barnaby shuffled himself up the bed nearer to her and, putting an arm round her shaking shoulders, blotted her eyes dry with a gentle hand. He could feel the tension in her easing. She leant against him trying to stop herself from crying, eyes closed tightly, hiccupping a little, and with her mouth pursed up with the effort of it all. Barnaby bent his head and kissed it lightly. She opened her eyes and there was such an expression of incredulous joy in them that he forgot to breathe. They stared at one another. Ruth looked away first and hid her face in his shoulder.

'You didn't really mean that,' she said in a muffled voice. 'You're just sorry for me.'

'You're wrong,' he said. He turned her face to his and kissed her again with determination, forcing her to respond. Then he looked at her searchingly. He had discovered already how sweet and gentle and essentially nice she was, but now he knew that there was more to her. In the moment of that one unguarded look of hers, he realized that he and she were made of the same stuff. They could *communicate*. It was like coming home. He was both astonished and elated. Nothing like this had ever happened to him before. Could he believe it? Yes, he thought. It's real.

'You do mean it?' Ruth whispered.

'Looks like it,' Barnaby said.

12

WHEN Imogen came back to her side of the hut that evening after supper, she had had a few drinks at the bar with Roger and was feeling relaxed and cheerful.

'Guess what?' she said as she opened the door and switched the light on. 'Roger says that Anse Georgette, where we're going tomorrow, is the most beautiful beach in the world.' No answer. Barnaby must be fast asleep already, she thought in disgust. She looked around. His bed was empty. He wasn't there at all. At once Imogen had escalating visions of disaster: Barnaby lost in the dark without his torch, Barnaby unconscious after a fall, Barnaby drowned . . . She thought, I may be fed up with him but I don't want him to come to any actual harm . . . Then she shook herself crossly at the absurdity of such imaginings and turned to go back outside to shout his name. Just as she did so, he emerged from the hut next door.

'What on earth were you doing in there?' she asked him.

He looked defensive. 'If you must know, Ruth found a cockroach in her bag and I went to get rid of it for her.'

'You?' Imogen laughed scornfully.

'Some people do value my help.'

'Bully for them. I somehow don't see you as some macho hero rescuing damsels by gallant insecticide.' She grinned at him, pleased with her own wit. He did not smile back.

'I don't think you see me at all.' He was taking off his shorts and shirt.

'What on earth do you mean?'

'Just that.' He pulled on his pyjama trousers.

'Oh come on, you can't say something like that and then not explain yourself.'

'I can, you know.' He climbed into one of the single beds and lay down.

'But if you're accusing me, I have a right to know what of.'

'It's late,' Barnaby said, 'and I'm tired. OK?' He closed his eyes. He hadn't even bothered to correct her grammar. It must be serious. Imogen changed tack.

'I was just worried about you,' she said. 'I'd no idea where you were. Naturally I was cross.'

'Naturally.'

'Let's get into bed together for a while, eh?'

'They're too narrow.'

'How do you know? We haven't tried yet.'

'It's obvious.'

Imogen tore her own clothes off in a rage and climbed into her own bed without another word. Hell and damnation! she thought. Why do I never learn? She turned over abruptly with her back to Barnaby and let out a long exasperated sigh. That's it! she thought. Anything that happens from now on is all his fault!

Roger led the way for the able-bodied group from the terminus where the local bus had deposited them, at the north-west tip of Praslin, walking along a road through well managed coconut plantation which had no undergrowth, and then on a track over a marshy bit with duckboards and little bridges, past two small huts, and finally along tiny hidden paths overgrown by dense coco-plum bushes.

'It'd better be worth it when we get there,' Janice said. It was.

Anse Georgette was deserted, a perfect arc of baking white sand, encroached upon at the top by dark green creeping plants, backed by dense shading trees and bounded on either side by jumbled masses of huge granite boulders amongst which low bushes and palm trees had a precarious hold. The sea was clear and brilliant, and the waves were small.

'Oh!' Dorothy said, wiping a tear of rapture from her eyes. She and Shirley, with sighs of pleasure, stripped down to their swimming costumes, covered themselves with factor 15 sunblock and lay down on towels with their eyes shut to grill gently in the hot sun. Janice, after a moment's hesitation to convince herself of the absence of skinks, joined them.

Roger and Imogen went swimming. 'Alone at last,' he said

to her half mockingly, as they floated on their backs side by side in the bay. He wondered, not for the first time, if she was playing hard to get or was simply not interested. He couldn't believe she wasn't. She had kissed him enthusiastically enough on their first evening on Praslin. So what was her gambit now? If she didn't make up her tiny mind soon, the holiday would be over and it would be too bloody late! He felt irritated by her vacillation. He wanted to say, For God's sake let's get on with it. There's no time to waste! If she messes me about today, he thought, then she can forget it. I'm not about to vandalize my hormones for anyone, least of all her.

'Isn't it heaven,' Imogen agreed. 'The perfect place for a honeymoon.'

Roger snorted. 'We had our honeymoon in Bognor,' he said. 'It rained.'

'We went to France,' Imogen said. 'It was wonderful.'

She turned over and started swimming to the shore on the other side of the beach from the sunbathers. She's decided against it, Roger thought. Oh well, sod it. She's too old for me anyhow. He rolled lazily in the water and then caught her up with a quick burst of crawl. 'Are you trying to tell me something?'

'No. Should I be?'

He grabbed her by the arm to stop her from swimming away from him, and they faced each other, treading water. Then Roger wound his legs round her body and pushed himself against her, keeping both of them afloat with his arms.

'Stop pissing me about,' he said. 'Are we going to fuck or what?'

'What a charming proposal,' Imogen said, 'and so poetically expressed. Is that a harpoon in your trunks, or are you just glad to see me?'

'I've a good mind to teach you a lesson once and for all.'

'I'd like to see you try!'

Roger pushed her under and she broke away from him laughing and began again to swim for the beach. Roger caught one foot and pulled her backwards. She kicked him hard with the other, but he held on.

'I want an answer,' he said, 'and I want it now.'

'OK, let go and I'll give you one. Let go! You're bloody drowning me!'

He did so. 'Well?'

'What exactly are you proposing? That we strip off right here and do it whale fashion?'

'No. In my experience salt water is a lousy lubricant.'

'You do surprise me.'

'So if you'd be good enough to accompany me to dry land, I think I can promise something much more fulfilling.'

Imogen looked momentarily wistful. 'It's a long time since I've felt fulfilled,' she said. Then she grinned, and beat the surface of the water with both hands, splashing his face. 'Race you back!'

Thank God for that! Roger thought as he swam after her. Now perhaps we can get on with it. Why does it take some of them so long? What is it that they're after; surely not true love?

Most of Claire's group had decided to have a rest day based at Grande Anse. Philip set up a hide by the fish market to try to get some good shots of the birds on the shore in front of it. Brian and Annabel settled themselves on the veranda of Shirley and Annabel's hut to do another pastel portrait and to talk. Leslie and Daisy sat at one of the parasol tables, looking out to sea, apparently deep in discussion. Simon had insisted on going off northwards on the bus with the others, but he had grumpily conceded in advance that the walk to Anse Georgette might be too taxing, so he had announced his intention to explore a more accessible beach. Claire, to her obvious disgust, found herself volunteered to accompany him.

Ruth watched as they all sorted themselves out, with an eagerness she could barely conceal. She was desperate to talk to Barnaby. They had a lifetime's experience to catch up on, attitudes to examine, discoveries to make, secrets to share, feelings to express. It had been so long since Ruth had basked in anyone's unqualified approval that the warmth of it overwhelmed and delighted her. Her newly boosted self-esteem made her heart beat more strongly than usual, her eyes grow more lustrous, and her skin glow. She even walked straighter and looked people more firmly in the eye. After that first moment of disbelief mixed with exhilaration when she and

Barnaby had suddenly come to understand each another, Ruth had felt remarkably, wonderfully, confident. I've earned this, she thought. It's mine by right. I deserve some happiness. Barnaby is the sort of man I should have married years ago. We have so much in common. He understands me. With him, I really do feel safe. To Barnaby, Ruth had felt able to explain herself openly at last. Even her feelings of humiliation at the knowledge that Shirley (and possibly others) knew about Roger's infidelity, had withered into insignificance beside this splendid new-found assurance of hers. Why should she care? Those feelings were transient and unimportant in comparison with what she and Barnaby now shared.

Ruth felt almost sorry for Roger, stuck as he was on his regular treadmill of pointless pursuit followed by calculated copulation. What satisfaction was there in that? What sort of terminally inadequate person would even want it? Did I ever love him? she wondered, or was it that I was simply swept along by his energy and his much-vaunted (but never actually achieved) disrespect for convention? I've been so busy being terrified of losing what I saw as my only security that I haven't taken stock of what it was that I was clinging on to. If only I'd known. If only I'd looked beyond my own pathetic proprietorship, my feeble dependency.

She could hardly bear to think of all the years she had wasted during this self-deception. Why couldn't she have met Barnaby when they were both young? More than half of his life had gone by, which she could never share. She must make up for lost time and she must do it *now.* She quizzed him about his childhood, his parents, his student days, his politics, his health, his attitudes to God, his taste in music and books, his fears and disappointments, and his hopes for the future. She remembered in shining detail everything that he told her, everything that he in turn had asked about her and her life, and every little nuance of their overwhelming new rapport. She studied his face and noted every fleeting expression. She resolved never to forget even the smallest detail.

They spent the morning walking slowly down the beach away from the village, stopping often for rests, paddling at the water's edge or lying in the shade holding hands. Then in the afternoon, in Ruth's half of the hut, they went to bed together. Barnaby afterwards confessed to the unexpected *frisson* that discovering sex in the afternoon (in too narrow a bed) had given him.

'It's a first for me too,' Ruth said, as they lay side by side, rosily exhausted. 'Doesn't it feel wonderfully wicked?'

'Incredibly immoral,' he agreed, getting up on one elbow and running a light hand over the curve of her naked hips, 'simply shameless, beautifully brazen . . .'

She reached for the hand and put it to her lips. 'I could get addicted to this, you know.'

He smiled down at her. 'Now there's a problem. What are we going to do about it?'

Shirley resolved not to cook herself in the sun too long and risk getting skin cancer, although a brief period of utter relaxation with the sun a red glow through one's closed eyelids, and the hot radiance beating down all over one's flaunted body, was surely nothing but a good thing? She had wriggled out a comfortable depression in the sand, but she was aware that her stomach still protruded too high above it and that her bosoms, held firmly in the grip of pre-formed cups with underwiring, stood proud like a pair of well-set blancmanges. At least her thighs had subsided a bit, spreading themselves comfortably sideways. I don't care! Shirley thought resolutely. Size isn't important. She was glad however that there was nobody about from Sheffield.

After a few minutes she checked on Roger and Imogen, shading her eyes with both hands to see where they were swimming. They appeared to be floating on their backs, talking. She could hear voices, but not what they were saying. Hmmm . . . Shirley thought. She propped her head up on her discarded clothes so that she could keep an eye on them without straining her neck muscles. Now Imogen was swimming across the bay and Roger was chasing her. He seemed to have got hold of her. What were they doing? Shirley wished Philip were with them, so that she could borrow his binoculars. Now they were larking about like a couple of kids, splashing one another. Shirley glanced at Dorothy and Janice to exchange 'Well really!' looks with them, but they were both concentrating hard on the business of sunbathing, eyes tight shut; silent worshippers.

Shirley looked back at the two swimmers. Roger was now chasing Imogen to the other side of the beach. Shirley watched them land and noticed that Roger got there first. He would, she thought. His sort always has to win. Good thing he never had any children.

Then Roger put his arm round Imogen's shoulders – *shameless!* Shirley thought, outraged – and they disappeared together behind one of the large boulders. It was more than a body could bear, Shirley decided, scrambling to her feet. Provocative, that was the word for it; shameless provocation. She draped her towel round her shoulders and set off across the beach at a lumbering trot towards the spot where Roger and Imogen had vanished.

Claire and Simon also went swimming, but on a beach near the bus stop. They took it in turns, leaving one of them guarding the other's clothes and both of the packed lunches, as there were other people about, some of whom were gangling adolescent males in loud undisciplined groups and, in Simon's opinion, potential thieves. Claire was grateful for their presence which allowed her to sunbathe in peace without having to parry Simon's aggressive comments. Then, when he came back with his black body hair all dripping with seawater like some large unwelcome dog, she could slip down the beach in a moment and let the warm sea embrace her all over and support her as she floated with her eyes shut.

Why on earth didn't I bring Murdo with me on this trip? she asked herself again. I'm a fool. What a wasted opportunity. For sun, sea, sand and sex, read separation, stalemate and solitariness. I just hope to God that no one on this beach thinks that Simon and I are a couple.

At Anse Georgette, Janice sat up suddenly and saw Shirley trotting away across the beach towards the rocks at the far side. Dorothy opened one eye and enquired lazily, 'where's she off to?'

'She never said,' Janice said, screwing up her eyes against the sun. 'Looks like she's in a hurry, though. I'm getting in under the trees now, or I'll be burnt to a crisp. I just hope my Leslie's got as much sense if he's sitting out in the sun too, but I doubt it.'

'Oh Daisy will look after him,' Dorothy assured her. 'She was a doctor, you know, before she retired.'

'I thought she was one of them psychiatrics?'

'A psychotherapist, yes she was.'

'Oh well, that's all right then. I wouldn't want him talking to a real doctor without me. You never know what they'll say, do you, men?' Janice got to her feet.

'Well . . .' Dorothy sat up too and started to gather her belongings, wondering if she could speak freely. 'You do know that Daisy has offered to give Leslie some counselling, then?'

'He said they were having a little chat, yes. You're not suggesting there's nothing wrong with that, I hope?' She lifted her chin with an offended jerk.

'Oh no,' Dorothy said hastily, 'nothing wrong at all. I just wondered if you knew what Daisy's speciality was?' The moment she had said it, she knew it was a mistake.

'Don't you know? I was told you two were close friends?'

'Oh yes, we are . . . and I do . . .' Dorothy's voice trailed away. Perhaps, she thought, we can just leave it there. There's no need to go into unnecessary details. It's up to Leslie himself to tell his wife. He's most probably done so anyway. There was a silence.

'Spit it out then,' Janice demanded abruptly.

'Oh,' Dorothy said, surprised, and unable to think quickly enough. 'What?'

'This speciality of hers. What is it?'

Oh dear, Dorothy thought, there's no going back now. No convenient white lie came to her aid, so she amended the truth just a little. 'Marriage,' she said.

Simon returned from swimming to where Claire was lying on the beach and sat down beside her, putting out a hand to detain her.

'Now don't you go rushing off again for another swim just yet. Stay and talk to me for a bit.'

'What about?' Claire said with her eyes half closed. He noticed that she twitched her shoulder to avoid his touch.

'Tell me about yourself. Live alone, do you?'

'I thought you didn't like polite conversation?'

'Not when it's imposed on me, no.'

'But you don't mind imposing it on others?'

'Well, everyone needs someone to talk to sometimes.' She didn't answer. Perhaps, Simon thought, I could semi-confide in her? He had an unacknowledged but overwhelming need for some human warmth and understanding. But even had he been able to analyse what it was he lacked, he would not have had the least idea how to go about getting it.

Of all the people on this holiday, Claire was the only one who appeared to him to be remotely on his intellectual level and, above all, reasonably discreet. Tell someone like Shirley your business, and you might as well take out full-page advertisements in the tabloids, he thought, raising his eyebrows in a dismissive gesture. He took his prescription sunglasses out of their case and put them on. Then he put his shirt on too, and an old khaki bush hat to protect his head from the sun. Claire still had not moved. Her eyes were closed but he knew that she was not asleep.

'I live alone,' he said to her. 'I prefer it that way. I like the freedom it gives me. Sometimes though I do wish I had someone to share experiences with. D'you know what I mean?' She remained silent. He pressed on, trying to find a way to get through to her. Perhaps he could intrigue her with a confession? 'I even invented a girlfriend to come on this holiday with me,' he said. 'I thought I'd be able to find someone to fill the role, but in the end I lost my nerve. I expect you think that's rather feeble?'

'Not at all,' Claire said, without opening her eyes.

Simon felt encouraged. 'I suppose you have a boyfriend,' he ventured, 'at home in Edinburgh?'

'Hundreds,' Claire said.

'Well there's no need to be quite so obnoxious!' Simon snapped, taking offence at once. 'Perhaps it's time we caught the bus back to Grande Anse.'

Claire opened her eyes and sat up. 'That's the best idea you've had all day,' she said.

'Now what?' Imogen asked, as soon as she and Roger were

out of sight of the sunbathers, behind a boulder. 'Truth, dare, kiss or promise?'

'How about kissing Mr Dare?' Roger moved towards her.

Am I really going to go ahead with this? Imogen asked herself. It's not the sort of thing I ever do. Perhaps I'm just flattered by the attentions of a much younger man (the first time it's ever happened)? Or perhaps I'm turned on by his directness and his refusal to use polite euphemisms? Oh what the hell! Barnaby doesn't seem to fancy me any more, and I wasn't made to be celibate. If he doesn't like what follows from that, he's only got himself to blame!

She turned her face up to be kissed, tasting the salt on Roger's lips and revelling in the sinewy feel of his arms and the confidence of his body, pressing against her. She willed him in that moment to declare his feelings for her, to confess to a growing passion, perhaps to articulate the reasons why he so urgently desired her above all other. I like sex, she thought, moving her arms to allow him to slip off the shoulder straps of her swimming costume. I like sex very much, but it has to come wrapped in something more than naked lust. I do need all the trimmings as well . . .

Roger said nothing. In the few moments when his mouth was not pressed down busily upon hers, he breathed heavily and squinted through half-closed eyes. Then he eased her costume down to her thighs, kneeling on the sand and burying his face momentarily in her stomach, squeezing her bottom with one hand as he pulled the costume right down to her ankles, with the other. She stepped out of it mechanically, and waited to see what he would do next, with a pussycat smile of complacency on her face. Men were so vulnerable at this stage, she thought, so conspicuously *unsubtle*. The thought made her feel both powerful and kind towards him. She watched his trunks join her costume in a wet heap on the sand, and noticed in passing that his pubic hair was as dark as her own.

She expected him to say something complimentary to her, confident that he wouldn't expect just to push her up against the gently sloping rock and enter her straight away, with no preliminaries. But when this appeared to be exactly what he was proposing to do, she prevaricated with the first words that came into her head.

'So what's wrong with seawater?'

His eyes seemed to have glazed over and he was still breathing heavily. He didn't reply. She put out both hands to his chest and held him from her, at arm's length. The rock at her back was almost too hot to bear.

'Uh?'

'Why couldn't you make love properly in the sea? Didn't Ruth like it?'

Conflicting expressions of avidity, frustration and disbelief crossed Roger's face in quick succession. 'It's got nothing to do with Ruth,' he managed to say. 'For Christ's sake don't – '

'But it was her you tried to do it with?'

'No of course it wasn't. Now shut up, and let's get on with it!'

Oh *Christ*! Imogen thought, as the shame of comprehension flooded through her. He doesn't care about *me* at all. He probably seduces some poor sucker on every holiday he leads. How could I ever have been so stupid as to think that I meant anything special to him at all; that it was me he wanted? Her understanding turned instantly to fury and to self-defence.

'You bastard!' she cried, propelling herself off the rock with one foot and pushing him violently away from her. 'How dare you treat me like some casual slag!' He stepped backwards, almost overbalancing and she noticed with satisfaction that his confidence was visibly waning. Then she snatched up her bathing costume and dragged it on, feeling the sand grains scouring her skin as she did so. She kicked his trunks towards him, so that they landed at his feet. He ignored them and stood looking at her with an expression of utter comtempt and disgust, shaking his head as if in sorrow.

'You poor, stupid bitch,' he said. 'That's just the sort of behaviour that gets pathetic cock-teasers like you raped and strangled. And serves them bloody well right, in my opinion. Well I've had it up to here with you and your middle-aged, middle-class, bourgeois respectability. So why don't you just crawl back to your amazingly mediocre husband? Or does he have trouble getting it up? Is that it?' There was a scrambling noise from behind the rock and Shirley emerged panting, with an expression of comic bafflement.

'Oh!' she said, 'I thought . . . What's going on?' She wiped the sweat out of her eyes and looked from Imogen to Roger and back again. 'Is this a private war?' she enquired, 'or can anyone join in?' Both Roger and Imogen stared at her.

So that's why she's been following me around, Imogen realized, with even greater mortification. It wasn't a pash at all. She must have thought that Roger and I were having an affair, and all this time she's been trying to catch us out!

Roger stepped into his trunks without a word and pulled them up. Shirley, temporarily recovering her aplomb, watched his every move.

'Mmmm,' she said, 'I always suspected you were a dyed blond, and now I know.'

13

'ANOTHER day already,' Barnaby said, 'and a visit to another tropical isle in another kind of small boat with yet another mode of landing. I'm sure I shan't remember in days to come, which day was which; that if it's day nine, it must be Cousin Island.'

'I shall,' Ruth said.

The transport that day was a local fishing boat with a small square awning to protect them from the sun, and also from a brief rainstorm which cleared to leave the day sizzling hot and so bright that the banks of sand ringing Cousin were blindingly white. The tracks of an egg-laying turtle from the night before were imprinted upon the beach like those of a miniature caterpillar tractor going up and (Ruth noticed happily) coming safely down again. They were all landed from the fishing boat as they had embarked, in two trips by inflatable dinghy in a flat calm, and were taken to a shelter at the top of the beach for a short talk on the island's history and status as a special nature reserve. Ruth, who had heard it several times before, sat dreamily looking out to sea oblivious of the hundreds of tame skinks which darted over every surface. Today, she thought, I'm completely happy. I'm involved with another woman's husband and yet I feel entirely free from guilt. It's a paradox. I know I'm absolutely justified in sleeping with Barnaby, considering what Imogen and Roger are doing, but much more important to me is the fact that my MS is no longer a one-sided liability. Barnaby and I are the same. With him, I'm not handicapped.

Ruth daydreamed about what would happen if she and Barnaby ever decided to make a go of it together. How would Roger take it? Knowing him, he would soon get over the shock. He certainly wouldn't have any trouble in finding someone to replace her. Might it even be Imogen? Somehow Ruth didn't think so. Roger had been in a very bad mood the afternoon before, when his group had got back from Anse Georgette. He hadn't stayed long in the bar for drinks after supper, and he'd barely spoken to anyone all evening. This made it all the more remarkable that he had wanted to make love in the middle of the night and had woken her up expressly for that purpose. Ruth had never known him to do this before, and was not impressed. She was exhausted, and sex at that moment (with Roger anyway) was the last thing on her mind. She had turned over crossly and gone straight back to sleep. This morning Roger had gone to breakfast on his own and without a word. Ruth barely noticed. She was on tenterhooks until she could see Barnaby again.

As the able-bodied group prepared to walk up through the trees to the top of the island, Barnaby watched Imogen covertly. He was now convinced that she was indeed having a fling with Roger and although at first it had been a considerable blow to his pride, he was now beginning to see it almost as a blessing. He had to admit that they hadn't been getting on at all well for years, and now here was the absolute justification for ignoring his commitment to her and pursuing his interest in Ruth, who was sweeter and more desirable by the minute. Imogen, as far as he knew, had not spoken one word to Roger all day so far. She even seemed to be avoiding him. She always was a good actress, he thought grimly. Well, two can play at that game.

Shirley felt confused, guilty, and aflame with curiosity all at once, as she stood at the top of Cousin with Roger's group and gazed out over the sea at the nearby island of Cousine and others on the horizon. She couldn't bring herself to believe that she had been wrong about Imogen and Roger, but they were definitely steering clear of each other today, and yesterday's evidence had been all against her. When she had burst upon them behind the rock on Anse Georgette, she had been prepared to find them *in flagrante*. She hadn't worked out in advance exactly what she was going to do about it when it happened; perhaps pretend surprise or outrage? But the scene that met her eyes had been entirely unexpected. There was Roger, stark naked, hurling abuse at Imogen who was perfectly decent in her swimming costume. What was going on? It looked very much as though she had entirely misjudged poor Imogen, who had clearly told Roger, in no uncertain terms, where he could go. As for Roger, didn't he look silly, all of a droop! At least, Shirley thought with a fleeting burst of pride, at least I managed to recover myself enough to give him some backchat. But then crucifying embarrassment had overtaken her and she had been obliged to pretend that she had just been going for a quick dip. She had turned and skipped towards the sea in a clumsy parody of youthful anticipation which she knew had fooled nobody, and looked ridiculous.

So was she wrong? And if so, what would the consequences be? She'd hinted of the affair to Ruth in Barnaby's presence. Had Barnaby picked it up? Had Ruth discussed it with him? Had Barnaby perhaps challenged Imogen? Would there be a big bust-up? Shirley couldn't help admitting to herself that this could be quite something to witness, but was inhibited from giving this feeling full rein by her bad conscience. Ruth and Barnaby were innocent of any wrongdoing. The last thing Shirley wanted to do was to wreck their holiday, let alone their marriages. As for Imogen and Roger? Well, Shirley thought, there's no smoke without fire. I'll bet I was partly right. In the meantime she decided it might be politic to keep her head down, discuss it with no one, and keep to strictly neutral topics of conversation like, for instance, mountaineering with Claire. Shirley sighed to herself. The study of human relationships as a hobby was all very well, but it could certainly land you in trouble if you didn't look out. Needlepoint would be much less fraught.

Imogen had watched Shirley the day before, prancing in fat confusion down to the sea, and hoped that it had taught her a lesson. She would now, with luck, realize that she had got it all wrong, and would in future leave her and Roger alone. Imogen was aware how close she had come to total humiliation and went crimson at the thought. What on earth had she been playing at, she asked herself? How could she have let herself down in that ludicrous fashion? How could she have been taken in by someone as facile and obvious as Roger Dare? She could see him out of the corner of her eye as they all stood at the top of Cousin, naming the far distant blue shapes across the sea: Recife, Mahé, Silhouette and North Island. Imogen had not acknowledged his presence all day and neither had he hers. Shirley was standing beyond him and was also avoiding her. This is a right old mess, Imogen thought wryly. So much for my famous interpersonal skills! Whatever's gone wrong? I wouldn't dream of losing control and screwing things up this badly at the CAB. I suppose on holiday all one's defences are down. Perhaps the real 'you' emerges at such a time. Imogen dismissed that last possibility as an unworthy thought. There was one thing though that she was sure of. She was quite determined that Shirley's misunderstanding and her own stand-off with Roger were not going to prevent her from seeing and doing as much as possible, and making the most of her time in Seychelles. She wasn't going to miss out on things just to make life more comfortable for either of them, and she certainly wasn't going to skulk about shamefacedly either. She had absolutely nothing to apologize for.

As they made their way down to sea level again Imogen forced herself to stop thinking about personal problems and concentrate on the splendours all about her. There were young fairy terns sitting on branches within reach. Huge tortoises ambled, sensibly in the shade only. Nearer to the shore white-tailed tropic birds were nesting in the forks of casuarina trees, as impressive close up as they were when soaring overhead. Cotton grew on bushes and coconuts were germinating on the ground. Imogen felt isolated from the rest of the group. Shirley was subdued. Roger was distant. Philip and Annabel were laughing over something. I can handle this, she thought. I'm more resilient than any of them.

After lunch, with some of the group who went snorkelling, Imogen immersed herself in the watery environment, floating above the coral and enjoying her newly acquired skills in fish identification while the greater part of her mind drifted in neutral. *Parrot fish*, she noted with satisfaction. What fantastic colours! *Short snouted unicorn*. She could feel the sun burning hot on her back. *Sulphur demoiselle and blue puller.*

Blue puller? When their two girls were small, she and Barnaby had had a blue double pushchair which Barnaby used to pull backwards up the hill to the house where they lived. Imogen could see it so clearly in her mind's eye. She remembered walking behind it, dodging behind pillar boxes and lamp-posts for the amusement of the two babies, making hideous faces and causing them to shriek with laughter. Barnaby had been much more even-tempered then. He had been a good father and his daughters were devoted to him. Imogen had loved him too, and since then they had shared so much. Perhaps, she suddenly thought, perhaps I've stayed with Barnaby all these years because that's where I truly want to be? For the last ten years I've considered myself to be tied down; prevented from ever leaving him because of his MS. But perhaps that was just a convenient rationalization? Perhaps I've been telling myself I can't leave, because subconsciously I really don't want to? It's true, she realized. At last I know what I actually do want. How ridiculous we humans are, she thought, smiling and almost letting water into her snorkel tube. So much of our life is pure self-delusion. Why should I discover the truth now, here, and for no apparent reason? Here's as good as anywhere, she decided. What better place for truth to emerge?

I've got to do better by Barnaby, she began to scold herself. We've been together a long time and we know each other inside out. He can't help being like he is. If I had MS, I know I'd be a million times worse . . . I'm sure if I tried harder, we could get our relationship back nearer to what it was in the beginning. In recent years we've barely travelled anywhere or done anything important together. Now we're both here in this wonderful place, and almost avoiding one another. It doesn't make sense. I can change that for a start.

Imogen floated almost motionless and recollected their honeymoon in France all that time ago. She remembered how on one memorable occasion she had forgotten to drive on the right-hand side of the road, and how Barnaby had reacted by taking all the rest of the driving upon himself; how she had sat back and gazed at the avenues of golden poplars in their autumn colours, the carts full of harvested corn cobs, the walnut trees by the roads, the sweet chestnuts in the woods, the caves and troglodyte houses of the Dordogne, the great winding river itself, the food and wine and all the laughter they'd shared. Barnaby had been good to her then. Perhaps she had taken it all too much for granted? I've been selfish, Imogen thought, and wilful, but now I'm going to make it all up to him. I really am.

'Seychelles brush warbler, and a wedge-tailed shearwater incubating under a rock,' Philip reported to Daisy, 'and a moorhen, of all unlikely things!'

'How strange!' Daisy said. 'It does make you wonder how they got here, doesn't it? Quite fascinating.'

Ruth, who was sitting beside them in the fishing boat on their way back to Praslin, smiled, and was pleased to witness such keenness. She glanced at Janice and Leslie opposite her and saw Leslie look across at Daisy and wink at her very deliberately. Then she saw that he was actually holding his wife's hand! All the positive emotion that Barnaby and I are generating must be infectious, Ruth thought. Janice caught her eye, and opened her mouth to speak.

'I'm not a fussy woman,' she began, 'but I liked that island the best of the lot so far . . .' Then she stopped in confusion as everybody else laughed. 'You know what I mean,' she said, smiling and looking almost girlish, 'but I really don't think we should've had to leave it so early. It's only half-past two now!'

Oh that's a relief, Ruth said to herself. I thought for one amazing moment that Janice had suddenly been transformed into a paragon of sweetness and light, which would have been too muddling for words. Something good has clearly happened between her and Leslie though, however unlikely that might seem. Ruth didn't dare to peep at Barnaby in case, in such a crowded place, her look might be intercepted and correctly interpreted, but she exchanged smiles with Dorothy, who was looking extra perky these days. Perhaps it's just my rose-coloured spectacles, Ruth thought, turning to smile forgivingly at Shirley as well. Shirley, however, merely looked unnerved.

The fishing boat dropped them back at Grande Anse, and they were taken ashore again by the inflatable, which had bobbed behind them all the way there and back. Roger, who in Ruth's estimation was clearly hoping to pull the wool over as many eyes as possible by diversifying his approaches to women, helped Annabel out. He made as if to carry her bodily to the beach, but she flushed scarlet and insisted upon being put down *at once*. Ruth watched with satisfaction. Some things never change, she thought; well they don't, and yet they do. Full marks to Annabel!

The afternoon was a lazy one. Even the able-bodied said they were tired and sat about on their verandas in the shade, reading and sipping long drinks. Only Janice, who had joined Leslie at one of the parasol tables with Daisy, was seen to be talking animatedly. Ruth waited in mounting frustration for Imogen to go off on a walk or *do* something, anything that took her away for a few hours. Instead, Imogen did some washing and hung the dripping clothes all round their shared veranda. Then she settled down next to Ruth in a deckchair to write a sheaf of postcards. Barnaby had started to read a book but had fallen asleep with his mouth open. Roger was nowhere to be seen.

Ruth tried to concentrate on her own book, but was over-taken by fatigue as well. Her eyelids kept dropping but she struggled to keep them open, just in case Imogen decided to leave. She didn't want to waste a moment of freedom with Barnaby. Any moment now, she told herself, Imogen will be off on some ploy or another with Roger. They've probably got it all worked out so that they aren't seen leaving together. If I can just keep awake, then at long last Barnaby and I can go to bed. We're both far too exhausted to make love and it's too hot to hold each other for long, but at least we can be together. That's all I want . . .

But Imogen didn't go. Worse still, she seemed to be making a big effort to appear charming, chatting brightly to Ruth about her daughters, her house in Somerset, and the difficulties of some of her clients at the Citizens' Advice Bureau. Ruth, who would normally have been quite flattered by such atten-tion, simmered with frustration and jealousy and wondered how anyone could have such a brass neck. Didn't Imogen know that virtually everyone suspected that she was carrying on with Roger? Claire certainly knew. She had said as much when she had come to comfort Ruth in the cabin of the catamaran two days before. And Annabel seemed to have changed her attitude to him, so perhaps she had guessed? I'd die of embarrassment if I were in her shoes, Ruth thought, with all those people talking about me behind my back. Barnaby is right. We must keep our own relationship completely secret. It's far too precious to be sniggered over.

Barnaby let out a loud snort, which jerked him into semi-wakefulness. Imogen reached over and shook him by the shoulder. 'You're snoring!' she accused him.

'Uh? . . . mmmm . . .' Barnaby closed his eyes and slept again. Why can't she leave the poor man alone? Ruth thought in a rage.

'I keep meaning to get him one of those special pillows,' Imogen said to Ruth. 'It's all right for him, poor love, he doesn't keep himself awake all night, roaring away! Do all men snore, I wonder?'

'Roger doesn't,' Ruth said crisply. The thought of Imogen and Barnaby in bed together was almost too painful for her to contemplate.

'Lucky you,' Imogen said, and there was such obvious sarcasm in her voice that Ruth frowned and looked sharply at her. Imogen closed her eyes and leant back luxuriously in her deckchair. 'It's a funny old life, isn't it?' she said, 'full of uncertainties. I don't mind that aspect of it though. The one thing I can't bear is stagnation. I do like to be kept on my toes.'

Claire stretched herself on a sun-bed under a palm tree at the top of the beach by their hotel with half an eye on the sea and half on the scattered accommodation huts. She had a book on her lap but she was feeling too lazy to read it, and the activities of the group were much more interesting anyway. Some distance away she could just see Barnaby, Imogen and Ruth on their veranda. Roger had gone off on a bus an hour before. Claire had been going to the shop in the village at that moment, and had seen him leave. That had given her pause for thought. The year before when she had finished what she termed their mini-flingette, he had apparently found someone local whom he had managed to persuade into providing the same service. He had even boasted to her of his resourcefulness. It looked very much to Claire as though the same thing was happening again this year, so perhaps Imogen hadn't come up with the goods after all? In that case, why had Ruth been so upset on the catamaran? She'd said she had a bad headache, but it was obviously not the whole truth.

This trip so far has been a doddle where illness is concerned, Claire thought to herself. Even Moaning Minnie's claims have subsided in the last few days. Perhaps Daisy is sorting her and Leslie out? They had all three been talking together earlier, but then Janice and Leslie had gone together to their hut (perhaps to put Daisy's sex therapy into practice? Claire boggled at the thought), and Daisy had gone to hers for a sleep. Poor old Daisy, Claire thought. She hasn't been herself since Dorothy rescued her on Aride. It must have been such a blow to her pride, and for her sort, pride is everything. In some strange way, as Daisy's assurance waned, Dorothy's seemed to grow. Claire could hear Dorothy laughing as she sat with Shirley on her veranda, and could see her fluffy white head bobbing up and down animatedly.

Brian was still drawing Annabel. He must have a great sheaf of portraits by now, Claire thought, of Annabel's head in every conceivable attitude. This time she looked as though she was fast asleep in the shade, head back, eyes shut, and with her red hair hanging over the edge of her reclining chair. Now there was another person whose confidence had visibly improved. Under Brian's aegis, she had blossomed in a quiet way. Claire could only admire such spirit in the face of an unknown and possibly crippling future. Perhaps these holidays do do good after all, she thought, in spite of being stressful so often.

Claire didn't think she would co-lead another trip, though. She had come to dislike the artificiality of the set-up, where a group of people could inhabit a place for a fortnight and yet live so superficially, like flies descending to eat just the cream off the top of the trifle, never penetrating to the varied layers beneath. Next time I go abroad, she decided, I shall make sure I meet the real people who live there and, if possible, go and stay with a family. This is too easy; too lightweight. And, she added as an afterthought, I'll take Murdo with me too.

Claire watched Philip coming back along the beach towards the hotel, hung about with all his equipment, and momentarily regretted her lack of success with him, before dismissing such an idea. Philip was an obsessional type, she had concluded from observing his passion for birds, the sort that, once involved, never let go; not her kind at all. She closed her eyes and sank into a relaxed daydream in which Murdo miraculously appeared and was flatteringly insatiable . . .

'Sorry, were you asleep?' Simon asked loudly, as if to make sure she wasn't.

'I still am,' Claire said jumping, but without opening her eyes.

'Very funny,' Simon observed. 'Do you do much travelling?'

Claire opened one eye and saw, to her irritation, that he was squatting down on the sand beside her chair. 'Isn't that on a par with asking "Do you come here often"?' she said dismissively.

'Not at all. It's a preliminary to asking you if you'd fancy a trip to Kenya with me in about a month's time.'

Claire opened both eyes, wide. 'What an extraordinary thing to suggest!' she said. 'I hardly know you.'

'Well you'd get to know me very well if you came.'

'And I couldn't possibly afford – '

'Oh I'd pay your fare if that's a problem,' Simon interrupted. 'I've got plenty of money.'

'I was going to say,' Claire said coldly, 'that I couldn't possibly afford the *time*. I'm a working GP, you know. We can't just swan off whenever we happen to fancy it. I bagged these two weeks months ago to make sure I fitted in with everybody else. I do have *responsibilities*, you know.'

'You shouldn't let your work run your life,' Simon said reprovingly. 'It is only a job when all's said and done.'

'Well yours might be, but mine isn't,' Claire retorted. 'Anyway, how can you manage to get away again so soon? I thought you said you worked in computing?'

'I do. I'm just sufficiently senior to do as I wish.'

'Bully for you. Is that where all your money comes from too? I wouldn't have thought bashing a keyboard would generate such an ostentatious excess.'

'Oh go to hell!' Simon snapped. He got to his feet rather awkwardly, brushed the sand off the back of his shorts and stumped off angrily and rather unsteadily.

It's high time I packed this in, Claire thought guiltily. I'm much too rude to the clients!

14

ROGER shepherded his charges from their hotel on Praslin on to the bus which would take them to the port of Baie Ste. Anne to catch the inter-island ferry for their day trip to La Digue. Only another four full days after this one, he thought, and then goodbye to Seychelles for another season. Would he even come again? He felt restless and dissatisfied. Leading holidays abroad had initially seemed glamorous and rather daring. It was the sort of job that dentists and insurance salesmen (and yes, probation officers too) envied and imagined to be one long holiday in itself. The reality was very different. It was a kind of juggling act trying, from half-way across the world, to organize transport, accommodation, services and trips out, so that they all meshed into a coherent programme. That was the easy bit. Then the punters arrived on the scene and made trouble. They interfered. They questioned his decisions. They deliberately got ill. They carelessly had accidents. They quarrelled with each other. They moaned. They ganged up on him. They were a pain in the arse. If it wasn't for them, he thought, it would be great. However laid back you were about the leadership thing, and Roger was studiedly casual, you were still in charge. You couldn't rush off on impulse or seize intriguing opportunities. You just had to stick with the itinerary and resign yourself to interposing your personality between warring factions.

This trip, Roger was forced to admit to himself, hadn't been so bad. It compared favourably with many of its predecessors and some of the punters were even quite nice. Don't be a whinger! he admonished himself. It wasn't the job that was getting him down, it was bloody Imogen. She had a nerve, that woman. She hadn't even the grace to look abashed or show any contrition for the run-around she'd given him. It wasn't often he was unlucky enough to lock horns with a frigid female like her, and a harridan at that. He admitted that he had allowed her rejection to unsettle him in an unprecedented way. He usually shrugged such things off; win some, lose some. He had gone off the afternoon before, seeking consolation, but even that had been denied him (they said the girl had never lived there) so he was on edge and resentful. The hell with it! he thought as the bus arrived at the harbour. Who needs a ball-breaker like Imogen anyway? It was a lucky escape. He sighed . . . Then he thought about his wife and frowned. It wasn't like her to turn him down. She must have been dog-tired last night. Yes, that must have been it. He glanced over his shoulder and saw her, three rows back in the bus, laughing with Brian and Annabel. He felt cheered and smiled complacently; good old Ruth.

There were a lot of locals also travelling on the inter-island ferry. Annabel found herself squashed in next to Philip, who was clearly frustrated at having his view of the skies obscured by other people, but was putting up with it. She found him difficult to talk to. He didn't give anything of himself. He answered her very civilly but didn't in his turn raise a thought, ask a question or keep the conversation going. In the absence of birds he was stumped. He has no social graces, she thought, and was surprised. She was curious to know how he coped with the uncertainty of life with MS; whether he worried about the future or tried to make plans to cover every eventuality, as she did. She wanted to try out her infant courage on him and see if it found favour.

'Do you know the one thing that always has quite the opposite effect on me than what was intended?' she asked him, to broach the subject. He raised his eyebrows, inviting her to continue. 'It's when people like Dorothy tell you you're wonderful. I'm sure they think they're being kind and encouraging but in fact they're just accentuating the chasm between ordinary people and "us". It's like patting the heads of dwarfs or talking above people in wheelchairs.'

Philip nodded. 'If there's one thing I'm certain of,' he said, 'it's that I'm *never* going into a wheelchair.'

'I've often thought that too,' Annabel admitted, 'but lately I've been trying to be more positive and look for any hidden benefits there might be in all possible outcomes. What do you think?'

'I think about it as little as possible,' Philip said. 'I just get on with my job, my bird-watching and my photography. I haven't time for pointless introspection.'

Oh dear, Annabel thought, then the blow, when it comes, will hit you very hard and catch you totally unprepared. 'I find it helps to talk,' she said.

'Fine,' Philip said, 'but it's not for me. Everyone has to handle things in their own way.'

'On your own?'

'Yup.'

Oh well, she thought, I tried, but I do feel that he'd be so much more fortified if he had someone to confide in, like I do with Brian. Thank goodness for Brian! She felt Philip craning his neck to try and identify a passing bird round the heads of the other passengers.

'Bridled tern!' Daisy's voice called from somewhere by the rail.

'Damn!' Philip muttered.

They were now within La Passe harbour on La Digue, passing a line of large yachts moored in front of a palm-edged beach, and then tying up at a small stone jetty. On shore, attending upon their arrival was a thicket of bicycles for hire and a wooden tumbril drawn by a depressed brown bullock.

'Choice of transport is up to you,' Roger said to the assembling group. 'Personally I'm going to amble along on foot to the Veuve Reserve and, if I'm lucky, see some black paradise flycatchers.'

'I'll go by cow cart,' Janice said at once. 'I've had quite enough of walking lately.'

'How could you?' Annabel protested. 'Look at that wooden yoke over its poor neck. Think how horrible it must feel. I bet it makes its hump all sore, pressing down on it like that. No wonder it looks so sad.'

'Have you ever seen a radiant bullock?' Simon asked, climbing into the cart and sitting down on one of its benches. 'Perhaps they're fractionally more common than porcine aviators but I doubt if it's statistically significant.'

Annabel scowled at him. Then she looked round for Philip,

whom she assumed had got off the boat at the same time as she had and should now be following Roger towards the bird reserve. He wasn't there.

'Hang on a minute,' she called to Roger, 'we've lost Philip.'

The Philip who eventually did join them was clearly most dreadfully upset, although he was obviously struggling to conceal his feelings. Annabel could see at once that something was wrong from the way he was staring at the ground and from the fact that his binoculars were bumping unused on his chest as he trudged towards them.

'What's the matter?' she asked, walking to meet him.

'Dropped my camera,' he said, tight-lipped.

'Oh *no*! Where?'

'In the sea, between the boat and the quay as I got off.'

'But did you manage to get it out? Is it ruined? Where is it?'

'In my pack, wrapped up. A kid in a small boat fished it out with a long stick, but seawater is so corrosive . . .' He looked away.

'Oh Philip I'm so sorry. Have you lost a lot of precious film as well?' Philip nodded. He was on the verge of tears.

'Come on!' Roger called, 'if you're coming.'

'Hang on!' Annabel shouted back, 'we've got a problem.' Then, turning to Philip asked, 'Can the camera be saved?'

'I suppose I could try washing it out with fresh water . . . but I don't know if . . .'

'Well that's what we'll do then. We must try *something*.'

Philip watched in a daze of misery as Annabel explained the situation to Roger and the rest of them. He was instantly surrounded by murmurs of sympathy. Daisy put her arm through his and squeezed it. Dorothy wept a little.

'Oh what bad luck!' Brian said.

'I know how you feel,' Leslie said.

'It must be like having your worst nightmare come true,' Imogen said.

Claire offered, 'You're welcome to use my little compact camera, but I know it isn't the same . . .'

'I suppose that's all your shots from the hide gone for a burton?' Simon asked.

'It's a good thing it wasn't your wallet,' Janice said.

'I knew there'd be a third disaster,' Shirley declared, 'I just knew it!'

Roger came back from somewhere with a bucket of fresh water and helped Philip to take the lens off, and bathe it gently. Philip opened the back of the camera. There was no hope for the film. It was nearly on the last frame and so was not even partially protected by its cassette. Philip took it out clumsily and threw it into a rubbish bin.

'When you've washed the camera out, I should wrap it up again,' Roger advised, 'and don't let it dry out until you can give it another good soak to get all the salt out.'

Philip did as he suggested, rolling it up in a spare T-shirt and pushing it carefully into his small pack. He was making a major effort to pull himself together. He followed Roger and the rest of the group and was grateful that they were sensitive enough not to try to sympathize with him any more.

Then it seemed to him as though the fates, having dealt him a crippling blow, were not content and had to mock him still further. As they walked slowly along the shady road there were perfect photo-opportunities, one after the other. Smoke from a sluggish bonfire in the garden of one house was filtering up through the trees and shining white in the rays of sunlight like a great starburst. A man holding a large fish by a string through its gills was caught in silhouette in front of the fire for a brief moment as he walked by. Another man walked past, steering an erratic calf. There were houses built of a charming mixture of grandeur and pragmatism, with flights of stone steps, balus-traded verandas, palm thatch, dormer windows and rusting corrugated iron. Then finally, in the bosky shade beyond the main settlement where the empty shells of hundreds of African land snails crunched underfoot, there was a pair of Seychelles paradise flycatchers flitting amongst the tops of the badamier and takamaka trees, elusive and infuriating but definitely there. Roger first picked out the shiny blue-black plumage and long funereal tail plumes of the male and pointed him out. The female was harder to see.

'But she's brown and white with a short tail!' Annabel exclaimed, at last locating the sparrow-sized bird, 'completely different. She can't be the same sort, surely?'

Why not? Philip thought. Sexual dimorphism is common in the natural world (ducks and drakes are the most obvious example), but most animals certainly do tend to behave true to type. Men and women, it seems to me, act more and more as if they were two completely different species. Take Annabel and me for starters.

'Isn't it amazing?' she said to him.

He managed a smile. He quite liked her. They were in the same predicament but couldn't be coping with it more differently. He didn't have to wonder how she would react to being in the situation in which he had just discovered himself. She had given a demonstration of it a few evenings before, at supper. It was all up-front with her, typically female; public panic. He could never let himself go like that for fear he'd lose control altogether. This was why he hadn't told anyone the reason *why* he'd dropped his camera in the first place; the fact that his right hand, so essential to both his job and his hobbies, had suddenly lost its grip, become numb . . .

'Oh well,' Leslie said to him, coming over and being matey. 'We wouldn't've been able to snap these damn things anyway, would we? I'm buggered if I can see them in all them leaves; makes the back of my ruddy neck ruddy ache.'

This is a much more inhabited place than some we've visited, Imogen thought as she walked with the group across the island, from its north-west port to its south-eastern coast. There was evidence of man's presence wherever you went: a roofed shrine on one of the granite boulders, banana groves, washing spread out on the grass to dry, white and purple bougainvillaea and passion flowers growing wild, bundles of palm leaves for thatching stacked beside the road and in one open space, mysteriously, a white chamber-pot balanced high on top of an eight-foot pole. It was uncomfortably hot as they walked over the plateau, past a lush freshwater marsh fringed with palm trees where shiny black cattle were grazing, and along a pale dusty road with occasional cuttings which exposed banks of bright orange soil. So it was with some relief that they eventually arrived at another wide empty beach, and sat down in the shade to recover.

'What's this one called?' Shirley asked.

'Grande Anse,' Roger said.

'They're not very inventive about names here, are they?' Dorothy said. 'Everywhere you go seems to be called Grande Anse.'

'Well I suppose every island has its own large bay,' Imogen said. 'That's what it means in French, isn't it?' No one replied.

'Who's for a swim?' Roger said.

'What about that notice?' Dorothy asked. 'It says it's dangerous.'

'It's fine,' Roger assured her. 'There's just a strong current, that's all, so don't go out too far.'

'I think I'll rest here,' Dorothy decided.

'I'm too hot *not* to swim,' Shirley said. 'I'm melting.'

Imogen changed swiftly into her costume. She wasn't going to miss out on an opportunity to cool off, even if it was only she and Roger who went in. For the first time in years, she wished that Barnaby were there too for moral support, to hold her towel for her, to confirm her translation from the French and to come back to, wet and laughing, after her swim. Perhaps tomorrow, she thought, I won't go off with the able-bodied group, but instead stay with Barnaby all day? It does seem mean to leave him behind all the time, even though that was originally the whole point of this holiday. Somehow I seem to have changed my attitude to him. I'm glad.

Imogen walked down the beach with Annabel as Philip set off along it with his binoculars. 'Funny, he hardly ever swims,' she said to Annabel.

'He's far too busy,' Annabel said. 'He's always afraid he might miss something. Poor old Philip, he seems to have taken his accident with the camera particularly hard, doesn't he? He's hardly spoken to anyone since it happened.'

As they got nearer to the water, they could see that it was quite rough. White spray jumped up the rocks on the south side of the bay and the breakers on the beach were huge. Imogen and Annabel were both knocked over by powerful waves the moment they got into the sea. Annabel scrambled straight out again.

'That's it!' she called. 'I've had enough.'

Imogen picked herself up and swam out a little further where she could ride the swell and watch what would happen to the others. Roger, without a glance in her direction, did a running dive through the waves and came up beyond the surf line with his back to her. *Diddums sulkyboots!* Imogen thought with some satisfaction before turning her attention to Shirley, who was hovering uncertainly at the water's edge. As Shirley nerved herself and stepped into the sea, she too was felled with one wave and wallowed like a beached jellyfish before crawling out, being knocked over twice more in the process.

'Oh hard luck!' Imogen called cheerfully to her.

'Oh . . .' Shirley wailed, kneeling in the receding shallows apparently feeling about for something.

'What's the matter?'

'My swimming sandals. They've both been sucked clean off my feet, and I did them up really tight, too.'

'Must be a strong undertow,' Imogen said. 'I'll dive and see if I can find them if you like.'

'It's not fair!' Shirley said, 'we've *had* our three in a row.'

Ruth watched with relief when the able-bodied group finally left on foot. Then the ox cart carrying the majority of Claire's group rumbled off, and she was miraculously left on her own with Barnaby.

'Be back in time for the boat, right?' Claire called. 'Sure you don't want a ride?'

Cave swiftlets swooped over the trees as the two of them walked slowly along the road in the shade. The mingled smells of woodsmoke and frangipani curled in the air and teased their nostrils. A brown cow tethered to a tree in a patch of sunlight had a hide that gleamed like home-made toffee. Ruth remembered the name of the bushes with the bright red leaves which were common around the houses, and she told it to Barnaby. 'And there's a kapok tree,' she added, pointing to a tall leafless skeleton covered in blobs of white.

'Good Lord!' Barnaby said. 'I always assumed it grew on bushes, like cotton.' She saw him look round to check that they were unobserved. Then he took her free hand and held it in his as they walked. I wish we didn't have to be so sneaky, Ruth thought. I want to *boast* about my feelings for Barnaby, not pretend I hardly know him.

'You're very quiet,' Barnaby said.

'I was daydreaming about being able to walk together like this in public.'

'Maybe one day,' Barnaby said, squeezing her hand. 'But for now, let's enjoy what we've got. Goodness, isn't it *hot*?'

'I'm hot and tired too,' Ruth said. 'Perhaps we could get a bus. They're supposed to be illegal on La Digue, but I saw one here last year.'

'Very civilized,' Barnaby said. 'Their illegality, that is. That reminds me . . . do you know this one?

> 'What is this that roareth thus?
> Can it be a Motor Bus?
> Yes the smell and hideous hum
> Indicat Motorem Bum!
>
> How shall wretches live like us
> Cincti Bis Motoribus?
> Domine, defende nos
> Contra hos Motores Bos!'

I've always liked that one. Isn't it a relief that in English, unlike Latin, we don't have a million endings to struggle with?'

Ruth laughed. 'Do you have a quotation for *every* eventuality?'

'For a lot of them,' Barnaby admitted. 'It doesn't annoy you, I hope?'

Ruth smiled up at him. 'Nothing you do could possibly annoy me.'

'You can have my job any time you want it,' Claire said in an undertone to Imogen on the boat on the way back.

'No thanks,' Imogen said, 'I've changed my mind.'

'Oh, really?' Claire looked at her with a knowing smirk.

Imogen did not rise. 'What's wrong with it?' she asked instead. 'Bad day?'

'Oh just bloody Simon! He really gets on my nerves. And then Janice went on and on complaining that the bullock had diarrhoea and shouldn't have been working.'

'Very compassionate of her.'

'Not at all. She said the smell made her retch. And then

when we got back, we found that Ruth had left her passport on a bus, and I had to go and sort that out.'

'Was it found?'

'Yes, but not on a bus, they said. There are no buses on La Digue, so it couldn't have been found on one, you see!'

'Impeccable logic,' Imogen agreed.

She had sat down next to Barnaby and now smiled at him, sharing her amusement. He looked blank. He had clearly not been paying attention.

'Shirley's jelly shoes got sucked clean off her feet today by the force of the sea,' she told him. 'Imagine!'

'Her what?'

'Jelly shoes; the plastic sandals she always swims in. You remember when our girls were small, they were always called that.'

'No.' Barnaby looked vague. Imogen found his expression thoroughly provoking, perhaps deliberately so? She tried harder.

'You *can't* have forgotten. It was you who first thought up the name. The girls loved it at the time. I can see them now, giggling together. They went through a whole week answering "Jelly shoes" to everything anyone said to them. You *must* remember that!'

'Sorry.' Now he looked bored.

Oh God! Imogen thought, aggravated but trying to keep it to herself. It was as if great chunks of their life together had suddenly fallen off the edge of his memory and melted away, like icebergs calving from a glacier. Somehow, she thought, I've got to teach myself not to resent this carelessness with our common past. I've got to be able to remind him of things without acrimony; reinvent 'us', if needs be. It's not his fault, after all. 'Those were happy days,' she said. He didn't reply. She felt intolerance rising within her again, in spite of herself, and wondered in passing whether people ever exploded through excessive self-control. She took a deep breath. Tomorrow, she thought, I won't go off with the group. I'll stay with Barnaby all day and we'll start again. We've been drifting apart for years and that's probably why he's forgotten things. If we were to become a united couple again, then joint experiences would lodge more firmly in his mind, I'm sure of that. I expect he's tired now. It's been an exhausting sort of a day.

Imogen glanced across at Philip, who had managed this time to find a seat near the outer rail of the boat and was holding his binoculars up casually in one hand and staring fixedly through them, not speaking to anyone. It had certainly been quite a day for him. Damaging his precious camera like that must have been traumatic for one so single-minded. She felt sorry for him, but didn't know what to say, and so in the end, said nothing.

That evening at supper she looked at him again, down the table. He seemed withdrawn and appeared not to be very hungry, toying with his food half-heartedly with just a fork. That's odd, she thought, I hadn't noticed before that he's left-handed. I wonder if he has to have specially made gadgets for use in his kitchen at work? She was about to ask him this, but was interrupted by a squeal from Janice.

'Ugh!' she cried, 'this food's got black bits in it that taste disgusting!'

'Where?' Roger asked, inspecting her plate.

'There. Oh, and there's another! I'm sure that wasn't there a moment ago.'

'Whoops!' Roger said. He looked upwards at the ceiling, and his face broke into a broad grin which he tried unsuccessfully to suppress.

'What's so fun – ' Janice followed his glance and then let out a shriek of outrage. There directly above her plate, stuck to the underneath of the sloping palm thatch by its clever suction feet, was a large bronze house gecko.

Claire said, *sotto voce* to Imogen, who was sitting at the far end of the table next to her, 'It seems poor dear Janice is having a rather shitty day.'

Most of the MS group were in the habit of going to bed immediately after supper, especially if there had been little opportunity to rest during the day. All the others tended to linger late in the bar, Roger and Claire mostly out of duty, and the rest of them for as long as they could keep their eyes open. This evening there was to be a local band playing sega music for the hotel guests to dance to. Ruth had stayed up for this the year before, but now as soon as the two men with guitars, the violinist, the drummer and the vocalist had set up and had begun to play, she crept away. Barnaby was supposed to follow her within five minutes, so Ruth got washed and undressed and lay down in her bed to wait for him, naked under the thin sheet and revelling in happy expectancy. She smiled to herself and cupping her hands, tried to check that her breath was fresh. The rest of her, she knew, smelt clean and wholesome. Both Roger and Imogen had separately expressed an interest in the dancing, so there was plenty of available time. With a bit of luck she and Barnaby could spend a whole hour in each other's arms. It might not sound long, but stolen opportunities like this were unbelievably precious.

After half an hour Barnaby finally arrived, full of apologies. 'For some extraordinary reason Imogen insisted on dancing with me,' he said. 'She knows that (a) I hate dancing and (b) that I can't do it without falling over, but she wouldn't take no for an answer.'

'How did you manage?'

'Oh we just stood on the spot and sort of swayed to the music; quite ridiculous.'

'I nearly went to sleep,' Ruth said, yawning.

'I'm sorry, darling. I couldn't just brush her off, could I? It would have looked very suspicious. At least we've still got some time left before the dancing finishes and everyone else goes to bed.' He was taking off his shirt as he spoke. Ruth watched, patient and amused as he carefully put all his clothes and his shoes together in a neat pile. She wondered idly whether he would ever get so carried away as to leave everything in a heap on the floor where it fell.

'Aaaaaaaah!' Barnaby let out his breath in a great sigh of pleasure as he slid into bed beside her and their skins began to fuse together in the hot voluptuousness of a long-anticipated embrace. 'I hope you aren't expecting miracles?' he said after a while, his voice muffled in her breasts. 'I can't always manage – '

'Sssh,' Ruth said, kissing the top of his head. 'It's not an endurance test, you know.' She felt him relax in her arms, and they lay quietly together. 'Aren't we lucky?' Ruth said after a while, with a sigh. 'Isn't this bliss?'

The door of the adjoining hut banged, and they froze, staring at each other with wide eyes.

Then Barnaby whispered, 'It must be Imogen. Perhaps she's

forgotten something? It's far too early for her to be going to bed, but I'd better get dressed p.d.q. anyway . . .' He made as if to get out of bed, but Ruth held on to him.

'Sssh! she'll hear you!' she whispered.

'She'll only think it's you.'

'And anyway, you can't leave without her seeing you.'

'You're right. We'll just have to sit tight then.'

They heard the next door being opened again and Imogen's voice directly outside called, 'Barnaby? Where are you? . . . *Barnaby*!'

Barnaby and Ruth looked at each other mutely. Ruth felt a quiver of hysterical laughter in the pit of her stomach, but kept it battened down. Barnaby's expression suddenly grew anguished. He whipped a hand up to his nose, but to no avail. A great roaring sneeze erupted from him.

Then their door crashed open and Imogen was standing there on the threshold, staring at them. Ruth's first thought was, Oh good! Now she knows, and we can all stop pretending. But then she saw the look on Imogen's face, and was frightened.

15

B RIAN had enjoyed his day on La Digue, but the heat had tired him out. He decided to have just one drink after supper and keep Shirley company while the dancing started. She was always nervous about being a conspicuous wallflower. He was beginning to think that it was almost time for this holiday to be over. He liked travelling, but after a week or so he inevitably began to think longingly of Sheffield and all the things at home that needed doing. I've had a nice change, he thought, but now I'd like to get back to something useful. He was pleased with the progress he'd made with his sketching in the past week. He had got some passably good portraits of Annabel. His sister, true to form, had teased him about that, hinting that he and Annabel must be forming a 'relationship'. Nothing could have been further from the truth. They were friends, simply that. Brian had been unattached for too long to start up with that sort of thing again. He was all for a quiet life.

'You've got a one-track mind,' he told Shirley with mock severity.

'Not true,' Shirley protested. 'I'm just interested in people. I should have been an anthropologist or a psychologist, although nursing is more useful, I suppose, when you come to think of it. But folk are so peculiar!' She lowered her voice so that no one else could hear. 'I'll give you an example – I came across Roger – quite by chance – two, no three days ago on Anse Georgette. Stark naked he was, and giving Imogen a right old slating! I couldn't believe my ears. Goodness knows what was going on, but now everyone's acting perfectly normal, like nothing happened, although Barnaby and Ruth *must* know . . .'

'So you slipped them a hint?'

'Well, no, not then. That was before – '

'You really must not interfere, Shirley! I said the same to you last year, didn't I? It's no business of ours.'

'Well I know that, of course, but it didn't seem right. I mean . . . it was so *blatant!*'

'If you're not careful, you'll end up with no one speaking to you, and you know how much you'd hate that.'

'But that's the whole point! Everyone *is* speaking to me, and I don't understand it. I feel . . .'

'Robbed of drama?'

'Well I suppose you could put it like that.'

'Best way to be,' Brian said soberly. 'I've always found a little drama goes a long way, meself.'

As she and Barnaby arrived at the dancing, Imogen had noticed brother and sister sitting cosily together at one of the small tables that had been set out round the circular concrete area in front of the main hut, which served as a dance floor. A few naked bulbs strung through the trees gave just enough light. Brian had been emphasizing whatever it was that he was saying by patting the table top with one hand as he spoke. Shirley was looking defensive. Perhaps she had confessed to snooping? She should have done it earlier, Imogen thought, and then Brian's common sense could have saved her a lot of embarrassment. She looked round the tables to see who else was there, that she could join. There wasn't much choice. She didn't think she could put up with Janice and Leslie, so that left only Claire, Ruth and Roger, all the rest of their party having apparently gone to bed. Right, Imogen thought, I shall just have to tough it out. That, she remembered, was an expression which her husband particularly disliked. She thought, It's going to be hard work having to adjust my language as well as everything else to accommodate Barnaby in our new-improved-marriage, but I'm sure it will be worth it. She glanced up at him. Even in the dark, she could see that he looked tired. She led the way forwards.

'May we join you?' she asked Roger. Roger was silent.

'Do,' Ruth said, smiling. 'Have my chair. I'm just off to bed.' She got up.

'I haven't been to a dance in years!' Imogen said, inclining her head in thanks and sitting down. 'I don't suppose any of us has, except perhaps you, Claire?'

'True,' Claire said, 'we dance a lot in Scotland.' There was a pause. This is going to be hard work, Imogen thought. Fancy Roger sulking for so long; it's so infantile! I wonder if Barnaby has noticed? She followed his glance and saw Ruth disappearing towards her hut, leaning on her stick.

'Let's dance?' she said to him.

'You know I don't dance,' Barnaby said testily. 'I can't think why you insisted on my being here. I'm exhausted!'

Imogen gave him a warning frown to indicate that such discussions should be held in private. 'Just stay for ten minutes,' she suggested. Barnaby sighed and got slowly to his feet again, and they walked a few steps out on to the dance floor. The sega music was bright and bouncy with an insistent beat, and the vocals contained odd recognizable words of French with some Americanisms. Barnaby stood apathetically as Imogen danced on the spot in front of him.

'You're not trying!' she said.

'I'm too tired,' he looked resentful.

'You don't have to move your feet. Just sway in time to the music; let yourself go.' She wondered how he could be so unresponsive. Even Janice and Leslie, who were not dancing, were tapping their feet to the insistent rhythm.

'This is silly,' Barnaby said, after a few moments. 'I've got to sit down.'

Imogen went to sit beside him. In the warm night air and subdued light, it could have been a perfect setting for the renewal of love; a little energetic dancing, followed by some slow, close, drifting, followed by a gentle walk hand in hand to the sea . . . Imogen sighed. They sat in silence and watched the others. Claire was dancing with Roger and looking almost as though she was enjoying it. Shirley had been propositioned by a stranger who clearly considered it his duty to involve all the hotel guests in the occasion. As they passed close by, Imogen understood the look of pained martyrdom on Shirley's face. Her partner exuded a powerful aura of rank sweat which hung about him like a personal microclimate.

'*Phwar!*' Imogen said in Barnaby's ear. 'What a pong!'

'What?'

'No wonder Shirley looks so affronted,' Imogen giggled.

'I'm off to bed,' Barnaby said, getting up abruptly.

'So soon?'

'Yes. I've had enough. Sorry and all that.' He left without waiting for her to follow. She didn't want to be seen to run after him, so she remained seated. In a few minutes, she thought, I'll get up and join him. I don't want to dance with anyone else, and I wouldn't mind an early night myself. She sat back, smiling determinedly and counted up to a hundred slowly. Then, as she got up to go, the smelly man bounded up and took both her hands, bobbing up and down and pulling her in to join him.

'No,' she said, 'I'm sorry, I'm not – '

'Dance,' he said, 'you dance. Music is good.' He had her hands so firmly in his own that Imogen could only have wrenched them free with difficulty, and too obviously. He smiled, a wide engaging grin, and danced even harder. Imogen, unwilling to make a fuss, allowed herself to be danced with, trying to breathe as little as possible and expecting at any moment to collapse in an anoxic coma. At last the music paused for a moment and she was able, decently, to withdraw.

She hurried back to her hut, hoping that Barnaby would not already be asleep. There wasn't anything she especially needed to talk about with him, but she wanted a relaxed mutual chat about nothing in particular, to round the day off. She opened the door of their hut, and it banged shut behind her. Barnaby was not there! She looked all around. His bed was still made. Imogen opened the door again and, careless of whether Ruth was asleep or not next door, shouted his name. There was no answer. Then somebody sneezed. It was a familiar man's sneeze and it came from Ruth's room. It wasn't Roger; Imogen knew he was still dancing. Surely it couldn't be . . .? She wrenched that door open, and stood there, holding its edge.

Barnaby and Ruth were in one of the beds together. He had his face squashed against one of her boobs. They were, Imogen noticed, ungenerous to a fault, and had *brown* nipples. She tried to organize her thoughts so that they became coherent enough for communication. Astonishment and shock gave way rapidly to a fierce anger which threatened to render her permanently speechless. She stared at them. Barnaby looked like a naughty schoolboy caught cheating at exams. Ruth looked unabashed. No, damn it, she looked positively smug!

Then the lie came to Imogen's aid like an alien spear, chanced upon *in extremis* and snatched up to deliver a mortal blow to the enemy.

'Oh God,' she said, 'not again!'

'Well, I'm not walking anywhere in *this*,' Janice announced at breakfast, 'and that's flat. I'm not a fussy woman but this is ridiculous!'

Day eleven had dawned, drowned in a tropical downpour. It was the day that Roger had planned a long walk, right across the middle of Praslin on a footpath from Grande Anse to Anse Volbert.

'We'll wait for an hour or so and see if the weather improves,' he said. 'It takes about two and a half hours over the top, and it's a walk well worth doing if at all possible. Claire's going to lead it today, for a change, and the rest of us will go round the long way by bus, so you can join us, Janice, if you wish.'

'I think I'll do the same,' Dorothy said.

'Right, so that's Claire, Shirley, Imogen and Annabel who are walking, yes? He looked round the table, collecting nods. 'And what about you, Philip?'

'I'll stay here if that's all right,' Philip said casually, 'and do some bird-watching.'

'Fine.' Roger glanced at Ruth, but she avoided his eyes. It was the conviction that something was upsetting her that had prompted his suggestion to Claire that they should swap jobs today; an offer that Claire was happy to accept. Roger was puzzled about his wife. She had woken him several times in the night, tossing and turning in the next bed, and this morning she looked as though she'd had no sleep at all. She had got a little upset on previous trips when he'd had the odd fling, but he knew she didn't take such lapses seriously, and she had never made a Big Thing of them. So why was she upset this time, when he wasn't even having one? She should be extra cheerful, not all pinched and worried looking. He had tried to jolly her along that morning, but she hadn't responded. Perhaps she was feeling ill? But she had assured him that she wasn't.

I don't have to go on the hike, he thought. I'll stay with

Ruth today and make sure she's OK. It unsettled him to see her like this. Claire of course had been delighted to take the opportunity for a proper walk – too bad the weather was so foul.

Ruth's heart sank as Roger announced his intentions. She was desperate to talk to Barnaby to find out what had happened when he and Imogen had gone back to their room the night before. After Imogen had said that dreadful thing, she had simply walked out. Then Barnaby had scrambled out of bed, dragged his clothes on, and had followed her with scarcely a word of comfort to Ruth.

'It's not true,' she pleaded as he left. 'Tell me it's not true?'

'Of course it isn't,' he almost snapped. 'The woman's off her head. Look, I'll have to go and sort this out. We'll talk tomorrow.' And remembering just in time, he had blown her a clumsy kiss and gone.

And now Roger was proposing to spend the whole day with them, so there would be no opportunity to talk privately with Barnaby. Why today of all days? She'd barely slept all night and she was exhausted. Surely Roger hadn't noticed? He never did as a rule. She hadn't told him anything, of course. She had to sort things out with Barnaby first, and decide jointly what to do. What would happen now? Ruth thought she really couldn't bear it. She thought she'd die of frustration. She couldn't believe that what Imogen had said was true, but why had she said it? Was it just spite? Could anyone invent something like that in the heat of the moment? Wasn't that when truth usually came out? And what would Imogen do now? Would she tell everyone, including Roger? Now that his undeception seemed imminent, Ruth couldn't imagine what he would say. How would he take it? He couldn't in all honesty denounce her for something he himself did all the time, but she was nevertheless apprehensive. It's ironic really, she thought, I used to spend all my time wishing that Roger didn't always go off all day, leading the able-bodied group, but now when he's decided not to, I wish he would. There's no justice!

Imogen decided to go with the able-bodied group after all. Her plans for spending more time with Barnaby would have to wait until the present crisis had been resolved. Above all, she needed space to *think*, and a walk, even in bad weather, would be good for that. She was not worried about leaving Barnaby and Ruth together, since Roger would be there too, as an unwitting chaperon. By ten o'clock it was still raining, and a decision had to be made.

'I say we should go,' Imogen said. 'So we get wet; so what?'

'I'm on for that,' Claire said, looking at Annabel and Shirley.

'Why not?' they agreed.

This is an ideal opportunity with no men about, Imogen thought, to go over everything in my head and decide what the hell I'm going to *do*.

When Barnaby had followed her into their hut the night before, she had been so angry that she barely knew what she was saying. How dare he be unfaithful to her, and with mousy Ruth of all people! A less convincing contender would be hard to find. What on earth did he see in her?

Imogen had managed not to shout, knowing that the thin walls of the huts would not muffle their voices, and unwilling that Ruth should hear anything that went on between them. She spoke in a kind of strangled whisper, rounding on him as the door shut behind them.

'What the hell's going on?'

'You tell me,' Barnaby said.

'And what's that supposed to mean?'

'Oh come on, don't play the outraged innocent. If it hadn't been for you and Roger, none of this would have hap—'

'Me and Roger what?'

'Look, Imogen, I'm not stupid and nor is virtually everybody else on this holiday, and for all I know, the hotel staff as well. It was perfectly obvious that you two were at it. You didn't even have the decency to conceal it. So how you can come over all . . . damn the word! . . . *sanctimonious* now, beats m—'

'You think I'm having sex with Roger?'

'Well you can't deny it.'

'I bloody can, and I do! You're just saying that to get yourself off the hook and it's pathetic. *You're pathetic!*'

'At least I don't tell outright lies. What was all that crap about me sleeping around? You know that's utter rubbish.'

'It wiped the self-satisfied smile off her stupid face though, didn't it? Wouldn't you have thought that life with Roger would have discouraged her from engaging in a sordid little intrigue herself? I – '

'Oh, so Roger *is* a womanizer, then. And just how do you know that?'

'Because he tried it on with me. Oh yes, he *tried*; people do still fancy me, you know. I'm not completely past it. And what happened? I told him to piss off and that was that. So where does that leave you, Mr Oh-So-Perfect; screwing some feeble, dreary female who hasn't even the guts to tell her ludicrously over-sexed apology for a husband to take a running jump. If I wasn't so bloody furious, I might even be fractionally impressed. I didn't know you had it in you. I mean, you haven't exactly excelled yourself in that department for the last ten years, have you?'

'Oh shut up! And don't talk like that about Ruth. I won't have it.'

'Quite honestly, I don't think you've got a lot of choice. I shall say just what I sodding well like!'

'I think you should know that Ruth and I are serious about each other.'

Imogen laughed, and then found it hard to stop, until she saw the look of actual dislike on Barnaby's face. Then she ceased abruptly, 'Oh grow up! For God's sake, Barnaby. You've just got trapped into feeling sorry for the woman. Why don't you admit it? Anything else is ridiculous.'

'I love her,' Barnaby said. He looked stronger than Imogen had ever seen him before. A splinter of fear pricked her.

'You don't know the meaning of the word,' she jeered.

'I do now.'

Imogen started to cry. 'How could you do this to me?' she sobbed, 'after all the years we've been together. What have I ever done to deserve it?'

'What have you ever done not to? It won't work, Imo. I'm not susceptible to tears any more, especially phoney ones.'

This was a new Barnaby, Imogen realized, and she would have to fight this threat in a different way. She wiped her eyes sharply with the backs of her hands, careless of smudging her make-up. 'Well I'll tell you one thing,' she said in her normal voice. 'You needn't be under any illusions about getting rid of me and making an honest woman of that wimpish creature, because I'm never going to consent to a divorce. So what would that do to your precious reputation, tell me that? From pillar of respectability to pillock in one fell swoop!' She saw she had scored a point, and held on to her advantage. 'Oh I get it now,' she said, 'you were planning to put all the blame on me, weren't you? *Poor man, deceived by heartless wife and lecher, finally finds solace with a second amazingly decent woman and retains his status in society.* Well, tough! You've blown it, and I hope you're satisfied!'

Now as Claire's group walked in single file along the path known as the Salazie track, Imogen went over and over the scene in her head, replaying it, analysing it, wishing she could amend it. She couldn't believe that Barnaby was really in love with Ruth. What was there in someone so negative that could inspire such devotion? Barnaby wasn't the sort who loved extravagantly anyway, he was much too controlled, too inhibited, too stuffy. She was convinced it must just have been a convenient lie to throw at her in the heat of the moment.

They had talked into the night, with Imogen getting more and more desperate as Barnaby remained obdurate. Nothing she said seemed to move him. She went through her entire manipulative repertoire, all to no purpose. It had never failed her in the past. She couldn't understand how he could have changed so radically in so short a time. In the end, when they were both too tired and too wrung out to say another word, they fell separately and uneasily asleep, and woke the next morning estranged and awkward, neither knowing what to say or how to behave. The only thing that they had agreed upon was that everything should be kept a secret from the rest of the group.

Now as she thought about it, she wondered whether she had read too much into the situation. She was sure that Barnaby hadn't even considered divorcing her in order to marry Ruth. She could talk him round. It was just a holiday fling, soon forgotten when back in the real world. The thing to do was not to over-react. It's a test of how tenacious I can be, she told herself, and with someone like Ruth, it will be no contest.

The rain continued undiminished as they walked up the track towards a verdant plateau where the vegetation was bushy and uncultivated and dotted with the occasional group of tall three-trunked screw pines. Imogen tightened the cord round her anorak hood and walked steadily behind the others. Raindrops collected in her eyebrows and eyelashes, stung her cheeks and dripped off the end of her nose. She was grateful to the weather, for once, for being in tune with her mood. The wet hard-beaten earth of the path in front of her was the same warm colour as unglazed terracotta. Rivulets of water were coursing across it, scouring the channels ever deeper. Colonizing offshoots of apple-green bushes crept low across it in places, but in general the path was open and easy to follow, and the gradient not difficult. Before the plateau they had passed through jungly places with rushing streams and warm orange and yellow rock exposures. Beyond it the track took them through a pass between hills and then down the other side of the island, past exposed multi-fissured granite crags, down which vertical stripes of water flowed, and beyond which their destination bay showed greyly through the clouds. Then after more jungle where the path was narrow and had become invisible beneath the stream of water flowing down it, they came to a wider track where there were clearings and occasional houses, and a couple of men felling a tree with axes.

Claire, Shirley and Annabel chattered as they walked, sometimes giving Imogen searching glances but otherwise leaving her to her own thoughts. She didn't care if they wondered what was eating her. She didn't care either if they had guessed. She was too busy thinking, and the more she thought of it, the more she was convinced that Barnaby could not possibly be serious.

Roger still seemed not to know. He had appeared to be perfectly normal at breakfast and surely even he couldn't be quite so laid back that he wouldn't turn a hair at his own wife's infidelity? So Ruth clearly didn't want Roger to know. Perhaps Imogen could threaten to tell him, and see what Ruth would do then; test her resolve? No, Imogen thought, better he doesn't know. Then there's more chance of everything returning to normal as soon as possible. I know Barnaby doesn't want a fuss. He has probably told Ruth to keep it quiet too. Well, that suits my purpose very well. With luck, then, it will all just fizzle out . . . Bloody man, how could he? How *dare* he?

'I'm starving,' Shirley said, suddenly next to her. Imogen jumped.

'Don't worry,' Claire assured her. 'You've got a three-course meal ahead of you and oodles of puds. It was fabulous last year.'

Oh Lord, Imogen thought. Lunch. I've almost come to the end of my thinking time and I'm not much forrader. How am I going to maintain some semblance of normality when I'm so churned up inside? How am I going to be able to be with Barnaby in public, and still appear casual?

The dining room where they were to have their lunch was spacious and comfortable, with a thatched roof built in high peaks. The blinds had been rolled up to reveal an open front, looking out on to a garden of palms with splendidly clashing scarlet flame trees and purple bougainvillea. The rain had eased off, and the air was fresher. The rest of the group were already ensconced in easy chairs on a terrace four steps below the main dining area, drinking cold beer, as the walkers came in, still dripping, and dragged themselves out of their clammy water-proofs.

'Well, was it worth it?' Brian asked, yawning and stretching lazily.

'Oh yes,' Annabel said at once. 'It was a lovely walk. I've got up a really good appetite and so's Shirley.'

Imogen looked across at Barnaby. He was sitting round a low table with Ruth and Roger, with Dorothy and Daisy on his other side. He looked relaxed and unworried. Ruth glanced up and caught her eye and held it for a moment longer than Imogen would have expected. It was a subtle but unmistakable challenge.

Imogen thought grimly, Right, we'll see about that!

16

ON the bus on the way back from the village of Anse
Volbert, Barnaby was too late to get a seat next to Ruth,
and had to content himself with sitting just behind her where
he could observe the top of her head with tenderness, and try
to organize his chaotic thoughts. When Imogen had snapped
at him in that sneering way the previous night, he had just
flipped. Quite without premeditation he had simply said, 'I
love her'. Now he realized that it was true. He had spoken
from the heart. He *did* love Ruth!

He was astonished at himself; amazed by the whole ostentatious theatricality of these new feelings. He'd never felt quite
so gloriously out of touch with himself. He was no longer an
old fogey. He'd been transformed inside his head into a romantic
hero, living a life tinged with such lavish voluptuousness and
brilliance that it made him dizzy. And all this because of love? At
his age? Fifty-year-old solicitors weren't supposed to experience
such things. Barnaby hoped his vital organs were up to the
excitement of it all. It would be sod's law if he went and died
of a coronary just as he had tardily started to *live*.

He now felt that every minute not spent with Ruth was a
wasted one. He fiercely resented the fact that Roger was sitting
beside her now, being attentive, damn his eyes! What right had
he to such pretensions, after the way he'd behaved? Barnaby
wanted to hold her hand, to apologize for rushing off so precipitately the night before, and to explain that he'd had to talk to
Imogen urgently to prevent her from doing anything damn silly
that might have jeopardized the whole situation. His dislike of
Roger mixed itself with resentment and agitated uncomfortably
inside Barnaby like indigestion. He could see the back of his
head next to Ruth's, and the emerging dark roots where the
blond hair grew in a whorl at his crown. Barnaby's lip curled.

He calculated the pleasure it would give him to inform Roger that his wife had finally had enough of him and that he, Barnaby, was the man who had enabled her to see just how contemptible he, Roger, was. It was almost tempting to do it now: LECHER LOSES LOVE TO LAWYER, or SATYR VS. SOLICITOR: SHOWDOWN IN SEYCHELLES, as the headlines might have it. He smiled at the absurdity of his thoughts. He was in love, but he wasn't completely out of control. He was faintly puzzled that Imogen appeared to be so angry. He had rather assumed that she was indifferent to him these days, but it was typical of her to take a contrary line, just to be awkward. Barnaby supposed it to be in character and, all things considered, he couldn't blame her, but he wasn't fooled by her denials. He knew she'd had a fling with Roger. The aspect of it all which most amused him, however, was her furious warning about never consenting to a divorce. What did she think she was trying to do? Surely not throw down a gauntlet?

Ruth was very conscious of Barnaby's presence in the seat behind hers, while at the same time being irritated by her husband's solicitousness. She didn't want Roger fussing. She didn't want him at all. She needed Barnaby to confirm that everything was still all right; that what Imogen had said really wasn't true; that she was still special to him. She knew rationally that all these things were so, but she needed reassurance. It made Roger's attentions all the more infuriating. He'd never shown such concern before. Why start now, for God's sake?

'You're sure you're OK?' Roger asked for the nth time.

'*Yes!* I'm fine. Don't keep on!' Roger now looked offended, and in the normal course of events Ruth would apologize and convince him yet again that all was well. Today she said nothing. She couldn't be bothered. Later on, when he had got over his initial huff he would contrive in some way to make her feel guilty, probably with his small-boy-unfairly-scolded look, which he could assume to perfection. Ruth knew that it would not work. It was fraudulent, and for the first time she would be able to treat it as such and ignore it. The realization gave her self-assurance an unexpected boost.

I'm going to need all the confidence I can muster, she thought. Imogen clearly isn't going to take this lying down (and who could blame her). If I want Barnaby, I shall have to fight her. It was a heady thought and for a moment Ruth was quite unnerved by her own temerity. Then she thought of Barnaby and the way they were together, and felt heartened.

Philip had waited with impatience for the group of walkers and those going by bus finally to leave him in peace. He reckoned that they would see very few birds anyway in all this rain, so he wouldn't miss anything vital by not going. As far as he knew, no one had yet sussed his problem. He had managed to hold his binoculars up, and eat, one-handed and no one had commented. He was glad of this. Sympathy had the effect on him of liquefying emotion; making it harder to contain, and that, he felt, he could do without. It was obvious to him that he was at the beginning of another attack. Would it be a major one? His right arm had become progressively numb and useless, but so far his left arm and both his legs were functioning normally. Would he manage to hold out over the last few days of this trip, or would he collapse in a heap? Could he keep going by sheer willpower? Would the attack take the same form as it had done the first time? Would he – Philip found himself trembling at the thought – would he go blind again? If he did, he might not recover from it this time. Most likely it would be permanent. That was what often happened with his sort of MS: the attacks got worse and worse and happened with greater frequency. You recovered in between them, yes, but never to the level you started from. It was down five steps, but only back up two or three every time; an inexorable decline. Why for God's sake does it have to affect my *eyes?* Philip wondered. MS doesn't always attack eyes, so why mine? I need them more than most. I'm different from most people because *all* my pleasures and inspirations are visual: birds, photography, land-scape, the presentation of food . . . Oh sure, if you can't see, you can still listen to birdsong, still eat the food, but that's not the point. I don't want to be just a recipient in this life. I'm a doer not a be-er. If all my potential for creativity is taken away, then for me there's no point to *anything*.

He tried to blank such thoughts out of his mind with rational reminders. They were purely destructive. He never allowed himself to wallow in such self-pity. He made a virtue of never exploring such possibilities. What was the point? I won't think about it, he told himself severely, *I won't*. He thought instead about his camera. Would it survive its inundation? He had taken out its batteries and washed it carefully with successive baths of fresh water, and had then set it down, open, to dry out. As soon as he got back to England, he would take it to a camera repair shop and get them to go over it for him. At least it hadn't been damaged in the fall. That was one piece of luck.

He felt tired. What should he do today? He could still use his binoculars one-handed and he could still walk. He decided that when the rain let up, he would go down the beach towards the village to the point where a small stream came out and met the sea. There were often good birds there. He had a packed lunch. He could just wander about and please himself. In the meantime though, he would just have a bit of a kip . . .

'Hello,' Brian said, coming into the hut which he shared with Philip. 'Oh, sorry, did I wake you?'

'Whaaa?' Philip said, dragging himself up from the depths of sleep. 'What time is it?'

'Tea time,' Brian said cheerfully, putting down his day-pack and scrabbling through his suitcase for a fresh tin of tobacco. 'We're all about to have tea and cake on the beach. Coming?'

'Be with you in a minute.' I must have slept though the best part of a whole day, Philip thought. God what a waste! He looked round at the hut, at the top of Brian's untidy grey head as he knelt on the floor by his bed, at the dark trees through the window and the brilliant sea beyond.

Well, he thought with relief, at least I'm not blind yet.

Imogen woke up the following morning with mixed feelings. It was to be their last day on Praslin, and in three days' time they would be leaving Seychelles altogether. She felt strongly that she didn't want such a perfect place forever associated in her memory with marital strife. She had three full days in which to reassert her rights over Barnaby and make him see sense, so perhaps she should stick with him all day? On the other hand, there was one last chance for some snorkelling that morning, round a small clump of offshore rocks known as St Pierre. She might never get the opportunity again . . . and anyway, she didn't know yet how she was going to tackle Barnaby . . . She decided that she would go snorkelling. Barnaby wouldn't be able to take time alone with Ruth whilst she was gone, because Claire and all the rest of the MS group would be there too, so she need not worry on that score.

Their transport that day was a small speedboat with a skimpy folding awning like a pram canopy, and two ostentatious outboard motors at its stern. They travelled at high speed, bumping over the tops of the waves and being soaked from time to time by cooling lashings of spray. Imogen sat partially in the sun on one of the pair of seats facing backwards over the outboards. Shirley sat in the other one, squeaking with pleasurable alarm when the ride was particularly rough or wet. The sky was cloudless, and the sun's heat bore down upon them fiercely.

'This is better than a rollercoaster, isn't it?' Shirley said, holding tightly on to the arms of her seat.

'Much,' Imogen said rather shortly. Shirley was clearly trying to be as pleasant to her as possible to expunge her former misdeeds. Imogen had already decided not to make it too easy for her, but today had other things on her mind. Six of their group had climbed aboard for this last trip: Roger, Shirley, Annabel, Simon, herself *and Claire!* This meant that there would be no organized activity for those left behind, and that Barnaby and Ruth would be free to do whatsoever they wished! Imogen seethed at the thought, but it had been too late to change her mind and get off again, and too difficult openly to question Claire's presence on board without revealing her own dilemma. There had been nothing for it but to carry on as normal, and hope that no one noticed how restive she was feeling. She could have kicked herself for handing the morning to Ruth and Barnaby on a plate.

She was increasingly unsure of her own judgement these days. She didn't normally get things so wrong. If she carried on as ineptly as this she would be in danger of having her morale seriously undermined. She'd got to get a grip on herself. She came to this conclusion as they dropped anchor just off St Pierre, a small rocky islet with a tiny beach and a few palm trees, but rapidly pushed it to the back of her mind as the magic of snorkelling took her over once again. The water here was, if possible, even clearer than elsewhere, and the multi-coloured fish swarmed everywhere in their millions. Imogen

182

marvelled at the sea urchins, the long pipe-fish, the sea cucumbers and the three sorts of starfish: bright blue, bright yellow and grey. Every now and again she came mask to mask with one of her fellow snorkellers or saw bits of them in her peripheral vision. She noticed that Annabel had got quite daring and was diving down below the surface, her red hair flowing behind her like finely divided seaweed, and her skin gleaming greenish white like marble. Imogen thought, I'm glad I'm not young like her. Maturity and experience do help at times like this. She glanced up above Annabel and unexpectedly saw a huge manta ray, gliding unhurriedly away with gentle undulations of its wing-like pectoral fins. After her first gasp of astonishment Imogen set off after it, but it put on a spurt and was gone. Imogen jerked her head out of the water and pulled her snorkel mouthpiece out, in triumph.

'Did you see *that?*' she asked Annabel who was surfacing close by, 'that enormous ray? It was amazing.' Annabel shook her head, disappointed, and went on swimming. Later when they had all gathered on the islet for a cool drink from an insulated box, Imogen discovered that no one but Roger and herself had seen the manta ray.

'It was my biggest one yet,' he said, speaking directly to her for the first time in four days. 'Wasn't it great?'

Imogen watched him as he stretched himself out on the sand, and wondered how he might take the news about his wife and Barnaby. She had a shrewd suspicion that he would be very angry indeed; double standards of behaviour being the norm for his sort. Perhaps she would be able to recruit him into her camp, so that he could exert some influence on Ruth? Maybe she had been wrong so far in agreeing with Barnaby and Ruth to keep things quiet, and had just played into their hands? Wouldn't it be better to amass all the ammunition she could on to her side; to take the war to the enemy? It was worth a try. Roger was going to know sooner or later anyway. Imogen reckoned that Ruth wasn't up to keeping intoxicating secrets for very long. She was the transparent type.

I'm not going to wait for events to overwhelm me, Imogen thought, that's not my style. I'm going to be up there, driving them. It may be that Roger and I can form an alliance (however uneasy) to cope with this mutual crisis. Better still – maybe I can prime Roger and launch him without ever having to get involved myself; just use him as a long-range missile instead! Why not?

She realized that she would have to get Roger on his own without alerting anyone else. At that moment everyone was ashore. Annabel and Claire had gone off to explore, climbing over the rocks and out of sight. Shirley and Simon were stretched out on the sand, sunning themselves, Shirley's acreage of skin gleaming with suntan oil, Simon's matt. Imogen thought that Simon's forehead was looking rather red. The sun was beating down unremittingly and it wasn't very sensible of him to risk such unprotected exposure, but it was his funeral. She decided to swim back to the boat where she had left her sunhat but as she did so, Roger got to his feet too, picking up his mask and snorkel again and making for the sea. Imogen seized her chance.

'By the way,' she said to him in confidential tones as they waded side by side into deeper water, 'I'd be grateful if you'd be good enough to call your wife off my husband. I mean, I know about birds of a feather and all that, but two of you in one family is ridiculous!'

'Just *what* are you gabbling on about?' Roger said, checking his step sharply and rounding on her.

'Ask Ruth. This compulsion you seem to have for screwing around appears to be catching.'

'You're off your head,' Roger snapped. 'I don't begin to understand what goes on in that twisted middle-aged cesspit which you're pleased to call your brain, but kindly leave Ruth and I out of it, OK? I've had enough.'

'Fine,' Imogen said. 'Please yourself, but I'm afraid in that context, it should be "Ruth and me", you know, not "Ruth and I".' She launched herself at the sea and swam rapidly towards the boat, wearing a smile of pure satisfaction which widened into a greeting as the boatman put out a hand to help her aboard.

Piece of cake! she thought.

Ruth and Barnaby lay uncovered on the outside edges of Ruth's bed with just the tips of their fingers touching. Any greater contact was too hot to bear.

'What d'you suppose the rest of our group are doing?' she asked him.

'Packing? Taking last-minute photos? Having a rest? Who knows. Perhaps Leslie and Janice are taking a leaf out of our book.'

Ruth giggled. 'Oi'm not a fussy wooman, but oi dew loike a bit'a nooky,' she mocked.

Barnaby smiled. 'Joking apart, sex does seem to work pretty well for us, doesn't it? It's a revelation to me.'

'And to me,' Ruth said. 'I think it's because you don't put any pressure on me to be something I'm not.'

'And Roger did?'

'All the time. I always felt outclassed by the competition.'

'Bastard!'

'Let's not talk about Roger, hmmm? Let's just be glad to be together.'

'He hasn't guessed yet, then?'

'I think he knows something's changed, but not what.'

'Good, let's keep it that way.' Barnaby let out a sigh of contentment, then turned to face her and said, 'I love you.'

He was so close that Ruth couldn't gaze into both of his eyes at once.

'So do I,' she said, 'love you too, I mean.'

'So, what next?'

'I don't know. I can't bear the thought of being apart from you when we leave here.' She buried her face against his chest. Barnaby stroked her hair.

'What would you say if we weren't?'

'Weren't what?'

'Apart.' Ruth jerked her head up and pulled away, so that she could look at him properly. 'We could live together,' Barnaby suggested. He looked shy.

'But I thought . . . What about your job?'

'What's that got to do with anything?'

'Well solicitors aren't supposed to . . . Wouldn't it look bad if you were separated . . . having an affair?'

Barnaby got up on one elbow and smiled down at her. 'Darling Ruth, I want to *marry* you! And anyway, no one gives a damn these days. Look, I've got it all thought out. I've got a cottage in Devon and it's not too far to drive daily from there to my office. We could go and live in it, the two of us. It's right in the country. Would you mind that?'

'Oh Barnaby . . .'

'Of course we might have to wait years before we can marry – if Imogen is obstructive – but that wouldn't bother me. Would it you?'

'No . . . no not at all.' Ruth felt quite overcome.

'It will take me a few days, when we all get home, to get organized,' Barnaby said, 'and then I'll drive down to the cottage, and you can join me there as soon as you can. How about that? I take it you do want to marry me?'

'*Yes!*' Ruth threw her arms round his neck. 'Oh Barnaby I didn't dare even to imagine that this might happen. I was so scared of tempting the fates.'

Barnaby kissed the top of her head. 'I admit it's rather out of character,' he said. 'Maybe it's a mid–life crisis? Suddenly I feel that I've been sensible and responsible for too long. Life's so short. To hell with everyone else! I haven't felt this wonderful since I was young.' Then he stopped and held her away from him, regarding her very seriously. 'No,' he said, 'actually that's not true. I've *never* felt like this before.'

Hours later, at twelve noon they got up, dressed in as few clothes as possible and prepared themselves for a difficult few days.

'Our rooms may be a long way apart in the hotel on Mahé,' Barnaby warned. 'We'll just have to be patient.'

'It will be worth it in the end,' Ruth assured him.

Then he kissed her and went through to his side of the hut to pack his things for the flight back to Mahé that afternoon. 'See you at lunch,' he said as he left. 'I gather it's to be a slap-up farewell affair with wine.'

Ruth had just finished packing her own things in a daze of happiness, when Roger returned. He seemed to be in a bad mood from the way he banged his holdall down on the bed and started chucking his belongings into it.

'What's the matter?' Ruth asked.

'Nothing.'

She decided to leave him to it, and didn't see him again until they were all seated round the table for their special lunch. The wine was uncorked and poured into glasses. Ruth noticed that

Roger had put himself at the far end of the table from her. His brow was furrowed and his mouth set in a hard line. He wasn't joining in the conversations around him. He looked intimidating and implacable. One of the group must have done something particularly annoying that morning, Ruth thought, glad it wasn't her.

'Cheers!' Imogen said, raising her glass in a toast to everyone.

'Cheers!' All the glasses were held aloft. Ruth looked at Barnaby who was directly opposite her, and tilted her glass slightly towards him. He reciprocated, twitching his mouth into the ghost of a grin, which was meant to be unseen by all but Ruth.

There was a crash as Roger's chair fell over backwards. He had got abruptly to his feet and was marching round the table to where Barnaby was sitting, with a look of fury on his face.

'On your feet!' he shouted at him.

'I beg your p—?'

'*Get up!*'

Barnaby put down his glass of wine with deliberation and was half-way towards standing up, when Roger punched him hard on the side of his jaw, and Barnaby collapsed back into his chair again, holding his face. There was instant consternation. Ruth screamed. Brian tried to pull Roger away. The waitress hovered uncertainly with plates of food.

Claire cried, 'For Christ's sake Roger, have you gone raving mad?'

Imogen was the only one who appeared to be in total control of the situation. As Roger angrily shook Brian off, and prepared for as dignified an exit as he could muster, cradling his damaged knuckles in the palm of his left hand, Imogen left her seat and bent over Barnaby, examining his jaw with cool, efficient fingers.

'Just bruised,' she said. 'You'll be OK. A dab of witch hazel would help, though . . .'

'*Gerroff!*' Barnaby pushed her brusquely aside and, tilting his chair so that he could still follow Roger's retreating back, called after him, 'I'd always suspected that violence was the last resort of the intellectually . . . lacking . . . missing . . . *inadequate*. Thank you so much for proving it to me so conclusively!'

Annabel was lost in admiration for Barnaby as he delivered his verbal retaliation to Roger. She longed for the gift of repartee. She would use it to prick the pomposity of rude people like Simon, and to impress attractive people like Philip... She glanced at Philip and felt a twinge of ill-defined anxiety. Something is wrong, she thought, I wonder what? He's not himself. It can't be just the camera...

'I looked up...' Imogen was saying to the group at large. She was now seated again and eating her lunch as though nothing untoward had happened. '... I looked up, and there was this *huge* manta ray! I've never seen anything so enormous. It seems that only Roger and I were lucky enough to see it.' She gestured towards the empty chair at the head of the table. 'Isn't that amazing?'

If I hear one more word from Imogen about that bloody ray, Annabel thought, then I'll personally throttle her! How dare she go on and on, rubbing people's noses in things they've missed and would dearly like to have seen? It's so insensitive, so malicious! And anyway, how on earth can she even think of carrying on a normal conversation when the leader of our group has just assaulted her husband?

Shirley tucked into her lunch with gusto, but all the while her mind was running in circles. Why had Roger hit Barnaby? Surely it should have been the other way around? So what had she missed? She felt out of her depth and it miffed her. It was like being a sentry on duty, surprised from behind; an insult to her vigilance. I wonder if Barnaby's jaw is painful? she thought. It was a right good thwack Roger caught him, just like on the films!

'Are you all right?' she asked him.

'Fine.' His manner was dismissive. Oh well, Shirley thought, in that case I won't waste my sympathy.

'Doesn't look as though Roger's coming back,' she observed. 'Someone ought to eat up his lunch. Seems a pity to waste it.'

17

IMOGEN went complacently back to her hut after lunch, for a short rest before the flight back to Mahé. Barnaby was already there, examining his jaw in the mirror, opening and shutting it experimentally and wincing.

'Was I right?' Imogen asked.

'What?'

'Nothing broken, is there?'

'No, but it still flaming well hurts,' Barnaby grumbled. 'What a moronic clown that man is.'

'Roger?'

'Who else?'

'He hasn't gone and hit you again?'

'Of course not! He caught me unawares at lunch, that's all. He won't get the chance again.'

'Where is he? D'you know?'

'Next door with Ruth. She was worried about him; insisted on trying to explain things. I think they're having a heart-to-heart.'

'I hope he doesn't hit her too,' Imogen said, relishing the possibility.

'He'd better not! He'll have me to deal with if he tries it.'

'Oh, very touching. Sir Galahad Redcliffe, not so much the knight of shining armour, more like the fight of shifting amour!'

'Not one of your best.' Barnaby declined to smile. He turned to face her. 'What on earth are you doing?'

Imogen was leaning against the dividing wall between the two huts, and cupping a hand round her ear. 'Sssh!' she whispered, 'I'm listening.'

'You can't do that!' Barnaby was scandalized.

'Oh don't be such a hypocrite. You want to know what's going on in there just as much as I do. So, if you'll kindly shut up, I'll give you a blow-by-blow account.' She giggled suddenly. 'How apt!' she said.

'You're drunk!' Barnaby accused her. 'Too much wine at lunch.'

'Rubbish. Now sssh! I think they're arguing.'

'And this whole pig's ear must be all your fault,' Barnaby persisted. 'I didn't blurt it out to Roger and nor did Ruth, so it can only have been you. What the hell did you think you were playing at?'

'I'm not *playing* at anything. Did you hear me mention it at all at lunch? No you didn't. I was doing my level best to distract everyone from your embarrassment, in case you hadn't noticed. And why should I tell anyone anyway, and make myself look a complete fool? Do give me some credit. Now will you shut up and let me *listen*. We'll have missed all the crucial bits by now.'

'I didn't plan things this way,' Ruth was explaining earnestly to Roger. 'I'm sorry but that's just how it happened. I fell in love.'

'*Love*,' Roger sneered, disgusted. 'Love, as all intelligent people know, is a much-hyped excuse for a chemical imbalance in the brain. It's quite random and meaningless and it doesn't last. You might as well get high on dope. It would be less expensive in the long run.'

'*He's whinging on about money*,' Imogen mis-reported to Barnaby from her position behind the wall.

'Expensive? Is that your only priority?'

'No of course not. It's you I care about, Ruth. You must know that.'

'How must I?'

'Well isn't it obvious? When you've been married as long as we have, it goes without saying.'

'Maybe that's the problem. Perhaps you should have said occasionally.'

'But Ruthie, you're not serious about *Barnaby?* The man would drive you bananas in a week.'

'*Now he's saying you're boring.*'

190

'On the contrary, he's everything I've always wanted. I'm sorry, Roger but My mind's made up. I love Barnaby and he loves me.'

'She says you're made for each other.'

'I can't believe you're doing this to me, Ruth, after all we've been through together; after all I've done for you. Didn't I look after you when you got ill? Didn't I even give up my job and start this business specially on your account? What more could anyone have done?'

'Now he's snivelling.'

'Well for starters you could have stopped yourself from having it off with every available female in sight for as long as I've known you. You must admit that you were unfaithful right from the word go; you can't deny it! And now, after all these years of putting up with it, when I've finally found the guts to retaliate, first you call me horrible names and then you go all reproachful on me. Talk about unfair!'

'She's saying Roger's a hypocrite too.'

'But you know very well that sort of thing's quite different for men. How many times do I have to explain that to you?'

'What, in the hope that if you say it enough times it magically becomes a fact? Is that what you told Imogen as well?'

'What's that cow got to do with anything?'

'Oh come on Roger, don't try to pretend that you didn't screw her too.'

'I don't need to pretend. I bloody didn't. I wouldn't touch her sort with a bargepole. You can see what she's like from a mile off, the deluded unstable bloody neurotic type.'

'She turned you down, then?'

'Now what's happening?' Barnaby mouthed at Imogen.

'Sssh! He's admitting how I told him to get lost . . .'

'What's got into you, Ruth? You never used to be so hard and unfeminine.'

'You mean I never used to stand up to you.'

'Look, I'm sorry I hit the stupid prat. I just felt so *wild*. And I'm sorry I called you all those nasty things at first, but you can understand why, can't you? I just can't imagine life without you. Ruth? *Ruth . . .?*'

'And now he's grovelling.'

'I'm sorry too, Roger. I really don't want to hurt you, but I've got no choice. At least it's all out in the open now. I hated deceiving you.'

'And she says, tough tit!'

'So you're really going to leave me? The minute we get back to Cheshire, you're going to walk out? Just like that?'

'He says he's going to find some way of damaging your career, since you've probably ruined his,' Imogen improvised.

'More or less, yes,' Ruth sighed. 'Look, there's no point going over and over the same ground, is there? I'm really sorry but that's it . . .'

'And she's telling him that you'll probably sue him for common assault.'

'Oh . . .!' Ruth exclaimed, 'what was that crash?'

'If there's any justice it will be Imogen next door, finishing off what I started.'

'I must go and see . . .'

'You stay right here!' Roger put out his hand to detain her.

'Now you've blown it. Why the hell can't you look where you're going?' Imogen hissed at Barnaby, who had tripped over the edge of a rug.

'Oh God,' Ruth said, bursting into tears. 'I can't bear all this awful *violence*,' and she covered her face with her hands and wept.

'*And now she's blubbing*,' Imogen reported.

The door to Ruth and Roger's room burst open and Barnaby lurched in. He went straight over to Ruth, pushing Roger aside, and put both arms round her. Imogen stood in the doorway and watched.

'Right,' Barnaby said, 'that's it! From now on Ruth and I are sharing a room and, as far as I'm concerned, you and Imogen can do the same. It's quite ridiculous of you to make a fuss, Roger, and it's utterly pointless at this stage to lie about who's slept with whom. We're clearly all as guilty as each other. Now wouldn't it make more sense if we all acted with dignity over this whole difficult business? I for one do not intend to make myself a laughing stock, and I trust you won't either.'

'Oh for God's sake,' Imogen protested, 'are you out of your mind?'

'Too right,' Roger retorted, 'you won't catch me sharing a room with that raving nymphomaniac, that self-indulgent hysterical old bag. I'd rather—'

'That's enough!' Barnaby cut him off. 'Whatever may have happened, Imogen is still my wife, and I won't have her spoken of in terms of such vulgar abuse.'

Ruth looked up at him in surprise, and then across at Imogen, who had assumed a martyred expression; proud and brave all at the same time. Ruth's heart sank.

Imogen pressed home her advantage. 'Thank you, Barnaby,' she said. 'And I trust you're not really going to abandon me publicly; show me up in front of the whole group? I think you owe me that much loyalty. And personally I'd rather our daughters were told about such things, before the Shirleys of this world.'

It got more confusing all the time, Shirley thought. On the plane to Mahé the Redcliffes were sitting together and so were the Dares. What was going on? How could Roger apparently get away scot free with punching a customer? What sort of a man was Barnaby to let that happen? And what was it all *about*?

193

Had Barnaby and Ruth perhaps . . . surely not! And was it all still festering away underneath, held down by a thick layer of snooty middle-class reserve? Shirley took a dim view of this sort of deceit. If you were going to go around hitting people in public, then the least you could do was to explain yourself openly too. If you didn't, then it wasn't much of an advertisement for Leisure Doubletrips, was it?

'Oooh I wouldn't go on that tour – the leader goes round thumping clients, you know.' 'He never does?' 'It's true; I've seen it with my own eyes.' Shirley anticipated such conversations keenly, and why not? She could feel no loyalty to Roger if he didn't come clean. Fair was fair.

Shirley tried to elicit as much information as she could from the rest of the group. Most of them were noncommittal or embarrassed by her blunt questioning, but she was unfazed. Only Claire appeared to support Shirley's growing suspicions.

'Looks as though the worm may have turned at last,' she said. 'Three cheers for Ruth!'

On the plane, Shirley and Brian found themselves sitting behind Imogen and Barnaby. Shirley eagerly awaited any snippets of overheard conversation, but even the best of these was disappointing.

'You'll be delighted to hear,' Imogen told Barnaby, 'that not only did I give Roger a flea in his ear, but I corrected his grammar too. You would have been proud of me.'

The rest of the day proved to be as unsatisfactorily inconclusive. At supper, back in their original hotel on Mahé, there was no more information forthcoming. Barnaby looked wary. Roger looked as though he'd lost all his stuffing. Ruth looked anxious, and Imogen inscrutable. They had coffee afterwards outside by the pool. The conversation was somewhat stilted despite Imogen's inconsequential efforts to jolly it along. In the middle of a tale of hers, Simon got clumsily to his feet and just made it behind a low wall in time to throw up all his supper into a flowerbed.

'I didn't think my story was that bad,' Imogen said, with a mock grimace.

'Sunstroke,' Janice said, identifying the problem. 'Cooked hisself today, didn't he? Some people haven't got no sense. Funny isn't it, Leslie? It's usually you who gets took with that.'

'Oh God,' Claire said, getting up wearily, 'I suppose I'd better go and get him a pill to prevent further sickness. It's unbelievable the lengths some people will go to, to get attention.'

By breakfast time the next day, Roger appeared to have got himself under control, and was performing his leadership duties as though nothing untoward had happened.

'Claire will be taking some of you for a walk at La Reserve,' he told them all. 'It takes about an hour and a half and is a steepish walk up through a mahogany plantation to the palm forest at the top, and then there are some fairly dramatic cliffs with views out over the low ground to Boileau Bay and the small islands beyond. I can recommend it for those of you who are not too knackered.'

I'm exhausted, Imogen thought, so how those with MS are managing, I can't imagine. It's much more humid here on Mahé than it was on Praslin; far more enervating. She was however determined to do this final walk. She wasn't going to hang around Barnaby like a supplicant. It wasn't her style, and in any case there was no need. He had given his word that he would act normally (for the girls' sake) at least until they got back to Somerset, and she knew that as an honourable man, he would keep it. She wasn't worried either that Ruth would steal a march on her that day. She and the others would all be going off with Roger in a second minibus on a tour round the southern part of the island, so it was unlikely that there would be any opportunity for intimate discussions.

Imogen felt encouraged. It had been a fillip to her morale to have Barnaby defend her in front of Ruth. Perhaps he was already starting to waver? She smiled at the thought.

Roger, despite outward appearances, was feeling shattered and bewildered. He had managed to persuade Ruth that he really and truly had not made love to Imogen, and so convincing was his denial that he had almost begun to believe himself to be completely innocent. He assumed that Ruth must now be labouring under an even greater burden of guilt than usual, so he determined to foster this emotion in her for all he was worth, to absolve himself from any responsibility for the mess they were all in.

He thought, Let's see how this *love* of hers deals with that! She can't possibly be in love with that pompous stuffed-shirt anyway. It's just a sort of madness brought on by the heat, like some unpleasant tropical disease, and as soon as we get back to Cheshire it'll vanish like a mirage in the rain. And anyway, people like Barnaby Redcliffe don't walk out on their wives. They're far too reputable; too *bourgeois*. Roger snorted as he remembered Barnaby's response when he'd purposely slagged off Imogen. That said it all! Ruth had noticed it too. Roger hoped it would give her pause for thought. At any rate, he wasn't going to give her and Barnaby any more chances. He was going to stick to his wife like a burr for the rest of the trip.

Now he stood by the door of the minibus and counted his group inside: Leslie, Brian, Ruth, Barnaby (who studiously ignored him), Simon, and Daisy who looked as though the combined heat and humidity had finally caught up with her.

'We'll have a gentle sort of day today, eh?' he encouraged her as he helped her up the steps.

'It's about all I'm good for,' she confessed.

'Tell you what,' Roger offered, 'we'll call in at the church at Anse Boileau. There's often a pair of Seychelles kestrels there, nesting on top of the tower, and we've had good views of them in previous years. That'll put you one up on young Master Philip, eh?'

Daisy smiled. 'Why not,' she said.

Dorothy toiled up the path behind the others as they climbed on foot in single file through the plantation. The mahogany trees were young and had not yet closed canopy, so the sun was able to concentrate its force on the crowns of their hats and on their shoulders, without respite. Dorothy put one foot in front of the other doggedly but without much pleasure. It really was too sultry and uncomfortable and she worried that the holiday had all been too much for Daisy. Perhaps they both should have gone to the Isle of Wight after all? This trip hadn't been such a success as others they'd been on with Roger, because of the perpetual heat. Oh, she personally had enjoyed every minute of it, and had seen some wonderful wildlife, but the MS group seemed to have spent a disproportionate amount of time sitting about, and they'd missed a lot of the best sights. Dorothy did hope that Daisy wasn't resentful about that. She didn't like to enquire in case Daisy herself hadn't thought about it and by doing so, put unsettling ideas into her head. That would be a great mistake. The whole idea of Leisure Doublet-rips was admirable, in that it enabled people to travel together, but it did rather emphasize, for those with MS, all the things they *couldn't* do. Dorothy wondered why Roger had chosen Seychelles in the first instance and then had come back several years running? It was a marvellous place for the fit and able, but he must have noticed the effect the climate had on his less fortunate clients. She thought, He probably comes because it's his own favourite place. I'm sure altruism isn't an overriding concern of his. Somehow I don't think we'll be doing one of his tours again.

Dorothy glanced ahead of her as the path curved up through the open forest, saw Philip and frowned. He seemed to be behaving rather erratically today. The way was well defined, but he had almost fallen just then, tripping over a branch at its edge. He looked hunched too, one arm holding the other and cradling his binoculars unused against his chest. It didn't look a very comfortable stance for walking in the heat. He looked, Dorothy suddenly thought, for all the world like a shy child on his first terrifying day at school. She wanted to talk to him, perhaps even to comfort him, but he was too far ahead and anyway she knew she wouldn't be able to find the right words.

Her attention was distracted by some bright red leaves with golden longitudinal veins, which were sprouting from the top of a shiny green bush by the side of the path. Young shoots of cinnamon! Dorothy identified them with pleasure, crushing a leaf and inhaling its perfume with closed eyes. Thus diverted, she forgot about Philip and trudged ever upwards until denser jungle closed round them, and they were in the palm forest. Here it was darker and cooler with the sun reaching them only after it had penetrated the greens, yellows and browns of palm fronds in all stages of growth and decay. Every now and again the path took a diversion to avoid vast moss-covered granite outcrops, and boulders as big as houses. Dorothy stopped to admire a delicate red flower (which she later to her delight discovered to be called flame of the forest) and when she caught up with the group again she found Philip bringing up its rear. He was now walking rather slowly with his left hand sometimes outstretched, brushing occasional tree trunks in passing, as though sampling his environment; rather like a snake tasting the air with its forked tongue, Dorothy thought.

'You all right?' she asked, feeling (in Daisy's absence) *in loco parentis.*

'Just a bit tired,' he said. He said it lightly enough, but she couldn't be sure whether or not he meant it.

'Here,' she said, slipping her arm through one of his, 'as my father used to say, "Take my arm and call me Charlie!" You can lean on me if you like.' She half expected him to pull away from her, but he appeared grateful and they began walking together more briskly than before, catching up with the rest of the group as they arrived at their destination.

The view from the vantage point was wide and beautiful and mostly wild. Morne Seychellois, nearly 3,000 feet above sea level, commanded the background. In the middle distance the cultivated mahogany plantation showed up as a patch of regular dotted lines amongst the random greenery and rocks of the rest of the hillside. Further round to the west by a small bay, the village of Anse Boileau could just be picked out amongst its trees, and beyond that bay the little islands of Thérèse and Conception showed mistily through the heat haze. The group was standing on an expanse of bare rock which stopped abruptly in sheer cliffs, so high that they could look down on the tops of the spreading white-flowering albizia trees below and imagine them to be circular rugs.

'I daresn't look!' Janice said, recoiling. 'Must be all of a hundred-foot drop down there, and I never could stand heights. I'm not just being fussy. I've always been a vertical sufferer. Can't do a thing about it; turns my knees straight to jelly.'

Dorothy, who was prone to vertigo herself, said rather nervously to Philip, 'It's certainly spectacular, isn't it?' but he didn't answer. He disengaged his arm quite gently from hers and strode forwards. 'Don't go too near the edge —' Dorothy began in alarm.

Daisy sat in the reviving pink and white interior of Anse Boileau church and felt her age. She was glad the holiday was almost over. It really had been rather too taxing. It was good to be able to sit somewhere cool and rest. Brian came in also and nodded at her without speaking, before sitting down somewhere behind her. Daisy could see that he was very fatigued too. She supposed all the MS group probably were. It had been that sort of a holiday. Certainly she had found it amusing to watch Roger's sexual forays, but on balance perhaps he wasn't the most suitable person into whose care to entrust oneself? Perhaps not again, Daisy thought. Maybe the Isle of Wight? She began to take in her surroundings.

Ahead of her, behind two carved, kneeling angels, and sheltered in an alcove above the altar, there was a cross draped in white linen and the figure of the Virgin Mary holding the spreadeagled crucified Jesus, faithfully reproduced even down to the crimson streak of blood from the spear wound on his breast. Carved in wood beneath, and partly obscured by candles was the exhortation VOILA VOTRE MERE – Behold your mother. Daisy sighed. She had not loved her own mother, which had been trying for them both at the time but had certainly given Daisy a very personal insight into other people's difficulties with theirs; invaluable for a subsequent practitioner of psychotherapy. Thinking of parents in general, Daisy was reminded of one of her patients many years before, whose neuroses she had discovered to have been almost entirely consequent upon his having been born to a couple who were both stupid and hysterical. He had grown up totally unable to form relationships of any kind, and thus had had a tortured and hopeless sex life, which was where she, Daisy, had come in. She remembered suddenly that he had also stolen money, large quantities of it, in an attempt to compensate for this emptiness of soul . . .

Simon came in through the church door at that moment and wandered down to the altar looking offended, and without acknowledging her presence there. That's it! Daisy thought. Of course, that's who Simon reminds me of. I wonder . . .? She watched him as he glanced up at the theatrical centrepiece with distaste and then, turning abruptly away, came to sit down beside her.

'You don't go in for all this body and blood communion rubbish, I hope?' he asked her. 'Personally I think it's grotesque.' Daisy gave a noncommittal shrug. 'You're surely not a God-botherer?' Simon was scathing. 'I had you down as a rational being.'

'I'm sure I could help you, you know,' Daisy said, pursuing her own line of thought, 'if you would let me?'

'Huh!' Simon said dismissively. 'Religion, psychiatry, hocus-pocus. They're all the same — crutches for the gullible!'

'Suit yourself,' Daisy said equably. 'It's entirely up to you.'

She closed her eyes to rest them for a moment and to conjure up the recent image of her latest 'tick': the small endemic kestrel and its almost full-grown chick on the church tower above. Daisy had seen enough of it to be able to identify it to her satisfaction and now she looked forward to scoring a small but exclusive point off Philip. He was way ahead of her in their contest, of course, but it would be satisfying not to be totally annihilated.

As they drove back to the hotel in the hired minibus Daisy dozed all the way, comfortably anticipating her small triumph, and so when she and some of the able-bodied group were reunited in the entrance hall her first words were, 'Where's Philip?'

18

SHIRLEY, oblivious of the rest of the group, stared out from the top of La Reserve and drank in the view. The day after tomorrow, she was thinking, we'll all be back in England and it will probably be cold and grey with driving rain. There may even be snow at home; there sometimes is in November. It seemed unreal, but she welcomed the thought. There was something very satisfying about being chilly and having to wear lots of all-enveloping cosy clothes to keep warm. That was, after all, the normal state of affairs and, in her opinion, much to be preferred to their present condition of sweaty semi-nudity. In the winter Shirley felt that her fatness was less obvious; well camouflaged beneath the layers. Here she felt exposed, like a hermit crab in a glass shell. I wouldn't want to live in Seychelles, she thought, even though it is paradise.

'*Philip!*' Dorothy suddenly screamed, 'Oh my God, *no!*' Shirley started out of her daydream so unexpectedly that she wobbled and had to grab at the rock to steady herself. She glanced round wildly to identify the reason for the scream and there below their feet, falling through the void, she saw him. Philip's body was plummeting silently, arms wide, puppet-like. The noise when he finally crashed into the upper branches of a tree and then fell through, jerkily, into the dense undergrowth beneath, didn't sound loud enough to be fatal, and yet Shirley knew straight away that he must be dead.

Janice said, wonderingly, 'He did it on purpose. He just walked off the edge. I saw him.'

'*No,*' Dorothy cried again, '*no!*' and staggered backwards with her hands covering her face. Imogen rushed to support her. Annabel had gone chalk white and looked as though she were about to faint. Shirley just stared down at the spot where Philip had fallen, although it was now impossible to see him. Then it seemed to her as though they were all stuck for moments on end in a kind of aghast, horror-stricken tableau, where no one was permitted to move or speak.

Then Claire took charge. 'I'm going down there,' she said. 'I'm pretty sure he can't have survived a fall like that, but just in case . . . Imogen, you and Annabel are likely to be the quickest. Both of you stay together and make your way back along the path to the bus. Get the driver to take you to the nearest phone and dial 999 for help, same as at home. Then bring the bus back to collect the rest. Shirley, you look after Dorothy. Janice, you keep your eye on me as I climb down, in case I get into trouble, and then the three of you make your way back to the bus. All of you, *do it now*!'

Shirley watched in a daze as Claire selected the most suitable route and began her descent, disappearing over the edge. She watched as Imogen, after a brief hesitation, lowered Dorothy gently into a sitting position with her back against the rock and started to retrace their steps along the path, looking round for Annabel as she did so.

'Come on,' Imogen called to her, holding out her hand, 'we've got a job to do', and she led her away.

Shirley came to with a jolt, her old training taking over. Dorothy had had a shock and she, Shirley must nurse her. She was glad she had something definite to do. Being useless at a time like this would be unendurable.

When Imogen thought about it all afterwards, great bits of the story were missing. It was impossible to quiz people in that state of shock, about what had or hadn't happened. Had Claire managed to climb right to the bottom of the cliff before the private helicopter (diverted on this mercy mission from its usual scenic flights) arrived? It had been foolhardy in the extreme, but at least she was an experienced climber. Or had it perhaps taken her off part-way down? Had it been difficult to find Philip in all that dense vegetation? Imogen supposed that they must have winched him up on a stretcher and then flown him and Claire straight to the hospital.

He was dead, of course. Claire had telephoned Roger with the sad news much later. Imogen hadn't expected anything else, but Dorothy had clearly hoped right to the last for a miracle,

202

and had been devastated when denied one. It was a dreadful thing to have happened, and apparently so unnecessary. What was one to think? On the bus drive back to the hotel, Janice had kept on and on about suicide until finally shouted into a huffy silence by everyone else. That sort of talk would help no one and was clearly having a disastrous effect on Dorothy. Imogen didn't believe it for a moment. Enthusiasts like Philip didn't kill themselves. It was just an appalling accident. She felt so sorry for Claire too, being in charge; responsible for their safety. She had done well, Imogen was bound to admit. She had reacted decisively and efficiently. Imogen was grateful not to have been in her shoes. The most emotionally draining time for Imogen herself had occurred before they had had confirmation of Philip's death. When the five of them had finally got back to the hotel, they were met in the foyer by Daisy, all smiles.

'Where's Philip?' she said. 'I've seen this marvellous bird – but Dorothy, you look simply dreadful. What on earth's the matter?'

Dorothy couldn't speak. She simply stood there looking haggard and hopeless; her halo of fluffy white hair incongruously perky. Imogen looked round. Claire and Roger were not there of course, and neither Annabel, Shirley nor Janice looked equal to the occasion. Imogen stepped forwards and, taking Daisy and Dorothy each by an elbow, she steered them towards the lift.

'I'm so sorry,' she said to Daisy, 'but I'm afraid there's been an accident. Let's go up to your room and I'll explain . . .'

'Philip's dead, isn't he?' Daisy asked.

So abrupt! Imogen thought. She doesn't shield herself with equivocation, just goes straight for the brutal truth. 'We don't know for sure, but it seems likely,' she admitted.

Daisy said nothing more as the lift took them up to the second floor. Her face was a mask of stoicism, but she put out a wavering hand towards Dorothy, who took it in one of her own and held it. When the lift doors opened, the two of them walked slowly hand in hand down the corridor, Daisy's stick thudding along the carpet. Imogen followed behind them. They both seemed to have shrunk in stature and had become two crumpled little old women. When they got to their door,

Dorothy produced the key, but fumbled ineffectually at the lock, and Imogen had to take it from her and open the door herself. 'Sit down,' she suggested to them gently, and the two of them sat down side by side obediently on one of the beds, and turned sad, grey faces up to her.

'So what happened?' Daisy asked, dignified to the last.

'We came to a very high cliff at the end of our walk,' Imogen explained, 'and Philip somehow fell over the edge. Claire climbed down while we summoned help, but we don't yet know . . .'

'Oh Daisy,' Dorothy found her voice again, 'it was all my fault. He just said he was tired. I should have known . . . Perhaps he's only hurt?'

'Nonsense,' Daisy said harshly. 'I'm sure it was nothing to do with you. It's I who should have seen it coming. He was having an attack, you know, but was trying to disguise the fact from all of us. I suspected it for the first time last night, but knowing how much he hates a fuss, I didn't speak about it. He's terrified of becoming helpless, you see; can't bear even to think of it. I should have talked to him straight away. If anyone is to be blamed, it is I. I should have stopped him from going. I could have prevented the whole thing.'

'But it was an accident,' Imogen protested. 'You can't hold yourself responsible for acts of God.'

'On the contrary,' Daisy said, 'it's abundantly clear to me that Philip knew exactly what he was doing. He isn't – wasn't – one for half measures. Perhaps he found his quality of life becoming intolerable, so he killed himself? That would be perfectly logical and in character, but I could have dissuaded him. I just didn't . . . anticipate it . . . today.' Her face contorted and she began to beat the bedspread with both hands, eyes tightly shut, mouth a thin line of unbearable tension. Dorothy stared at her, mutely in desperation. They both looked, to Imogen, to be at the end of their tether.

Imogen placed a comforting hand on Dorothy's shoulder. 'I'll go and fetch a doctor to give Daisy a sedative,' she told her.

It was a relief to get out of that room and an even greater one (after she had organized hotel reception to find a doctor to treat both Daisy and Dorothy) to retreat to her own room and lie quietly on her bed. Even then, troubled thoughts went round and round in her head. How could Daisy be so fatalistic? How could she be so sure that Philip was dead? Wasn't there still an outside chance? Was it really true that Philip had been ill? Wouldn't she herself have noticed it, if so? Was Janice right all along about it being suicide? Shouldn't everyone have tried harder to talk to Philip? *I should have*, Imogen castigated herself. She was amazed that someone could get to that depth of despair with none of them realizing. Didn't it make them all guilty of an appalling indifference and lack of humanity? But perhaps he hadn't planned it at all? Perhaps it had been a momentary impulse? Perhaps Janice and Daisy were both wrong and it really was an accident? Surely it must have been? But Janice was so sure . . . Either way, I should have picked up the signs and worked out what was happening, Imogen told herself. I should have seen that Philip was seriously disturbed. I thought he was just upset about his camera. I should have *talked* to him.

The bedroom door opened and Barnaby came in. 'I've just heard,' he said. 'I came up straight away to make sure you were all right. What a ghastly thing to have happened.' He stood there, large and dependable, his worried expression instantly endearing. Imogen, oblivious of her carefully planned strategy where he was concerned, knew only that she needed comfort and a familiar refuge. She scrambled off the bed and ran straight into his arms.

'We couldn't *do* anything to stop it happening,' she said, her voice breaking, 'none of us. We were all so *useless*', and she subsided on to his chest and bawled like a baby.

It was a depleted and subdued group the following day that wandered round the capital, Victoria, ostensibly doing some last-minute shopping and sightseeing, but mostly drifting about in a daze. A minibus took them first to the Botanic Garden where they came across a friendly man with a telescope trained upon a roost of Seychelles fruit bats, high in the trees. Barnaby focused the instrument for his own eyesight and found that they were charming creatures with golden brown foxy heads and chocolate-coloured wing membranes which became translucent in the sun when they flew. He watched Imogen as she too had a look. He felt closer to her today than he had for years, in spite of his new devotion to Ruth. It was a sort of protective feeling of the kind he hadn't experienced since their children were small. When she had cried and clung to him the evening before, her tears had been of genuine grief, not self-pitying or manipulative. She had been crying for Philip's mother, for Daisy, for Claire, for the whole pointless waste of it all. Barnaby had held her closely for a long time, had murmured encouraging nothings into her ear and then, without really meaning to, had slipped easily into their old routine and had made love to her.

Of course, he now told himself, it didn't mean he'd changed his mind or anything like that. He didn't feel as though he'd been exactly unfaithful to Ruth. After all, he and Imogen had been together for thirty years, give or take a few . . . and after all that time each had become a habit to the other. It wasn't as though it *meant* anything; it was simply reassuringly familiar – much in the same way that his old cord trousers were. All the same, he didn't think he'd mention to Ruth what had happened. She might not understand.

'What were you thinking about?' Imogen now asked, at his elbow.

'Oh this and that. It would be nice to have one's own wing-blankets to wrap oneself in at night, like the bats, wouldn't it?'

'Only if they could zip together to make a double,' Imogen said, with an attempt at a smile. Barnaby relaxed into a brief grin too, and was still half smiling when he looked up and found Ruth staring at them.

Ruth had been very tired, so she and Roger had gone up to their room the previous afternoon, some time before the remnants of the able-bodied group had returned from their ill-fated walk. Consequently they had both been unaware of the drama until Claire had telephoned from the hospital to say that Philip had been killed. Ruth thought that she had never seen Roger so upset, and then felt bad that it didn't engender in her a greater sense of solidarity with him. She went with him nevertheless, when he set off at once to check on Daisy and Dorothy, but they turned out to be heavily sedated and not in need of any immediate help. Roger spoke to Janice in the corridor in passing but didn't believe her story of suicide. The only other group members around the place were those who had been with them all day, the rest having taken to the privacy of their rooms to get over the shock. Ruth felt hurt that none of them had apparently thought it necessary to inform her and Roger about what had happened. She could see that Roger's inability to *do* anything was causing him great agitation, but there was nothing for it except to wait until Claire returned and the authorities arrived. When they did, they naturally only wanted to interview those who had witnessed the accident. Ruth, failing to find Barnaby anywhere downstairs, and unwilling to encounter Imogen in their room, went back to her room alone and waited with growing impatience for Roger's return and some clarification of the story.

When Roger did get back, he told her very little, and said only that he was afraid their insurance company didn't cover suicide, only accidents. 'So I hope to God bloody Janice doesn't go around shooting her mouth off,' he said. 'There's absolutely no call to do so. I've told her so, but I've got little or no confidence that it will have sunk in. The woman's not only as thick as two short planks, but she's a deliberate pain in the neck as well.'

'But you can't be held responsible,' Ruth protested.

'Leisure Doubletrips can. Do you realize this could be the finish of it; sued into bankruptcy? God, what a thing to do, eh? How bloody selfish can you get?'

'Who?'

'Well Philip, of course. Whether it was suicide or an accident, it's still down to him. There was absolutely no need to get that close to the cliff edge, was there?'

Ruth was silent. It's just shock, she told herself. He's not really so callous or so egocentric . . . or maybe he is? Thank goodness I shan't have to put up with him for much longer. Only a few more days . . .

She slept badly that night and the next day felt depressed and exhausted. Roger and Claire would be involved in the official investigation all morning, and in making arrangements for the body to be flown home. The rest of the group were free to board the minibus for Victoria and amuse themselves as they wished. Daisy and Dorothy unsurprisingly did not appear, so the complement was down to nine. Ruth wondered what

Shirley, Imogen, Annabel, and especially Janice had said in their statements the night before, but she felt she couldn't ask. No one wanted to talk about it.

What if Leisure Doubletrips did go bust? It was a scenario Ruth had often needlessly worried herself over. Now that it seemed all too possible, she felt curiously unconcerned, rather like the old countryman who, when asked how he manages when it rains, says 'Aaaar, well I lets it.' If Leisure Doubletrips went to the wall, Ruth expected that Roger would find something else to do and someone else to do it with. He was an optimist. Today was a bad day, but by next week he'd already be bouncing back.

Ruth was the last one off the minibus at the Botanic Gardens, and the last to look through the stranger's telescope at the fruit bats. With the naked eye they looked simply like a crowd of small, badly folded umbrellas, dangling from the branches high above, but through the telescope she saw that they were really upside-down teddy bears encased in vine leaves with just their heads sticking out, like half-wrapped dolmades . . . Then she had straightened up, full of remorse for having been able to enjoy such a ridiculous flight of fancy so soon after Philip's death, and was caught off-guard by Barnaby and Imogen's exchange and by Barnaby's warm response. She thought, How can they make jokes after what's happened? And then, They're acting just like a couple again. What's going on?

Janice was glad to get into Victoria proper and get on with some serious shopping. She considered the Botanic Garden a drag. She'd already seen enough tropical plants to last her a lifetime, and she would much rather have spent the time searching for mementoes of their holiday to give as Christmas presents. As it was, she managed quite well and arrived near the agreed rendezvous, the Queen Victoria memorial clock tower in the centre of town (followed by Leslie who was weighed down with packages), ahead of some of the others.

'What have you been buying?' Shirley asked.

'Don't ask,' Leslie said. 'All I know is it weighs a ton.'

'T-shirts, a palm leaf hat, a batik dress, Indian Ocean tea and these – ' Janice said, ferreting about in a bag and then brandishing several large and beautiful sea shells with pride.

'You shouldn't buy those!' Annabel rounded on her. 'It encourages unscrupulous people to kill the animals on purpose just to sell their shells. Why, in the Caribbean they even dynamite the reefs to satisfy the tourists' demand for souvenirs. They destroy whole ecosystems!'

'Whoever told you that?' Janice demanded. 'I know for a fact that these were found empty on the beach. I was going to get some of that tortoiseshell stuff, but these are nicer. Leslie liked them better, didn't you ducks?'

'Just as well,' Brian said. 'Tortoiseshell would have been even worse!'

'What did you get?' Janice asked Imogen, unabashed.

'Just this, for Barnaby. Quick, because I don't want him to see it yet.' She opened her bag to reveal a small wooden box with an intricately patterned lid. 'It's inlaid with a whole lot of different local woods, and it smells divine inside. Have a sniff?'

'Toothache,' Janice said at once, remembering an old remedy of her mother's.

'Cloves, actually,' Imogen said. 'Trust you!'

Barnaby went to buy a couple of first-day covers, having noticed that Seychelles stamps were particularly attractive, and on his way back to the clock tower he came across Simon and then Ruth, and walked with them.

'Some capital city,' Simon scoffed. 'I've seen better hamlets.'

'I think it has charm,' Barnaby said, and to Ruth, 'All right?'

'Not really.' She clearly wanted to say more, but felt inhibited by Simon's presence.

Barnaby gave her an encouraging smile. 'Buy anything?'

'Only a few postcards. My heart wasn't in it.' It seemed she wasn't alone. When they rejoined the group, Janice and Leslie were the only ones burdened by conspicuous consumption. They were also the only ones acting normally. Everyone but them seemed to be blaming themselves in some degree for Philip's state of mind. Annabel voiced it first, over supper.

'I wish I'd taken the trouble to *understand* him more,' she said. 'I know I could have made more of an effort.'

'I feel the same,' Imogen said.

'It probably wouldn't have done any good,' Barnaby said, and was rather miffed when both women rejected his offering.

'It might have helped,' Ruth said, taking their side too. Poor love, Barnaby thought fondly. She looks so wan in spite of her suntan. He gave her a fond look, but she barely responded. Later when he went over to the side-table where all the puddings were laid out invitingly, to help himself to some fruit salad, he found himself standing next to her.

'Barnaby, I need to talk,' she said in an undertone, glancing over her shoulder to check that they could not be overheard. 'I can't stand this artificial separation. Couldn't we meet on the beach after supper?'

'Wouldn't that be a bit obvious?'

'It's pitch dark! And surely it doesn't matter now; the holiday's virtually over.'

'True.'

'See you by the big badamier tree, then? You've got a torch?'

'Yes I have. All right then love, I'll see you there.'

When Barnaby returned to the table with his bowl of fruit, he found a furious argument going on between Simon and Imogen over the ethics of computer hacking, and became involved in defending Imogen's contention that however clever it might be, it was never morally justifiable. They sat long over coffee as they continued the discussion; most of the group ending up ranged against Simon, who nevertheless defended his position with some skill. So engrossed were they that Barnaby didn't notice the non-combatants slipping away, and when Imogen said much later, 'We'd better have an early night, since we've got to be up at five o'clock tomorrow morning', he allowed her to lead him upstairs to bed without demur.

It was only when he woke suddenly in the middle of the night, that he remembered with a start that he'd clean forgotten to go and meet Ruth.

19

IMOGEN woke abruptly at four in the morning with that feeling of urgency she always had, when occasionally obliged to get up extra early to catch a train. She reached for her travelling clock from the shelf beside their double bed and by holding it very close to her half-opened eyes, she could just make out the time. She was reassured that she need not get up for another hour, and lay back comfortably with a sigh. Barnaby was fast asleep beside her and snoring lightly. For once it did not annoy her. She was feeling very benevolent towards him, and very understanding. Their marriage had been tested in paradise (surely the greatest form of challenge?) and it was going to survive. She felt it in her bones. She and Barnaby were close again. They knew each other so well. It was just that their spark had got smothered in the tedium of the daily round, and it had needed a crisis like Philip's death to rekindle their undoubted feelings for one another. Imogen was sad to be leaving such a wonderful place, but glad that she had managed to reclaim her husband before doing so. She looked forward to beginning their partnership all over again with renewed empathy and compassion. She didn't blame Barnaby for his one lapse. After all, she too had been very tempted and had nearly given in, so how could she in all fairness criticize him? Thank God he wasn't like Roger! She certainly wouldn't be able to stand for that. Imogen grimaced, and allowed herself to feel just a little sorry for Ruth.

Ruth was going to get a nasty shock when they all got home, if she was expecting Barnaby to run off somewhere with her. Imogen didn't bother to try to imagine this scenario. There was no point. Although she and Barnaby had not had much opportunity to discuss the future, she was quite sure that as soon as they got back to Somerset, Barnaby would settle back into his cosy routines, into his comfortable house, into his job that fitted him perfectly like those dreadful old corduroy trousers that he loved so much and refused to let her throw away . . . Then next month the girls and their men would come over for Christmas, and everything would revert to recognizable order again. Affection and indolence will keep him with me, she thought, I can depend on that, even though romantic love has long since faded. She let out a small sigh of regret at the necessity for the abnegation of passion, and then caught herself up briskly. What nonsense! she thought. I've had all that stuff. It was wonderful then, but now I'm nearly 50 and there are other compensations. I'm experienced. I'm confident of who I am. I have a modest amount of talent and I'm still vigorous. After all, I'm only half-way through my adult life. I have a difficult but generally rewarding part-time job with the potential to do all sorts of good in society. Who can say what other challenges there will be? She turned over and cuddled up to Barnaby's naked back, smiling to herself in the semi-darkness. For all she knew, there might soon be grandchildren too.

Ruth was waiting for Barnaby downstairs in the dining room at 5.30 a.m. sharp. It was light and there were already three joggers pounding along the beach outside. Roger had gone to check that Daisy and Dorothy were going to be up in time to catch the bus for the airport at 6.15. They'd had meals taken up to their room ever since Philip's death, so no one except Claire (who was keeping a doctor's eye on them) really knew how they were. Ruth felt deeply sorry for both of them, but at the moment her full attention was concentrated upon Barnaby. She felt a numbing mixture of anger and anxiety, but most of all of disbelief. How could he have failed to appear the night before? Had Imogen prevented him from doing so? And if he couldn't stand up to her now, what chance was there for them both in the future?

When he did appear, it was certainly in advance of the rest of the group, but Imogen was right behind him, and Ruth didn't know what to do. She was reluctant to let Imogen see that Barnaby had let her down, knowing how much Imogen would gloat, but she *had* to know what was going on.

'Morning!' Imogen looked bright-eyed and sickeningly

jaunty. She was one of those people who leap from bed in the morning with all their faculties on *full ahead*, Ruth thought glumly. Barnaby looked less assured; in fact he looked positively shifty. Ruth felt her determination swell. She ignored Imogen's greeting and spoke straight to Barnaby.

'I need a word,' she said, 'and I need it *now*.' She was astonished at her own assertiveness.

'Yes, of course,' Barnaby said at once. 'Where d'you think – '

'Hold on,' Imogen put in. 'We've got a moratorium on all that, remember? You can't rat on our agreement.'

'Well . . .' Barnaby looked from one to the other.

'For God's sake!' Ruth exploded, 'what the hell does that matter now?'

Barnaby looked even more uncomfortable. 'Look,' he said, 'please don't let's have a scene here in public. We'll be home later on today and – '

'I need to know,' Ruth persisted. 'Who's more important to you, her or me?'

Barnaby frowned as though puzzled. 'But that's not the issue, is it?' he said. 'Look . . . we really can't discuss it now, and anyway things aren't as black and white as all that, are they? I mean, I feel I owe Imogen . . . after all, she hasn't done anything wrong . . .'

'And I have?'

'Good news!' Roger interrupted breezily, appearing beside them. 'The old girls seem to have got themselves together. I don't think they'll collapse on us on the way home now.'

'Well, how convenient for you,' Barnaby returned, acidly.

Ruth could see that he was relieved to have had the subject changed for him. She knew for the moment at least that she was stymied, and her rudimentary confidence seemed all at once to be evaporating, like white spirit from a neglected paintbrush in a jamjar, leaving the misery within her to dry up and set hard.

Claire was impressed with Daisy's fortitude. When she had come round from her sedation that morning, she had been in a great state of wretchedness and shock, and inconsolable with remorse at having failed to prevent the catastrophe. Claire had succeeded in calming her down sufficiently to allow her to

speak coherently, but it was Dorothy who had risen magnifi-
cently to the occasion. Far from collapsing herself, she seemed
galvanized by her friend's despair, into becoming an unlikely
tower of strength. She let Daisy talk and talk until a modicum
of catharsis had been achieved, and then she took upon herself
all the practical tasks for the rest of the holiday. When Claire
went back to check on them a little while later, Dorothy was
finishing the packing for both of them while Daisy sat stiffly
in an upright chair, staring out of the window and not interfering, even when Dorothy answered for them both.

'I'll send a porter up for your things, shall I?' Claire asked.
'The bus is leaving for the airport in a few minutes, to get us
there by 6.30. Now, is there anything else you need?'

'No dear, thank you,' Dorothy said. 'There's nothing more
you can do here, and we're both very grateful. But if you could
just tell us about the arrangements for . . . for when we get
there?'

'A neighbour is going to drive Mrs Blunt, Philip's mother,
to Gatwick, and there will be a private room laid on for you
all to meet in, and you can stay there as long as you need to,
before the neighbour drives you home. I'm so sorry. I'm afraid
it will be very upsetting.'

'I shall look after her,' Dorothy said, with a gesture of her
head towards Daisy. 'She's done the same for me for years and
years — although most people thought it was the other way
around — and now I shall repay the debt and do it gladly. Don't
worry dear, you've done your bit faultlessly; it's up to me now.'

Claire withdrew, but not before she had seen Daisy turn to
her friend and smile at her tremulously. The bravery of that
expression stayed with Claire for a long while, and every time
she recalled it, it brought the same constriction to her throat.

Barnaby was relieved to be going home at last. Now that he
had decided to start life afresh with Ruth, he didn't want to
waste any more time about it. He wished he'd had the opportunity to apologize to her about being AWOL the previous
night, but perhaps it was just as well, until he had sorted out
what he was going to say. He decided that he would be ill-
advised to confess to her that he had quite forgotten their
assignation. That would be unnecessarily unkind, even though

it was the truth. He remembered his father's maxim, *Never apologize, never explain,* and then thought, I must look up who first said that. It had never seemed particularly apt until now. He sighed. Perhaps in future he would have to resign himself to doing what Imogen had been nagging him to do for so long, namely to write everything down on a notepad in order not to forget it. He let a little snort of air escape down his nose as he envisaged the entry: *8 p.m. beach 3rd badamier along, Friday – conference with R re love.* Poor darling Ruth, she seemed to be finding this limbo time harder than he did. He had been surprised at how easily he had coped so far; buoyed up by thoughts of the future, no doubt. She, on the other hand, had been so heated at breakfast. He hadn't realized that she had it in her to be so bossy! He was sure that underneath she did appreciate Imogen's need to maintain appearances, and was generous enough to allow her rival some self-respect. He didn't blame Imogen at all for keeping him up to the mark. A promise was a promise. Then it did belatedly occur to him that Ruth might have waited for him in the dark for some time the night before, getting more and more worried and upset. Barnaby frowned and resolved to make it up to her the moment he could.

He fidgeted in his airline seat. They were in a Boeing 707 again and it was uncomfortably cramped. He couldn't even see Ruth from where he was, with Imogen snoozing on his window side and Simon on the other, and the Cromwells and Brian across the aisle. They had taken off only twenty minutes late, but it was going to be a long haul. Barnaby passed the time by drawing a map of the route to his cottage from the M5, on the back of an old envelope, shading it with his left hand so that Imogen wouldn't be able to see it if she opened her eyes. She dozed on. Breakfast, lunch and tea came and went. A film was shown; the same one as on their outward flight. Barnaby peered over Imogen and saw dried-up river beds in Egypt and the Pyramids twice, as they circled. They were diverted to Athens to refuel, before offloading all the Germans at Frankfurt. Janice, who had complained all the way that her seat was broken and wouldn't recline and that the discomfort was killing her, moved to a different one. Barnaby got up too, stretched himself and went to the lavatory.

When he emerged, he found Ruth outside, waiting anxiously.

'I'm so sorry about last night,' he said to her at once, keeping his voice low, 'truly I am. Look, I'll explain it all when we're together. Also I've been meaning to give you a map and this, so you can phone me at work, in an emergency.' He handed her the envelope and his card, which had Butcombe Nempnett & Thrubwell's telephone number on it. 'Not long now, my love,' he said, squeezing her arm gently.

'Oh Barnaby!' she took the card, biting her lip. 'I thought . . .'

'What?'

'Never mind. You're sure everything's all right?'

'Everything's going to be fine. You'll see.'

Shirley sat next to Annabel on the plane, and at Frankfurt a large man came and occupied the third of their trio of seats, taking the place of a German who had just got off. Shirley studied him with interest. He wasn't dressed like a holiday-maker, but didn't look like a businessman either. She noted his sandy hair and his striped shirt bulging through the front of his dark suit. He had white eyelashes, a snub nose, a sweaty, unsmiling face, and a standoffish manner. He looks just like a peevish pink porker, Shirley thought, pleased with the alliteration; a ginger Tamworth at that, *and* he's even fatter than me!

'Shirley?' Annabel said beside her, rather hesitantly, 'Brian and I have been talking . . .'

'Oh?' Shirley was instantly alert and hoping for intimate disclosures.

'Yes. You know you've always wanted to go to the Himalayas?'

'Yes . . .?'

'Well, Brian and I thought that perhaps I could go and stay at your house while you went, maybe next year sometime. And I could look after it and do meals for Brian, and it would give you a chance to travel somewhere you've always wanted to. Brian says he's tried to persuade you to go before, but there's never been anyone who could deputize, so to speak, and he'd be so pleased . . .'

'Oh . . .' Shirley was dumbstruck.

'It's only an idea.' Annabel looked unsure of its welcome.

'But that'd be . . .' Shirley said, finding her voice and then scenting a catch all at once, ' . . . but what would you and Brian do?'

'We'd be fine. He said he'd show me some of Yorkshire, if I'd do the driving. We could do the museums and the sculpture park and go to concerts, that sort of thing. We're just friends, you know. There's nothing else . . .'

Shirley had the grace to feel ashamed. 'Well I reckon that's a marvellous offer,' she said, recovering herself, 'and thanks ever so. Oh my goodness!'

'What?'

'I've to lose some of this weight then if I'm to go trekking, haven't I?'

'You could always become a vegetarian,' Annabel suggested.

'Well I doubt if I'd take it that far,' Shirley said thoughtfully, 'but I suppose I might have to consider giving up sausages.'

Annabel smiled and then, feeling about in her hand luggage, produced *Middlemarch* in paperback, removed her bookmark and began to read.

Shirley stared out of the window and imagined that the clouds below her were really mountains covered with snow. She was pleased and yet astonished that someone she barely knew should offer to put themselves out, so that she could achieve her long-cherished ambition. Oh no! she thought, her courage already failing, I'll never get fit enough, and everybody else on the trek is sure to be half my age, and what if we don't get on? I've never been off all on my own before . . . She realized that Brian and Annabel between them had called her bluff. Of course she could have gone years ago, had she been determined enough. Having to look after Brian had mostly been an excuse and a sympathy-inducing ploy, enabling her to be both wistful and stoical; encouraging people to say 'Shirley's wonderful, you know – so selfless.'

But didn't Annabel say that Brian would be *pleased* if she went? It now occured dimly to Shirley that perhaps such heroism on her part might actually have become a burden upon its recipient; that Brian might in fact *prefer* her to abandon him sometimes. She felt hurt and relieved all at once, and then audaciously resolute. *I shall go*, she decided.

Then she sighed and thought, Oh my, I'm that tired. Surely

we must be getting there soon? It's over thirteen hours since we started, and there's no room to swing a mouse in here, let alone a cat. All my joints are seizing up. I shall need to go to a gym or aerobics or somesuch; get into training! The absurdity of the thought tickled her and she chuckled aloud.

At 5.30 British time, the plane landed at Gatwick in pouring rain and taxied to the airport buildings. Before it had been connected to the exit tunnel, Shirley noticed that a police car with its blue light flashing was driving up right beside their plane. Its doors opened and two uniformed policemen jumped out.

Oooh! she thought, I was right all along. I'll bet any money they've come for Leslie Cromwell. I *knew* he must've thieved the money for this trip! She waited agog to see what would happen next, while obeying, with all the other passengers, the pilot's Tannoyed instructions to remain seated. Peevish Pink Porker, however, got smartly to his feet and walked purposefully up the aisle to where Imogen, Barnaby and Simon were sitting. He bent over and spoke quietly to Simon, too softly for Shirley to catch what he was saying. Then Simon stood up, and Shirley saw to her astonishment that he was now *handcuffed* to the other man. Then she heard Imogen laugh and call out loudly as the two of them made their way out,

'Oh I get it, now it's *intellectual* property that's theft, is it?'

Simon and his captor must have left via a staff exit leading straight down on to the wet tarmac, because Shirley next saw him being put into the back of the police car by a policeman with a large hand on Simon's head, and being driven off at speed in a shower of spray.

Well! Shirley thought, chastened, I was wrong about that then, wasn't I? I was wrong about Imogen and Roger too, and about disasters coming in threes. I really am going to have to watch myself in future; be careful what I say to people. Brian was right (as per usual). How sickening!

'Who would have thought it?' she said to Annabel. 'Simon wanted by the police! I'm gobsmacked, me.' Annabel seemed more amused than amazed. 'What's set you off, then?'

Annabel smiled even more widely, and said with great satisfaction, 'I've just seen my first ever flying pig. Now for a radiant bullock!'

Imogen would have preferred to go straight home as soon as they had collected their bags from the carousel, been through customs and emerged into the main concourse at Gatwick, but Barnaby said they ought to stay and have a final coffee with the group, just to round things off properly. So here they were, minus of course Simon, and Daisy and Dorothy whom Imogen had witnessed going towards their private room to meet Philip's mother, as if being led off to an execution. Poor things, she thought, I wonder what will happen to them. I don't suppose I'll ever know. I'll probably never see any of these people again. So she looked carefully at them to get a final impression.

Janice was in her element, complaining first how *cold* it was, and then even more vociferously that their son hadn't bothered to get off his fat backside to come and meet them.

'I'm not a fussy woman,' she said, 'but handsome is as handsome does.'

Claire was the only one who had been met, and it had clearly been unexpected and very welcome. She had introduced her man to the group with obvious pride. Murdo had long legs that seemed unable to fold up small enough to fit into the space under the table, and he appeared shy, hiding his expression behind a thick red beard and a lot of brown curly hair. His voice was sibilant with the gentle inflexion of the outer Isles, and Imogen was surprised to find herself charmed by it, and astonished that frigid-looking Claire had managed to bag herself such a trophy. She reluctantly identified her predominant emotion as envy, and looked away hurriedly.

Brian was telling Annabel one last story from his past, when he was a sanitary engineer. 'Seeing all this mucky weather, reminded me,' he said. 'They'd put this new septic tank in, you see, but they hadn't filled it up. Then it rained cats and dogs in the night, and in the morning they saw this huge white mushroom had popped into view at the bottom of their garden. It had floated up on the rising ground water, see, and burst through the topsoil with all its pipework trailing, a bit like a wrenched-out heart! Funny the things you remember, isn't it? I used to have that much information and know-how at my fingertips in those days, but it's as if I'd never learnt it at all now.'

'Education is what survives when what had been learnt has been forgotten,' Barnaby put in, 'according to B. F. Skinner.'

'Oh!' Ruth said, 'how clever of you to know that. It couldn't be more appropriate!'

Imogen snorted inwardly and wondered idly just how Barnaby was going to break it to Ruth that it had all been a mistake. He was leaving it a little late, wasn't he? Perhaps he was hoping that things would die a natural death as soon as they were safely home? That would be in character, she thought wryly. Barnaby is the sort to avoid a showdown at all costs. Imogen glanced across at Roger to see how he was taking Ruth's sycophancy, and saw that he was about to react in his usual way by changing the subject. He had drained his coffee cup and put it down with a clatter.

'Well,' he said authoritatively, 'I suppose this is it, then. Our trip is over, and all that remains for each of us is a fading suntan and the sand in our luggage. At this stage I usually suggest that we all get together somewhere central in a few months' time for a reunion, to swap photos, show slides, and perhaps meet up with another of my groups to compare notes, that sort of thing. So if any of you – '

'Not us,' Janice interrupted. 'Me and Leslie's going on the *QE2* next, in style, aren't we duck? We're going to make the most of what we've got. After all, t'isn't every day you win the Lottery.'

There was an audible intake of breath from Shirley. 'Oh,' she breathed, 'Now I *see*.'

Well thank God for that! Roger had thought as they disembarked from the plane, Not much bloody longer. Just as well; I don't know how much more of this miserable whingeing rabble I could take. Before they had even sat down to a farewell coffee, they'd all individually got at him about Simon being carted off by the police. As though Simon's private life was in any way under his control! He was a tour operator, not a flaming nanny. Good God, if you had to vet all your clients' financial affairs and parentage before accepting them, you'd never even leave the country. It's not worth the hassle, he thought. I've been thinking so for a long time, but now I've had it up to here; I'm totally pissed off with the whole damn thing.

He had gone through his customary spiel about a reunion, but half-heartedly, and was almost grateful when no one took him up on it. Let's get the hell out of here, he thought to himself. I've had just about as much as I can take of my wife sucking up to Barnaby bloody Redcliffe, with his precious know-it-all quotations. Best thing I can do is to get her home and talk some sense into her. Then we're going to have to do a major reassessment. I'm not sure that Leisure Doubletrips has a future . . .

Claire and Murdo were the first to leave, and their departure precipitated a general rush. 'I'll be in touch, Claire,' Roger called after them.

'Fine. Good luck, then. I hope things work out OK.'

'Goodbye Roger,' Barnaby said, and added mockingly, 'it's been a pleasure.'

'But not one we intend to repeat in a hurry,' Imogen said, *sotto voce.*

'Paradise certainly has its moments,' Shirley said stolidly, shaking his hand. 'A bit like the curate's egg.'

'Very memorable,' Brian said, shaking it too.

'Don't blame yourself,' Annabel said, 'about Philip, I mean. It wasn't your fault', and she patted his arm.

'Back to Brum,' Janice said, 'and civilization. I can't wait.'

'You really put us through it,' Leslie said. 'It was definitely an experience.'

And then they were all gone, and just he and Ruth were standing there beside the table full of empty coffee cups and dog-ended ashtrays. And Ruth was trying to pretend that her eyes were watering just because of other people's cigarette smoke.

Roger looked across into the distance and saw Janice and Leslie finally disappearing, burdened with suitcases and bags but still managing to walk hand in hand. Jesus wept! he thought. There's no justice.

20

'OH Barnaby,' Imogen said, 'isn't it wonderful to be home!' She collapsed onto the sofa, eased off her shoes and lay back, sighing with pleasure.

'Mmmm,' Barnaby said absently. He had collected a wad of accumulated mail from the hall floor, and was leafing through it.

'What do you think then, on reflection?' Imogen asked.

'About what?'

'About the holiday of course – apart from Philip's death, I mean, which obviously cast a dreadful shadow over everything. It certainly wasn't quite what I expected, but on balance I'm still glad we went. Seychelles are so marvellous, aren't they? I wouldn't have missed them for anything. And then there's us. I don't know about you, but I really feel I've learnt a lot. In a funny sort of way, I feel as though I've grown up. That sounds ridiculous at 48, doesn't it? Do you understand what I mean?'

'Mmmm?'

'You're not listening to a word I'm saying, damn it! You know I really can't be bothered to say that all over again.'

'Right.'

'Well I'm going to bed then,' Imogen said, peevishly. 'I fancy an early night. D'you want a drink or anything?'

'You go on up,' Barnaby said. 'I'll just finish looking through these.'

Five minutes later, Imogen lay in a hot bath, surrounded by scented foam, with her spirits restored and luxuriating in familiar surroundings. She was thinking. She decided that it had been more than a holiday; it had been a voyage of self-discovery where she had had the leisure to examine her innermost needs and hopes. She had even thrown off the albatross of niggling discontent which had hung about her for so many years. She had reassessed her priorities. She had set off on holiday wanting to find out whether Barnaby had any *spirit* in him. Well she'd done that all right, and he had surprised her in a way she could never have anticipated. Far from rejecting him for being unfaithful, she felt more than usually drawn to him, as though his attractiveness to another woman had somehow validated her own attachment.

Am I peculiar? she asked herself. Shouldn't I be telling him never to darken my door again? She smiled at the ceiling. If anything was peculiar, it was love itself. Who would have thought that Janice and Leslie would prove to be the happiest pair on the trip . . . Imogen speculated about Brian and Annabel as potential lovers, and wondered whether Shirley would gossip about them too and perhaps burst in upon them in the spare bedroom? She had a suspicion that Dorothy and Daisy might be a couple too, and hoped they were, so that they would be able to comfort each other better . . . She hoped strenuously that Philip's mother (whom she had never met, but felt such sympathy for) would be all right in the end, although she suspected that this was impossible. The death of a child wasn't something you ever got over . . . Then she thought a little about pain and isolation, and even managed to feel slightly sorry for Simon, stuck in a cell somewhere awaiting trial. Of course, she thought, he was trying to lie low and escape detection. That explains why he would never have his photograph taken! It also explains how he's wealthy enough to go on endless expensive holidays. She wondered if it had proved worth while? Judging from his ill temper in Seychelles, probably not.

Imogen yawned. She was suddenly very tired. She sat up to wash herself and, reaching for the soap, got a good lather on both hands and began to rub it under her armpits and around both breasts. Then she stopped abruptly, and began feeling the top of her right breast cautiously with the fingertips of her left hand. She had not been mistaken. There it was again. It was quite small, only pea-sized really, but it was unmistakably a lump.

Ruth got back exhausted, but was still able to muster enough energy to get to the telephone ahead of Roger, when it rang soon after they arrived home.

'Hello?'

'Darling,' Barnaby said, 'it's me. Are you alone? Can you speak?'

'No, not really,' Ruth said, glancing over her shoulder at Roger.

'I just wanted to say I love you and that it won't be long – only a week – until D-Day, our deliverance day!'

'Yes!' Ruth said. 'That's wonderful!'

'Who is it?' Roger intervened rudely, snatching the receiver and speaking into it. 'If it's bloody Redcliffe, you can damn well fuck off!' He crashed the phone back on to the rest and turned a furious face to his wife. 'What's going on?'

'You know very well what's going on. I'm leaving you.'

'When?'

'In a fortnight.' The lie should prevent him from using any spoiling tactics.

'You're not serious!'

'Of course I'm serious.'

'So what about me?'

'What about you?'

'It doesn't matter to you that Philip's mother will probably sue Leisure Doubletrips for negligence, and that my whole business (which I built up entirely for your benefit, as you well know) looks set to go down the tubes? That doesn't bother you at all, huh?'

'You're fed up with it anyway. It was only a matter of time.'

'And that's all you've got to say?'

'What more can I say?'

'Well I hope for your sake that you can keep up this façade of indifference; don't try to con me, I know that's all it is. I just hope you can keep it up when you discover what all this is doing to me; when they finally drag my bloated corpse out of the River Dee, half eaten away by scavengers and very very *dead!*'

'Oh come off it, Roger! I didn't think even you could be that tacky. You make simple bad taste appear positively admirable. Now I'm exhausted, and I'm going to bed.'

'I can't sleep,' Imogen complained to Barnaby, turning on her bedside lamp and blinking crossly. 'What on earth have you been *doing* all this time? What time is it anyway?'

'Only eleven o'clock.' He had hoped to slip into bed in the dark, without having to talk to her.

'So what have you been doing?'

'Just reading my post.'

'Is that all?'

'Yes.'

Barnaby thought, I could say – actually I've been phoning every quarter of an hour, waiting for Ruth to answer, to be reassured that she's safely home; that I've made a date with her for our rendezvous at the cottage, and that I can't wait to get there – but on balance, I don't think I will say that!

'Well now you're here, why don't you come and give me a cuddle?'

Barnaby hesitated. 'I'm fit to drop,' he said apologetically. 'If you don't mind, I think I'll go and sleep in the spare room. That way we'll both get a decent night's sleep.'

'But I do mind!' Imogen protested. 'I need you to hold me.'

'Why now especially?'

'I just *do*! That should be enough for any proper husband. I shouldn't have to spell it out to you.'

'But I'm afraid I'm not a proper husband, am I?'

'What do you mean?'

'We both know what I mean.'

'Oh Barnaby, you are sweet. You don't have to go through the sackcloth and ashes routine, you know. I've forgiven you your trespasses. Now come and give me a cuddle!'

Barnaby frowned. 'You surely don't think . . .' he began. 'You can't imagine . . .'

'Look it's all right,' Imogen said. 'I realize that it was just a passing aberration, and I'm not going to hold it against you for ever. Every dog is allowed one bite, isn't he?'

'But Imo, what makes you think . . .? I never said . . .'

'You didn't have to, you old silly. We went to bed and made love two nights running, didn't we? That told me more than any words could; that we're back together again. And since then we've been better friends than we've been for ages.' She smiled lovingly up at him.

'But you were very upset,' Barnaby said, confused. 'Naturally I had to comfort you . . .'

Imogen frowned. 'What are you trying to say?'

'You said you wanted to keep up appearances,' Barnaby explained, 'until we got home, so I – '

Imogen sat bolt upright in bed. 'You're telling me it was all a fake; that you slept with me quite cold-bloodedly; that all the warmth and companionship since then were meaningless?' she demanded. 'Well I just don't believe you!'

'Well . . .' Barnaby floundered, 'if you put it like that, no . . . but . . .' he took a deep breath. 'I'm sorry,' he said. 'I had no idea that you thought I'd changed my mind; that you weren't acting a part just like me. If I had, I would have got things straight before. The fact is, Ruth and I are going to live together, and I want a divorce. I'm sorry to put it so baldly, but that's how it is.'

Imogen picked up the bedside lamp and threw it at him. It fell short, tethered by its flex, and crashed on to the floor, plunging the room into darkness.

'You bastard!' she screamed at him. 'You filthy rotten two-faced *bastard*!'

In the days that followed, Imogen lurched between fury and depression. She tried to stop shouting at Barnaby, because it had no effect at all. (It was almost as though he were accepting her invective gratefully, as part of a penance which might eventually purge him from all guilt.) But she couldn't stop herself, and he *was* guilty. It was the one fact that Imogen clung to, in her battle to regain her self-esteem. She was in the right; the innocent party. Barnaby, the so-called pillar of respectability, was a commonplace adulterer, just another weak man who had no compunction about running off and leaving his wife . . . But for whom was he about to leave her? Ruth could hardly be described as a Scarlet Woman. There would be no comfort there for Imogen to salvage. Already she felt shamed.

She tried talking to Barnaby, but that only made things worse. He told her home truths that she would never have entertained; that she didn't wish to hear, but once articulated returned over and over again to undermine her. As if it wasn't bad enough to discover a lump in one's breast; having to cope with this as well was all too much.

She had decided not to tell Barnaby about the lump until she had seen a specialist. She would go privately of course; the

National Health Service was hopelessly overstretched these days. It took far too long to be seen, and some things couldn't wait. Unbeknown to Barnaby she took time off from her voluntary work, and discussed it with no one, not even her colleague Carol. A call from the consultant's secretary, who called her 'Deah', told her the time and place of her appointment. It was for the next day.

The consultant's name was Mr Ulysses Corn, which in other circumstances would have amused Imogen greatly, but now only caused her alarm. This was one time when she didn't need a clown. She need not have worried. Mr Corn was quiet assurance personified. His consulting rooms were part of a large and elegant Victorian house. His secretary moved noiselessly over the thick carpet like a well-oiled precision instrument. Her surroundings spoke to Imogen of efficiency, authority and competence. Mr Corn's hands, when they touched her breast, were warm and dry and comfortingly impersonal.

'Mmmm,' he said, 'ah yes, here it is, mmmm . . . good . . .' He straightened up and looked her steadily in the eye. 'Fine,' he said, 'it is a lump, you're quite right about that, but it feels smooth and harmless and is in all probability an innocent cyst. Cancer usually feels 'craggy', you know, and this definitely doesn't.'

Imogen refastened her bra and put on her blouse and jacket again, feeling enormously relieved.

'Come and see me again in a fortnight,' Mr Corn suggested, 'just to check it's still the same size.'

But what if it isn't? Imogen wondered in the car on the way home. If it's grown bigger, will they have to cut it out? The thought appalled her.

She got home to discover Barnaby packing books into ex-supermarket cardboard boxes on the sitting-room floor.

'Why aren't you at work?' she demanded. 'You told me that masses of stuff had piled up in your in-tray while we were away.'

'Not to worry,' Barnaby said, lifting down Trevelyan's *History of England* from the shelf. 'I'm intending to stay late some nights next week to catch up, but in the meantime I've taken the rest of the week off, to sort myself out. Bob Thrubwell was very understanding.'

'Oh wonderful!' Imogen said sarcastically. 'So now he knows all about our personal business, which is absolutely nothing to do with him. How do you think I feel about that? And how am I supposed to get on with anything worth while if you're here all day under my feet?'

'It's not for long, and anyway you'll be at the CAB some of the time, won't you, that is, unless you've suddenly got tired of giving advice to people?' He put the book on to the pile in the top box.

'That's mine!' Imogen said accusingly

'No it isn't. We both had a copy, remember?'

'Yes, and that one's mine.'

'Oh well, you'd better have it then,' Barnaby said irritably, throwing it on the floor. 'I couldn't care less.'

'And you can unpack all the rest too,' Imogen demanded, 'so I can check what you think you're taking.'

'Oh for Pete's sake!' Barnaby snapped, 'can't we be adult about this? I do not intend to make off with *anything* that belongs to you. You can keep all the joint things: wedding presents, cooking things, bedclothes, the television and the video – the lot. All I'm taking is my own books, my clothes, a few paintings and the odd piece of furniture. Satisfied?'

'Which bits of furniture?'

'My mother's bureau, my father's desk, and the inlaid table which came from my great-aunt. Even you can't lay claim to those.'

'And which paintings?'

'The harbour at Pittenweem, the watercolour of Ireland, the woman in purple and the portrait of the girls as babies.'

'*No!*' Imogen said. 'You can't take that portrait. It belongs in the family home. It's got to stay here.'

'You haven't worked it out yet, have you?' Barnaby looked pityingly at her. 'Once we're divorced there won't be a 'family home'. We'll have to sell it and split the proceeds.' Imogen looked stunned. 'You've got to face up to things, Imo,' Barnaby said, a little more kindly. 'It's no use pretending that this just isn't happening, you know.'

'Don't patronize me!' Imogen yelled at him. 'You're so bloody pompous. You think you know it all. Well you don't; you don't know the half of it!'

'Let's face it,' Barnaby said, 'at least I'm not swanning about in Cloud-cuckoo-land for most of the time.'

'And just what d'you mean by that?'

'I mean frankly that I can't conceive how on earth you manage to achieve any do-gooding at all with your totally egotistical outlook on life, or how your colleagues at the CAB perceive you – let alone your motives for working there. Perhaps they take you at face value? I'm just saying that I can see deeper than that. I've lived with you for too long, and I know only too well what's behind that habitual sweet smile and that solid brass neck of yours . . .'

'*Shut up*! If all you can do is call me names, then I don't want to know, OK? You can take your stupid books and bugger off and good bloody riddance!'

'Nevertheless,' Barnaby said, apparently unperturbed, 'for your own good, my considered opinion of you is this: you have no self-knowledge at all, and absolutely *zero insight* into the human condition. The only thing you are wonderful at is . . . blast! . . . yes, is *manipulating* others and getting your own way. Well I'm sorry, but as far as I'm concerned your innings is over. A man can only be pushed so far, and I passed my limit years ago.'

'You're well past your sell-by date too, you pig-ignorant, self-important, pathetic *cripple!*' Imogen screamed at him. 'Damaged bloody goods, that's what you are. Ruth's welcome to you! Why wait until the weekend? Why don't you just sod off now?'

'Good idea,' Barnaby said, 'but before I do go, has anyone ever told you that you conduct arguments with all the finesse and subtlety of a retarded eight-year-old? You know the sort of thing:

'I'm the tallest' – 'No you aren't' – 'And you're an effing wanker', or to analyse it it more precisely: statement – counter-statement – personal abuse. What was it you said earlier about growing up? Don't make me laugh!'

Ruth began at once to pack her things surreptitiously whenever Roger went out, which wasn't often. He was supposed to be preparing for his next trip and catching up on paperwork, but after a strong initial attempt to ridicule her plans for the future, he now seemed to be spending much of his time in his office in the spare room, drinking too much black coffee, looking peaky and sulking. He reminded Ruth irresistibly of Suckling's poem 'Why so pale and wan?' especially the second verse:

> Why so dull and mute, young sinner?
> Prithee, why so mute?
> Will, when speaking well can't win her,
> Saying nothing do 't?
> Prithee, why so mute?

She smiled to herself, surprised how calmly impervious she had become to all Roger's tactics. She longed to be with Barnaby already, to share poetry with him, to exchange quotations, to have the quality of her life transformed from constant anxiety to serene contemplation and adult bookishness. She pined for the sound of his voice, and when she hadn't heard from him by Thursday, she convinced herself it was an emergency and tried to telephone him at work. They told her he was on leave and refused to give her a contact number. She got his home number from Directory Enquiries, but Imogen answered, and Ruth put the receiver down without speaking. She began to worry.

Perhaps Imogen is working on him not to go? she thought. Perhaps she'll prevent him from doing so? She is very powerful, after all . . . What shall I do if I leave Roger and get all my things taken to Barnaby's cottage, and then he isn't there, and I can't get in? Or what if Imogen's there too? Ruth fretted along these lines all week, and when finally the time came to go, the following Saturday, her nerve almost failed her.

She wasn't able to drive easily any more, and anyway she and Roger had only one car between them, so hiring a small van and a driver was the only way she could manage to move her things to Devon. She had timed its arrival carefully, hoping against hope that Roger would go off as usual on Saturday morning to do their weekly shopping at the supermarket. Normally she went with him to remind him of what to buy. Sometimes she stayed sitting in the car while he did it, if she was feeling particularly tired. Today she planned to cry off at the last moment, just as they were about to drive off, plead exhaustion and hope that he would go anyway.

'We could always go this afternoon instead,' he suggested, leaning across the passenger seat to speak to her. 'Makes no difference to me.'

'Oh you may as well go, now you've got the car out,' she said, closing her door and hoping her words sounded casual. She crossed her fingers inside her skirt pockets and tried not to hold her breath too obviously.

'Well . . .' he said. Then he opened his door. Ruth's heart sank as he got out of the car and went back into the house. She began slowly to follow him inside, but when he re-emerged a very short time later, it was all she could do not to laugh. He had unplugged both of their telephones and wrapped them in their flexes to form a bundle. Then he threw it on to the back seat, smirking triumphantly at her as he did so.

'That'll stop the bastard from pestering you, won't it?' he remarked.

'Has he already tried?' Ruth asked.

'Wouldn't you like to know?' He put the car into gear and roared off. Ruth felt weak with relief.

The removal man was due in a quarter of an hour, but he didn't arrive for thirty minutes, by which time Ruth was quivering with angst all over again. He parked unobtrusively on the road outside, at her request, although there was plenty of room on their drive. Ruth had been afraid that he would argue about that, but she need not have worried. He turned out to be a rather elderly, but still athletic Scotsman who followed her all over the house, shouldering the things she indicated, and carrying them out, supplying her with wardrobe bags for her hanging clothes, and politely asking no questions. It took much longer than she had anticipated, even though she was taking very little. She began to feel desperate, imagining Roger returning early and ordering the Scotsman to put it all back again. What would he do? Would he obey? Would Roger perhaps tell him that she was stealing it all? Would he call the police? Ruth could feel herself getting more and more fearful as each minute passed. Finally, thank God, it was all aboard and the back of the van firmly closed up.

'Very guid,' the Scotsman said cheerfully. 'Wull we be awa' the noo?'

Ruth picked up her handbag from the kitchen table and had one last glance around at her past life. She took a deep breath.

'Yes,' she said. She followed him outside and climbed awkwardly into the passenger seat beside him, handing him her stick first, and then opening her window for some air. He started the engine and they began to move off from the kerb.

'Stop!' Ruth exclaimed. She'd forgotten to leave the note she had written for Roger. She scrabbled about in her handbag, found it, and made as if to open her door.

'Hold on,' the Scotsman said, understanding. 'Gie it here. I'll be Postie jist noo, wull I?'

Ruth nodded thankfully and watched him as he left the engine running, walked up their path and bent down to drop the note through the letterbox. As he was coming back, a car drove up to their garage – Roger's car.

'Can I help you?' Roger asked him rather truculently, getting out.

'Niver mind,' the Scotsman said, sidestepping neatly, heading for the van and jumping nimbly inside. Roger looked across at it, puzzled, and then seeing Ruth, understood. He came running down the path towards them as they accelerated away. He was shouting, but it wasn't with grief or rage or even in supplication. It was with exasperation.

'You told me a fortnight!' he yelled. 'You can't leave me *today*. I've just bought us two fillet steaks for a treat.'

Ruth burst into tears and tried unsuccessfully to disguise the fact, bowing her head as they drove rapidly down the street, and wiping her face covertly with the sleeve of her jersey.

'Here – ' the Scotsman said kindly, driving one-handed and passing her a man-sized box of tissues from the shelf above the dashboard, 'Have a guid cry. Dinna mind me. I'm used tae it. 'Tis a vexatious pastime, is flitting.'

21

BARNABY had gone two days earlier than he had planned to the cottage in Devon, in fact the day after Imogen had screamed at him to get out. As he saw it, there was no reason not to. He'd got time off from work. Home life was becoming ever more intolerable. He was all packed up and had already arranged for his three pieces of furniture to be taken into temporary storage that morning, so why prolong the agony?

He waited until Imogen went out for something, and then he simply moved all his boxes and bags into the back of his Volvo estate and drove away with scarcely a backward glance. In the end he had left behind the much-loved portrait of his little daughters, and he hoped that that would go some way towards mollifying his wife. He had no stomach for a prolonged feud. As he drove down the M5 to Exeter and beyond, he found himself singing aloud; silly songs whose words he could only sketchily remember, to the tune of 'Men of Harlech':

> 'Dum de dum de dum dum,
> Woad's the stuff for Foe Men,
> Boil it to
> A brilliant blue,
> And paint it on your head and your ab-do-men . . .'

He felt foolishly as though he had escaped from a dark and forbidding institution, and was now free to wander at will and unendingly in sunlit meadows. Never mind that the weather was grey and threatening rain, or that these days he rarely walked anywhere for pleasure, he was driving westwards to a new life.

233

' "Come live with me and be my love,"

he declaimed to the steering wheel,

> "And we will all the pleasures prove
> That hills and valleys, dales and fields,
> Or woods or steepy mountain yields."

Steepy? Some poets don't half exceed their licence!' Then he sighed and thought, This is all very fine, but I must also be practical. Imogen will still have her keys to the cottage, so the first thing I must do when I arrive is to get the locks changed.

Imogen couldn't believe that Barnaby had gone, just like that, without a word. She came back from a prolonged shopping session rather pleased with herself, having bought three pairs of shoes in one go and spent a lot of money. Shopping always cheered her up. Some women ate too much when they were unhappy; Imogen bought things.

And there Barnaby wasn't! She had been cheated of her farewell scene, in which she stood bravely on the doorstep, making no fuss whilst he slunk off, feeling and behaving like a cad. She realized that she hadn't ever accepted in her heart of hearts that he really would leave her, and now she couldn't begin to imagine a life without him to fall back upon. She rushed wildly round the house to discover what he had taken with him. Hollow drawers rattled and opened too easily. The wardrobe was only half full. Empty bookshelves looked like dusty ladders. He had taken his pewter tankard, the barometer and the hall clock . . . Not much had gone, but to Imogen it was as though the entire house had been pillaged. Inconsequentially, she recalled Brian's recent septic tank story, and instantly identified herself with it. She too felt as though her heart had been uprooted on a groundswell of emotion, had burst out, and was lying there on the surface with all its tubes ruptured; useless, even risible. She wandered apathetically back into the dining room and suddenly noticed that Barnaby had left her the portrait of her babies, after all. How condescending can you get? she thought furiously. Am I supposed to be *grateful*? Anger engulfed her. She lifted the painting from its hooks and dashed it to the ground. The glass broke, and a small sliver of it ripped through one of the chubby painted arms, tearing the paper in an ugly scar.

Imogen found herself sobbing bitterly, down on her knees beside the broken glass, and trying desperately to rectify what she had just done, but achieving only a worse mess by getting blood on to the painting from a finger she hadn't even realized she had cut.

Oh God, she thought, I'm cracking up! I must pull myself together. She got to her feet, carefully picked shards of glass off her skirt, and went to find a dustpan to clear them all away. She bound up her bleeding finger in a folded piece of kitchen towel. She blew her nose and wiped her eyes. Now, she thought, sweeping the last of the glass up, in a couple of days' time, if I can get myself back on an even keel by then, I shall find out where Barnaby is and phone him and tell him about the lump. Then he'll have to see that I really do need him.

Barnaby had tried many times to telephone Ruth, but her moronic husband kept answering, and cutting him off. Barnaby noted with some amusement how limited Roger's vocabulary was. He hoped that Ruth might think to get the cottage number and phone him there, but then he remembered that he wasn't supposed to be there until Saturday, so she was unlikely to do so until then. Perhaps she had already phoned his home and got Imogen? Perhaps Imogen had refused to speak to her? Anyway, now it finally was Saturday, so she probably wouldn't bother. She'd just arrive instead. As he was thinking this, the telephone beside him rang, making him jump.

'Hello?' It was only Imogen. 'Oh, it's you.'

'Thanks for the wild enthusiasm.'

'How did you know I was here?'

'Well it wasn't hard to guess. You're so bloody predictable!'

'What d'you want?'

'Barnaby, please don't be so curt and unfeeling. I've got no one to talk to but you.'

'You want to talk?'

'Yes I do.'

'You mean you want to wheedle and cajole, throw in a bit of flattery and then, when that doesn't work, offer actual violence, just to show how false all the flattery was in the first place?'

'No. Look, can we please forget all the aggro and begin again? I'm sorry . . . It's just that I'm in trouble . . .'

'What have you done?'

'I haven't *done* anything . . . I've found a lump in my right breast.'

'Is it serious?'

'I don't know yet. I've got to go and see the consultant again on the seventh of December.'

'Well I wouldn't get in a panic until then, then. Most lumps are entirely benign, I believe.'

'Is that all you can say?'

'What more do you want me to say?'

'I want . . . *need* you to come home. I'm going mad here all on my own, . . . worrying.'

'Sorry. No can do,' Barnaby said.

'But Barnaby, you can't desert me. I might have cancer! I might even die of it and how would you feel then? I haven't told you this before, but I nearly left you years ago, and d'you know what stopped me? Simple: no decent person leaves a husband who is incurably ill. I just couldn't do it. I wouldn't have been able to live with myself.'

'Very noble,' Barnaby agreed.

'So now if I'm terminally ill, you can't possibly leave me, can you?' Barnaby was silent. 'Barnaby? For heaven's sake *talk* to me!'

'It's not on, you know,' he finally said, 'and getting hysterical won't help.'

'What isn't on? And I'm *not* hysterical.'

'Emotional blackmail,' Barnaby said, and put the phone down.

It rang again a couple of times in quick succession, but he ignored it and got on with the job of making the cottage as welcoming as possible for Ruth. He went out into the garden and found a few pink sprigs of winter flowering viburnum, and put them in a vase in the small bedroom. When he went back upstairs later, the room smelt sweet and spicy; inviting. Barnaby stood at the window with his palms flat upon the sill and stared contentedly out at the view across the lane to the hills beyond.

Ruth and the Scotsman stopped at a motorway service station for some lunch, and to enable her to telephone Barnaby at the cottage. There was no reply, and she felt the panic that was never far from the surface, beginning to rise again. Once back in the cab and on the road again, she waited and waited until they were almost at Exeter, and then consulted the directions on the back of Barnaby's envelope with trembling hands. It was a tiring journey which took over five hours, and by the time they arrived at the top of the narrow lane leading to the cottage, Ruth felt totally done in.

'If I wisnae tolt there wiz a hoose doon here, I wouldnae credit it,' the Scotsman observed cheerfully.

'I hope to goodness there is,' Ruth said. Her throat felt dry.

They turned a corner and there it was, a small whitewashed cottage with an old green porch covered in the leafless thorny stems of an ancient rose, and above it an open window and Barnaby's face, smiling . . .

'*Yes!*' Ruth exclaimed, 'we're here. This is it!'

She loved the place at sight: its setting, its wild garden with a small brook running through it, the view, everything. She forgot how exhausted she was and wandered round in a daze of pleasure whilst Barnaby organized the unpacking and tipped the Scotsman.

'It's a very modest load,' he said, coming back to her as the van drove away. She waved until it had disappeared and then turned smiling to him.

'I'm a very modest person!'

'Yes,' he said thoughtfully, 'that's another of your undoubted qualities. What a lucky fellow I am.'

'Where is all your stuff?'

'Mostly still in boxes in the back bedroom. I haven't brought my furniture yet. I thought I'd store it until we saw how and where it would fit in.'

'How very considerate of you. When did you arrive? I tried to phone . . .'

'I've been here since Thursday in fact. I tried to phone you too, but dear Roger was obstructive, and then today I've had Imogen on at me . . . I'm sorry, I'm afraid I let it ring a couple of times today, in case it was her again. It was you?'

'It's all right now,' Ruth said, 'now that we're both here and everything's wonderful. I'm afraid I'm a dreadful worrier. I hope you can put up with that?'

'If you can put up with my forgetfulness,' Barnaby said, putting both arms round her and kissing her.

'Let's sit down,' Ruth said. 'I'm suddenly whacked.'

'Yes of course, thoughtless of me.' He led her into the sitting room. 'Tea?'

'Tea is exactly what I need.'

Barnaby brought ginger biscuits, and they sat side by side on the sofa, dunking them in mugs of Earl Grey.

'Is Imogen being a problem?' Ruth asked.

Barnaby made a little huffing noise in his nose. 'When was Imogen not a problem?' he said, 'But yes, she's putting on the pressure.'

'Anything specific?'

'She *says* she's got a lump in her breast.'

'Oh *no*!'

Barnaby raised his eyebrows at the vehemence of her exclamation.

'That's something I've always been terrified of,' Ruth said. 'Poor Imogen, if it's true. Do you think it is?'

'Who knows,' Barnaby shrugged. 'I wouldn't put anything past her.'

'Perhaps you should find out?' Ruth suggested. 'If it is true . . . and it proves to be cancer . . . I mean, I wouldn't wish my worst enemy to have to cope with that alone . . .'

'Hummm,' Barnaby said, 'perhaps you're right. You're a very generous creature, aren't you?'

Ruth thought, *What have I said*? What am I encouraging him to do? I must be mad. I was just feeling so relieved and happy to be safely here with him that for a moment there I forgot how much I dislike the wretched woman! I'll bet her lump story isn't true anyway. It will just be one of her stunts.

'Oh I don't know though . . .' she said quickly.

'No,' Barnaby said, 'you're right. I am being callous. Perhaps I'll call in and see her after work next week some time, just to check that she's OK.'

Imogen was outraged by Barnaby's defection, and knew it to

238

be far more of a betrayal than anything she herself might have contemplated. In retrospect she was triumphant that she had managed to withstand Roger's blandishments, but was mortified that she had actually called Barnaby a 'cripple' and 'damaged goods'. I was severely provoked, she reassured herself. I wouldn't normally dream of saying such a thing. It wasn't my fault . . .

Over the following days she felt an unaccustomed emotion she gradually came to recognize as loneliness, and was eventually driven back to her voluntary work just to have someone to talk to. At the Citizens' Advice Bureau she confessed to her friend Carol, the debt advice worker, over a snatched mug of coffee between case conferences, that Barnaby had left her for another woman.

'Great,' Carol said cheerfully. 'I've always thought he wasn't nearly good enough for you.'

'You never said!'

'But why the long face and the puffy eyes? You don't want him back surely? Not if he's been screwing around with someone else? I know I wouldn't. You're the winner, you know.'

'How do you make that out?'

'Well, Barnaby and this female of his are just doing the same old thing all over again, aren't they? But you've now got the chance to start afresh, break new ground, be yourself!'

'Is that what you did?'

'Yep. I got my divorce and then I got this job full time, and I've never looked back.' She glanced over her shoulder. 'Don't mention this to anyone else here though, will you? It's hardly the official CAB line. That's why I stick to debt; relationships were never my strong point!' Imogen laughed. 'Just think,' Carol went on, 'there are endless possibilities for a future a damn sight more rewarding than being a part-time housewife, even in these days of unemployment. You could retrain, go into teaching, get a paid job here at the CAB, maybe even become a magistrate!' She looked at her watch. 'Got to go. I've got some poor bugger coming for an appointment who's run up a 30K debt, and is only now addressing that fact. God! there really are some hopeless, feckless people about, aren't there? Good thing they've got us to sort them out, eh? Now I must go and find his case sheet . . .'

Imogen was still smiling as Carol left the room. She's right!

she thought. I'm being much too negative. Previously she had scorned people who tried to 'find' themselves, but now she was beginning to acknowledge the need to do just that, even to admit her faults. I've been shallow and juvenile, she thought, but I'm not completely worthless. I can recover from all this (especially if Mr Corn is right and the lump is nothing to worry about). I'm a survivor, and I'm still very privileged. Perhaps full-time work is the answer, and the satisfaction of achievement? Jobs may be hard to get, but they are always short of social workers, for instance. I could train and get an inner city job; be *useful*. Carol's right, I don't need Barnaby as some sort of a prop. I can look after myself perfectly well, and I will. I have my pride. If he wants to crawl off with rabbity Ruth, then bloody good riddance!

She was still in militant mood that evening, when Barnaby appeared on the doorstep. 'Good Lord!' she said. 'That was quick. Have you and Ruth called it a day already?'

'Very funny,' Barnaby said, unsmiling.

'What, then?'

'Well let me in first. It's freezing out here.'

'Just quickly, then,' Imogen said. 'I'm off out in twenty minutes.' It wasn't true, but it gave her the satisfaction of seeing Barnaby look disconcerted.

'Oh . . .'

'So, what d'you want?' Imogen sat down on the edge of the sofa and glanced at her watch.

'Well, you sounded . . . I thought . . .'

'Did your conscience prick you?'

'I just wanted to make sure you were all right.'

'Well I shan't know until a week on Wednesday, and maybe not even then. I'll send you a postcard.'

'Oh . . . right.'

'Is that it then? Only I've got to get changed.' Barnaby got up to go, and she let him do so without bothering to see him off. As she heard his car driving away, tears pricked her eyes but she sniffed them back crossly. Honours even! she thought. Now the next thing to look forward to is sorting out this damn lump and after that, Christmas with my two best beauties and their blokes. Perhaps I'll go to one of their houses this year for a change, and then they can cook for me? Sound idea.

By the week before Christmas, Ruth had relaxed into her new life so completely that she had almost forgotten old anxieties. The cottage had felt like home from the outset, but now she had paid for the walls to be painted and for some cupboards to be built, and she had made and put up new curtains, and it really had become her territory. She blessed the small legacy which had enabled her to make it so, and also provided her with the wherewithal to buy Barnaby a beautiful leather briefcase as a Christmas present. In the past few weeks, whenever she went food shopping, she had bought something extra to ensure that their first Christmas alone together would be very special.

Ruth also joined the local MS group, and persuaded Barnaby to go along with her to their meetings. She became known as Mrs Redcliffe and didn't bother to correct the error, hugging the name to herself like a hot bottle on a cold night. She knew genuine happiness almost for the first time, and discovered that it wasn't a state of continuous bliss. Rather it was manifest in odd moments; small revelations that came unsought, and spoke to her of contentment and an inner peace: lying in bed next to Barnaby, snug and warm, with the winter rain hammering against the window – sitting on the sofa in front of a log fire, listening to Vivaldi – or remembering out loud some of Barnaby's quotations while doing the ironing ... She thought to herself, I'm not stranded any more. Barnaby was the spring tide which came and swept me away. *I'm so lucky.*

When Mr Corn stuck the needle into Imogen's left breast, she expected it to be exquisitely painful, and was surprised when it was no worse than any commonplace injection. This time of course he was extracting fluid, rather than putting it in, and the stuff that rose into the barrel of the syringe from the centre of her lump, Imogen noticed, was a very small amount and milky white.

'No blood,' Mr Corn said encouragingly. 'That's a good sign.' He felt over the top of her breast again. 'And the cyst seems to have gone down a bit too,' he said. 'Come back and see me in another fortnight, so I can check whether it's gone. If not, we'll snip it out.'

By the 21st of December when she had to go and see him again, Imogen was confident that all would be well.

'Yes,' Mr Corn said, his warm hands squeezing and searching, 'yes . . . good . . . The lump now feels more like a ridge . . . Probably only mastitis . . . Good.'

'So you won't have to cut it out?'

'No lumpectomy required,' Mr Corn agreed, smiling.

'And what about the stuff you sucked out? Was there a result?'

'Due back today,' Mr Corn assured her. 'I was hoping it would be here before you arrived, but no matter, I'll write to you. Now, if you'll make another appointment to see me in three months' time . . . where are we . . . yes, March the 21st, then I expect we can conclude things satisfactorily. Good. Goodbye.'

The next day, his letter arrived. Imogen tore it open at once and read it in the hall. It said:

Dear Mrs Redcliffe,
Just to let you know that there was no evidence of anything untoward going on, on examination of the needle specimen which I took.
Yours sincerely,
U.N.I. Corn, FRCS
Consultant Surgeon

Imogen allowed her back to slide down the wall, so that she ended up sitting on the bottom step of the stairs. Phew! she thought. Thank God that's that. Then she read the letter again and laughed aloud at its astonishing illiteracy. It was a laugh which soon changed into a sigh of regret. Tears filled her eyes.

'Oh dear,' she said aloud, 'Barnaby would have had such a wonderful jeer at this. I do wish he was here.'

EPILOGUE
TWO YEARS ON

22

IMOGEN walked along the street in Bristol, smiling to herself. She had another lecture in an hour, but there was just time to pop into Blackwell's to see if the book she had ordered had arrived yet. Life begins at 50! she told herself. She felt jubilant, and the reasons were obvious. She was fit and well. She was grandmother to a charming little boy, and another baby was due soon. She was a full-time mature student at Bristol University. She had bought herself a neat little flat in Clifton, and she hadn't thought about Barnaby for weeks. I'm cured, she thought. I've got my confidence back. I've been given the chance to start life again, and I'm going to do it better this time. I'm even relishing how hard it is to force my brain to study, after all these years. Never mind that most of the other students are too young to be my children! They're so full of energy and ideas; such fun. It lifts the heart and makes me glad to be alive. It's good to have one of them as a lodger too. I'm even learning to like her music . . .

That morning, coincidentally, there had been two postcards from people on her Seychelles trip. Imogen remembered them all rather as one recalls characters in a play; as caricatures of real people with whom she had shared a brief interlude, but would never particularly want to see again. As she thought about them, she found it hard to remember their names, especially that ghastly couple from Birmingham. The name Oliver came to mind? No, that wasn't it. Shirley, of course, she remembered only too well and the red-haired girl with the classy French surname, Annabel de . . . something? Annabel's card came from Sheffield and proudly announced an exhibition of paintings by Brian Gage. Never heard of him, Imogen thought. Oh – that Brian. Good for him! Shirley's was from Katmandu (and someone had stolen the stamp). It said:

Having a lovely time here! The mountains are even more wonderful than I thought — they knock spots off Seychelles! I've recently lost over three stone! You wouldn't know me! Just thought you'd like to know that Brian's art has now got the recognition it's always deserved and is actually selling! and he and Annabel are engaged! (or as near as makes no difference!) Hope you are well.

Best wishes,
   Shirley Gage.

P.S. I heard on the grapevine that Roger Dare lost his court case, but has taken up with a rich widow and is now living the life of Riley in California! Trust him!

Ruth woke and lay in bed for a few moments, knowing that this was a special day, but not remembering at first, why. Of course, she thought, it's my birthday! Sun slanted in through the bedroom window on to the empty pillow next to hers. Barnaby was already up. Ruth could hear noises in the kitchen below as he turned taps on and off and threw wood into the boiler. She lay there comfortably warm and wondered whether he would remember the date. He had twice forgotten the anniversary of their moving to the cottage. It's not important, Ruth told herself. He brings me tea in bed in the mornings, which is more than Roger ever did . . . She thought about Roger every day and was always troubled by guilt. They hadn't been in touch or spoken for over a year now, and she had no idea what he was doing, except that Leisure Doubletrips was no more. She imagined him pale and thin, and having to do some rotten menial job just to make ends meet. She felt bad about the way she had left him, and wondered if he would ever forgive her.

'Tea,' Barnaby said, coming in with a tray and putting it down on the windowsill with a clatter.

'Lovely,' Ruth said, yawning. She looked over at the tray. There was no card on it.

There was no card later that evening either, when Barnaby got home from work. Ruth felt hurt in spite of herself.

'Good day?' Barnaby asked her. He always said that.

'So, so.' Usually she said yes. Barnaby raised his eyebrows at her. 'It should really be a special one,' Ruth said.

'Oh Gawd,' Barnaby groaned. 'What have I forgotten now?'

'It's nothing much. It's only my birthday.'

'I'm sorry,' Barnaby said. 'I'm afraid my family never made a thing of birthdays. That's why I never remember how important they are to you.'

'It really doesn't matter,' Ruth said.

'So, what did you do today?'

'Went into town on the bus and bought us some food; nothing much. There's a worrying rumour going round, that they're thinking of cutting down our daily bus service to twice a week, or maybe even discontinuing it altogether. I'd be really stuck without it. It's my lifeline. What would I do?'

Barnaby began:

> 'What is it that roareth thus?
> Can it be a motor bus?
> Yes the smell and hideous hum
> Indicat mo—'

'Not now, Barnaby,' Ruth interrupted, 'if you don't mind.'

'Imogen?' her lodger asked her after breakfast. 'You're divorced, aren't you?'

'Nearly.'

'So you know a lot about relationships and splitting up; stuff like that?'

'I suppose so.' Imogen made a face. Absently, with one hand, she stroked the small wooden box with the beautifully inlaid lid, in which she kept postage stamps. Then she straightened it up on the mantelpiece.

'Did he leave you, or did you leave him?'

'Oh I left him,' Imogen said at once. Then, 'No . . . to be strictly honest, he left me . . . Why? Are you having trouble with your boyfriend?'

'Sort of.'

'And you need to know one way or the other, whether you're really suited to each other?'

247

'That's the kind of thing, yes.'

'Easy,' Imogen said, with a rueful smile. 'It never fails – go on holiday together.'